DARKWALKER

DUNCAN EAGLESON

DARKWALKER

DUNCAN EAGLESON

PINK
NARCISSUS
PRESS

DARKWALKER
© 2014 Duncan Eagleson

Cover illustration & design by Duncan Eagleson.

Published by Pink Narcissus Press
P.O. Box 303
Auburn, MA 01501
pinknarc.com

Library of Congress Control Number: 2013914501
ISBN: 978-1-939056-04-7
First trade paperback edition: January 2014

Now in the night,
the dark walker came,
gliding in shadow;

-- Anon., *Beowulf*
translated by Howell D. Chickering

1. WOLF

"We're being watched," said Morgan, her voice tight and low. "From the bluff, ten o'clock."

Rok slowed the jeep imperceptibly. I sat up from where I'd been dozing in the back seat. I peered at the bluff on the left ahead, and after a moment, I saw it. A flash of sunlight reflected off something, probably field glasses.

"What do you think?" said Rok. "Welcoming committee? Or Ravager ambush?"

I thought it over. Zone towns weren't as paranoid as they used to be. These days, travelers were more likely to be traders than raiders, so most places didn't keep regular lookouts anymore. But we'd heard Apache Run was having trouble with Ravagers, so it could be either.

"Good spot for an ambush, between those two bluffs," said Morgan.

"We're still out of range," I said. "Pull over, pop the hood. We'll make it look like we've got engine trouble. Give us a minute to take stock. If it's a lookout from the Run, he'll hail us, or come down to offer help."

"If it's Ravagers, they might pretend."

"They might."

Rok pulled over and got out. I went to the back of the jeep and made sure the heavier weapons were easily accessible. Checked the loads on the two shotguns and slammed a clip into Rok's sniper rifle. Morgan joined me, slipping Darkwater into her back rig. Railwalker swords are short, like ninja-to, short enough that most of us can draw them from a low-slung back rig.

"Take your husband his," I said, holding out The Fury.

"I'll put it in the back seat," she said. Swords were not

Rok's favorite weapon. She climbed back in the car, and from the shadows inside, scanned the bluff with her own field glasses. I joined Rok at the front. He was leaning under the hood, wedging a large cooking pot between the DC inverter and the electric traction unit. There were several small rocks in the pot.

"They've got to figure we're armed," he said. "If they're Ravagers, and they're smart, they won't come to us. Not yet, anyway."

I looked at the desert between us and the bluffs. He was right. They'd be too exposed. "You think if we don't go forward, they'll wait until dark."

"Wouldn't you?" He straightened, stretched. "Wish we knew how many and what weapons."

I scanned the skies. To our south, there were two black specks sailing west. "Lemme go ask," I said.

I climbed back in the jeep. Morgan just nodded— she'd seen the two crows on the horizon as well. I settled myself, closed my eyes, slowed my breathing.

Flying—there just isn't any feeling like it. It's too easy for me, when I do this, to get caught up in the flow of air through feathers, the wind in my face, the sheer joy of soaring in any direction, in four dimensions. I had to really concentrate to preserve my human agenda. I let myself go now for just a moment, reveling in my flight. I could feel the crow's awareness of my joining him, and something like amusement. I brought my mind back to the job, and glanced toward the bluff. We banked and coasted toward it. The other crow, winging along beside us, sensed what was going on. She flew a little closer, tilting her wings at us, and I knew she'd stay with us and be patient with my use of her partner as long as I didn't overstay my welcome.

I opened my eyes in the dim interior of the jeep. Shook myself. Morgan looked a question at me. I waited until Rok slammed the hood and got in behind the wheel.

"Six of them," I said. "Four on the left bluff, two on

the right. They've got two three-wheelers and a truck of some sort. Truck's positioned ready to roadblock. Only saw one long weapon, on the left. The rest look to be handguns."

"They'll want to get in close, then," said Rok. "See a convenient drop point?"

"Yeah. That big rock there on the right. With the creosote bush. You could get up the back of the right ridge unseen that way."

"Left would be better. I could flank the larger group. And they've got the rifle."

"Terrain doesn't have enough concealment. They'd see you coming."

"Okay," he said, getting out. He kissed Morgan quickly.

"Take care, bear," she said.

Rok climbed into the back, and I took the driver's seat. Morgan and I slid our swords into the clips mounted above our heads, pommels toward our doors. That makes it much easier to draw as you exit a vehicle.

I started the engine. When I pulled back onto the road, the electric engine, normally a quiet purr, jangled and clanked.

"What the fuck?" said Morgan.

I laughed, remembering Rok's pot full of rocks. "Why does the lion limp?" I said.

Morgan sighed. "Right, grasshopper," she said. "To make the antelope think it's safe." She racked the slide on her Gunspire to put one in the chamber, dropped the clip, replaced the chambered bullet, and slapped the clip back in. I drove in fits and starts, trying to mimic an ailing engine. Near the big old stone and its creosote bush, I veered a bit, slowing down, and throwing up a lot of road dust. I felt the jeep shift as Rok's weight left it.

When the rocky walls of the bluffs rose up on either side of us, I saw the battered old truck they had rolled across the road. The doors and one side panel were missing; it was barely a cab and a short bed on wheels, so rusted and dirty I wondered if they'd towed it here rather than driven it. When we were five or six yards from the clunker, a shot rang out. The bullet kicked up dust in front of us. I floored it for a second as if startled, bringing us within a couple of yards of the truck, and stopped. Figures appeared from the rocks on our left, three of them, pointing pistols in our direction. Gods, they were just kids, barely out of their teens. No one appeared from the right. The three, looking nervously at each other and glancing up to our left, ranged themselves out, one approaching me, the other two headed for the front of the jeep. One of them would have kept going to Morgan's side, but she stepped out, Gunspire held low at her side, hidden by the jeep's open door. He stopped, covering Morgan. The second kid, a pimply-faced blond, stood directly in front of the jeep, but couldn't decide whether to cover me or Morgan.

"Sounds like you're having a little trouble," said the first guy, as he stopped by my door. He was the oldest, obviously the leader. My own Gunspire was in my hand, hidden below the window, trained on him through a hole we'd cut in the driver's side door for just this purpose. You could shoot through the tin of the door, but it slowed the bullet's travel slightly, and could affect its path a little, too.

"You don't want to do this," I said.

He laughed. "What's up with the eye tattoos?" he said. His pistol drifted a bit as he squinted, peering at my face. "Some kind of gang sign?"

"You might say that," I said. "Ever hear of the Railwalkers?"

He snorted. "Bullshit," he said. "The Railwalkers are all dead and gone." He stepped forward, bringing the old six-shooter to bear on my face. I was about to fire when a shot rang out, and his head exploded. I stamped on the accelerator as I heard Morgan's gun bark. The jeep jumped forward, pinning the blond guy against the old truck. He screamed, then jerked as Morgan put a bullet in his head. I leaped from the vehicle, drawing Windsteel. A shot pinged off the jeep, cracking one of the roof's solar panels. I heard

another shot from behind me, and a scream from up the
bluff. Then all was quiet.

Morgan and I glanced at each other. Rok was coming
out of the rocks on our right, carrying his rifle. He jerked
his chin toward the bluffs on the other side.

"Pretty sure I got him," he said.

"I'll check," I said.

As I started hiking up to the top of the bluff, I heard
Rok say, "Shit. They were just kids."

Morgan replied, "Rollins said their Ravagers were
juvies. This must be them."

Apache Run was on the edge of the zones, where the
desert began to give way to a greener, damper climate.
"Began" being the operative word. It was still dry and
dusty by most standards, though the locals managed to
raise corn and beans, and there was even a vineyard. By
the time the outlying farms came into view, the landscape
was less flat, the rising hills showing patches of green
amidst the browns and golds. We were glad to be here. The
jeep had needed some solar cells replaced even before the
junior Ravager's bullet had cracked one, and those were
hard to come by out in the zones.

When our jeep came over a rise to give us our first
glimpse of the town proper on the horizon it was still early
afternoon, the sun spilling down into every niche and
cranny. Which was how we saw the dust.

"Uh-oh," said Morgan. "Two o'clock. Dust."

I looked in the direction she'd gestured. Here and
there in the mostly pale brown landscape you could just
make out traces of the unnatural reddish-purple dust. In
some spots it had turned brick red, like the natural dust
you'd find to the northeast of here, as if it had dried out in
the sun.

"It's turning red already," I said. "The storm was a few
days ago."

She held out a breathing filter. "You wanna roll those
dice?"

I didn't. Scaledust isn't something you take chances

with. At the sight of those distinctive purple clouds, you put your gas mask or breathing filter on and head for shelter. A day or two after the storm has passed, the dust it deposited undergoes some sort of change—the poisonous organisms in it die, or mutate, or something, and it turns from purple to a dull, rusty red. At that point it's no longer dangerous. Scientists assure us that after the change, you could safely eat the stuff if you had a mind to, though it likely wouldn't taste very good. Far as I know, no one has ever made that experiment.

As we rolled into Apache Run, you could tell right away we were on the fringes, leaving the zones. The local ball court showed patches of pale green grass in the outfield. There were actually a few planters with feeble flowers growing in them, and one or two attempts at something that might have been intended for a lawn. Out the other side of town, a dark shape against the horizon, a single Tesla distributor loomed. The few folks on the street were all wearing breathing filters or gas masks, though there was no sign of any scaledust on the streets. Crews with hand blowers would have chased it to collection points as soon as the storm had passed.

The proprietor of the one hotel checked us in.

"Where would we find Christine Rollins or Ivan Rowley?" I asked him.

"First Chair Rollins?" he said. "She's most likely out to the plant." He jerked his thumb in the direction of the Tesla distributor we'd seen on the outskirts of town. "Ivan, he'll be at his place, the Korner Kitchen, serving lunch." He was staring at the tattoo over my left eye.

"Does Ms. Rollins carry a handset?"

"Yeah, but she usually leaves it switched off. You could try her, if you've a mind." I nodded at Morgan, who brought out our handset and dialed Rollins.

"Offline," she said.

"You're the Railwalkers," the clerk said. I nodded. "I'll send the boy to fetch her," he said.

"No big rush. We'd like to see our rooms, clean up."

***

Wireless signals get pretty spotty in the zones, but the closer to the cities, generally, the better luck you have with them. When she set up in the hotel room, Morgan picked up our messages. She was seated at the rickety hotel table with her equipment spread out on it. Rok had stretched out on the bed, hands behind his head, and closed his eyes. I knew he wasn't asleep, though.

"What have you got?" I asked.

Morgan didn't look up from her screen. "Services for Wiley and Brock. Twilight tomorrow. Nothing about any more information."

"Let it go, Morgan," I said.

"Come on, guards from both Santa Brita and Monteague, along with a couple of Railwalkers? And no survivors on either side? Man, at least one Ravager, or maybe a turncoat guard, had to have hightailed it into the zones."

"Hicks Junction is not our responsibility. What else you got?"

She scrolled the screen. "Roth requests our presence. Urgently."

"Micah Roth? Bay City?"

"Wants us to meet his ornithopter at Maricopa Flats, ASAP. Damned city bosses think they own everybody's time, like any obligations we have in the zones don't mean anything."

"We don't have any obligations right now, so what's the problem?"

"Don't you think the locals expect us to be here for Summersend Night?"

"They didn't formally request us for that, and Roth did. They called us to get rid of their Ravagers, and we've done that. Once we report that to one of the consensus chairs, our work here is done. Time to move."

"That's assuming those kids were the Ravagers they meant, right. Also, there was a message from Dahlia. She wants to know when you can visit Cairnhold." Cairnhold was the headquarters of the order's Western Warden.

"Tell her we don't know."

"It's not like she's calling you in for a reprimand. How

long are you going to keep avoiding her? She's older than
Traveler. We don't go see her soon, she could be gone."

"That would be a pity," I said, and I meant it. I liked
Dahlia. She was one of the most moderate and level-
headed of the order's Ravens. But it was becoming clear
she had her eye on me to replace her when she retired, and
that kind of authority was the last thing I wanted.

I heard Rok give a soft snort. "What," he said, "you
want to see Grout as Warden? Or Kane? That would be
real good for the order."

"I don't want that kind of post. I'm not Raven material," I said. "My decisions affect enough people as it is. I
don't want more responsibility than I've already got."

"But—" said Morgan

"End of discussion."

The town had been trying hard to get into an appro-
priately festive mood for Summersend, with corn dollies
hung about the streets and wheat wreaths on the doors.
The news that the gang had been killed helped, though
there was still a melancholy undertone to the air of celebration. They'd built a big old Corn Guy, one of the biggest
I'd seen in a while. Most small towns out in the zones content themselves with a life-sized Guy, stuffing some old
clothes with straw and cornstalks, adding a stuffed bag for
a head, and tossing it onto a bonfire. Apache Run had
built a Corn Guy nearly twelve feet tall, all cornstalks
bound together on a bamboo frame.

Ivan Rowley walked up to where we were packing the
jeep, getting ready to head for Maricopa Flats. He was staring down the street at the Guy as he spoke.

"Don't seem fair," he said. "We were all looking forward to having you folks do the Blessing of the Harvest for
us. Summersend's only a few days away."

"Communication said it was urgent," I said. "We got a
responsibility to city folks, too."

"They got all kinds of priests and officials in the city
to do their blessings for them."

"It's not about Summersend," I said.

"No it ain't," said a woman's voice. "It's about killing." Christine Rollins was precise and clipped behind her glasses. "You've heard the rumors, same as me," she said to Rowley. "Killings in the streets of Bay City."

"Those killed won't be any more or any less dead after Summersend."

"But others may die before then. Let's be thanking the Railwalkers for what they done for us, and let them be on their way."

"Folks," I said, raising a hand, "I know City Boss Roth a little, and I don't believe he'd call a situation urgent if it wasn't. Truth is, it really doesn't matter anyway. Our presence has been formally requested, and we're going. End of story. I'm sorry we won't be here for Summersend."

"Hey," said Rok, leaning out from the other side of the jeep. "Size of that Corn Guy, at least we'll be able to see the flames all the way to Bay City." Everyone laughed, or at least chuckled. "We'll think on you."

Storm clouds were gathering as we loaded our gear into the 'thopter. Fortunately they were the gray of the zone's rare rainstorms, rather than the purple of scaledust.

We climbed in, and Guardsman Geary fired up the engine. There was a brief shudder as the wings shifted into flight position and began to pump, first slowly, then faster, as fast as the small propeller at the back. The 'thopter gave a lurch, and we lifted off, swinging around to head north by northwest as the first raindrops began to spatter the cupola. Geary said nothing, but his grim demeanor suggested Roth hadn't been kidding about the urgency.

I had met Roth a few years back. As city bosses go, he seemed hard but fair. I wondered if Roth had summoned us because he knew me, or because we're one of the last full Railwalker teams.

All three of us were in the regulation coats tonight. Yeah, they were a little dusty and wrinkled—what do you want from three Walkers out for weeks in the zones? Except for Rok's. To look at him in work clothes or fighting leathers, you'd think he was just a big dumb woodchuck who didn't care about how he looks. But of the three of us, Rok's regulation Crow coat was the one that always looked like it just came from the dry cleaners. Damn if I could tell you how he managed that. Morgan's head was on his shoulder, her portable comp unit in her lap.

It was weird to be headed into a city again, after so much time in the zones. I hoped we hadn't grown arrogant from being final authorities for so long. In the city, we'd be the pros from Dover, but not the final word. We could expect the City Guard to treat us as respected colleagues, but generally they would keep themselves distant and not a little suspicious.

A Railwalker does not seek to grandify the self. A Railwalker seeks only to get the job done. A Railwalker seeks Soul-Are.

INTERLUDE: BRICKS AND CROWS

Although many, if not most, biographies claim Brick never received much formal schooling, did not attend or graduate from any school or academy, and many passages in the *Book of Brick* and *Arteology* seem to be expressed in an academically naïve, if street-wise, voice, it should be noted that aside from the rendering of certain contemporary slang or street phrases, most of the grammar in these passages is essentially sound, and that in some places, simple words are misspelled, while more complex words are spelled accurately. This suggests a writer at least moderately well educated adopting an uneducated voice and tone. If we accept that the Red Raven himself penned the *Book* and *Arteology*, we must also accept that he was perhaps better educated than many sources have led us to believe—indeed, more than Brick himself wanted to appear. Some authorities, like Siblene James, argue for what is known as the "Amanuensis Theory," which holds that some associate—perhaps even one of the First Five of Ravens—performed the actual writing, either recording Brick's discourse from memory, or from dictation on which the *Amanuensis* consciously or unconsciously acted as a sort of copy editor.

With regard to Brick's parentage, we have three conflicting legends. The first is that he was the son of the beloved pre-Crash spiritual leader and popular singer Sariel Mamaji. Another tale relates that he was found floating in a basket in Manhattan's East River. Yet a third casts him as the son of the Crow Goddess, Morgana.

Since the "baby in a basket" story has no accompanying detail, the Mamaji story is the only one that can be ex-amined for historical veracity. Unfortunately, while much of Mamaji's life may be well documented, the period in question was one during which she traveled on the road, performing and preaching her way across the then-united country. She worked with a variety of small bands, and records of this period are severely fragmented (see Grafton's *Life with Mamaji* or Altran's *SM: A Biography of Sariel Mamaji*). There is no record of any child other than Christopher Johns, born during Mamaji's Mexico tour, who grew up to take the reins of her Wheel of Life Church from Mamaji's death until the time of the Crash. And Johns, however admirable a character in his own right, was clearly not Brick. Nevertheless, we cannot rule out the possibility of another child born during Mamaji's early wild period.

There are, of course, many "Brick tales," stories of various episodes in Brick's life, which may take place before, during, or after the Crash. In the years following Brick's death (or disappearance; see below), the Brick tale entered the arena of popular culture, spawning many short stories, DVs, and comanga. The vast majority of these tales may be discarded as the compositions of imaginative authors, artists, and screenwriters. Within the Railwalker Order itself, orthodox dogma was clear on this point: these tales, even those of the Canonical Raven Texts, as well as the stories of Brick's miraculous birth, were to be regarded as metaphor, and not literally true. The popularization of Soul-Are and the rise of the Soul-Areists have muddied the waters on this point considerably, since fundamentalist Soul-Areism tends to treat all of the Canonical Texts as received Truth, and literal history. But despite the order's emphasis on the metaphorical nature of the tales, most authorities today acknowledge the stories written by the First Ravens to be largely legitimate (although some believe that even these tales had historical incidents as their starting point only, and were overlaid with motifs from earlier mythologies).

As might be expected, the best documented years of Brick's life are his last. Once the aftermath of the Great Crash was past, and the Order of the Railwalkers became something like an established institution, finding

their niche in the newly evolving society of mid-period
Merica, the gradual rebirth of record-keeping and media
technology provided for materials that would allow schol-
ars to build a larger and more detailed picture. (For an
extended treatment of this period, see M.E. Grant's *Red
Raven Twilight*.)

Yet, after a few brief years of reliable records, the
very last years of Brick's life are again poorly documented. After stepping down as Elder Raven, and seeing
the installation of his foster-son Ryon in his place, Brick
seems to have gone walkabout in the zones. What he did
there in those last three years is a complete mystery. It is
known that he surfaced at the Nestudio in New Frisco
once during the second year, and again toward the end of
the third year, when he informed Elder Raven Ryon that
he would not be returning again. One month after Brick
left for the zones that last time, Ryon called for the Chant
for the Dead to be sung for Brick.

For more detailed treatments of Brick's life, and critical analysis of the historicity of various tales, see the bib-
liography.

Preface to the Second Edition
The Book of Brick (Annotated)
Anthony Lumiere & Daniel Peirce, Editors
Corvine Books, New Frisco, 0304 AC

INTERLUDE: MAD BALLET

The Universe is a ballet of chaos, set in motion by a mad director. Thing is, the director being mad, once the show got started, he wandered off somewhere and forgot about it. Now, any time you set something in motion and walk away, you gotta expect it's gonna develop in its own patterns. That's how order and sanity come about at all. Life reaches toward it naturally. You look at any chaos closely enough, you'll see order, and vice-versa. But if life reaches toward order, at the same time, it reaches toward chaos, since part of us always wants to go back to our roots.

And who knows? Maybe the director comes by now and then, remembers the mad ballet, and throws some more madness and chaos into the mix. Not always a bad thing, necessarily.

Soul-Are is the light and order that evolve out of that mad ballet. Soul-Are is the chaos that breeds, and breeds in, the light and order. Soul-Are is the fact that all the dancers are one troop, one tribe, one family, not separate at all from each other, or from the stage they dance on. It exists whether the dancers recognize it or not, but recognizing it can free you from the choreography of insanity.

—The 23 Blessings, *The Book of Brick*

2. WOLF

Back around the time of the Great Crash, a huge earthquake knocked a big chunk of what was then the western coastline into the ocean. A whole bunch of places that had formerly been desert waste became beachfront property in a hurry. Probably would have done wonders for the real estate market, had it existed post-Crash.

Bay City grew up during the Reconstruction on the ruins of a smaller city. Couldn't tell you what that older city was called, though I'm sure you could find a historian who knows. I hear there was a pre-Crash "Bay City" somewhere in the northeast, but I couldn't tell you anything about that one either, other than that they apparently once had a famous rollerblading team.

As we soared over the desert, I could make out a glow on the horizon. Lot of power in Bay City. With its lights blurred by the rain it looked like a big glowing crescent, cupping the landward end of Baja Bay, spreading out for a couple of miles on either side of the Coronado River where it empties into the ocean.

"Look at this." Morgan raised her voice, turning the comp unit so I could see the screen. "You know Bay City produces so much electricity, they actually sell the surplus to other cities and zone towns nearby?"

I glanced at the screen. Looked like the city had some huge wind farms, and immense fields of solar collectors. By the sea it would get wind constantly, and except for the brief seasonal storms, they had sun pretty much all the time. The article said the city had been rich to begin with, but after the People's Takeover some 27 years ago it had surged ahead to rival Gatesville as one of the west's major tech centers. I would have been nine at the time, traveling with my Pa, a couple of years or so after our first encounter with Micah Roth.

"Anything about killings?" I asked.

She flicked through several screens. "Serial killer," she said, handing me the unit. "Call him 'The Beast.'"

I glanced over the articles, got the general idea, and handed the unit back. I didn't want to study the media on it until I'd had a chance to study the actual evidence.

Normally, after the time we'd spent in the arid zones, I'd have welcomed a little rain, but this gray night-drizzle was depressing for some reason. One of the things I liked about being in the zones was the herbal smell that rose up off the desert whenever it got one of these rare rainstorms. Just now, all I could smell was motor oil and the ozone scent of the 'thopter's electric engine. The sounds of the engine, the clatter of the wings and the propeller were all too loud for extended conversation. I stared out through the 'thopter's scratched perspex cupola. The lights of Bay City were diffused and piss-yellow in the distance, and I could now make out individual buildings, at least the taller ones, like the massive City Administration Tower.

Looking at the blurry skyline of Bay City, I was remembering other sounds, other smells... cigars and liquor, clinking ice cubes and flipping cards, grunted remarks. It had been in Bay City I'd first experienced the visions that would eventually put the tattoos on my face and the black coat on my back. I was just a kid then, trailing around after my itinerant gambler father, Pa following some obscure path on a chaotic map drawn by the gods of chance, a map that only he could read, leading from poker here to crops or jackflash there, from a back room or a fancy casino to a back alley or a gaming hell, from destitution to piles of cash and back again.

There had been a poker game that night, and I was alternating between sleepily watching the play and dozing off curled up in the corner. I came a little more awake at one point, wandered over to Pa's chair and looked over his shoulder. The game was down to my father and a big fat fellow across from him, and the fat guy had called. I was sure Pa was a shoe-in with his kings full house, but the fat guy grinned and laid down a suicide jack-high straight flush.

I was smelling oranges and burnt hair. When I looked up at the fat guy, instead of exulting at his win, his face was a picture of despair. He drew out an automatic pistol and put the barrel against his own temple. A second before he pulled the trigger, I screamed—I think it was "No!" or "Don't!" or something like that. Then suddenly the world shifted, and there wasn't any gun, the fat guy was grinning like a loon, and everybody was laughing.

"Don't sweat it, kid," someone said. "Your Dad can afford it."

I looked at my father and saw he wasn't happy; but it was clear to me that he was more disturbed by my outburst than by the result of the game. It was also clear that the whole bit with the gun had been some sort of vision or hallucination; no one had seen it but me.

"It's okay," Pa said quietly.

A month or so later I would learn that the fat guy had killed himself—not over cards, but over a woman. Or at least most folks thought the woman leaving him was the last straw in a series of bad news items in his life that led to his suicide.

At the time I had no concept of what this whole business of visions was all about, and for some years I would struggle with trying to live a normal life, or as normal a life as an itinerant gambler's son can live. Worked at shutting out the weirdness of having visions, seeing ghosts, hearing voices, and having animals talk to me. Eventually I couldn't shut it out any longer, and I turned to the Railwalkers for help. Little did I know that I'd end up joining the order.

When the ornithopter finally landed on the roof of the City Administration Tower, we climbed out and crossed to a covered walkway leading to the elevator. Six uniformed guardsmen stood at attention under the plasglass awning, led by a short, well-built young Hispanic woman wearing a sergeant's bars. Her black hair was tied into a bun, pulled back so tightly it looked like it must hurt. Eyes so dark brown they looked black in this light stared across the rooftop through the mists as we approached. The whole group stood at attention as we came up to the awning, and she saluted as if we were visiting guardsmen from another city. Guard usually treats us like civilians—civilians of rank, perhaps, but still civilians, for all that.

As she opened her mouth to speak a man pushed past the guards, a figure in a long coat that resembled a Crow coat, but without the patches.

"Who the hell are you?" he asked as we reached the stairwell.

There was a Force to his voice, a minor magick, one that any of us would disdain to use in such a manner. You put a Force in your voice to quiet a panicked crowd or tame a wilding animal, not to impress somebody at a first meeting. And with our coats, eye tats, and head scarves, it had to be pretty obvious what we were, if not who. I chose to answer him formally, as though he'd spoken the ritual question.

"Wolf am I, Walker of the Rails Between the Worlds, charged by Ianeh, seventh of her line from Brick, the Red Crow. Say your need."

I could feel the look Rok was giving the back of my head. Technically the ritual doesn't require the phrase "Twenty-three blessings of Soul-Are upon you and yours" between the kinline and "say your need," but it's customary. Don't get me wrong, Rok is not one of those anal, by-the-book types, mostly. He's just a bit particular about the rituals of the Order. My guess was that if it had been Rok, he'd have just ignored the guy and brushed by him.

The guy looked at me and gave a smirk. "Not the same Wolf who got lost in the Otherworld for three days trying to find Oakwood?" he asked. "Hear that was the talk of the Railwalker Academy back then."

It was true. As a student at the Railwalker Academy I was a real woodchuck sometimes, like any student is. I was older than most of the other students, but apparently not much wiser. So when Brecht came up with his challenge, like an idiot I accepted it.

I was second degree at that time, looking at taking my third. We'd been hanging in the student lounge, and Dirk was all full of first-degree enthusiasm about traveling the Otherworld physically. We all do soul travel in the Otherworld from our initiation on, but to qualify for third, a second degree has to move physically between worlds, as well as astrally. Dirk had just been introduced to the concept. Brecht had laughed at Dirk's newbie ebullience.

"It's not such a big deal, little otter," he said. The otter was Dirk's ally. "Bricks do it all the time." Brecht was aiming for a position as a Brick, though most of us figured he'd end up a Bear.

"Yeah," I said, "Brecht's a real expert at it. He's traveled there, what, at least two or three whole times now."

"Five times. Twice by myself." Which was absolutely forbidden, unless you'd made third degree.

"You're an idiot," I said. "You're still only second."

"Oh, right, Wolf, like you're ready to go walk the rails tomorrow."

"Readier than you are, numbnuts."

"Yeah? Prove it."

"Fuck you, Brecht. I got nothing to prove."

"Methinks the Wolf doth protest too much. You may have traveled the planes more often, but I got a natural talent for it. You'll never be as good as me." He stood and began pumping a fist in the air to a beat only he was hearing. "I am a rail-walking super-brick, a raven among crows. My ally is the mountain lion, as everybody knows. We eat otters for breakfast, and wolfies for lunch. I got a prof's mega-brain and a bear's killer punch. I got the power of Soul-Are a-rippin' through my mind, and in walking the rails I leave y'all behind. So don't pit yourself against the champion Brick, 'cause we already know you got a little tiny dick."

He finished leaning over me, his hands on the arms of my chair, his face inches from mine. If I'd jerked my knee up I'd have caught him right in the crotch, and I had a half a mind to do it, and hard.

"I repeat: You're an idiot. Get out of my face before I hurt you."

He looked down at my knee, straightened up, and stepped back. "A contest," he said. "You and me. Traveling in body. Here to…. We come out at the Rustic. Last one there buys a round."

I know, I should have told him to fuck off. Instead, I said, "You're on."

Every Railwalker sees the Otherworld differently. It can be a world of light, or one of fog and shadow, a world made of crystal or glass or neon. It may imitate this world, or present a surreal, distorted aspect.

I see it as a version of this world painted in strange. There are buildings and roads that roughly correspond to ours, but they always look not quite the same, oddly off, in a way I can't remember the particulars of when I'm back in this world.

When I opened my eyes in the Otherworld, Brecht was nowhere to be seen. I left the building and headed quickly toward the place I thought in this world would correspond to the Rustic Tap in ours. I was feeling extremely queasy, my guts rumbling and turning over, my skin seeming hypersensitive. My body knew it didn't belong here, and wanted to get the hell back to the normal world. I hurried faster, even though this made me feel sicker.

I didn't recognize the girl who came running from the Oakwood Bridge, but I knew immediately she was a lost soul. Her eyes were wild as she ran at me. I caught her as she caromed into me, and it was like grabbing hold of cotton candy—there, but not quite. She wasn't here in body, like I was.

"Breathe," I said. Having no lungs, she couldn't breathe, of course, but she could mimic the action, something that tends to calm you down, and she did, taking several long, deep breaths.

"Help me," she said. "I think this is death, and I'm not dead. I can't be dead."

They all think that at first. But sometimes it's true. Regular people with no training do soul travel here by accident. Now, I could create a door for her, let her move on to the land of the dead, something I'd been taught, though I'd never done on it my own. But what if she really was still alive? That would be bad. If I backtracked her to her body, I'd know for sure.

"What's your name?" I asked.

"Polly."

"Okay, Polly, I want you to close your eyes and think about when things were last normal for you. Can you do that for me?" She nodded and closed her eyes.

It was the better choice. When we located Polly's body, she was indeed still alive. Once she was sorted out and back in her body, I was feeling sicker than ever. By the time I made it across the Oakwood Bridge to the building I thought was probably the Rustic, I was staggering and finding it hard to breathe. I made the shift and sank to my knees on the sidewalk outside the Rustic Tap, and vomited onto the pavement. I was heaving in great gulps of air, sweat pouring off me. Gradually, I got hold of myself.

When I'd shifted, it had been night. It was now broad daylight. The afternoon sun made sections of the street glow like gold. I had been gone all of last night and most of today, probably seventeen hours or so. The extreme nausea was gone now, replaced now by an intense hunger.

I got to my feet. Walking to the door of the Rustic felt like walking across a trampoline. Inside it was as dim as always. There were four or five customers in booths, locals, and one guy at the bar. It was Rok. I dragged myself to the bar, sat down. The bartender came over to take my order, and I asked for a shot, a beer, and a burger. I turned to Rok.

"No hello? Nothing to say?"

"Figured I'd let you order first. You're probably starving."

"Yeah, actually, I am." The bartender delivered my beer and shot. When I reached for the shot, Rok gripped my arm.

"Get some food in first, or it will hit you too hard."

"Okay," I said, lifting the other glass, "but beer this dark qualifies as food." I wanted to gulp it, but made myself sip instead. "So, you're skipping classes today?"

"Waiting on you."

"What, so I miss a couple of classes this morning, you get all paranoid?"

"You've been gone for three days, brother."

I gaped at him. I'd known, in theory, that the Other-world could do that when you went there in body, distort time in all sorts of ways. I'd never experienced it first hand before. Subjectively, my mind was convinced the trip had taken an hour or two, three at most, but my body knew it had been three days. It made for a very schizophrenic feeling.

"No wonder I'm starving. And you've been waiting here the whole time?"

"Hell, no." He laughed. "The story was all over the school, and after you didn't show yesterday, a few of us started taking shifts, so nobody would miss too many lessons."

"Thanks. What about Brecht?"

"He was here an hour after you guys shifted. Guess you owe a bunch of people a round."

When my burger arrived, I very nearly lived up to my name with it, but forced myself to eat slowly. You vomited in the Rustic, you got tossed out.

I didn't get tossed out. I put down a second burger, a bowl of soup, and two more beers telling Rok the story of what had happened, and getting filled in on how Brecht and I were the talk of the campus.

Standing in the rain on the CA Tower roof, I wasn't about to get into all that with this jabone. Before I could respond, the leader of our escort spoke up.

"Sir, Mr. Roth requested we bring the Railwalkers to join him as soon as they arrived."

The man raised an eyebrow at the sergeant. "Don't tell me. Roth asked them here to deal with the Beast?" he asked, and then looked us over again. "I suppose we'd better go, then."

As I turned to follow the uniformed guard, Rok got right up in the jabone's face. I heard him say quietly, "He was guiding a soul home. How many souls have you guided, Grackle?"

A grackle is a bird that, to those who don't know any better, might look like a small crow. It had become a derisive term for Railwalker wannabes. I didn't catch the guy's reaction. I just followed the escort into the building. Behind me, I heard Morgan's voice say, "Collar's too big. Epaulettes are mounted the wrong way."

The conference room we were led to was large and nicely appointed. One long wall was an enormous window looking out over the winking lights of the city and the bay beyond. On the other was mounted a large reproduction of Bay City's official seal, a gold ring enclosing a stylized wave design. There were two other people waiting there with the city boss.

Micah Roth's dark suit was expensive, with fashionably wide lapels, the shirt crisp and blindingly white, his tie perfectly knotted. But his face looked rumpled and worn. Meeting him, you could see how the man could have inspired a mixed bag of city people, politicians and bureaucrats as well as merchants and labor forces, to take up arms against an entrenched regime. He was not tall, but barrel-chested, and carried himself in a way that gave the impression of height. His hair and beard, jet black when I'd encountered him years ago, were now mostly gray and white, but his eyes were still sharp, large and dark with a piercing look. When he turned that laser gaze on you, he made you feel like the only important person in the world—a useful tool for a politician, and an effect that could be very reassuring or extremely uncomfortable, depending on why you had his attention. At the moment he was glad to see us, and in spite of myself I found I hoped we could keep it that way. When I greeted Roth, I left in the "Twenty-three blessings" line.

"Micah Roth I am," he said in proper reply to my ritual greeting, "Boss of Bay City. Welcome to our city, Railwalker. Come freely, go safely, and bless us with your corvine council."

Next to Roth sat a massive woman in a gray knit dress, a silk scarf pinned at her shoulder. She was a head taller than the city boss, even seated. I'd have guessed she'd be at least six feet if she were standing, and built to go with the height, a cataract of wavy hair as black as Roth's once was only beginning to show some gray, and a face more handsome than beautiful. At the moment she looked tired, concerned, and kindly, but I had a feeling she could do forbidding just fine when she needed to.

"Sarah Weldt, my chief policy advisor," Roth said. We shook hands. She had a firm, dry grip, and a level gaze. I seemed to recall she might have been married to Roth at one time, but I wasn't certain. Neither of them wore a ring.

I introduced Morgan and Rok, and Roth introduced Merrin Gage, the chief of the city guard, and Guard Investigator Rainer Auden. Auden was the fellow who had challenged us on the roof, the one Rok had called "grackle." Chief Gage was a tall, athletic man in his mid-thirties. Worried eyes peered out of an aquiline face; the short Mohawk above it would provide an opponent nothing to grab in a fight. Tattoos peeked out from the collar

and cuffs of his dark blue uniform. It seemed unlikely that
he's achieved his post through politics. He looked like a
man who would be absolutely confident on the street, but
was afraid he might be out of his league in a council
chamber. Roth drew us to sit at a large conference table,
and Weldt called for coffee and tobacco.

Sarah Weldt acted the JavaMama. The ritual serving
set she used hadn't been bought at a discount shop. The
tray was walnut, inlaid with silver. The cups and pot were
a strangely delicate-looking earthenware in the same
shades. The communal cup had a shape like a cauldron on
a short stem, while the individual cups were tall, cyl-
indrical things, flaring at the top like the mouth of a trum-
pet. Each had a silver slotted spoon placed across it, a
small cube of sugar standing upon it. The big woman
gracefully raised the pot and slowly poured the black
liquid over the sugar and into the communal cup, until the
sugar dissolved. An experienced JM, she timed her pouring perfectly, so the last of the sugar vanished as the cup
was just about full, the final drop sweeping away the last
brown grain. The aroma of the coffee filled the room.

She dipped the small silver ladle into the bowl of
cream and placed a dollop in the cup. It spread slowly,
marbling through the black liquid before dissolving completely, leaving the coffee a rich, dark walnut brown.

Weldt raised the cup to the sky, then offered it to
Roth. "May your inner eyes be opened as your need
requires." Roth took the cup, sipped, returned it. With the
same formula, she offered the cup to me. It was good coffee, hardly cut with chicory at all, eighty percent pure,
unless I missed my guess. When all present had sipped
from the cup, Weldt repeated the pouring again, this time
into the individual cups, which she offered to all.

When we all had coffee, Roth took the pipe and filled
it from the bowl of tobacco. He lit it, puffed, and delivered
it to me. When we had all shared of the smoke, pipes and
cigars were offered for those who wished to continue
smoking. Roth and Weldt lit their own pipes, Gage and
Rok each took a cigar.

"Down to business." Roth sat back with a sigh. "I suppose you know there is a killer loose in Bay City."

I allowed as how we hadn't known until today; we'd been in the zones for several months, and mostly out of touch with the newsfeeds.

"He began by taking people off the street—fisherman, teacher, prostitute. Now he's killed two guardsmen, one of them the late Chief Adams."

Well, that explained why Gage looked a little uncomfortable. He'd only become the chief quite recently.

"In summoning you to help, I hope everyone understands I mean to imply no offense to Chief Gage, or the men and women of the City Guard," said Roth.

Auden shifted in his chair, and Gage fixed him with a look.

"None taken," Gage said, still looking at Auden. "We all loved the Old Man..." He hesitated, glanced at me. "Well, maybe not everyone, but even the ones who didn't like him respected him." He stopped, went inside himself for a moment, sighed, and then continued. "The whole guard is foaming at the mouth to take this bastard down. But to take him down, we've got to find him, and the plain truth is, we've gotten nowhere on this, even while Chief Adams was still alive. Our best Investigators have come up empty. If you can help us find this killer, that's all that matters."

"That's all that matters to you, maybe," Morgan said.

If Gage knows his own men, I thought, he knows about the attitude problem on Investigator Auden. Chances were Auden wasn't the only one.

"It's not unreasonable we should expect to encounter some resentment among your guardsmen," I said, keeping my eyes carefully on Gage, not looking at Auden.

"Maybe," said Gage. "But they'll keep shut about it and give you full cooperation, or they'll answer to me, and they all know that."

"Fair enough."

Auden's communicator gave a soft buzz and he excused himself.

"Have there been no demands from this killer?" I asked. "No one claiming responsibility?"

"So far," said Gage, "confessions have been a handful of kooks, their stories easily disproven. And no, no demands. No notes, no vids, no audios, no nothing."

The phone on the conference table rang. Roth picked it up, said "What?" As he listened his expression went from slightly annoyed to absolutely grim. He said, "They'll be right there," and hung up.

"Well," he said, looking at each of us in turn, "I guess you'll get a firsthand look at the Beast's work. He just killed Phillip Czernoff, the city treasurer, in the lobby of this building."

4. THE BAR OF GOLD

"What do you mean, he disappeared?" Dobbs demanded.

Carter Evans cringed. He didn't mind so much getting yelled at when he'd fucked up; that was natural, you had to expect that. But he hated it when his boss blamed him for things he couldn't control. And he wished Dobbs would sit down. When the tall, gangling bar owner waved his big, bony hands around like that, Evans was reminded of his old man, the way he'd wave his big hands around just before he'd start cuffing you.

"I mean he friggin' disappeared!" Evans insisted. "He goes inside the fuckin' jakes, and he never come out. I watched for a while, didn't I? Then I goes in, and looks around, see? And he ain't there. Nothing. Nobody. Zip, zilch, nada. Into thin air, like."

The very air of Dobbs's private office, reeking of cigar and bourbon, evoked Old Man Evans as well. The beery, cigarette smoke-fogged atmosphere of the Bar of Gold itself, with its overtones of unwashed bodies and grace notes of vomit and antiseptic, was comfortable and familiar. When swimming through it, Carter Evans felt like one of the sharks. In Dobbs's office, on the other hand, he felt like a delinquent kid.

Hanover Dobbs sighed, set his cigar in the ashtray, and sat down. He'd been thinking he could have had this interview at a corner table in the bar, but with the turn it had taken, he was glad he'd brought Evans back to his small private office. He looked steadily at Carter Evans. The scruffy little turd blinked, but he didn't back down. He believed what he was saying, that much was clear.

Mutants were often rumored to have strange powers, but Dobbs was not ready to believe that even a mutie could walk into a men's room and vanish. Evans wasn't the sharpest knife in the drawer; the mutie could have slipped by him.

"Anyone else come or go from the jakes?" Dobbs asked.

"Sure, several guys, but not the mutie. I'd have seen him. I were watching close, Dobbsey, swear to the gods I were."

Dobbs mulled this over. A few of the men Dobbs employed on errands were either so completely intimidated by him, or else so worshipfully devoted to him, they would do his bidding to the letter. Evans fit into both categories. If Evans said he watched close, he had watched close. Dobbs felt sure of that.

The little man had followed the mutie from the bar last night to an apartment—presumably the mutie's own, though it was a bit more upscale than most mutants could afford. Evans hadn't been able to tell which apartment he'd gone into, but the mutant had stayed there the night through and left in the morning. Evans had followed him to a dentist's office, where the mutant spent an hour or so, and then to the Bock Street tram station, where he'd pulled his vanishing act. Dobbs considered the possibility that Evans had missed the mutie's exit from the jakes because he was tired from watching the apartment all night. Possible, he thought, but less than likely.

"You sure you didn't just nod off and miss him?"

"Absolutely. Oh, I might have dozed a bit while I was watching the apartment, but not once he left in the morning. Popped a couple of crackers about four-ish, just so's that wouldn't happen."

Crackers, Dobbs thought. That's why he looked so wired. Dobbs wasn't into uppers himself, but he knew enough about the drug to know that if Evans was on crackers when he was watching the jakes, there was no way he'd have dozed off. Nevertheless, even muties couldn't vanish into thin air, so the fucker had to have snuck by

Evans somehow or other. Had the fucker known he was
being followed? Evans broke in on his ruminations. "I
didn't think I should follow him into the jakes. That
woulda give the game away, wouldn't it?"

"Shut up," Dobbs snapped, and Evans cringed. Fuck,
Dobbs thought, I shouldn't blame Evans. If the mutie was
a clever dick, it was Dobbs's own fault for setting Evans to
follow him, instead of someone with two more brain cells
to rub together. "No, Carter," he said finally, "it's alright.
You did right. Go have yourself a drink, whatever you
want. Tell Briggs I said it's on the house. Then go home
and get some sleep."

Evans burbled multiple thank-yous and bowed his
servile way out.

Hanover Dobbs poured himself a drink from his
private reserve and re-lit his cigar. He hated mutants. He
served them in his bar because the law said he had to, as
long as they could show they were properly registered with
the city. Once upon a time Dobbs would have scoffed at
the law, and any mutie who dared enter the Bar of Gold
would have found themselves unceremoniously chucked
out. But since he had decided to run for council two years
back, Dobbs had changed his policies. He didn't buy from
runners anymore, his hooch and pot had all the proper
paperwork and taxes paid on them, his little kitchen
passed muster with the health inspector, and his games
were all straight. Well, mostly straight. If his resident card
sharp was caught cheating by city officials, Dobbs was prepared to fire him and pay the appropriate fines.

Still, although he might be compelled by law to serve
the muties, he didn't have to make them feel welcome, and
he didn't. Yet this particular mutie continued to visit the
Bar of Gold each Thursday and Friday night. Dobbs
guessed the guy was just used to the stares and cold reception and didn't give a shit. He didn't stay long, anyway.
He'd come in, have a couple of drinks, and leave. But his
continued presence had drawn Dobbs's interest. One time
Dobbs had gotten behind the bar and served the guy himself, just to get a close look at him. He was tall—almost up

to Dobbs's own 6' 1". And strong. Dobbs had spotted the body of an athlete beneath his nondescript clothing, long and lithe, like a swimmer or a runner. He had no tail, no extra limbs; he wasn't obviously distorted or crippled like some mutants. His mutie status was betrayed only by his albino coloring: pale, white skin and hair and pink eyes. For Dobbs this somehow made it worse. Mutants whose knees worked backward like an animal's or who sported other obviously nonhuman traits were bad enough, but those whose appearance made them seem almost normal really twisted Dobbs's short hairs.

Dobbs couldn't have said exactly why he was so interested in this particular mutant, except for the question of why the fucker kept coming to a bar where he obviously wasn't welcome. But now he had a reason. You didn't vanish—or appear to vanish—from public restrooms unless you had something to hide. And Dobbs had a feeling he knew what the mutie was hiding. There was a killer loose in the city, and given the nature of the killings it was a good bet the Beast was a mutant.

By six o'clock the following friggin' bleary gray morning, Dobbs sat in his runabout outside the City Arms apartments. He wasn't really a morning person, but he could drag himself out early when he needed to. Evans had seen the mutie leave his apartment at eight to go to the dentist, but dental appointments meant variations in schedule; there was no telling what time the mutie customarily left his place in the morning, so Dobbs was there extra early to make sure he didn't miss the fucker. Dentist appointment, Dobbs mused, that's pretty mundane for a mutie serial killer. He supposed even the Beast had to get fillings now and then, but wondered if there were something darker behind it. Have to look into the dentist. Meanwhile, he thought, keep your eyes glued to that front door.

Watchful as he was, Dobbs might have missed the bastard if it hadn't been for the coat. It was about eight when he noticed the stylish blue trench coat. There was no doubt in his mind that the coat on the man coming out of the Arms belonged to the mutie; Dobbs had seen it too many times to mistake it. He set down his paper cup of coffee in the runabout's drink holder and stared. The dark hair and glasses and the olive skin tone were wrong, but once he'd recognized the coat Dobbs ignored the man's appearance and concentrated on his movements. The body language was right, he decided. It was the mutie disguised as a normal.

That had to be how he got past Evans. The mutie had gone into the jakes and changed into his normal disguise. This was getting better and better. The mutie—he had charged his drinks once, and Dobbs had discovered his name was Aguilar Cordoba, but Dobbs still thought of him as "the mutie" or just "the fucker"—headed off toward the tram station. Dobbs got out, locked the runabout, and followed.

5. WOLF

Neither Roth nor Weldt felt the need to be present, so it was just the three of us and Chief Gage who walked into the lobby of the City Administration Building, the scene of the killing of Treasurer Czernoff. Cavernous and marble-clad, two stories high, the lobby was split by a broad central stairway, with banks of elevators to either side and a security desk at the front, where a group of guardsmen clustered. Outside the thick glass doors, wide steps ran down to an open plaza. To one side of the steps lay a bloody corpse, presumably that of the treasurer. The place had already been cordoned off by the guard, essentially making the whole front of the building inaccessible from the plaza side.

The corpse lay in a pool of congealing blood, several steps down on a broad step that was virtually a landing. It was barely recognizable as human. One arm was twisted beneath it; the other, severed, lay two steps down from it. The chest was opened as if for an autopsy, white ribs gleaming amidst red and brown muscle and fat. The face had suffered several parallel slashes, exposing eyeballs, nose cartilage, and teeth. We'd seen worse, but not often. On the pavement beside the body a mark was painted in blood—three vertical slashes above a squat oval, presumably the "mark" we'd heard referred to. Investigator Auden joined us as we surveyed the scene.

"Chief," he said to Gage.

"Auden," the Chief nodded in return.

The investigator favored me with a slight head movement that, had it been allowed to live, might have grown up to be a nod. He turned back to Gage.

"Czernoff was apparently on his way home for the

night," he said. "Perp caught him coming out of the elevator. Looks like a quick job, no sign of struggle. Man on the desk heard nothing. Tyburn came down five minutes behind Czernoff and found him this way." His nod indicated a man in the over-robe of an Allworld priest who sat to one side of the broad stairway. The man was tall, his hair long but thinning on top, and he had a mournful look that I suspected was as much due to his customary demeanor as it was to the tragedy of the killing.

"No witnesses? Who was on the desk?" asked Gage.

"John Hamblin. Swears he didn't hear a thing."

"Hamblin?" said Gage suspiciously.

"Yeah, I know," Auden sighed. "Ran a breathalyzer on him. He's clean."

"And we're sure it was the Beast?"

"No question. Like his technique isn't distinctive enough already, he left his usual mark."

Gage regarded the mutilated corpse in silence for a moment. Finally he took a breath. "Are all the pieces accounted for? Do we know yet?" he asked.

Auden scrubbed a hand across his face. "We'll know for sure when the coroner gets here," he said. "But you want my guess? No. There's... parts unaccounted for."

There was an awkward silence.

"Kind of blows our theory to hell, doesn't it?" Gage said at last. "Czernoff was well known as an atheist."

"Theory?" I asked.

"We hadn't got to that yet," Gage said apologetically. "The only connection we've made so far among the victims has been that each was involved in some sort of religious activity. We were considering that if the Beast's killings aren't just random, there might be some religious motivation behind them."

"There still might," said Auden, staring at the body. "There are religionists who can't stand the idea of an atheist." He looked at me.

"I suppose," Gage allowed. "So why's Tyburn still here?"

"Some sort of ritual thing, helping his friend's spirit

move on. Thought it was polite to let him stay, seeing he's a city official and Czernoff was a close friend. He promised to stay out of our way, and he did."

"I wouldn't be too sure of that," I said. "We could have contacted the dead man's spirit and had the best witness of all. If this guy has seen the victim's soul off to the other side, he's just made collecting evidence from the spirit impossible. Excuse me a minute."

I walked over to where the mournful-looking Allworlder sat. "Brother Tyburn," I said, using the Allworlders' title for their priests, and held out my hand. "Wolf am I, Walker of the Rails Between the Worlds. Twenty-three blessings of Soul-Are upon you and yours."

He responded with the customary Allworlder greeting as he shook my hand. "Never thirst, Railwalker. I am Thudisar Tyburn. What can I offer?"

"Byer leave," I said as I sat down next to him, "Share words with me. I understand Treasurer Czernoff was a friend of yours. My condolences."

"Thank you. Yes, Phillip was a close friend." He glanced toward the body, and then quickly away, as if not wanting the sight of his friend's remains to replace the mental image of the person he'd known. "A true man of the spirit, for all he professed disbelief in souls or godhead. In the sense of being a generous, caring person, he was more spiritual than many who wear the cloth of their own denomination. I'm sure you know what I mean; you have undoubtedly met such in your own travels."

"That I have. Forgive my intrusion on your grief. Investigator Auden tells us you were here seeing to your friend's soul?"

"That is true." He gave a brief, rueful smile. "I imagine he was rather surprised to discover he had been wrong in his opinions about the existence of the soul."

"You imagine? You didn't speak with him, then?"

"Allworld priesthood does not train us in spirit travel, or speaking with the dead the way you Railwalkers do, but we have rites and rituals to help the soul pass on. I believe he has truly passed on now. I even took steps to be sure his shade dispersed."

That didn't bode well. I suppressed the urge to strangle the bastard and kept my face carefully neutral. "If you did not speak with the soul of your friend, I suppose you didn't learn anything about his killer?"

"Oh..." He blanched. "Oh shit... I didn't even think of that..." He looked at me, clearly flustered. "It was the Beast, surely...?" Recognition dawned in his eyes. "You... you have been asked to aid the guard in apprehending this killer? And you would have questioned Phillip's spirit about it? Oh, my. I have obstructed your investigation, haven't I? I am so very sorry, Railwalker Wolf. It never occurred to me. I was so concerned about Phillip's transition, the health and well-being of his soul, I never thought... My profoundest apologies."

It could have been that he was lying, that he was allied with the killer, but I doubted it. My sense of when someone was lying wasn't infallible, but it was pretty good. I thought it more likely he was a well-intentioned blunderer. Either way, it wouldn't achieve anything to let on how angry I was. We could possibly have sewn this thing up then and there, if it hadn't been for his meddling. Instead of shaking him until his teeth rattled, I again expressed my condolences. This man would bear watching, but I wasn't about to jump him to the top of the suspect list, at least not yet. I walked back to where Gage, Auden, and my partners stood.

"This Tyburn," I asked Gage. "Who is he?"

"He's the head of the city's technology bureau," Gage told me.

"And an Allworld Priest? He have a temple here?"

"He did at one time. I think he just assists there now. Allworlders don't pay their clergy, so they all hold down regular jobs as well." I had known that, but most of the Allworld priests I'd known had part-time jobs, or did consulting work. Allworlders tended to work well with technology, especially higher tech like computers and communications. Not many of them held full-time positions as prestigious as a city tech officer. I explained briefly what

I'd learned from Tyburn.

"Stupid dick," said Morgan. I frowned at her. She grimaced, but said nothing more.

"We'll have to deal with what we've got." I took in both Gage and Auden with a look. "But I'd keep an eye on Tyburn, if I were you. I don't think he was lying, but you never know. He might have had a reason for sending his friend off so quickly."

Gage nodded, and Auden looked speculatively in Tyburn's direction. Gage sighed.

"Well," he said, "our forensics people are nearly done here." He looked at Auden for confirmation, and the investigator nodded. "Unless there's something else you lot think you can learn from this location, I'd like to get the cleanup crew working. Roth did say he'd like this site cleared up as soon as possible. I can have one of my men show you to your accommodations."

"Not yet," I said. "Since we can't consult the spirit of the late Phillip Czernoff, we should try our luck with the next to last victim, and as soon as possible. I'd appreciate it if you could take us to the site of Chief Adams's murder."

"That would be our wardroom."

I had expected the City Guard wardroom to be a bland, institutional gray, with a dribble of ancient coffee slowly burning to carbon on a hot plate, a deck of cards on a metal table, and not much else. All three of us stopped dead as we entered the place, which looked almost like a small apartment. There was a kitchenette with a large table that could have served as a conference table as easily as a dinner table, with a speakerphone in the center of it. The lounge area held a couch and chairs, television and DV player. Calendar, cork board, and duty roster hung on the near wall, one picture hung on another, a view of the bay by Euri Pappas, a sergeant who was also a weekend artist. There were none of the motivational posters you saw in other guard wardrooms. I walked about, surveying the room. Rok actually almost smiled as he looked around.

"Nice," he said quietly, nodding.

"And empty," I said. Late on a week night, the ward-room would normally be fairly quiet. Tonight it was deserted.

"Since the Chief's murder, a lot of the guard have been finding other places to spend their break time," said Gage. That made sense. Once forensics had finished, the place had been cleaned up, but you couldn't clean the memories of what had happened there out of the mind.

Gage stood back and watched silently as we set about our tasks. I set up a small brazier in the center of the room, loaded it with pieces of charcoal, and lit them. I took out several small packets of herbs, which I placed beside the brazier, along with the blood samples we'd collected from the evidence room, and the slip of paper torn from the bottom of a day roster with Adams's signature on it.

Morgan approached the wall phone, then glanced around the room. She noticed the phone on the table. "Speakerphone," she said. "Score!"

She unplugged the speakerphone and, producing a screwdriver from her pack, removed the casing to expose its inner works. She removed the phone cord and replaced it with a short cord with the wires of the far end exposed. These she attached to a small battery.

Rok looked quickly through the cabinets in the kit-chenette, found a bowl, and filled it with water from the sink. Into the water he emptied a packet of graveyard dust. He took out a small rectangle of metal, about the size and shape of a stick of gum, placed it in the water, and muttered quietly over it. He left the metal piece in the bowl and went around the room, unplugging electrical devices—toaster, microwave, television.

Gage was watching me as I stood back, waiting for the charcoal to catch. "If you don't mind my asking, what exactly are you doing?" he asked.

"We're going to try and contact the shade of your murdered chief."

Of all the murder victims, Guard Chief Adams was not only among the most recent, but was also the one most likely to be able to give us useful information. I had little doubt that even as he died, some part of the old chief's mind would have been recording all the relevant information—his attacker's height, weight, eye color, distinguishing marks, all the little details a good investigator registered automatically.

"You think he's still here?" asked Gage. "I mean, yeah, the men don't hang out here much these days, but I haven't heard rumors of mysterious cold spots, or voices, or shadowy figures or anything."

"Uncomfortable with this, Chief?" I asked.

"Not afraid of ghosts, and certainly not the ghost of Chief Adams." Adams had apparently been a mentor to Gage. "In fact, the idea of the old chief still being around in some sense, watching over the guard, is kind of cool." He thought for a moment. "But I'm not so sure I like the idea of his being stuck here. Once you're done, you'll send him on his way, right? To the other side, or whatever you call it?"

"Probably he's already gone," I told him. "Ghosts aren't souls, anyway. When a person dies, the departing soul sheds a sort of psychic residue, like a shadow of itself; we call it a shade. Normally the shade just sort of disperses once the soul has moved on to the land of the dead. But there's something about violent death that makes it possible for the shade to hold itself together for a while. That's what people call a ghost."

Rok had returned to the kitchenette and taken the piece of metal from the bowl. He now handed it to Morgan. She inserted it carefully into the workings of the phone, and the mechanism gave a short tone. She nodded to me, and I crouched down and began adding the herbs to the coals in the brazier. As they caught fire and began to smolder a pungent smoke billowed up. Its smell was not repulsive, but it was not entirely pleasant, either.

Morgan set up a small portable computer next to the speakerphone and booted it up. Rok had stepped back to a point beside Gage; he leaned against the wall, arms folded, watching me.

"So," Gage asked, "how do you...?"

I held up a hand to forestall the question. Crouched down by the brazier, I opened the small plastic evidence bag and sifted some of the dried blood onto the piece of paper with Adams's signature. I spoke the ritual formula quietly. I heard Gage whisper to Rok, "This will bring the Old Man's shade?"

"It's a long shot," Rok answered quietly. "Even if we connect with the shade, it may not be able to tell us anything useful. Shades ain't exactly what you call conscious entities. They're like the smell in the air after a fire—it ain't the fire itself, or even the smoke; it's just, like, a fading memory of the fire."

I looked over at Morgan, who nodded. "We're good," she said.

I lit a pair of candles and Rok killed the lights.

Gage looked at Rok, raised his eyebrows. "So it's like a séance?" he asked. "Are we going to hold hands?"

"Nah." Rok laughed. "The more electrical stuff is working nearby, the more interference. So we unplug everything, turn out the lights."

"What about the computer?"

"Low voltage, direct current." Gage frowned, as if he didn't see why that should make a difference. Rok didn't elaborate.

I carefully laid the blood-dusted paper on the coals. It didn't flare up, as paper usually does; it too simply began to smolder and burn slowly, as if it were damp.

"So why don't you try to contact his actual soul? Wouldn't his soul be more coherent?"

"If he was stuck between, in one of the shamanic realms or in limbo, we might be able to find him and talk to him. But it looks like he's moved on, y'know? Gone into the light, to the land of the dead."

"I thought Railwalkers could travel to the land of the dead."

"Nah. Every Railwalker goes there once, during their initiation. But you can't ever go there a second time while you're alive."

I stood up and stepped back from the brazier.

"So how do you contact this shade?" Gage asked Rok.

"We don't," I said. "We get him to contact us."

The speakerphone rang.

Despite the number of times I'd done this sort of thing, at the ringing of the disconnected speakerphone, something fluttered in my diaphragm. No one said a word. We all froze, looking at the phone. I held up a hand. You always wait for the third ring in these cases. It rang a second time. One knock for chance, two coincidence, thrice is... There it was. I stepped to the table, leaned forward and hit the "connect" button on the speakerphone. With the volume turned all the way up, a static hiss filled the darkened room.

"George Frederic Adams?" I asked loudly.

The reply from the speakerphone was indistinct, scratchy, as though the connection was bad, torn by interference.

"It's all I know," a voice said.

I looked at Gage. He was staring wide-eyed. I knew he could feel a tingling throughout his body, as if the room were filled with static electricity, just like I could. Your heart begins to race, and it gets hard to draw a breath. Your palms are sweaty, and the coppery taste of adrenaline is in your mouth. It hits everybody that way, every time, but the first time was always a real bitch. I felt for him.

George Adams was dead. Gage had seen his bloody, mutilated body in this very room, had seen it again at the autopsy, and with other guardsmen he had carried the casket containing that body in solemn ceremony to the funeral pyre, watched it reduced to ash. And now he was hearing the man's voice issuing from a speakerphone—a disconnected speakerphone in a darkened wardroom. I wanted to remind him that if this wasn't Chief George Adams, his friend and mentor, it was some fragment of him, and there was nothing to fear from the Old Man. But I knew his body would not be convinced. His body knew this was just wrong, unnatural, a cause for flight or fight. I waited, watching Gage. He forced himself to breathe slowly and deeply. That was good.

The voice spoke again.

"I'm dust in the wind. French Canadian bean soup."

Gage made a choked sound that might have started life as a laugh. I exchanged glances with Rok and Morgan. We were none of us so jaded we were unmoved by the voice of the dead, but this wasn't terra incognita to us as it was to Gage. The guardsman did seem to find some reassurance in the three strangers' calm, "business as usual" outer demeanor.

"We need your help," I said to the shade.

After a moment, there was a whine-like feedback from the phone, and the voice came again. "She told him father would be proud. The evil one is not for you, not yet."

I frowned. Was the Chief telling us we couldn't catch the Beast? Or that we couldn't catch him yet? That something else was fated to happen before we could hunt down the killer? I found myself staring unseeing at the opposite wall, where the bloodstains had been scrubbed off and the wall repainted. The bloodstains were back now, and fresh; I could see the drops crawling slowly toward the floor.

"Can you tell us about your killer?" I asked.

The lights flickered on, then off again. A burst of static crackled from the speakerphone, and the tone sounded once. I felt a clammy chill on the back of my neck.

"Andy wasn't there," the speakerphone crackled. "The clothes are in a rucksack. Kindly take my shoes off."

Gage shook his head. "Andy's the guard station janitor," he whispered. "It's was true he wasn't there the night of the Chief's murder."

I tried again. "Who killed you?"

"There is no self to know." Another loud burst of static. Suddenly we found ourselves blinded, as if we were surrounded by a storm of electric snow. Every hair on my body stood up. Distantly, I heard the Chief's voice say, "Mother knows best." I gasped, shook my head, and my vision cleared as the speakerphone rasped, "Memory is gone, on a work release."

I wondered if Gage had experienced the same weird static storm we had.

"Did you know your killer?"

"The sun is set, set on it. A boy has never wept, nor dashed a thousand kin."

Behind the voice, I thought I could hear the sound of a baby crying. Despite the closed doors and window, a definite cold breeze moved through the room.

"How did he get into the wardroom?"

The television in the corner flickered, uttered a scratchy burst of music, a vague, snowy image of face appeared on the screen—not Adams, but a thin blond man's face, animated, apparently speaking or singing. It vanished, appeared again, became what looked like Adams's face for a moment, and then turned to snow. Another short burst of music came from the speakerphone, and it stuttered, "Ch-ch-ch-ch" as this time the dead chief's voice came from the television. "Turn and face the strange. It's changes; it's the training, y'know," it said.

The screen lit up again, this time showing a black and white image of a man with hair growing rapidly over his face. This was replaced quickly by a color shot of a corridor, where a large suitcase quickly morphed into a strange, pasty-faced man in a uniform I didn't recognize, before the television died again. The microwave gave forth popping noises, as if someone were trying to cook something foil-wrapped in it; then there was a bang as its door flew open. "Don't make any bull moves," the speakerphone urged.

"Can you tell us anything about the Beast?"

"It's duty, to serve and protect." The voice was fading now, overtaken by staticky white noise.

"George?" I said more loudly. "George Adams, can you hear me?"

We could barely make out the reply.

"I was once, but I can't talk long. Move on, Mamma."

The quality of the static changed, and there was a buzz, almost like a dial tone on a normal phone. I looked at the brazier. The paper was now completely ash. On the wall behind us the bloodstains were gone again. I took a deep breath, sighed, and turned the speakerphone off.

I collapsed into a chair, scrubbed my hands over my face. Morgan looked up at Rok, then left his side to walk to the table, where she sat down before the computer.

"New shielding hold okay?" I asked.

"Puh-lease." Morgan rolled her eyes.

"So did we get it?"

She nodded. "End to end."

"You were recording it," Gage said suddenly. "But what's the use? It doesn't really tell us anything much."

"Well," I said, "it does tell us a few things."

"Like what?"

"Like for one thing, your killer is a shapeshifter, and I think possibly a professional assassin, trained for this sort of work."

"I didn't hear him say anything like that." Gage looked at each of us in turn.

Rok smiled. "You gotta know how to listen to a shade," he said.

6. THE CAVE

He sat in the cave, staring into the darkness. The morning's meditation had not gone well. His mind kept sliding back to the mistake he had made last night.

It was not a huge, horrible mistake. It had not affected the outcome of his mission particularly, but the implications worried him. He stood, moved forward, and began his basic katas. Block, step, punch, block, kick... The familiar patterns and movements brought some relief from anxiety. Here, within the realm of physical flow, attack and defense, he was in his element, completely in control. He moved through the pitch black of the cave with utter assurance, not because he could see, although his eyes could pierce the darkness far better than human eyes, but because he knew without seeing where every flat place and steep pitch was, every boulder and stalactite, every rock and stone. Still, as he moved through the forms, the questioning face of the man from last night still arose before his eyes.

He had been approached on the street by a laborer, who had posed a question, and he knew not how to answer. He glanced up and down the street—they were virtually alone. He considered killing the man just for the fun of it, slashing his throat first so he could not scream, and then... But no, that would have broken the pattern, and the pattern was important. He had recovered by pretending he could not speak, using sign language to suggest he was in a hurry to get somewhere, and the man went away. No real harm was done. Still, it was worrisome. When he had been in Santa Brita, he had known the city and its people, the rhythm and melody of their language, their slang, their accents. He had remained an outsider, of course, and did not fully understand what all their various interactions really meant, but he was a careful observer, and an excellent mimic.

Though he had grown up in this cave, not far from Bay City, and he knew his way around the city streets, he had never lived among its people. He did not feel in his bones the throb of the city's heart, did not know the dialects of the various social realms, the music of their speech, the way he had in the brief years he had lived in Santa Brita. He would not allow himself to feel any nostalgia. To wish for a time that was gone was a pointless indulgence, a weakness, a way of turning your face from what is; and facing that which is at every moment was crucial to his survival and the success of his mission. Still, it had been easier in Santa Brita.

Finished with the kata sequence, he shifted to what he thought of as his true killing form. Teeth grew into fangs, hands became claws, skin thickened and hardened to horny plates. He was proud of this form. He had worked hard at developing it over the course of several years, and it had not been easy. The hide had to be thickest and hardest where it protected vitals, and where arms and legs would be used for blocking, yet it had to be flexible enough in the right places to allow him a full range of movement. The claws had been the most difficult task, and it took him months to perfect them. He could never tell when he might need dexterity in his hands, and not have time to change. The claws had initially made it difficult to use his hands for anything other than rending and tearing. Over time, however, with practice and experimentation, he arrived at a claw design that he could manage quite well. A big breakthrough came when he realized claws did not have to be needle-sharp to be deadly. By slightly roughening the very tips, he discovered he could employ them like tweezers or forceps, and eventually he was able to manipulate the tiniest objects far better than blunt human fingers could. And they could still disembowel a human with a single slash.

The shift of form finished, he moved into his own

unique kata series, which he had devised especially for this form. His killing form did not move exactly as a human body would. Now, after years of practice, he was as fluid with these kata as with the others. He had not revealed his killing form to the Ravagers at first; his human form was more than adequate to their purposes. After he had traveled with them for several months, he had ensured that he could trust them to keep his secret by the simple expedient of killing all those he did not trust, either by engineering accidents or picking fights with them. He was careful to make sure that when their raiding was done, no one was left alive to recount tales of a monstrous creature that traveled with the Ravagers. He did not want rumors reaching Bay City until he was ready to reveal himself there.

When the time came, he had watched with interest as the guard destroyed the remnants of his Ravager band. In company with the guard had been two strange men, not guardsmen but members of some other brotherhood. Each wore a long, black coat, and a tattoo over one eye. Each carried about him the aura of the Otherworld, the scent of magic and mystery, and each fought with a spirit and discipline beyond even the best among the guard. He had heard tales of the Railwalkers, but he had never seen them before.

When it was over, in solemn ceremony, he sang to their spirits, and ate their brains.

7. WOLF

Like most of the city's government, the guard had their headquarters in the City Administration Tower, the same building we'd landed on. The CA Tower, as it was known, was the largest building in the city, and within its precincts were not only many offices and conference rooms, but also suites for visiting dignitaries and for city officials who might be working overnight. The tower pre-dated the Great Crash, though what it might have been in those days—corporate office building, expensive apartments, or civic offices—was no longer evident, given how thoroughly it had been revamped and redecorated many times over the years.

The suite we'd been assigned was not exactly palatial by city standards, but it was far more luxurious than any of us were used to. There were three bedrooms and a common room with armchairs, couch, and DV unit. On the table was a bottle of moderately expensive hooch and an invitation to the Bay City Summersend Festival, with a note from Roth asking if I would give the Harvest Blessing. Of course, in a city, the Harvest wasn't so much corn and grain as the city's economic index, but they'd use produce to stand in for that. The idea was the same.

Preoccupied with the murders, I'd forgotten the festival was so close. It was traditional for communities to ask any visiting Railwalker to give the Blessing, and I'd done it plenty of times, though never for such a large crowd as would probably be assembled at this event. I told myself I'd get through it fine. What I really wasn't looking forward to was the reception afterward. Diplomacy is part of the Railwalkers' job; you had to do the meet and greet. But just now I begrudged the hours away from the investigation.

Morgan sat down at the table, swept the bottle and invitation to one side, opened up her portable unit, and started to work on the recording. Rok and I knew what she'd be about. Shades are disconnected from the normal flow of time. Frequently they answer questions backwards. Morgan would be taking the responses from George Adams's shade and re-ordering them, so that his first answer would match my last question, his second my next-to-last, and so forth, until his last answer matched my first question. Hopefully at that point the whole thing would make much more sense. She'd also be running the recording through a battery of tests, enhancements, filters, and analysis, slowing it down, speeding it up, running it backwards, to see if anything other than the obvious voices turned up.

"What do you think?" I asked Rok.

"Well," he said, "Gage is alright—a straight arrow, not real long on imagination, but I think we can trust him. The other guy, Auden... He's gonna be trouble."

"You think so? I dunno. He resents our being here, yeah, but I don't think he'd actively interfere. Seems to me he wants the Beast stopped as bad as anyone. He may grumble about us, but I'd bet on his cooperation." Rok shook his head skeptically.

"He's a dick," Morgan said, her eyes still glued to the screen, where multiple windows showed various waveforms and charts.

"Didn't say he wasn't," I said. "But I don't think he'll cause us a problem."

"Coyote's balls," said Rok. "Will you look at all that paper?" The stack of files on the table was a good three inches thick. "I've never seen a city use this much paper."

Morgan said, "Hemp paper. There are huge hemp farms to the northeast of Bay City. Acre of hemp produces as much paper as ten acres of trees, and you get a new crop every four months."

"So Bay City doesn't care how much they use," said Rok. "Amazing." I joined him as he opened up the sheaf of files. Here was Auden's report on his encounter with the Beast, the one eyewitness we had so far, aside from the fragmented testimony of the shade of Chief Adams.

Auden's description said the Beast was over six feet, two hundred pounds or so, very powerful, unnaturally fast. Bald, with the mark he'd left at the scenes on his forehead—whether tattoo, birthmark, or paint, Auden hadn't been able to tell. With claws, and something odd about the eyes. Auden had speculated that he might be a mutant. I had thought mutants were barred from the city, but Gage had informed me they were only required to register themselves.

The muties lived mostly out in the zones. That's where they came from, after all. In the Great Crash there had been a nuke dropped, and there were areas beyond the zones where it still wasn't safe for any living being to go; you'd die of the burning sickness. Scientists said that same energy changed human genes so they'd produce mutants, which was why they mostly appeared in the zones.

You hear ancient legends of mutants with strange powers, but I haven't seen that very often. Mostly, muties are just shaped weirdly, or missing something, or have some strangeness about them that cripples or disadvantages them. Occasionally it gives them advantages as well, but generally mental ones—they're outstanding at mathematics or pattern recognition or something. Usually there's some physical problem to go along with it. Very rarely, it gave them some physical edge: great size or strength, night sight, claws, whatever. I'd only seen that sort of thing a few times, but of course those were the types of things that got people talking, telling stories; so that was the popular impression of muties in the cities, where they weren't seen as often.

Some folks pity them, some despise them. Me, I figure they got dealt a lousy hand, but they're mostly like the rest of us on the inside. Unfortunately, I've seen the insides of enough of them to know.

The Beast Auden had seen, with his size and claws, could have been a mutie, but if so he was a rare one.

Something the shade had said made me think the Beast was a shapeshifter, instead. Shifting your shape was an acquired skill; shapeshifters were made, not born. It wasn't one of those apparently occult powers that muties were sometimes born with. A shapeshifter was a magic user, which could possibly imply other uses of magic as well, though that wasn't a given. Changing shape was a major operation. To do it well took lots of training, will, determination; it occupied lots of your time, so most shapeshifters I'd encountered weren't exceptionally skilled at other types of magic. They tended to be specialists.

Patrolling the streets, Auden had come across the Beast at his work—killing a professional harlot named Suzi Mascarpone. It was the first time anyone had seen the killer. The investigator had been certain he had hit the Beast with all three rounds, yet the killer had jumped up again, disarmed the investigator, and then run off. It wasn't likely an experienced investigator would be wrong about hitting his target. It was possible the killer could recover quickly from wounds by shifting just the flesh around them, but it would take enormous energy and concentration. More likely the Beast had been wearing body armor, or the shape he'd shifted to might have had its own built-in armor: thick, tough hide covering its vitals.

Reading between the lines of the report, it seemed almost as if the Beast were playing with Auden, taunting him. The fact that he'd done that, and refrained from killing the investigator when he probably could have done so fairly easily, along with the leaving of a mark near each victim, suggested a definite agenda. The harlot, Mascarpone, had been his intended victim and the investigator had not; the Beast had killed only his target.

Looking over the files on the victims, I could see why Auden and Gage were considering the religious angle. But although many of the victims had been active in one religious cult or another, they all followed different religions.

The first kill had been a fisherman, Arnold Hawthorne. His professional life had been pretty innocuous—he ran a small fishing boat that he'd inherited from his father, had four employees whom he apparently treated well, no complaints registered. Spent his weekends surfing. He was also the priest, or "Core Charger," of a small circle of worshipers of Huey Otiz, God of the Sea. According to the notes, his congregation, or Brasse, had all been quite happy with him, and were grief stricken at his demise.

The second victim had been an archaeology teacher named Juan Castro. He was well liked by students and other teachers, although thought of as a little weird and eccentric. In his youth, Castro had headed up the Bay City College's Campus Crusade for Cthulu, and was apparently still sometimes seen at their events. There was some debate amongst historians and mythologists as to whether Cthulu had been an actual ancient god or a product of a pre-Crash novelist's imagination. The guard investigators seemed to have taken the impression that Castro was quite serious about Cthulu, but I had my doubts. Castro was also a big Roth supporter, had volunteered in Roth's last campaign. Considering Roth stood for order and democracy, and Cthulu was generally taken to stand for chaos and apocalyptic disaster, it seemed to me Castro probably had his tongue in his cheek about the CCC. Of course, you could never tell for sure.

Guardsman James Fitch had come third. Fitch was a Soul-Areist. To the Railwalkers, Soul-Are is not a god, but a principle, the animating energy of the multiverse. We don't invest Soul-Are with personality; it's more like the Tao or the Force. Soul-Areists worship and pray to Soul-Are as a personal deity. Originally they approached the Railwalkers to act as their priesthood, but the order had refused. We couldn't prevent them from disseminating a wrong-headed interpretation of our philosophy, but we didn't have to support it.

The harlot, Suzi Mascarpone, had recently joined the Marilynists. That was a new one on me, but according to the information in the guard file it was a growing cult among the harlots, based on the idea of the Sacred Prostitute.

The last two victims seemed to break the pattern. Chief Adams had been a Christian, but not an ardent one. Attended his Church irregularly, mainly at the high holy days. Czernoff had been an atheist, although his friend Tyburn had called him a spiritual man.

I didn't see that the religious angle was really holding much water. But then my own idea, that the Beast had some score against Roth, didn't appear to be holding up well, either. Chief Adams and Treasurer Czernoff fit that pattern, and maybe Guardsman Fitch; and then the teacher, Castro, had worked on Roth's campaign staff. But the others had no obvious connection.

All the victims had been mutilated in various ways. In most cases, pieces of them were missing, and never recovered.

Morgan looked up from her comp unit and pulled out one of her earbuds. "I think that's it," she said. "Not much beyond the shade's answers. A few of those random vocal fragments you always get in recordings like this, but that's pretty much it."

She hit the playback.

"George Frederic Adams?" my voice asked.

"I was once, but I can't talk long." Morgan's filters had cleaned it up some, but the voice from the speakerphone was still scratchy. "Move on, Mamma."

"We need your help,"

"It's duty, to serve and protect."

"Can you tell us about your killer?"

"Ch-ch-ch-ch.... Turn and face the strange. It's changes; it's the training, y'know. Don't make any bull moves."

Rok held up a finger, and Morgan paused the recording. "That was the point where the DV came on," she said.

Rok nodded. "The image was from an old black and white movie, *The Wolf Man*. It's about a shapeshifter."

"And the color image?" I asked, "where the suitcase turned into a guy?"

"Not sure."

"TV show," said Morgan. "I think it was one of the Trek franchise programs had a shapeshifter in it."

"So it's pretty clear what Adams means," I said. "Our killer's a skinwalker."

Morgan started the recording again.

"Who killed you?" I heard myself ask.

"The sun is set, set on it. A boy has never wept, nor dashed a thousand kin."

"Did you know your killer?"

"There is no self to know. Mother knows best. Memory is gone, on a work release."

"How did he get into the wardroom?"

"Andy wasn't there. The clothes are in a rucksack. Kindly take my shoes off." This time I was the one held up a hand, and Morgan paused it again.

"Gage said Andy's the janitor," said Rok.

"And he wasn't there, he was out sick or something," said Morgan.

"'The clothes are in a rucksack,'" I quoted. "Want to bet our shapeshifter got in masquerading as Janitor Andy?" No one did. I nodded, and Morgan hit "play" again.

"Can you tell us anything about the Beast?"

"She told him father would be proud. The evil one is not for you, not yet."

"George? George Adams, can you hear me?"

"I'm dust in the wind. French Canadian bean soup. It's all I know."

And that was all we had. Some of what we'd heard we recognized as random, nonsense phrases we'd heard before from other shades, like the one about the boy who dashed a thousand kin, or the French Canadian bean soup. Why certain phrases like that should keep cropping up over and over in dialogues with shades is beyond me, but they do.

Eliminating the nonsense, what we were pretty sure of from this one was that the shade of George Adams was doing his best to cooperate ("It's duty, to serve and protect"), and that the killer was a shapeshifter ("It's changes, it's the training, y'know"). "There is no self to know" probably indicated some form of psychic training. He'd likely come into the wardroom in a disguise of some sort ("The clothes are in a rucksack"), possibly shapeshifted to the form of a janitor named Andrew Foreman ("Andy wasn't there"). Foreman, it later turned out, had spent the evening in question in an emergency room, victim of a hit-and-run accident.

The jury would be out for a while on some of the other remarks. References to Mother or Momma were quite common in shade contacts, but it was hard to know in any given case whether they were nonsense babbling or had some actual relevance. Comments about fathers were more rare, and I wondered about "She told him father would be proud. The evil one is not for you, not yet." Was Adams telling us that we couldn't stop the Beast yet, or was the "evil one" someone else? Could this have been addressed to the Beast himself, by the "she" who told him Father would be proud? It seemed to me that the victims were getting a little closer to Roth with each subsequent killing, and I wondered if the Beast was maybe working his way up the food chain to the City Boss. Was Roth the "evil one" in the Beast's mind? "Father would be proud..."

"Wait a minute," I said. "Run the recording back a bit." Morgan backed it up, playing bits and pieces until I heard my own voice ask, "Who killed you?"

"Right there," I said.

"The sun is set," Adams's scratchy voice told us. "Set on it."

Maybe Adams hadn't meant "sun," but "son." Suddenly, something clicked in my brain. The son was set on it... Father would be proud...

I grabbed the phone and called Roth. When he picked up, there was no "Hello," only, "It's nearly three A.M. This better be damned important."

"Did Wendell Crichton have a son?" I asked.

"Railwalker Wolf? What? No, no children."

"Are you sure?"

"Absolutely sure. It was one of the real tragedies of the

Takeover. Crichton and his wife had problems having children. She'd finally gotten pregnant, but she was killed in
the fighting, and the baby died with her. Why is this
important?"

"I guess it's not. Sorry to have disturbed you."

"Oh, no problem. I had to wake up to answer the
phone anyway."

I hung up on Roth's sarcasm.

"You were thinking the Beast might be Crichton's
son?" Morgan asked.

"Or connected to him somehow, working for him or
something. But Roth says Crichton had no kids. His wife
was pregnant at the time of the Takeover, but she and the
baby both died in the fighting."

"Figures," said Morgan. "That would have been too
easy."

Morning sun streamed in the large windows to paint gold across the ranked desks of the investigators' bullpen. There weren't many people there at this time of morning, three or four of the investigators drinking coffee at their desks and doing paperwork, Sergeant Robles talking to one of them. We crossed the room through the bands of sunlight to where Rainer Auden's desk sat.

"Morning, Investigator Auden," I said.

Auden eyed us from behind his desk. "Roth called you guys in," he said without preamble, "and the Chief says we all gotta cooperate with you. I'm a paid employee of the city, and orders are orders. I'll do what I'm told, but I don't have to like it. The guard can look after its own."

"Well," said Morgan, "two of you killed, the Chief right here in your own wardroom. I'd say you've done a bang-up job so far."

Auden sat forward in his chair, fists balled, and for a moment I thought he was going to stand up and take a shot at her. Then I saw something shift in his eyes. He knew that however much he hated the truth, Morgan was right.

"Look, man," I said, "we're only interested in finding this guy. We don't have any agenda about making the collar. If we can find him for you, you're welcome to bring him in or take him down."

Auden raised a skeptical eyebrow. He didn't say anything, though, so I continued. "You need our help to find him. We've got ways and means you don't, but to use those skills, we also need all the information we can get. For us to be able to help you, you've got to help us."

"You've got copies of my reports."

"Reports are nothing but facts. We need more than that. You saw this Beast face to face. You can tell us things the written report can't. As an investigator, you've gotta know that. Reading a written report is different from hearing a witness's story firsthand. And a professional investigator is the best witness we could hope for."

Auden stood. "You've got my reports. Read 'em." He shouldered past me and left the bullpen. The door didn't exactly slam behind him on the way out, but nobody in the room had any doubt that it had closed.

Morgan opened the file with Auden's reports. "Six-four or so, maybe two-thirty, two-fifty pounds," she read. "Dark skin, but not like a black or either kind of Indian, more grayish. And fast... He was, and I quote, 'hellish fast. A couple of times, I could barely see him move, he was just a blur, like.' When Auden ordered him to freeze, he smiled."

"With that speed, and being bulletproof," said Rok, "I'd smile, too."

We all thought about this for a moment.

"We need to get to his motive," said Morgan. "Why does he kill the people he kills? How does he pick them? When we find out how he finds them, we'll find him."

"Don't sound like Chief Adams was real big on religion, and the treasurer was an atheist," said Rok. "Looks like the religious angle isn't holding up."

"I dunno about that." The sergeant who'd led our welcoming committee had crossed the office to join us. Her name tag said *Robles.* "Excuse me for intruding, but Investigator Auden had me looking into that a little this morning. Seems Treasurer Czernoff had been particularly hard-nosed about tax exemptions for churches and temples. Turned down a bunch of recent applications. Several groups were pretty pissed off about that. There were even a few demonstrations, and calls for his resignation."

"Any chance of that happening?" I asked.

Robles chuckled. I liked the sound. "Well, he's permanently resigned now, isn't he? But, no, Czernoff laughed in their faces. He wasn't about to resign."

"What about Roth?" asked Morgan. "Would he have asked for Czernoff's resignation, if the political pressure was stiff enough?"

"No chance. Roth and Czernoff went back; he was one of Roth's main men during the Takeover. Maybe if the council voted for it, Roth would consider it. But the churches involved didn't have enough clout to take it that far."

"Any of 'em might be angry enough to hire a killer?" Rok asked.

Morgan looked at him. "You thinking this guy might be for hire?"

"I'm just saying," Rok said.

"Professionals don't usually leave a calling card, do they?" asked Robles. "And that's an awful lot of jobs in a short time."

"Calling card might be good for business. Maybe some were random, just to add to the rep." Rok was trying, but I could see he didn't believe it either. "Okay, so it ain't likely, but it ain't impossible, either."

"On the religion angle, the other thing is," Robles continued, "I was looking into the former chief's finances..." She shook her head. "Seems shitty, like spying on your own chief, but you gotta cover all the bases. Anyway, I find out he'd been making large contributions to a couple of charities—the Rock Soup kitchen, and the Graceland Rehab Center."

Rok shook his head. "Contributions to charities? That don't seem very suspicious... Or are they bogus charities? Were they unusually big contributions or something?"

"They're legitimate, and no, the sums weren't that big. No real stress on the chief's wallet. The weird thing is, the chief was Episcopal, and both these places are run by the Church of the King."

That wasn't totally outrageous, but it was a bit odd. The Church of the King accepted Christians well enough, but the good feelings didn't tend to go the other way. CoKs saw their god, Elvis, as just another incarnation of the same dying king they saw in Osiris, Dionysus, Jesus, or

JFK, but the Christians tended to see theirs as the one and only, and regarded such syncretic sentiments as blasphemy.

"What about the other victims' friends, family?" I asked Robles. "Your people interviewed most of them, any of 'em seemed like there was more there, worth following up on?"

"Maybe." She consulted her notebook again. "I sorta thought it might be worth taking a closer look at the harlot, Mascarpone. She only joined the Marilynists recently, but she'd held several elected posts in the Guild. A real activist, and it sounds like she was kind of a spitfire. Probably pissed off any number of people along the way."

"Activists usually do."

"Could be a real rat's nest there. I wonder about the teacher, too."

"Juan Castro?"

"Too clean. Everybody we asked thought the sun shone out of his ass. Sounds too good to be true to me. Not a soul walking the earth hasn't pissed somebody off, got some kinda dirt in their closet. Either some of these witnesses were lying, or we didn't dig deep enough, talk to enough people."

"Unless it really was random," said Morgan.

"You want to assume it was random, Ma'am, you tell me, where do we start with an investigation?"

The "Ma'am" might have been respectful, or it might have been sarcastic; it was hard to tell. I could feel Morgan bristling. This could quickly get ugly again, so I held up a hand.

"She's right, Morgan," I said. "If it's really random, we've got no place to go with this. For the moment, we have to assume there's some kind of method to the Beast's madness." Morgan scowled at me, but didn't push the issue further. "Anything else?"

"Don Whitehouse, second mate of the *Bay Queen*— that's Hawthorne's boat. He seemed like he was holding back on something. I'm thinking maybe they were doing a little private import-export on the side."

"Smuggling what?" asked Rok. "I thought everything was legal here."

"Legal, yeah, but taxed. Booze, tobacco, pot, you name it, if there's a tax on it, there's a profit in smuggling. Could go either way, too—tax-free coming in, or might be going out, to one of the ports where they're not legal at all. Small-time fisherman like Hawthorne, even just a small shipment now and then could make a big difference to his bottom line."

"Might be worth a follow-up. What about Guardsman Fitch?"

Robles shot me a look that told me she wasn't happy I'd brought that one up. "He was a right guy, a straight shooter. Everybody liked him."

"They all thought the sun shone out of his ass?" asked Morgan. "Sounds too good to be true."

Robles looked at Morgan with a laser gaze. After a beat, she said, "I'll thank you to remember you're a guest in my city, Railwalker, and these are my people you're talking about."

Morgan came away from the wall and stepped toward the desk. "If it's your city, then they're all your people, aren't they? Including the fucking Beast."

"Enough!" I put a Force into my voice as I spoke up and stepped between them. Morgan stepped back and Robles sat down again before either of them realized what I'd done. Out of the corner of my eye I saw Rok trying not to smirk. "You," I said to Robles, "don't need your City Boss on your case because you picked a fight with a Railwalker. And you," I turned to Morgan, "know better than to antagonize a city guardswoman when she's cooperating."

Both were breathing a little heavy and glowering, though they were each now studiously looking anywhere but at the other.

"My associate's rude way of expressing herself aside," I said to Robles, "she's right. Guardsmen make enemies. It comes with the territory."

"I never said he didn't," the sergeant allowed. "Sure,

there might have been a few lowlifes who didn't like Fitch much. But, hell... Even though he was career guard, nearly the Old Man's age—due for retirement in another three years, he never made it above Guardsman First Class. He was never involved in any big cases, except as backup. Never made any important collars, nothing like that. Not too many people willing to kill over a few minor citations or traffic fines."

"Well," I said, "we've got enough to get started on, anyway. We can leave Guardsman Fitch for the moment, and get working on the others—but we'll come back to him. What were you thinking was your own next step?"

"I was figuring on talking to Czernoff's associates."

"Okay. Byer leave, Rok can join you on that. Morgan and I should check the sites of the murders. It isn't likely we'll find shades or spirits hanging around there at this late date, but you never know."

Morgan and Rok both gave me a quizzical look, but I ignored them. I wasn't going to say out loud that working with Sergeant Robles would be too distracting for me. Rok had eyes for no woman but Morgan, so it was safer this way.

INTERLUDE: THE GREAT CRASH

Volcanoes, earthquakes, hurricanes, crop failures, economic collapse, riots, bombs, EMPs, monsters and zombies and domestic terrorists, oh, my. Where does one begin with the Great Crash? Why did it happen? Why all of it at once? Which parts were random disasters, and which human created?

Some historians would assert it was all human created. Fiscal and environmental irresponsibility certainly prepared the way for the disasters of that period. The economic situation in the states was already perilous when Hurricane Arthur hit the Gulf Coast. Arthur devastated much of Louisiana and Texas, areas barely recovered from Katrina a generation or so before. The oil distribution system collapsed, and riots began even before the bombs began exploding.

Terrorists, taking advantage of the mounting chaos, set off bombs in seven American cities, including one small nuclear bomb in a place called LA on the west coast. Another nuke was intended for Washington, but was intercepted by federal agents. The LA nuke was a low-yield, one-kiloton suitcase bomb, dropped from a civilian aircraft and detonated in the air. This had the result of spectacular and horrifying immediate local effects, but resulted in fewer casualties in the long run, since there was less widespread fallout.

The death toll was in the hundreds of thousands. Arizona, New Mexico, and northern California were flooded with refugees. Arizona was particularly hard hit, as prevailing winds had brought the plumes of fallout to some sections of that state. The scientists all predicted it would be twenty years before the area could be reclaimed, but they were wrong. Southern California would never be reclaimed. The following year, an earthquake resulted in much of Southern California being swallowed by the Pacific Ocean.

Crops were already failing around the world, a plague known as "colony collapse disorder" having wiped out most of the planet's bees. Agricultural crops were not being pollinated. The effect of the LA nuke on the climate was not the nuclear winter a larger bomb would have produced, but harvests the world over were thinner in the following years, and within five years there was widespread starvation around the globe. Despite all this, recovery was considered possible until the volcanic eruptions.

Volcanoes throughout the Pacific Ring of Fire suddenly became active, spewing ash and smoke into the air that accomplished what the LA nuke had not. Global warming was no longer an issue, as temperatures cooled by an average of seven degrees for the next ten years. The death tolls would mount into the millions.

Finally, the anomalies began. Monsters appeared. Places slipped in time. Whole areas experienced an apparent twisting of the laws of physics.

The Great Crash: An Historical Perspective
Ronald Olsen, Errant Press, New Washington, 226 AC

9. THE BAR OF GOLD — *Five Weeks Ago*

He was in the shape of a Mayacan sailor—there were many of those who hung around the Bar of Gold, so he'd be perfectly inconspicuous. The target was sitting with his first mate in a booth at the back. The place wasn't crowded, and the booth next to them was empty. He ordered a beer at the bar, and then took it to the empty booth. He brought out a newsfeed, unrolled it, and laid the plastic sheet on the table. He began tapping his way idly through the pages as he pretended to sip the beer. Behind him, the captain of the *Bay Queen* and his mate were becoming quite drunk. There was something going on with them. Usually when these sailors got drunk they became louder, more boisterous. These two became quieter, their tones more serious and intense. But he could not make out more than a few words.

He closed his eyes for a moment and concentrated. Shifted the shape of his inner ears, making the left one less sensitive, to screen out the general noise of the bar, the right one more acute, so as to pick up the quiet conversation.

"What?" The mate's voice sounded incredulous. "You've got to be shitting me."

"Keep your voice down," said the captain. "You knew I fought in the Takeover, right? Happened that toward the end I was with the group took Crichton's headquarters. You've seen the CA Tower?" The captain paused, and the secret listener could imagine the first mate nodding. "Big place, like a rabbit warren inside. Well, I get separated from the other guys, and I find myself in a suite of offices that seems deserted. I'm about to leave, try to find the other fellas, and suddenly here comes this big galoot around the corner, a huge fuckin' monster of a gun in his hands. I seen the guy before he sees me. I squeezed off a shot and dove behind one of the desks. I'm sweating so hard I can hardly keep hold of my gun, and I'm expecting the guy's monster weapon to go off like a bomb and blow me and the desk both to bits. But alls I hear is a groan. I peek out around the edge of the desk, and the guy is on the floor, in a huge pool of blood. At first I thought he could be faking to draw me out, but then I realize the blood's not fake.

"Now, you gotta understand, we was just regular workin' stiffs facing Crichton's trained bullies. We was all sorta on edge, a little jumpy on the trigger. Me, I'd never killed anyone before in my life. I was so shook up I didn't know whether to shit or go blind. So I walk over to this dead guy, right? Turn him over with my foot, and lo and behold if it ain't the old Crichton himself. I left him there, found my way back to the rest of my crew and never said a word. Crichton was reported as being killed in the fighting, and no one ever knew who it was actually killed him. 'Cept me. And now you."

"No shit?" said the mate. "So why'd you keep this a secret all these years? Anybody else woulda been boastin' and puffing themselves up about such a thing. Me, why I'd have been drinkin' for free on a story like that the rest of my life. I mean, I know you're a modest man, Cap, but shit…"

"Tell you the truth, I was ashamed. I didn't feel like a big hero, just liked I'd fucked up. I shot first and didn't try to capture the guy alive. That was cowardly."

"That was fuckin' smart, you ask me."

"Didn't feel that way to me. Roth was hot to bring Crichton up on charges, see him go to jail. He didn't want a dead city boss as a possible martyr his people might rally around. I screwed up, ruined Roth's plans. Never wanted Boss Roth to know I was the guy did it."

"People still would have called you a hero. They'd have carried you through the streets cheering."

"I never wanted anything like that. Only reason I was

in the fight was to see the Takeover happen, get Bay City on a democratic basis. Roth was a hero, and Adams, guys like that. I was just a working Joe who was unlucky enough to be in the wrong place at the wrong time, and shot first to save his own skin."

"So why you telling me this now?"

"You're my man, Don. I'm an old man now, and I expect you to take over for me when I'm gone. Take care of Christine, and take care of the *Bay Queen*. I don't want there to be any secrets between us."

In the next booth, the man who looked like a Mayacan sailor sat frozen, staring straight ahead, gripping the handle of his beer mug with white knuckles. Slowly and carefully, he released his grip on the mug. Yes, he thought, I made the right choice. This is the one. Whether his story was true, or just an empty boast to his first mate, he would be the one to start with.

10. WOLF

We left Rok and Robles heading for the motor pool, and Morgan and I went downstairs to the evidence lockers. From the boat captain's effects we selected a medallion made of shell, with an image of a sea turtle—one of Huey Otiz's avatars. From the harlot's we picked up a Marilyn pin in the shape of an off-center heart with eyes and lips inscribed on it. From the teacher, a pocket protector containing several pens and pencils, and from the guardsman, his badge.

The *Bay Queen*, Arnold Hawthorne's fishing boat, was no longer docked at the site of its captain-owner's murder. After the initial investigations on site, it had been towed to the guard's impound dock, where it stayed pending judicial disposition—apparently there had been a challenge to Hawthorne's will, and the ownership of the boat was still being debated in the courts. The impound dock was just north of the shipping docks, in the no-man's land between where the shipping docks ended and the docks for fishing boats and other small vessels began. It was protected on the street side with a high chain-link fence topped with razor wire, and I eyed it wondering what, if anything, protected the approach from the water.

A bored city employee tore himself away from the bladeball game on his handheld long enough to glance at our identification, unlock the gate, and point in the general direction of the *Bay Queen*. Not that she was hard to find—most of the boats in the impound were small pleasure boats; there were only a couple of commercial vessels. Still, although she was small for a commercial boat, only forty feet or so, she was the biggest thing currently in the impound. She was a combination trawler and purse-seiner, with her superstructure forward, the trawl-seine winch just behind the wheelhouse. We clambered over the gunwale onto the deck and looked around. Though there was no doubt that the hold would be empty, the odor of dead fish permeated the vessel. Hawthorne had been killed in the wheelhouse, so we threaded our way to the forward hatch.

Morgan set her portcomp unit on the dash and powered up. She plugged in the small electromagnetic field meter and gave me the nod. I produced the Huey medallion and held it up by its leather thong, slowing my breathing and reaching out with my mind. I could feel the leftover resonance of violent death, almost like a smell in the air, but that was all. No sense of presence, no lifting of the hair on the back of my neck, no whispering voice. After a suitable interval I opened my eyes and looked at Morgan.

She shook her head. "Not a thing," she said.

I looked around the wheelhouse, at the control panels, the windshield. Something was wrong. Something was missing.

"Crime scene photos—of this bridge," I said.

"Two seconds..." said Morgan. Her fingers fluttered over the keyboard, and she turned the comp unit toward me so I could page through the photos. I went through them forward, then, more slowly, backward. Each time, the same image caught my eye. It was a view through the forward windshield. I turned to look at the real thing, moved back to stand where the photographer had stood. Ignore the picture outside the windshield, I told myself. What was inside the wheelhouse, something added, something taken away, something different? It wasn't the outside background, and it wasn't the bloodstains. I looked back at the photo on the screen. The pendant.

In the photograph, a Huey Otiz pendant hung in the center of the windshield, suspended from a peg or a hook in the woodwork above. Now it was gone. I looked more closely at the photo, zoomed in. It was a different pendant from the one I was holding. We were carrying the captain's personal Huey talisman. I suspected the one in the photograph was the *Bay Queen*'s. Morgan looked over my shoulder at the screen. Looked from screen to windscreen.

"You think the Beast came back to take the boat's pendant," she said.

"Possibly. Someone took it, anyway."

"Why? Could you have gotten something off it?"

"Not sure. But apparently he thought someone could."

"Maybe he wanted a souvenir."

I shook my head. "He took pieces of the victims' bodies. Why would he want the pendant? No, this was an afterthought. I'm betting he infiltrated this place and took it after he heard there were Railwalkers here."

We packed up and headed out.

The college teacher, Juan Castro, had been killed in a raised, covered passageway, like a bridge between two of the buildings on campus. When we arrived we discovered a small shrine had been set up there, flowers, pictures of the teacher, cards and corn dollies gathered on one side at the middle of the passageway. I brought out the pocket protector, Morgan fired up the electromagnetic frequency meter, but nothing showed here, either. We had carefully timed our arrival for shortly after the beginning of a class period, so as to minimize the possibility of interruption, but as we were packing up, a short, burly young man with wild black hair and beard appeared at one end of the passageway and stood looking at us.

"Can I help you?" I asked.

"I was going to ask you that. You're Railwalkers, hunh?" I nodded. "Come to look for Juan's spirit? Or some astral record of his murder or something?"

"Something like that," I said. "You knew Juan Castro?"

"I was his grad student assistant, so, yeah, I guess I knew him about as well as anyone here. Something in particular you want to know?"

"Anything you can tell me about him. Any enemies? Anything he said or did generate hard feelings anywhere?"

"Well, he was a passionate guy. Some of his ideas about literature might be called controversial—he was a little to the right of Singer, super conservative—but I can't see any of his professional rivals having him killed over it." He sighed and hesitated for a moment, then added, "He was active in politics, off and on."

"And he was a conservative, politically?"

"No. Y'know, it's funny, Juan was real progressive, politically."

"Why is that funny?" asked Morgan.

"Well, he was such a traditionalist when it came to his classes, the literature he taught. He'd reprinted some of the really old pre-Crash classics at his own expense. Twain, Joyce, deLint, Rowling, Michener, people like that. But politically, well... He supported Roth before the Takeover, and worked Roth's Boss campaign at least once afterward. He used to quote ancient radicals, too, like Paine and Leary, Marx, Ventura. What was that Moore quote he used to use? 'People should not be afraid of their government, the government should be afraid of its people.'"

"Are people afraid of the Roth administration?" Morgan asked.

"Nah." He chuckled. "Oh, there are probably a few, holdovers from the Crichton years, but mostly, no. People trust Roth."

"So Castro was an activist? Any of his work threaten the Roth administration? Would someone in the government have wanted him dead?"

"I'm a radical, not a conspiracy nut. No, I don't think Roth or any of his people had it in for Juan Castro. You have to understand, he didn't set himself up as an opponent to Roth and his people. He wasn't calling for another Takeover or anything. Juan and Roth had similar ideals. Juan just thought the city could move along faster toward being a true democracy."

We thanked the young man for his time, took his contact info in case we had any further questions, and went on our way.

***

Guardsman Fitch had not been on duty when he was killed, but had been in the tram station at Central and Fifth, waiting to transfer to the downtown line. There was no way we were going to get any privacy there unless we waited until the wee hours of the morning, when the guardsman had been killed. By now it was mid-afternoon, and the station wasn't full; there were a dozen or so people on the platform waiting for the tram. Since we didn't want to wait, we set up in the quietest corner we could, but had no better luck here than we had at the previous two locations.

At the tram overpass where the Harlot Mascarpone was killed Morgan got some blips on the meter, but in an open public street there was no telling what could occasion that. If the spirit or even the shade of Suzi Mascarpone had been hanging about, we should have gotten a bigger reaction to the Marilyn pin.

All in all, a pretty disappointing day. Not that we had expected dramatic results. Hawthorne, Castro and Fitch had all been killed three weeks or more ago. This long after the deaths, unless people had reported a haunting of some sort, chances were that there'd be no sign of shades or spirits. We'd had slightly better hopes for Mascarpone, whose death was less than a week before, but we weren't counting on anything. Even the shade of Chief Adams, who had been killed only three days back, had been weak and almost dissipated. Still, we had to check. It would have been foolish and negligent not to.

When we arrived back at the CA Tower, Rok and Robles were still out. I changed into workout clothes, left Morgan scanning the net, and went down to the guards' underground gym. It was a good-sized space, well equipped with weights, boxing ring, heavy bag, standing bag, several wakimara. It was practically empty at this time of day. There was one guard whose name escaped me working out in a sort of desultory way with the weights. I stretched out some, and then moved into what we call "the crowbar," a series of exercises combining elements of calisthenics, yoga, and various martial arts—especially baritsu, the martial art that's the closest thing to an "official" Rail-walker style of fighting (hence the slang term among walkers, "crowbar").

Finishing my series of exercises, it was time for my run. I barely looked at the three treadmills set to one side. I never liked running on a treadmill. I preferred Parkering (what some call free running) anyway. I approached the guy on the weights.

"'Scuse me," I said.

"Yeah?"

"There someplace I can run around here that isn't totally paved, like a park or something?" I'll run on pavement from time to time, but as I get older I become more aware of the effects of the repeating impacts on concrete or asphalt. You can't really Parker very extensively without spending some of your time running on pavement, but I've come to prefer the feel of real earth under my feet, at least part of the time. The guard chuckled.

"You running to something, or from something?" he asked.

"I'm running from amateur psychologists. They scare the piss out of me."

He pulled a face. "You could try Riverwalk Park," he said. "Go out the tower's south entrance, follow your nose for three blocks, you can't miss it."

"Thanks."

I took the stairs, jogging up and out into the street to stay as warmed up as possible. He was right about not being able to miss it. South Street dead-ended right into the park. Riverwalk Park was maybe fifty or sixty feet wide at that point, and ran three blocks or so east, and quite a bit farther to the west, where it paralleled the riverbank, running down the hill toward the waterfront. I turned right and headed west.

I vaulted a fence, ran along a bench and jump-stepped to the top of a retaining wall, running along it until it swung north, where I left it to continue parallel to the main path. Some of this wasn't strictly kosher by real Parker standards. The whole point of Parkering is to travel along the most direct, efficient, and natural route possible, flowing around, over, or under obstacles along the way. In deliberately choosing a path full of obstacles when a clear one was immediately to hand, I was sort of stretching a point for the sake of staying in training.

The nice thing about Parker running is that unlike just plain running or jogging, your mind can't be anywhere but focused in this very moment of the run. You can't be re-playing an argument you had with someone that morning, or thinking about what you're planning for tomorrow. It takes mindfulness and full concentration. If you go over a wall, there's no telling what you might encounter on the other side of it, but whatever it is, you've got to be ready to deal with it. For the length of my run, at least, I would have to forget about the Beast and his victims, and exist wholly in the here and now.

Most people seem to prefer to run in the morning, or maybe it just seems that way 'cause mornings are more convenient for most folks. Me, I prefer the afternoon. I like ending my run with the Salute to the Setting Sun. I retraced my path back up the hill. My back was now to the west, and in front of me the park was lit with an intense red-orange light. I arrived back at the top just in time to turn and see the sun's disk beginning to sink into the western sea. I raised my arms and performed the Salute. As the disk sank into the horizon, it seemed to grow larger, and its orange glow turned to deep red, as though it was absorbing blood from the sea. Several minutes later it was just a line, and then a pinpoint of light. And then just a glow in the sky.

The twilight times are when the walls between worlds become thinner. Points where the flow changes. It happens at noon and midnight, too, but not so strongly. Even without any special training, at noon and midnight you can sometimes sense these changes. At dawn and dusk, you can see them.

I turned from the now-vanished sun to find an elderly mutant sitting on a bench staring at me. He was one of the ones they called a "gray" type—skinny limbs, long fingers, largish head with big, dark eyes, evocative of the popular conception of a space alien. He was wearing several layers of filthy clothing, and shoes that did not match. Beside him on the bench was a stuffed duffel bag, which he rested an arm on. It was tied closed with a piece of stocking.

"You worshiping Soul-Are, Railwalker?" he rasped.

"We don't think of it as worship, grandfather," I said. "Soul-Are isn't a god, it's just the way of things. We try to work with it, instead of struggling against it."

"Mutual respect," he grunted, nodding. "Diggit. Heard you talking to that falling sun. He talk back?"

"Sometimes."

"You ask him about the Beast?"

"No."

"You figure the Beast's part of Soul-Are?"

"Everything is." I was wondering if this was going somewhere, or the old one was just rambling, making conversation. His serious stare seemed to make that unlikely, but sometimes you can't tell with a mutant.

"Your Old Man Sun can't tell you anything about a creature o' darkness." He levered himself to his feet and shouldered the bag. "Sun, he don't know from darkness. He only know from light. But light, he shape what the darkness is."

I wasn't sure what to say to that. He turned and walked off into the darkening park.

"Thank you," I finally said to his retreating back. "I'll try to remember that."

When I got back to our rooms in the CA Tower I found Morgan sitting on the couch, cleaning her sword. We're all pretty good about maintaining our gear, but Morgan's very particular about Darkwater. She had one ankle propped on the opposite knee, and her foot was bouncing. She was either angry or ambivalent about something, possibly a little of each.

"What?" I asked.

"Nothing. I was having a crass, selfish moment."

"About what?" I couldn't see her eyes for the poofy black bangs she wears, like a character out of one of those animes she likes to watch. The rest of her hair hung down her back in a long braid. Despite the bouncing foot, her hands moved slowly and evenly as her long, thin fingers drew the cloth across the shining blade, almost caressing it. I looked at her bouncing foot again.

She stopped polishing the blade, sat there with it on her lap, looking at it. "Nobody's talking about it, y'know? 'Cause it would sound bad to say it out loud. But at Hicks Junction, we lost more than two brothers. We also lost two swords."

Morgan held her sword up, looked up and down its length. Darkwater was damascened, almost charcoal gray, with slightly lighter liquid patterns. Her style with it was like dark water, sparkling and powerful and treacherous. Every Railwalker is matched to their blade by a sensei; but the sensei do not assign a sword to a person. The sword chooses the person.

"They're works of art," she said. "Works of spirit. They're supposed to be destroyed with their bearers or returned to the Roost." It wasn't as if a Railwalker blade had never been lost, but it was a rare thing.

"They're also weapons of death," I said. "And those who carry them should be accountable. But even the order can't guarantee that."

"Yeah, well it sucks. And that's 'what'..."

"Okay." I thought about what she'd said. "Well, obviously someone's talking about it, or you wouldn't know they hadn't recovered the blades."

"I talked to Omnia. She was on the team that went down there after."

"Twenty-three Blessings on her for it. It's not a job I'd want."

"Like you wanted this one?"

"Right."

INTERLUDE: BLADE WEAPONS

Isao Suddeth was nearing 80 years of age when Bane of the First Five brought him to the Railwalker Roost in upstate New York. Suddeth had been taught the art of bladesmithing in Japan, by his maternal grandfather, the great Hideo Nakamura, and he had been making swords for most of his adult life. His blades, while based on Japanese models and principles, also showed the influence of American culture, though more often in their decoration than in their form.

Suddeth established his forge at the Roost and taught his craft to three apprentices, all of whom were mutants. After Suddeth's death, when the order opened their chapter house in New Frisco, two of Suddeth's apprentices, John Hobbs and William Osoto, relocated to the nearby Sierra area, where there was a large mutant population. At their forge there they took apprentices of their own, and within two generations metalwork (most particularly swords and knives, but also other metalwork) from what would be called the Sierra Mutants would gain an almost mystical reputation.

Nor was that reputation undeserved. Isao Suddeth may have worked with and for the Railwalkers, but Hobbs and Osoto were most certainly initiates to the order, branded with the famous eye tattoo, and there is no question that they and their apprentices were trained in shamanism and magick.

A story popular around 200 AC or so depicted Suddeth embedding the first Railwalker blade in a cement block, and although many tried, only Brick could draw the blade. This rather obvious grafting of the Arthurian "sword in the stone" legend to the story of Brick seems like transparent mythologizing. Yet more reliable accounts do suggest that Suddeth subjected Brick to some sort of test or trial before presenting him with the sword Ravenwing.

Dudley Boer,
Blade Weapons of Post-Crash Merica
Salle Publications, Newyark, 321 AC

The surface of the chest-high cement block was scored to imitate a wooden crate.

"With your bare hands alone," said Suddeth, seating himself on the bench.

"I know your rules," said Brick. He walked slowly around the block, studying it. He came back to stand before the old man. "You created this yourself?" he asked.

Suddeth nodded. Brick studied his face for a while, and then nodded himself. He walked back to the cement cube. He circled it more slowly this time, stopping to peer closely at the engraved lines that imitated the edges of boards. Finally he stepped to one corner, placed a hand low on one side, and applied pressure with one finger high on the opposite side. A large section, comprising most of the top and one side, slid smoothly free and pivoted away. It revealed, in a hollow in the base of the cube, the silk-wrapped form of a sword.

"Very good, Railwalker," said Suddeth. "The crow grows into a raven."

Ravenwing: A Railwalker Novel
Gordon Gray, Coldspring Press,
Newyark, July 287 AC

11. SANTA BRITA

Lantz sipped his scotch and followed the burn down. It was nice, the warmth moving at his center. Like a sense of belonging was nice, having buddies you could count on. Guys like Jack Pauls, guys who had your back when you went down, into the dark, like that shot of whiskey going down, into the guts of things, bringing maybe not light into the darkness, but warmth, a hot burn of red at the end of a long, dark path. Lantz liked being a Santa Brita guardsman. Their name tags only showed their first initial, so to the uninitiated, he was Patrolman "Q. Lantz." Most of the boys called him "Quid," which was the common term for the Santa Brita dollar, so that was alright. Better than Quentin, which is what it said on his birth certificate; only the administrative types ever called him that. Even the chief referred to him as Quid.

Santa Brita was a guardsman's town. The city boss, Jaworski, was a former guardswoman herself. After the Union Riots, Jaworski had run on the law and order platform, and had taken power in a landslide-election. Anti-union, pro-industry, Jaworski kept the trains running on time. And she employed lots of guardsmen.

After a long silence, letting the sounds of the bar wash over him but not really hearing the chatter of the other customers or the twangy music on the juke, Pauls had turned to Lantz and said, "Lemme ask you something."

Lantz looked at Pauls, wondering what was so serious all of a sudden.

"If it's none of my business, feel free to say so. But I am your partner. You know I'll be cool, and nothing will go any further."

"Yeah, sure..." said Lantz, making a "go on" motion

with one hand.

"So, what went down with you and the Grinder, any-way?"

Lantz felt himself following that shot again, down into the dark, and instead of standing by his side, this time his partner was pushing him there. Not that he blamed him. If their positions had been reversed, Quid Lantz probably would have asked the same question some time earlier. He was actually surprised at Pauls's forbearance in waiting this long to press the issue. He stared at his reflection in the mirror behind the bar, wondering if that same mirror had been there five years ago, at the time of the Union Riots, back when Jaworski first came to power. Probably it had been replaced, at least once, that mirror. Crazy times back then, chaotic times; probably every damn mirror in the city needed to be replaced, and some of them never had been, by choice. There were people had problems looking in the mirror the first year or so after the Riots, Lantz among them. He'd had some sleepless nights, but he'd got over it. He knew his stories were far from the worst. Although this one was bad enough.

Somehow, he didn't think the Bone Grinder had ever lost any sleep, or had any trouble with mirrors. They'd called the man "the Monk" in those early days, before the Riots. He was dubbed "the Bone Grinder" afterwards. His name tag said "V. Caine," and that was all anyone knew. It was his habits, of course, that earned him the tag "Monk" among the guard. Didn't drink, didn't fuck, as far as anybody knew, women or men. Always on time, precisely. Worked out regular, regular practice on the gun range, knew the regs book forward and backward. You'd think a guy like that would be a stickler for procedure, but he wasn't. When the chief first assigned the Monk to be Lantz's partner, Lantz had no idea just how far outside the rules the Monk was willing to go.

Lantz stood, sighed, and looked at Pauls. "Let's take a walk," he said.

Outside the air was cooler, the late summer breezes coming in from the zones. It was late, only a few people left on the streets. As the two guardsmen walked slowly down the street, Pauls said, "I'm sorry, I shoulda thought of that. You didn't want to talk about it in there."

"I ain't exactly falling all over myself to talk about it anywhere, Jack," said Quid. "But I figure you got a right to know."

"Okay," was all Pauls said, letting Lantz find his way to the story in his own time. They walked in silence for a block or so.

"You remember that guy, Amira?" Lantz said at last. "Worked for the Unions?"

"Real heavy duty fighter, martial arts and all that? Used to bodyguard sometimes for that Union leader, what was his name, Kwant or something?"

"That's the one. You know the Monk was the one took him down?"

"Yeah, I heard that. Shot resisting arrest, right?"

Lantz chuckled, but there was no humor in it. "Yeah, the Monk shot him. Eventually.

"It was back about the time the Riots started. Amira had become a real pain in the ass, and the powers that be had decided to 'bring him in for questioning.' The Monk and me were assigned to it. Unofficially, we were told, it didn't really matter what his condition was, even dead was okay, as long as we brought him in. At the time, I wondered if they meant they'd rather we brought in his corpse, but I was a guardsman, not an assassin, and besides, I figured the Monk would want to do it by the book, so I was looking at we were gonna bring him in alive, if we could. Messed up, maybe, but alive.

"So we go down to the place we were told he was staying—a little transient hotel off Becker. Grungy little joint, dunno if the bell worked or not, but we didn't bother trying, y'know? We just head in and up the stairs to the fifth floor, where Amira's supposed to have a room.

"Well, we get to the fifth floor, and somebody must have tipped him off, because guy's coming out of his front door, a backpack over one shoulder. I've got my piece out, but the Monk still hasn't touched his. Amira turns and sees us, he just drops the pack and stands there with this cocky smile on his face, and he goes, 'What, only two of you? My reputation must be slipping.'

"Now, here's where it starts to get weird. The Monk, he takes off his gun belt and hands it to me, and I'm looking at him like, 'What the fuck?' and trying to keep one eye on Amira at the same time, and the Monk goes, 'No. Only one of us.'

"And then I get it—the Monk wants to go one-on-one with this guy. Amira's got a rep as the most badass fighter the union guys have, and the Monk is gonna measure himself against him. Or that's what I thought.

"'Hold your fire,' the Monk tells me. 'No matter what happens.' Well, I nodded, but inside, I'm thinking, shit on that, if this thing goes bad, I'm gonna plug this union bastard. So I set down the Monk's gun belt, but I keep my own piece out and ready.

"They circled each other in that hallway for a minute, and then they went at it. Man, I tell you, I've never seen anything like that in my life. I'm thinking, shit, this is like an exhibition fight people would pay big bucks to see, and it's going on in this grungy little hallway with nobody watching but me. Up and down that little hall, with kicks and punches and head-butts, faster and harder than you'd believe, and moves I never seen before, on both of 'em.

"But that part of the fight, it don't last all that long. Pretty soon, the Monk gets in a kick to Amira's knee, and I could hear the bones snap. Must've hurt like a sonofabitch, but Amira just grunts when he goes down, and he never loses his guard. He's down there on one knee, skootching around to face the Monk as he circles him. I open my mouth—I'm gonna tell the Monk okay, man, he ain't going anywhere on his own; you beat him, let's take him in. But I seen the look on the Monk's face, and I shut my mouth again. The Monk takes a couple more shots, which Amira manages to block, and then gets in a good kick to the head. Amira's down, one hand and one knee, and the Monk stomps on that hand, all he can give it, and I hear more bones snapping and crunching.

"This time I do speak up, and I go, 'Okay, Caine. Enough, man. Let's take him in.'

"He looks up at me, and he don't say a word, but I swear, the look in his eyes, he was ready to come after me, never mind I had a gun in my hand. So I shut up again. I go to turn away, 'cause whatever the Monk's got in mind, I know I don't want to see it, but then I realize, if I'm gonna stand by and do nothing, if I'm gonna let this happen, the least I can do is have the guts to watch this poor fucker's last moments.

"They were long last moments.

"Y'know, we talk about somebody taking someone apart in a fight, but I don't use that expression anymore, 'cause I've seen it done literally. The Monk must have broken every damn bone in Amira's body, one by one, taking his time, letting the guy suffer. And Amira, he never makes a sound other than a grunt now and then, like he won't give the Monk the satisfaction of hearing him scream.

"Finally, when Amira's nothing but a pile of ground meat, lying there in that hallway, the Monk walks over to me and picks up his belt. He buckles in, takes out his gun, and shouts, 'City guard! Don't try to run, or we'll shoot!'

"And then he shoots the guy.

"To be honest, I don't know if Amira was still alive or not. The Monk walks over, picks him up, and throws him out the fifth story window, right through the glass. He looks down there for a minute, and then turns to me, and says, 'He shouldn't have tried to run. Bad luck he was making for the window. Drop like that, he probably broke every bone in his body.'

"Then he grins, and walks past me down the stairs."

"Holy fuck," said Pauls. "That's some cold shit."

"Yeah."

"And you stayed partners with this guy for how long after?"

"Couple of months. Never saw him do anything like that again. Oh, he was pretty brutal in the Riots when they actually started, but no more than some of the other guys, at least not that I saw. Then come the fighting down by the power plant. Some of the union boys had guns, and I took a shot in the thigh. Laid me up for over a month. When I come out, the Monk had been assigned a new partner, and they put me with you."

"Right," said Pauls. "By that time, they were calling Caine 'Bone Grinder' instead of 'Monk.'"

"Yeah. I dunno how he came by that tag, but I can guess."

The two walked another block in silence, each wrapped in his own thoughts.

"When Grinder disappeared after the Riots," Pauls said at last, "I never did get the whole story on that. You figure some of the unionists got him, or maybe some of Amira's friends or family?"

Lantz shook his head. "Nah. Take more than an angry crowd of unios to take that bastard down. My guess, he figured even Jaworski had limits, and he couldn't get away with shit like that forever. I think he blew town, maybe out to the zones, where there ain't any law to speak of. Long as the Railwalkers didn't catch up with him, he could do whatever the fuck he wanted out there."

They stopped walking and stood in silence for a moment. Finally, Pauls asked, "Are you drunk?" They had been drinking long and hard that night, neither of them walking an even keel when they left the bar, but both stood steady and straight now.

"No," said Lantz.

"Me neither," said Pauls. "What do you say we do something about that?"

Lantz nodded, and the two guardsmen began to walk toward a smear of neon that could be seen down the street.

One of Morgan's talents is she's what they call a "comber." She hooks up to the net and searches. She's got several programs she sets up with different search parameters. Sets them searching, and sits there watching the screen. There are four windows open on screen, with text and pictures flashing by faster than you or I could take them in. But Morgan's in this sort of fugue state, where she'll pick up on relevant items out of the thousands flashing by on the screen. While the programs refine their results, Morgan's refining them, too, and the combination of their results is winnowed through again. She finds some amazing stuff this way.

This morning Morgan would be doing her combing thing on the victims. With so many, it could take a while. Rok and I decided to head out. We were pretty useless while Morgan was doing her thing, and we wanted to look into what had happened with Andrew Foreman. We were going on the theory that the Beast had snuck into the CA Tower disguised as the janitor, and the hit-and-run accident that had put the real janitor in the emergency room seemed a little too convenient.

We stopped at the main desk. Pappas, the older sergeant who'd painted the watercolor we saw in the wardroom, was on duty. He was a small, thin guy with a large head and a lined face, who smiled easily and pleasantly. I asked him about the vehicle in the hit-and-run.

"Have to query Traffic for that," he said, and held up a palm. "Don't worry, I'll get it for you." He tapped at the keyboard of his desk unit, peered at the screen. "They nailed the vehicle. Fifteen year-old Quantum Roller. Registered to a Jemison Farris, 348 C Street. Owner claims the vehicle was stolen, but he didn't bother to report it. He does have an alibi: he was at work. His boss and the time clock both vouch for him."

"Thanks, Pappas."

"Hey... you guys going down there? To see Farris?" I nodded. "That's Alphabet City—Mutant Central. Watch your backs down there."

We said we would.

We set out on foot. It was a longish hike from One City Plaza out to Alphabet City, but we both wanted to get more of a feel for the city than we were getting while holed up in the tower, or being ferried to incident sites in guard vehicles. Around the Bay City area it generally stays pretty warm for a month or so after Summersend, but today it seemed like Old Man Autumn wanted to give us a little preview. As we walked up Third Avenue, the sunlight was pale, if bright. The slanting light turned the buildings on one side nearly white, while the buildings on the opposite side cast bluish shadows halfway across the street. I noticed people were tending to walk on the sunny side. It wasn't actually cold, but the shadows held a cool nip that folks weren't acclimated to yet.

Before too long the buildings were getting shorter, and there were fewer granite, concrete, and plasteel structures, and more brick and adobe. At 35th Street we crossed a wide, open plaza with a farmer's market, filled mostly with Oriental and Latino faces, where women in black carrying string bags weighed and judged tomatoes, corn, rice and beans, while kids ran or skateboarded between the stalls.

Within a few more blocks we were entering the ghetto.

Every city has its ghettos. Historians tell us that before the Crash the country attracted millions of immigrants, and it was usually the most recent immigrants who occupied the ghettos, while the previous inhabitants of the bottom rung moved up one social station, from abject poverty to merely poor. Irish were replaced by Eastern Europeans, who were replaced by Italians, and then Orientals. Africans, of course, were being brought over as slaves during a lot of that time, but really only entered the social structure as though they were immigrants after the Freedom War. And so the cycle went, from the Founding Times until the Crash. There aren't nearly as many immigrants anymore, so ghettos since the Crash have been made up of a haphazard cross-section of groups, depending on the location. In San Angelo it's mostly whites. Santa Brita's ghettos are Chinese and Russian. In Gatesville, where the ruling classes are mainly Indian and Chinese, it's mostly Latinos and black, with a scattering of whites. Places like Bay City, which allowed mutants in, usually had a mutant ghetto.

As we drew further into Alphabetland runabout traffic slowed, then ceased. There were fewer wreaths, corn dollies, and other seasonal decorations, too. Less of a sense of celebration. Foot traffic thinned out until, as we approached Avenue C, there was only a group of five walking a block behind us. We unbuttoned our tunics for easy access to our guns. Rok muttered, "Next corner," and I nodded.

Before we got to the next corner, though, a woman in a motorized wheelchair came around it and stopped, facing us. We slowed as we got within ten feet or so of her. She was bald, marble-white skin gleaming in the weakening late summer sunlight. One of her huge, pale eyes was made to look even larger by a lens, like a giant jeweler's loupe, held in place by leather straps. Her upper body, wrapped in several layers, looked powerful, but her lower body vanished beneath a blanket, showing no feet below. The way the blanket occasionally shifted, I was guessing there was something that was not quite legs under there. I was also guessing she was old. It's hard to judge sometimes with mutants; in this case, she seemed to have no eyebrows, so her baldness probably had nothing to do with her age, but the wrinkles and age spots were pretty indicative.

She leaned to one side, looking around us to the figures behind, and called out, "Put your toys away, boys, and leave them in your pockets. These are Railwalkers. They could kill you twice before you got off your first shot, pledge and promise on it." She looked at us. "Ain't that so, gentlemen?"

"Might be," said Rok. "If they're good." He looked over his shoulder, then back at the chairbound mutant. Gave a little sideways nod. "Or might be we could kill 'em three times."

The old woman chuckled. "So how's that saying go? You come from the East?"

"Wolf am I, walker of the rails between worlds, and he is Rok. Twenty-three blessings, grandmother. Say your need."

She laughed again. "Say my need? You don't got that long to listen, Normie. Tell you what I'd like, though. Like to know what you want here, Railwalkers. You didn't come down sniffing for no mutant pussy."

"Looking for a man named Jemison Farris. Had his runabout stolen a couple of weeks back."

"Farris?" she laughed. "If that piece of shit Stroller of his got pinched, he's better off without it. Why you care, anyway?"

I answered her question with another. "What's it to you?"

"Jemison had enough trouble with the guard already. Don't need no more official crap coming his way."

"No crap involved, just some questions."

The old mutant eyed us suspiciously. Then she nodded. "Ephram," she said to one of the mutants behind us. "Go get Farris, tell him I said come on over to Deke's." Then she called over her shoulder, "Waldron! Go tell Deke to put on the coffee." She turned back to us. "Won't be but five percent, but it's the thought that counts, ain't it?"

"That it is," I said.

She spun her wheelchair and led the way. The fellows behind us came up closer as we began to move. We kept a weather eye open, but it seemed that the woman's tentative approval of us was accepted, and their formation was protective—apparently we were now guests rather than potential enemies. Closer up I could see that these were indeed mutants, though more sound of body than many I'd met. Three of them appeared relatively normal if you didn't count the lack of a nose on one, and a tail on another. The fourth was a lumbering behemoth, not above six foot, but weighing over three hundred pounds. He had rough, scaly-looking skin, and his fingers were wed, forming something like lobster claws. Except for the big one, they all carried weapons, though they followed the old mutant's instruction and kept them in their pockets.

The boarded-up storefront she led us to had "Deke's Place" written in spray paint on the window's plywood. It had been some sort of convenience store or groceria at one time. You could still see the marks on the stained linoleum where display shelves had once stood, the empty space now taken up with a half-dozen mismatched sets of tables and chairs. The refrigerator cases along the back wall were dark and empty, no colder than the rest of the place. The room was vacant except for a thin mutant behind the counter, whose eyes were on the sides of his head like a horse. The old woman wheeled across the floor to take a place at the sturdiest-looking table. She gestured for us to sit.

"Take a load off, Railwalkers. Fair to say you, Terrapin Jones am I. These folks call me Oculus." She gestured at the others in turn and introduced them. The one with the tail was Jed, the noseless one Marlus, the huge one was called Lob, and the fourth man, who showed no malformation except for a wall eye, was known as Pinko. The four didn't join us at the table, but took up positions around the room, Pinko at the window near a gap in the boards, Lob beside the front door, Marlus and Jeb at the back. The horse man, who Oculus introduced as Deke, brought a tray with heavy white chipped mugs, a pot of coffee, and a bowl of loose tobacco to the table. Oculus took the pot from him.

"I'll Mama that Java," she said, and poured for the three of us. Deke took cups to each of the other four as well, but most set them down untouched. Oculus brought out a stone pipe and began to fill it from the bowl.

"Seems like you're ready for a war," I said to the woman. "Trouble with the guard?"

"Not the guard so much." She shook her head. Fired up the pipe, handed it to me. I took a token puff, handed the pipe to Rok. "Bay City used to be a decent place for mutants," she continued. "Got to register, you know, but the laws give us our rights, assuming we got the where-withal to use 'em. Oh, like anyplace else, there's plenty of normies don't like us much, but mostly they let us be, until recent."

"Since the Beast appeared?" I asked. She nodded. Rok stood and offered the pipe to Pinko, who puffed quickly and passed it on.

"Ain't been a single mutie killed by the Beast so far. Lots of normies assume the Beast is a mutie his own self. Mebbe some think we might be helping him, or sympathetic, anyway. Things been a little tense, as you might say."

"I can imagine," I said, and I could. When people become frightened they look for scapegoats, and become suspicious of anything that smacks of otherness. Next to the malformations of most mutants, differences of skin color and cultural heritage among the normals would become insignificant.

"What about you, Walker of Rails?" she asked. "You think the beast is a mute?"

"Not sure yet."

"But Roth called you here about the Beast, no? Why you down here lookin' for Jemmy?"

"Farris's runabout was involved in a hit and run."

"The night Chief Adams died," she nodded. "Guards sweated Jemmy good about that night. He was workin'. What's that run down got to do with the Beast?"

At the door Pinko stirred and said, "Jemmy." The front door opened and another mutant entered, dressed in a laborer's denims. He had a Neanderthal look about him: an overhung brow ridge and lots of hair. His hairline reached halfway down his forehead, and his five o'clock shadow nearly reached his eyes. He didn't have the appropriate physique, though—he was thin and weak, and with an incongruous-looking pair of glasses perched on his nose, he gave the absurd impression of a techno-nerd caveman. He nodded at the woman. "Oculus."

"Jemmy," she said. "Pull up a chair. These are Railwalkers Wolf and Rok. They was about to tell me why the guard thought you and your runabout had something to do with the Beast."

Farris nodded but said nothing else as he pulled a chair up to the table. I looked from Jemison to Oculus, considering how much I should tell them.

"The man the runabout hit," I said, "was a janitor at the guard station at City Center." Oculus smiled slightly, but Farris' eyes widened. The guard apparently hadn't mentioned that while questioning him. "We think the Beast stole your runabout to put that janitor in hospital, and snuck into the station disguised as him."

Oculus laughed out loud at this. "So that Beast, he's a skinwalker," she said, using the Namerican term for shapeshifters. "Oh, don't look at me like that, Railwalker man. You didn't have to say it, Oculus was born at night, but not last night. Roth call you folks in, gotta be he thinks there some hoodoo in this Beast. Ain't no guardo janitor got claws like the Beast supposed to have, ain't no disguisin' that kinda thing, unless you're a shapeshifter."

I turned to Farris. "I know the guards grilled you for hours about this. I don't want to add to your troubles, just want to know if there's anything about that night you can tell us, anything at all that seemed strange or off, maybe something you didn't tell the guard, or didn't think of at the time."

Jemison looked from me to Rok to Oculus, and back again. He looked at the table.

"Only one thing," he said. "Didn't know it until after. Tommy Chang." He glanced at Oculus. "You know, Annie's kid? He says he seen a big bald guy hanging around Chalmers Street, where the Roller was parked. Said he looked like a mutie, but Tommy didn't know him."

"Tommy gets around," Oculus explained. "Knows just

about every mutie in Alphabet City."

"Only thing I can tell you I didn't tell the guard," Farris added with a shrug.

A big bald guy sounded like it could have been the Beast Auden saw, but it was iffy, a slim connection. This didn't add very much to our knowledge, but talking to Farris had been a long shot anyway.

"Thanks Jemmy," Oculus said. "You go on back to work now."

Jemison Farris got up, avoiding eye contact, nodded to us, and to Oculus, and made his way to the door.

Oculus looked at us. "Tell you what, Railwalker man," she said. "I can see Jemmy didn't tell you nothing you didn't already guess. But I'll give you a new toy to play with. That weren't the first time someone seen a bald mutie nobody knows. He's a ninjaman, walks the night like a shadow. But there's eyes in Alphabet City see through the dark, and we watch out for our own. That bald ghost, he be seen one too many times 'round a squat over at Chalmers and A Street. Most of the squatters there, they found other places to habit, you get my meaning? Might be you want to check that place out."

"Might be," I agreed.

We were rising to leave when Ephram burst in, out of breath.

"Jemmy..." he gasped. "Guards... C and Montrose."

We followed out the door and down the block to where a small crowd was developing. The dozen or so people—mutants all—backed up suddenly, and the air became tense. I could see at the center a burly guardsman holding Jemison Farris up against a wall.

The crowd had backed up because the guard's partner had drawn his gun. Other guns and knives were appearing, most still held down, away from the guards' line of sight, but exposed to us as we approached from behind.

I shouldered my way between the mutants, and ignoring the partner, who looked like a middle-aged lounge lizard with too much pomade in his hair, I walked to the one holding Farris.

"What's the problem here, guardsman?" I asked.

"Guard business," he growled. "Back off unless you want a..." At this point he turned and looked at me for the first time, and then trailed off.

"It's the Railwalker," the gigolo said. The burly fellow, dark of hair and mustache as well as expression, shot a look at his partner, but didn't bother to answer. Below his badge, a nametag read "C. Remming."

"Let him go," I said quietly.

"Drunk and disorderly," said Remming loudly. "He was harassing people." Then he lowered his voice, and said to me, "This is the mutie whose car hit Andy. We want to question him again about that."

"One of the investigators put you on that?" I asked.

"Don't need no authorization to question a fuckin' mutie," he growled.

There was a shuffling noise, and I looked around. One of the watching mutants had raised a gun, and Rok had taken it away from him, putting the guy on the ground in the process. The crowd stirred. I heard at least three guns cock, and the lounge lizard went on high alert, gun ranging back and forth over the crowd. As he turned, I could see his nametag read "N. Turrin."

"PEACE!" I shouted, putting a Force into it. The guns all pointed to the ground, and the tension in the air dropped perceptibly. Rok grinned at me. I turned to Remming again.

"In the first place," I said, "I was just talking with this man, and he was perfectly sober. He didn't magically become drunk in the few steps he took from there to here. In the second place, this man is now a witness in a Railwalker inquiry. Do I have to quote you the title and section that give me jurisdiction and authority in this?"

He glowered at me a moment more, then grudgingly released Farris. The mutant nodded his thanks at me, then scurried off down the street.

"What are you all looking at?" Remming demanded of the crowd. "Move along. Excitement's all over. Be about your business." As the people began to slowly disperse, he turned his glare on me again. "Good luck with your inquiry," he said, with emphasis on the last word as if it were an insult. Then he nodded at his partner, and the two of them walked off.

Rok stood beside me, watching them go. "Bay City's Finest. Gotta love 'em."

"No, I don't," I said.

"Hmm." Rok pretended to think that over. "Guess you don't at that."

The squat at Chalmers and A Street had been an office building at one time. The front doors were firmly boarded up, but in a trash-filled alley that stank of urine and garbage we found a side door that had been broken open. We ranged carefully through the building, guns drawn. Many of the rooms were scattered with trash, but the departing squatters had taken anything that might have been useful to them. There was no sign of their occupancy except for a few blackened spots where fires had once been lit and some empty tin cans and food packages.

On the fifth floor we found it: a corner room, where pieces of the plas-ply boards had been removed from windows looking out over both Chalmers and A Street. There was a rickety card table with a few power bars and a couple of water bottles, several articles of clothing: some shirts, a pair of pants, and a couple of denim jackets on hangers hooked over nails set into the wall. A canvas duffle sat on the floor. Inside it was a uniform with "Andy" embroidered over the pocket.

"No ID card," Rok observed. The uniform by itself, even on a body that looked like Andy Foreman, wouldn't have gotten him into the guard station without an ID card. The uniform was easy; the ID would have been the hardest part of an impersonation for a shapeshifter. Chances were the Beast wouldn't use Andy's identity again, but he'd have kept the ID card somewhere safer than the squat, just in case. "He's probably not coming back here."

"We'll have Gage put some surveillance on this place anyway," I said. "You never know."

"Yeah," said Rok, surveying the nearly empty room. "You never know."

13. BAY CITY

Sometimes John Hamblin thought they ought to just hose the damn locker room down with disinfectant—then he'd remember that Andy actually did pretty much exactly that every other day, and it didn't make a hell of a lot of difference. The place still smelled like... Well, like a locker room; what else would describe that perpetual dirty socks-and-jocks funk? He closed his locker and hooked the hanger his uniform was on through the latch while he finished changing into his civvies. Hamblin took his uniform home each night, because otherwise it picked up the funk of the locker room, and he'd have to smell it for the first hour or so of his shift till the stench wore off. It was partly the damp, he thought. He could hear the shower still running, and he could smell that funny herbal soap Nick Turrin, who was always longest in the shower, was using. It was the steam, he thought; the steam carried that funk, caused uniforms and other absorbent materials to pick it up. Behind him Remming was still holding forth. Blunt, bald, mustached and bullet-headed, Cort Remming always seemed to be angry about something, and today it was the presence of Railwalkers in Bay City.

"You think this looks good for the guard?" Remming was demanding. "These fuckin' outsiders comin' in to do our job for us?"

"Hey," said Hamblin, turning to join the discussion, "maybe they can actually help. They know about shit we don't."

Cort Remming rolled his eyes and slammed his locker door. It sprung open again, spoiling the effect somewhat. "Oh, man," he said. "Tell me you don't buy into that spooky horseshit."

The shower cut off. Hamblin shrugged, and Calb Whaling offered, "The new chief said they talked to the Old Man's ghost."

Remming turned on him. "Get a clue, moron. Gage fuckin' worshiped the Old Man. They coulda waved a picture of him and had somebody say 'not on my watch you won't' on the intercom, Gage woulda peed his pants and bowed down."

Looking over his shoulder, Hamblin could only see the back of Calb Whaling's curly blond head. Big as he was, Calb seemed to shrink before the shorter, darker Remming's anger. It was an old sore point. Whaling was notoriously naïve, willing to believe, as the Old Man had once said, six impossible things before breakfast. Whaling wanted to qualify for investigator in the worst way, but no one believed he'd ever make it. Naiveté was not a desirable quality in an investigator.

"Hey," said Nickas Turrin, who had just come around the corner wrapped in a towel, "Gage is alright." He opened his locker, took out a bottle of aftershave, and leaned against the row of lockers as he twisted off the cap. Hamblin thought he looked like he was striking a pose, waiting for someone to challenge his assertion, but the effect was spoiled when he surreptitiously checked his reflection in the mirror hanging inside the locker door.

"Yeah," Whaling added, "Gage is street."

"Damn straight," said Turrin. He straightened up, slapped on some aftershave, then dropped his towel on the bench and started dressing in his street clothes.

"Yeah, yeah, fine, Gage is a right guy," Remming allowed. "But we're not talking about doin' something about Gage, are we? We're talkin' about them fuckin' high-hat Railwalkers. I say we oughta show 'em whose city they're in."

"Same city we're in," said Turrin. "Micah Roth's fucking city. And Roth invited them here."

"Yeah, well," said Remming, "I'm sure he meant well, but Roth don't know shit about guard work. And neither do them fuckin' Railwalkers. I dunno about you guys, but the streets I know, that weirdo shit don't cut it. You need to know what you're doing out there. You gotta hang tough. These Railwalkers dunno shit from Shinola when it comes to the streets of Bay City, and we're supposed to kowtow to them? Fuck that! I say we teach 'em a lesson."

"He may have a point," Turrin offered. "I mean, lookit what happened last spring at Hicks Junction. I heard it was the Railwalkers screwed the pooch, led the guards from Monteague and Santa Brita right into a trap."

"That's just what I'm talking about." Remming slammed his locker door again. This time he held it closed as he gave the combination lock a twirl. "These arseholes think just because they can play sheriff with those hicks out in the zones, they got the moves to come into a place like Bay City and lord it over the regular guard?"

"I dunno, man," Whaling said. "Fuckin' with a Railwalker, that's like fuckin' with a priest. Besides, I heard they got all sorts of special training and fancy moves."

"What, you're afraid they're gonna turn you into a newt?"

"That's not what I'm talking about, man. They're not just, like, spooky stuff, y'know? I mean like, serious martial shit. My cousin Fred seen..."

"Your cousin Fred don't know crap," Remming interrupted. "Ain't he the one got took in that pyramid scheme last year?"

Hamblin was starting to feel pretty uncomfortable with the whole trend of the conversation. He swung his legs over the bench, turning around completely to face the others. "How tough they are isn't the point," he said. "The point is, Nick's right. The Railwalkers are here because Roth invited them. It ain't our job to second guess the city boss."

"Fine," Remming growled. "You just go ahead and let these outsiders walk all over you. Some of us have some pride left, and the balls to do something about it." He stalked to the door.

The Tankard was just around the corner from the CA

Tower, seven steps down from street level, a long, narrow, low-ceilinged room with the bar running down the left wall and a line of booths down the right, two pool tables and a few more booths at the back. Later on, the clientele would consist mostly of city guard and a handful of private security people, but at just after six P.M., the place buzzed with the noise of the more mixed early evening crowd.

"What's Dobbs doing here?" Nickas Turrin elbowed Cort Remming and nodded toward the door. The two guards peered through the smoky atmosphere at the lean figure of the proprietor of the Bar of Gold as he surveyed the small crowd, noticed Remming and Turrin, and headed in their direction.

"We'll know in a minute," said Remming.

As Dobbs pulled up to the bar, Turrin asked, "Whatcha doin' here, Dobbs? Wanted to find out what real liquor tastes like?"

Dobbs ignored the dapper guard and focused on Remming. "We need to talk."

Remming looked pointedly at his beer and said, "So talk."

"Privately."

Remming looked at Dobbs, then nodded to Turrin and led the way to an empty booth at the back. "So," he said when they were settled, "what's up your backside?"

Dobbs took out a cigar and lit up. "Suppose I were to tell you that I could lead you to the Beast?"

"I'd ask what the hell you've been smoking besides that foul cigar."

"I'm serious. Word on the street is, the Beast is a skin-walker—a shapeshifter."

"And you believe that scuttlebutt?"

"There's a mutie comes into the bar..."

"Is this a joke?" asked Turrin. "'Cause I think I heard this one."

Dobbs glared at him, looked back at Remming, and continued, "Something about him struck me wrong, so I had him tailed. Turns out he's a shapeshifter. He goes about disguised as a normal."

Remming snorted.

"You saw him change?" Turrin asked.

"No, but I know it was him. Went into a public jakes, came out as a normal. Nobody else in or out in that time." It had been Evans who saw this—or didn't see it, as the case may be—but Dobbs didn't see why he should let the guardos in on that little detail. He was certain, after all, that was what had happened.

"He shaped normal? No tail or nothing?" Remming asked. Dobbs nodded. "Don't have to be no supernatural thing to put on some makeup, look like a normal." Remming turned to Turrin. "What do you think?"

Turrin did his best to disguise his surprise at Remming actually asking his opinion. "Me? I dunno. Could be he's the Beast, could be he's got some other sort of scam going."

"Yeah." Remming glowered at Dobbs. "Of course, there ain't actually any law against a mutie going about disguised as a normal. Now, if he stole some normal's identity, that would be something else again."

"But guaranteed something's not right about it," said Dobbs.

Remming shrugged. "Why bring this to me?"

"Why not? We've had arrangements in the past. Just because I'm a legit businessman now, don't mean we can't still do business. If I manage to win a seat next election, it couldn't hurt to have friends in the guard. And it couldn't hurt a guardsman to have a friend on the council."

"So this mutie—assuming he really is the Beast—what's he gonna cost me?"

"Nothing. Nada. Free of charge. Just remember who pointed you to him. Be good for my press, come election time, if it's known I helped the guard nail the Beast."

"You know, you're not real popular around One City Plaza these days. Gage and some of the others think your Citizen's Safety Committee are just a bunch of damned vigilantes, deserve to be popped."

"Exactly my point. If the chairman of the Safety

Committee contributes materially to the apprehension of the Beast, a lot of that bad press could just go away."

"As far as the public's concerned, maybe."

"Public are the ones who vote." There was a long pause. Finally, Dobbs said, "If you're not interested, I could take this to Kabanov."

"Right." Remming laughed. "That'd do wonders for your PR." Kabanov ran the Russian mob out of the northeast quarter.

"Let me tell you something, guardo." Dobbs leaned across the table, punctuating his points with stabs of the cigar. "I'm a selfish man. I know which side of my bread is buttered. The Beast is bad for everybody, not least of all for my business. I want to see the Beast go down. Kabanov's got muscle, and he's got a vested interest in this city. He'll want the same. If I can get some good press out of this, fine, all the better for me. If I can't, that's just peachy, too—as long as the Beast ends up gone."

14. WOLF

Summersend morning found me sitting in the main room of our suite, surrounded by a mess. I had printed out a lot of the records and pictures of the victims and the murder sites, and they were spread around the living area of our rooms, piled on chairs and table, sideboards and sofas.

"Festive Summersend," Morgan said from the kitchenette, where she was brewing coffee. "Get any sleep at all?"

"Yeah, some," I said. I had napped for an hour or two, but before the sun had risen I'd found myself wakeful again and abandoned my bed to study the evidence. The coffee smelled great. Like the hooch Roth's people had left us, the coffee we'd found in the kitchenette was high quality, maybe half real coffee, as opposed to the seventy percent chicory you got in most places. Carrying two cups of the fragrant black brew, Morgan stepped carefully between piles of photos and transcripts and handed me one. It was nicely warm in my hand.

She peered around the room. Rok had occasionally grumbled about the mess, but Morgan would just dump whatever inconvenienced her off a seat or a table, though she was careful to put it in an appropriate spot. One-handed, she shifted the treasurer's photos off a chair and slumped them against a pile of transcripts of interviews with his associates. She plunked down in the chair and shoved some files aside to set her cup down on the table.

I sipped appreciatively at the coffee. Remembered belatedly to mutter, "Thanks."

Morgan chuckled. I could hear Rok stirring in the other room, and the shower went on.

"You getting anywhere?" Morgan asked.

"Dunno yet," I muttered. "Maybe."

Morgan nodded, got up with her coffee, abandoning any attempt at conversation. She knew what I was like at times like this. "Parade's at ten," she said, heading for their room.

"Ceremony is at four," I said. I had my dress tunic already laid out on my bed. "I already told Roth we might not make the parade. You go without me if you want."

Morgan laughed. She knew I hated parades. She said something else as she vanished into the room she shared with Rok, but I didn't catch it. I was already back to my contemplation of the Beast's calendar.

When the Beast takes his first victim, the fishing boat captain, Summersend is five weeks away. It's not quite first quarter past the full moon, a Thursday. It would have been bright that night, the three-quarter moon shining off the water. The Beast walks onto the boat and kills him there. Eight days later he takes the teacher, Juan Castro. The weather was bad that night, no view of the last quarter moon. Castro was killed in an enclosed bridge between two of the college buildings. Private, like the boat, and indoors. Fitch, the guardsman, is taken the night before the dark moon, a Sunday night. He's on patrol, apparently gets dragged into the shelter of a tramway station. This is a little bolder, more exposed. He's taking his victim off the street, not coming to him in a place he thinks of as secure. Then nothing for almost two weeks, the whole of the waxing moon, until two days before full, a Monday. That's when Suzi Mascarpone of the Harlot's Guild gets taken in the street, out in the open, and Auden attempts to capture the Beast. The timing blows the "waning moon, baneful magic" connection all to hell. Two days later, the Beast walks into the guard's wardroom and kills the chief. Moon's just past full, waning again, one week to Summersend.

If you're looking for baneful magic, you usually look at the waning moon first. But could the Beast be running on the sun instead? Midsummer is the equivalent of the full moon, while Summersend is the equivalent of a moon in its first waning quarter. I wondered what, if anything, we could expect of the Beast on Summersend.

The Summersend ceremony commenced at four P.M., but it was already feeling like sunset in the square, shadowed as it was by the tall buildings on all sides. Central Square was a wide open plaza in front of the main entrance to the CA Tower. For the city's Summersend celebration the big fountain in the center of the plaza had been emptied of water and a huge Corn Guy had been set up in it. At least, I assumed it was a Corn Guy. The figure must have been twenty-five or thirty feet tall, but as we entered the plaza that afternoon it was still shrouded by what appeared to be a parachute. On the side of the square opposite the CA Tower a temporary stage had been set up, hung with speakers and sound equipment, but it was empty at the moment, and the crowd's attention was focused on the steps of the CA Tower, where Roth, Weldt, Gage, and several other city officials were gathered, along with the three of us, and the priests and ministers of the city's major churches and temples. Among the black robes and suits of the more conservative denominations I saw Thudisar Tyburn in his pale-blue over-robe, a woman in the orange robes of a Buddhist monk, and the representative of the Church of the King in his formal white spangled jumpsuit. Between the tower steps and the fountain with the shrouded Guy stood a huge cart filled with produce: bundles of corn, wheat, baskets of fruit and vegetables, and of fresh fish on beds of ice. I knew that beneath this pile would be dozens of financial statements and year-end reports, representing the less tangible fruits of the city's harvest.

Speeches were made, of course, though there was nothing particularly memorable about any of them, and certainly no mention made of the predations of the killer we were calling the Beast. I didn't think the Beast would appear and wreak havoc at the public Blessing ceremony. That wasn't his style. But even though it was unlikely he'd

appear, he was clearly on everyone's mind. Everywhere
you looked there were tight mouths, haunted eyes.

When the appropriate time came, city guards moved
the closest of the crowd back, the priests and ministers
ranged out in a circle around the Harvest Barrow, holding
their hands out toward it, and the entire crowd seemed to
hold its breath as I stepped forward to pronounce the
Blessing of the Harvest. I had never performed the blessing for a crowd as large as this, nor had I ever used a
microphone to do so, but I didn't feel particularly
nervous.

I wasn't quite prepared, however, for what followed.
At the end of the Blessing the assembled community traditionally joins in a tone, and the crowd assembled in
Central Square did so with great enthusiasm. I'd never
heard a tone chanted by a crowd that large, and I could
feel their joined voices vibrating through the pavement
beneath my feet. For a moment I wondered if the vibra-
tion might actually cause some damage to the structures
around, it was so loud, and then I realized that was silly.
Bay City had been celebrating Summersend in just this
way for many years; surely there was no danger of such a
thing. There were probably outdoor concerts that had a
higher decibel level. What I was really reacting to, I reflected, was the intensity of emotion the crowd put into their
tone. A whole city that had been living in fear was putting
their hopes and desires into this great sound, wishing for
blessings on the results of their labor, as well as relief from
the threat that hung over them.

At the other side of the square a band had climbed
onto the stage, and as the ceremony came to its end they
began to play. I saw bottles being handed out, and people
began dancing, despite the lack of space to move around
in. The various dignitaries on the steps began to move
around me, filing back into the tower, or down the steps
through a cordon of guards. Now I had only to get
through the formal reception upstairs, in the penthouse
ballroom of the tower. I wasn't looking forward to that.

Politics and diplomacy can be a bitch. They come

with the job, of course, and we're all trained to that stuff, but I've only ever met a couple of Railwalkers who actually liked that end of the work. The rest of us deal with it just because we've been drilled in the necessity.

Across the square I noticed a father and son. Dad was apparently explaining about the Corn Guy as Son stared up at the giant, shrouded shape, glancing between it and a corn dolly in his hand. I wondered what it was like to grow up with a knowledge of these ceremonies and traditions.

My Pa had never stood before a town's Corn Guy and explained it to me. We never had a Yule tree, hunted colored eggs on Osterday, never hung corn dollies. My father considered all that stuff superstitious nonsense. As a kid, they were strange foreign practices that I never quite understood.

In the square, Mom joined Dad and Son, and I watched them vanish into the crowd together. My mother left when I was barely three, and from what I learned later in life, I can't say I blame her. Oh, I suppose there's some residual resentment left in me that she didn't at least try to take me with her. But if she was anything like the other women I saw my father with over the years, that would have been at least as big a disaster as leaving me with my Pop turned out. Women like that, they just had no real "mother" genes in them. They'll ooh and aah over a baby, sure; they'll pinch a kid's cheek and call him cunning and cute as a button. But don't ask them to change a diaper, or clean the kid's spit-up. I don't really know if my mom was one of those women or not, but I guessed she probably was. There's not much I do know for sure about my mother; my Pa never talked about her.

Pa wasn't much better at being a father than his girl-friends were at mothering, come to that, but we got by somehow. He thought of himself as a professional gambler, and it was true he knew the games inside and out. There's an old song about gambling, how you gotta know when to hold, and know when to fold. Pa knew all that shit. He knew the percentages on every game of chance there was, knew how to play 'em, too. But knowing is a different thing from doing. Gambling is an addiction, just like hooch or poppyshot, and however much intellectual knowledge an addict has about his chosen poison, he's never really in control. All that knowledge just makes him think he is.

When I was a kid we were always on the move. Sometimes Pa was just feeling the urge, needing to move on to greener pastures, convinced that his luck would be better in the next town or city. Sometimes we were doing what he called the Kansas City Shuffle. Doing the KC Shuffle always meant that Pa had been losing bad and didn't have the money to pay off his losses. That happened almost as often as him just getting itchy feet for their own sake.

I was woolgathering, I realized. Staring out unseeing over the desperately celebratory crowd, dancing and drinking before the shrouded figure of the giant Guy, I was thinking back to my days on the road with Pa. I felt a touch on my elbow, and turned to face Micah Roth.

"Coming along with us?" he asked.

"Of course," I said, and turned to join the procession to the elevators. Why was my father so much on my mind these days, I wondered. It wasn't like I'd seen him in... how many years was it? Ten at least, probably more like twelve or thirteen, if I'd stopped to do the math. Perhaps it was just being in Bay City, or perhaps contact with Micah Roth was provoking old memories, though Roth had said nothing about our previous meetings.

Waiting for the elevator in the vast lobby, the burble of conversation going on around me, I settled my Crane Bag more comfortably under my tunic, feeling the shape of the small rolled paper cylinder inside it. Yes, I'd been in Bay City with my father several times as a child, but the last time I'd actually seen him, it had been in further north, in Alturo. Which was ironic, I suppose, considering. The first time I remembered being in Alturo I was about eight or so, I guess.

Our travels had brought us back north again, and we had landed at the house of one of my father's older friends, a couple by the name of Bill and Patty Morris. The

Morrises had a largish spread just outside the city, a ram-shackle farmhouse and several outbuildings, all of which were filled to the brim with old junk and bric-a-brac. The farmhouse was chock full as well, both with old furniture and odds and ends, as well as with live bodies—the Mor-rises, their four kids, two dogs and six cats.

The couple were a study in contrasts. Patty was as broad as she was tall, a miniature mountain of a woman with a sharp, beaklike nose in the middle of her soft, round face. Bill was medium height and thin, bearded and balding, with a pug nose and blunt features. They scraped a living for their large family with a variety of small busi-ness ventures—besides dealing junk (the hand-painted sign declared "Anteeks," but hardly anything in the place really deserved the name), Bill did a bit of small engine and appliance repair and hired out for haulage with his oldest son, using Bill's beat-up panel truck. Patty took in washing and did a bit of seamstressing, read tarot cards and cast horoscopes, and acted as midwife and herbal doc-tor for the local women.

Everything in the Morris place was strange to my youthful senses. Traveling with my Pa I'd met rich people and poor, stayed in palatial suites and fleabag hotels, but I had never spent much time in an actual home, never met people who were both so poor and so happy, had a life so rich. The smell of the place was a strange stew of spices and herbs, incense and old cooking smells, dogs and cats and dust and other things I couldn't identify.

I'd also seldom had home-made food, unless you count the peanut butter sandwiches or beans out of a can that we dined on now and then when Pop's luck was run-ning bad. Dinner at the Morris's house was lively and fairly noisy with five kids at the table, even though I didn't contribute that much to the noise. I had spent very little time around kids my own age, and was more than a little wary of them.

After dinner I followed Bill and my Pa outside, Bill carrying a large flashlight, my father smoking a cigarette. Bill led the way to a small, padlocked shed beside the swaybacked barn.

"I'm really sorry, Doc," Bill said. "But it's been four, almost five years, and we really need the space." My father's name was Bryce, but no one ever called him anything but "Doc." Since he knew nothing about medicine, to this day I have no idea why they called him that.

"S'okay, Bill," my father said. "I understand. Appreciate you keeping the stuff this long." He stared off into the distance, smoking, while Bill fumbled through a ring with what looked to me like about a million keys on it, until he found the right key to fit the padlock.

Inside the small shed were a few chairs, a table and dresser, a disassembled bedstead, and a pile of boxes. Unprepossessing, maybe, but I was fascinated. Here was all I would ever see of my father's past, of my own life as it had been before my earliest memories decomposed into fragmentary, dreamlike images. Before my mother left us. I stared at the collection. The headboard against the back wall looked like a wide tombstone standing mute watch over the remnants of my father's past.

"Sorry there's no light," Bill said as he held out the flashlight, and Pa took it. "You sure you don't want to wait 'til tomorrow, do this in the daylight?"

"We gotta be in Freno tomorrow night," said Pop. "May's well git 'er done. Not much of it worth keeping anyway. Can you an' Patty do anything with the furniture?"

"Yeah, I s'pose," said Bill. "That club chair would bring a buck or two, and you don't see many of them old carved headboards anymore. Sure, we can unload that for you. We make anything on it—"

"You keep it," my father interrupted. "Call it rent on the storage space."

"We couldn't—"

"Sure you could. Betcha Patty would agree with me."

Bill smiled and shrugged. Pop went to the top box on the pile, lifting a flap with one finger and shining the flashlight inside.

"Well, I'll leave you to it. Give a holler if you need

anything," Bill said, and headed back to the house. Pa began pulling the boxes out of the shed and going through them.

Soon his previous life was spread out on the grass under the flashlight's beam, all sorts of the things that go to make up a household: dishes, pots and pans, clothes, papers, books, discs, even some actual printed photographs. He sorted through it quickly, retaining only two small boxes, one not quite full of papers and things; I didn't quite catch what they all were. Another box held some of the clothing. The rest he repacked, some to be burned, some for Bill and Patty to sell.

I looked into one of the boxes of discards. It was mostly papers, a few old photo prints sitting on top. I leafed through the pictures. A couple showed my father as a younger man, horsing around with some guys I didn't recognize. Another showed the same group gathered around an ornithopter. In a third my father sat on the hood of an older styled runabout. There were a couple of postcards from Freno and Two Suns. And one picture of a woman.

The photo had been taken outdoors, near the zones. I could see buttes and scrub-brush and cactus in the background. She was wearing a white blouse, the collar turned up. Her light-brown hair was being lifted slightly by the wind. She looked at the camera with a rueful smile, as if she didn't really want her picture taken, but was fond of the photographer and knew she couldn't dissuade him from taking it. Although the picture was in color, she looked to me like a movie star from one of those old black and white pre-Crash movies. Something tingled in my gut.

"Pa? Who is this?" I asked, holding the picture up.

When his eyes alit on the photo, he looked like he'd been kicked in the stomach by a horse. He dropped the paper he'd been reading back into the box and sat up straight. Took a deep breath. "That's your mother," he said.

Now it was my turn to feel like I'd been kicked in the stomach. There must have been some suspicion in my young mind as to who this was, but my world still turned on its side to have the suspicion confirmed. My mother was a strictly forbidden subject. I gripped the photo a little tighter, with both hands now, afraid he was going to rip it out of my hands and burn it before my eyes or something. I took a step backwards.

"Can I keep it?" I asked, sure he was going to refuse.

He sighed, then looked at me silently for a long time. Sighed again. "Yeah," he said. "Just don't ever let me see it again, okay sport?"

I nodded gravely.

I still carry that picture of my mother, rolled up in my crane bag, what the Indios call a medicine pouch. Regular folks don't often see a Railwalker's crane bag, but we all carry them, generally on a thong around the neck. The formal tunic even has an inside pocket that the crane bag slips into, so it rides right where it usually hangs, in the hollow of your breastbone, and doesn't move around or cause a bulge. Mostly your crane bag is filled with pebbles, little feathers, tokens and fetishes—small objects that hold a piece of your memory, a piece of your magic. The rolled-up picture in mine was a little larger than most such fetishes, and I could feel it riding there under my tunic as I stepped through the doors of the big function room on the fifth floor of the CA Tower, into the noise and motion of the Bay City Summersend reception.

The reception was typical, if larger in scale and more glittery than most I'd attended. You didn't see many tuxedos or ball gowns at Summersend in the zones. Fortunately we'd been in the city long enough for me to get the dress tunic cleaned and pressed, so I looked almost as respectable as Rok. I enviously watched Rok and Morgan slide out onto the dance floor.

The Allworlder Tyburn was rambling on about the city's zoning ordinances. One of the other officials there, I think it was a fellow from the Crafter's Guild, started hectoring Tyburn about dual-purpose zoning (he thought crafters ought to be allowed living space as well as sales and manufacturing in the same building). As their dispute heated up, a new voice said, "We would welcome the arriving stranger."

It was the first line of the really formal version of the traditional greeting. I hadn't heard it in years. I turned to face an elder woman, white of hair and pale of skin. Thin as a starving zone wolf, she stood as straight as any of the guardsmen there. She wore a floor-length gown of scarlet and black, and on her breast was a cloisonne pin with the sigil of the Harlot's Guild.

"Come you from the east?" she continued.

"I come as the crow flies, and would not remain a stranger. Wolf am I, Walker of the Rails Between the Worlds, charged by Ianeh, seventh of her line from Brick, the Red Crow. Twenty-three blessings of Soul-Are upon you and yours, sister. Say your need."

She smiled, stepped forward and took my arm. Despite her age she was a handsome woman, and had no doubt been in great demand when actively working for her guild. I was sure better men than I had been overwhelmed by that intimate, quietly glowing smile.

"Hannah Caine am I, Guildmadam of the city's Harlot's Guild." I had guessed as much. There were younger members of the guild in attendance, most on the arms of various city functionaries, but she was the only older guildswoman I'd seen, likely to have been officially invited as one of the guild's officers. "Welcome to our city, Railwalker," she completed the formula. "Come freely, go safely, and bless our homes with your corvine wisdom." She sighed and smiled again. "As to my need, no more than some pleasant and diverting conversation in the midst of a boring social function full of self-important people. And perhaps a few minutes on the arm of a handsome young man, to remind me of the glories of days past."

"Not so young, I fear," I said. "Nor do I believe for one moment, looking at you, that your glories are all in days past."

She laughed. Her laugh wasn't silvery; it was more like

the rattle of ice cubes in a glass of fine bourbon.

"Ah, the Railwalkers were ever well spoken. We've not seen a Railwalker in Bay City these many years. It was a true delight to see the Blessing of the Harvest performed in the traditional manner. Tell me, how is it you return just now?"

"We don't get here often, but technically, Bay City is on our usual round," I said, "and it's not often we arrive just in time for one of the great festivals."

"Or that you arrive to find the city so desperately requires your corvine councils?" She raised a quizzical eyebrow at me. "Tell me for a truth, Railwalker Wolf: Roth summoned you to help with the problem of the Beast, didn't he?"

"If he said so, Lady, I would not contradict the word of the city boss."

"Oh, pshaw." She laughed again. "Roth said no such thing, nor would he—though I imagine I could coax that admission from him, if I had a mind. No, Railwalker, Micah Roth is far more subtle than you give him credit for. He would not be seen running to the Railwalkers for help, as if he and his government could not keep the peace in their own city. He would much rather the general public see the arrival of the Railwalkers as a fortuitous synchronicity—as if the gods themselves, noticing their favored Bay City was troubled, had arranged things to our advantage."

"He didn't seem to me a particularly religious man," I said. "Or a secretive one, for that matter."

"Oh, I don't doubt he would confess he called you here, if anyone questioned him directly on it, yes or no. But consider your own answer to my question just now. You would not have answered me with such careful circumspection if you had not noticed how he explained—or did not explain—your presence at the Ritual of Summersend this afternoon."

I had to allow as how she had me there. "You think this is a bad decision on his part?"

"What, summoning you here? Or do you mean concealing—perhaps I should say neglecting to reveal—the fact that he has done so?"

"Either."

She thought that over for a moment. "These are terrible days, Railwalker," she said. "Not just with regard to the crimes of this killer, horrible though they may be. Our city may be flourishing economically, but it is rotting away inside. We struggle to resurrect the technology of our ancestors, with no regard for the disasters that technology wrought in their time. Our youth have no respect for their elders, or for the traditions and customs that made our city great. Civility, honor, fair dealing, common courtesy, even good sense and serious reflection fall before the onrushing juggernaut of commercial progress. Look to the newsfeeds and you will see it. Journalism and reportage give way to huckstering and sound bytes, serious consideration of important issues is nowhere to be found, only the shrill caterwauling of partisan pinheads, lashing the public with shallow sloganeering."

It sounded a little like a speech, and one she'd given before. The smile was gone now, replaced with a look that reminded me of a raptor. Not one on the hunt, but one who had sensed an invader in its territory. Then she sighed. "There was a time," she said, "when there was order in the world, and sanity. Honor and nobility meant something; breeding, manners, customs and traditions were not just empty forms."

"And you think," I asked, "that Micah Roth contributes to this degeneration? That the People's Takeover and the creation of more democratic institutions signaled the downfall of honor and nobility?"

"Micah Roth is a man of his time."

"Perhaps so. But do honor and nobility exist in an institution, in a form of government, or in the hearts of the individuals who make up a society?"

"The efficient function of any form of government requires good intentions, honor, and honesty in the hearts and minds of those at the top. History has shown us that a corrupt democratic leader can do as much damage as any hereditary monarch."

"And you would have me believe that Roth is corrupt?"

She looked at me for a long moment, her head cocked to one side. "I did not say so," she said at last. "But if I were you, Railwalker, I would go carefully, with both eyes wide open. Corrupt or not, no politician is without his agendas. The Walkers of the Rails have a reputation for integrity and incorruptibility. If some in this city do suspect Micah Roth to be corrupt, the appearance of a close association between him and your order might well persuade them otherwise. Have no doubt the city boss is cognizant of this."

The music had turned to a waltz, and Hannah Caine gestured toward the dance floor. "Will you dance, Rail-walker?" she asked. I said I'd be honored.

I'm no great dancer, though I know the steps to the traditional dances of most regions and can manage not to trip over my own feet. Guild harlots were trained in far more than sexual skills, of course, so it came as no surprise that the guildmadam should be a marvelous dancer. As we moved across the floor, she compensated for my little inadequacies so smoothly and subtly, if I'd been just a little less self-aware I might have thought I'd discovered a previously unknown natural ability for dance. I had little doubt that her skill at manipulation extended to other areas as well, and it was unlikely she'd have to take a city official to bed in order to lead him around by the nose. And the guild was a powerful force in Bay City.

I put those thoughts aside. There would be enough time for grim and suspicious musings on the morrow. For the moment I let myself go and just enjoyed dancing as I seldom had before.

At midnight a bell summoned us out to the penthouse terrace to watch the burning of the Bay City Corn Guy. I made my way to the railing, looked down. Many stories below I could see Central Square, where the draped parachute had been removed, revealing the huge Corn Guy set up in the dry fountain. On the stage the band was playing, traditional seasonal tunes interspersed with what I assumed was their own original stuff, since I hadn't heard it before. They weren't bad, actually. The square was still crammed with people, some of them dancing, some of them just standing around. Here and there people held up smaller Corn Guys of their own, or little Corn Dollies, which they'd toss on the bonfire once the big Guy went up. For the moment, guards on watch at the sawhorses kept the crowd back from the fountain and its giant figure. I was thinking the leaves and stalks on the Guy looked kind of oversized when I became aware of a tall presence beside me.

"Hannah's a trip, isn't she?" Sarah Weldt asked.

"You could put it that way," I said. "I take it she and Roth have a somewhat adversarial relationship?"

"Not always," she sighed. "She cooperates a lot of the time. But she can be a bit rigid about certain things."

A girl, maybe twelve or thirteen, came rushing up to Weldt, and then, noticing me, abruptly shifted to a slower, more stately approach. She was wearing a rather adult-looking gown, but a conservative one.

"Mother..." she said, smiling and glancing at me. I had a feeling had they been alone it would have been a delighted, energetic "Mommy!"

Weldt nodded and turned. "Railwalker, this is my daughter, Rochelle. Rochelle, Railwalker Wolf."

"Twenty-three blessings," I said, as I took her hand. She curtsied and said, "And to you. You honor our house with your corvine presence." I bowed. "Though I suppose it's technically not 'our' house," she added, with a glance at her mother, "except in a sort of metaphorical way."

"Thank you for your welcome," I said. "To whatever place you are in."

She blushed and nodded. "Mother," she said, turning back to Sarah Weldt, "I've got my corn dolly. May I go down and throw it in the fire? Alissa will be with me, and we'll be ever so careful."

Her mother nodded. "But be back in twenty minutes or so," she said.

"You bet." The girl pecked her mother on the cheek and curtsied again to me.

"Alissa is an older girl from her classes," Sarah Weldt told me, her eyes on the swiftly disappearing girl.

"She's precocious, isn't she?"

"She is that. She's had good training, I think, but she isn't ruled by it, which is good."

"It is," I said.

"We're proud of her." She beamed.

"We?" It probably wasn't politic to ask, but I had a feeling that Weldt could be a plain talker when she chose to be, and might not mind. I was right.

"Micah and I."

I'd thought I remembered they had been married. Neither wore a ring now, though.

"I take it it was a pretty amicable separation?"

"Mostly. And what wasn't amicable back then, we've worked out by now."

Down below another band had gotten on the stage, and they kicked off into a raucous, electrified version of "Cornmash Johnny," the tune that traditionally accompanies the burning of the Guy. It was pretty good, if you like that sort of thing, but I found myself wishing I was back in Apache Run, listening to the tune played by a bunch of enthusiastic amateurs with acoustic instruments. We watched in silence as the Corn Guy blazed up, to cheers from the crowd below and a rumble of approving noises from the group gathered on the terrace.

"It's actually a metal sculpture," Sarah Weldt said, looking down at the square. "A fellow by the name of Sargasso built it. Fired by gas, mostly, and designed to collapse in on itself as the burn goes on. Supposed to look like a real Corn Guy."

"Does it?" I asked.

She nodded. "Pretty much."

She was right, more or less. At least from that distance, it was pretty convincing.

At a certain point, not long after the Guy had flared up, I excused myself and faded from the company. I made my way to the deck on the southern side of the building, opposite where the square was. Rok and Morgan were there before me, leaning on the railing, looking out toward the south, toward Apache Run, as if they might actually see the flames from that zone town's oversized Guy. Morgan turned and nodded as I walked up and joined them. We stared at the darkened horizon in silence for a while. Finally Rok straightened up and stretched.

"I didn't really expect to see it," he said. "I just thought it was worth the gesture. We did say we'd look, after all."

I nodded my agreement and the three of us turned to go back to the reception, and Bay City's burning Corn Guy.

Much later, I found myself wandering the halls of the CA Tower, too tired to do any serious work, but too keyed up to sleep. I still didn't know whether to expect another killing tonight. The guard were on high alert. As I turned down a corridor, I noticed a dim light coming from the conference room where we'd first met with Roth and Gage. Then I noticed a guardsman standing by the door. It was a patrol guardsman named Karstairs. I'd seen him around once or twice. I nodded to him; he nodded back. I shot my eyes at the conference room door. He just shrugged. I stepped to the door and looked in.

As gently and quietly as I'd moved the door and peered around it, Micah Roth either heard me or sensed that I was there. He looked up from the end of the long conference table, a glass and a bottle before him.

"Railwalker Wolf," he said. "Come in, sit. Join me for a drink?"

"Don't mind if I do." I stepped inside. I had drunk only a few sips of champagne early in the evening, the better to keep my head clear for dealing with the city notables. Maybe a shot of whatever Roth was having would help me relax and sleep. A carafe of water and several clean glasses stood on a tray in the middle of the table.

"Grab a glass," he said. He gestured toward the door

as I did so. "Guardsman Karstairs refused my hospitality."

A quiet voice came from the doorway: "I appreciated the offer, but I'm on duty, sir."

I sat. Roth chuckled as he poured a couple of fingers of amber liquid into the water glass.

"I suppose I should be grateful my guardsmen are conscientious," he said. "Gage assigned him to me for tonight, wouldn't take 'no' for an answer. Decidedly firm with his boss for a new guard chief. He thinks the Beast may be going to kill again tonight, so he wanted me guarded, just in case."

"He may be right," I said, accepting the glass from Roth. "Thanks." The amber liquid burned going down. I'm not a connoisseur of hooch any more than of tobacco, but judging from the medicinal taste it was probably expensive scotch, so I tried to look appreciative.

"Gage said something about the Beast being on some kind of solar cycle," said Roth. "What do you think? Is he prowling for another kill tonight?"

"Honestly, I'm not sure." I sighed. "I kind of doubt it, but I can't say definitely. Gage is right to be careful, stay prepared."

Roth nodded slowly, thoughtfully. "Unlike your father, you're not a gambling man," he said.

"No sir," I said. "I'm not, not generally."

"Tell me something, if it's not prying. What did you do between the time you left your father and the time you entered the Railwalker Academy?"

"I worked construction, mainly. Santa Brita, Two Suns."

"You know what I did before the Revolution?"

"Something in the labor unions?"

"Before that, I meant."

I thought about it for a minute, searched my memory. "You ran a restaurant?"

He chuckled. "Yeah. I started out as a chef. Worked for a guy named Goodman... who wasn't. A good man, I mean. Treated people like shit. He ran a restaurant called the Coronado."

I'd heard of the Coronado.

"Y'know, Railwalker, in my experience, most people want to do the right thing. Oh, you get your arseholes here and there, your monsters like the Beast, your jerks like Goodman. But most people, you treat 'em fair, give 'em a job they can get some satisfaction out of, and a reason to do it well, and they'll give you the best of themselves. Goodman didn't understand that, but I did. And I ran the kitchen in the Coronado. When the restaurant had made a name for itself, and Goodman was ready to open a hotel, I'd saved enough to buy the Coronado from him.

"We did okay, better than okay. I demanded a lot from my people, but I treated them well, and gave 'em plenty of incentives to do the best they could. And they did. With their help I built the Coronado into a very successful place, made a lot more with it than Goodman ever had.

"Eventually I figured out that the principle worked just about anywhere, in any aspect of life. You treat people with respect, give 'em their dignity, reward 'em for good work, they'll bend over backwards for you. They'll do even more than they ever thought they could.

"Of course, eventually I got it in my head that the whole city could be run the way I ran the Coronado. Got into politics, ran for office. But Crichton wasn't like Goodman. He wasn't about to hand me Bay City and go off to boss some other city-state. I hadn't planned on a bloody revolution, but before I knew it, it was here, and people were looking to me for leadership."

"Well," I said, "bloody conflicts are always a tragedy, but it does seem like Bay City ended up better off in the long run."

"I hope so. But I'm tired of it, Railwalker. We've got elections coming up next year, and I'm not going to run again. I'm ready to retire and go back to the kitchen. Got a little place set up for myself, actually, just outside the city. Hartshall, it's called. When this is over I'll have to take you folks out there for dinner. You ever have venison chili?"

I never had. Chili is a staple in the area; I'd had beef and turkey and even meatless chili, but never venison. I shook my head. He smiled.

"I was born up north, where venison is more common. Nowadays I have it shipped in. Great stuff. You'll have to try it.

"Right now, one of the fellows who worked for me at the Coronado is running Hartshall, and he's done good. I think when the time comes I'll let him continue to manage the place, and just spend my time in the kitchen again."

He was silent for a long time, and we both sat there in the semi-darkness, wrapped in our own thoughts, sipping the scotch. Finally he turned to me and said, "I noticed you dancing with Guildmadam Caine earlier. Has she convinced you that I'm not to be trusted?"

I looked at this slightly drunk older man, trying to see him the way the Guildmadam of the Harlots seemed to see him—a master manipulator, using me for his own ends. That picture wouldn't quite come into focus, which had nothing to do with the scotch, since I'd only had a couple of sips. No, I thought, taking another sip, this isn't about Roth's political advantage. Oh, I had no doubt Roth could play the manipulator when he wanted to; I'd already seen how he got what he wanted out of his people. But right now all I saw was a tired old man who wanted to see the city safe before he dropped the reins and went home to relax.

"Can't say she has," I said.

"Well, that's good, I suppose. Still, whatever advice she gave you, you shouldn't discard it out of hand, Railwalker. She's a wise and cagey old woman. And what's more, I'll admit to you, she's not entirely wrong about me. I can lie and cheat with the best of them, if the occasion calls for it. But I will promise you this. I won't drag you into any political contretemps, try to use you for my own political ends, not just now. Stopping the Beast is too important to the health of this city. I don't want your attention divided between the case at hand and the political factions in Bay City."

"I'm not convinced that the Beast is apolitical, that the factions and conflicting interests in the city don't have some influence on his actions."

"Okay." He nodded. "But for what it's worth, I'll promise you this, too... Once the Beast is caught or killed, all bets are off. If you hang around here, I'll make whatever political hay out of you I can. But until then, I'll make sure the Beast is all you have to worry about. Fair enough?"

"Fair enough."

15. PLUMBLINE CREEK — *Six Months Ago*

The vehicle the Ravagers called "the Hammer" had begun life as an oversized armored truck for transporting gold into the cities from mines north of the zones. How it had ended up in retirement hauling chickens and goats on some farm near the Sequoia River, Scather had no idea, but the minute he saw it, he knew they had to take it. In the years since, it had become nearly unrecognizable. Armored to begin with, it had acquired additional home-made plating and gun turrets, along with a makeshift luggage rack that held supplies. Several paint jobs over the years, as well as adornment with obscure personal sigils and slogans, had created a patchwork of colors that also helped disguise the vehicle's lineage.

Just now the Hammer squatted in the center of Plumbline Creek's town square like a massive leaden monument to truculence, flanked by a half dozen scruffy, arrogant Ravager cars and a jeep. The smaller ATVs were all in use, as Ravagers scouted the outer portions of the town making sure no one escaped. This was Scather's policy, although it really wasn't necessary for safety's sake. There was no help to be found less than a full day's drive away, and the Ravagers would be long gone before any such help could arrive. But you never knew what good shit an escapee might carry out with them. Fact was, the Hammer itself was a bit of overkill, purely an affectation, since the Ravagers hardly ever did battle against opponents who had any real capacity to fight back.

Scather had climbed onto the roof of the Hammer's cab, watching his men go to town on the town. He laughed at his own mental wordplay as he uncorked the last of their stash of liquor. No need to be frugal with it anymore; they'd be set for all sorts of supplies when this raid was done. If the general store didn't have hooch in stock, there'd be some in the little saloon at the end of the street.

Scather knocked back a slug of the rude homebrew, wiped his mouth, and eyed Burly and Snakebite, who were heading toward the general store. "Hey!" he yelled down at them, and then again, louder, "Hey, you two!"

Burly stopped and turned. Snakebite hesitated and then looked around.

"Don't kill the store guy! We want him alive!" Proprietors of general stores in these shit-feed towns knew everybody, all the gossip and dirt—like who had what sort of good shit stashed away, and where. Scather had found in his years of ravaging the zones that it always paid to question the general store guys.

He looked down the street and noticed Bone Grinder. As usual, the guy wasn't tearing around crazy-arsed like the other Ravagers, but instead stalked down the center of the street with a measured pace, his head slowly turning side to side. The motion reminded Scather of a lizard, taking everything in, missing nothing. Scather knew what Grinder was up to. He was searching for the townie with some balls, the one who would try to stand up to the Ravagers, pull a gun or a knife to try to protect his wife or his daughter, or just his own self-respect. He was looking for a challenge. Scather knew he wouldn't find it, not really. He'd find some rube to kill, no doubt, but Scather had seen what the Bone Grinder could do. There was nobody in any of these backwaters who could give him any sort of challenge. Maybe if they stumbled across a Railwalker, or a city guardsman who was visiting relatives or something— and even then, Scather's money would be on the Grinder.

He sighed and slugged from the bottle again. Things were starting to get a little bit hairy. Scather wasn't sure he himself could take the Grinder on, come to that. Not that Grinder had ever challenged Scather's leadership, not outright, and certainly not in front of the others. The Bone Grinder had been with them for almost eight moons, and after the third moon, he'd challenged Walrus, Scather's Secondman. Their combat had been short, nasty, and bloody. Too quickly to be believed, Walrus was lying there dead, and the Bone Grinder wasn't even breathing hard. Walrus had been the toughest sonofabitch any of them had ever seen. It might have been pure dumb luck, of course, but everything Scather had seen of Grinder since proved it wasn't. Now Grinder was Secondman, and truth be told, he might as well be the Honcho.

Scather had started out following the Grinder's advice because it seemed like he always had good ideas. He was sharp, Grinder was. He knew which towns were best to hit at which seasons, depending on the crops they grew or the animals they raised. He knew when trade caravans traveled through the zones, and which routes they'd usually take. The gang had certainly profited from Grinder's schemes. It was Bone Grinder who came up with the idea of having the buggies range out to nail any escaping townies. More than once that had turned up some old coot blowing town with a bag full of money. Truth to tell, it had been Grinder who'd pointed out the value of the store proprietors. But it was getting so Grinder seemed to take Scather for granted. Even though he gave Scather his props in front of the gang, more often than not these days in private conversation he was telling rather than asking, and Scather wasn't sure he was comfortable with that.

"Fuck," Scather mumbled, and took another slug. He hoped they'd find some tobacco in this burg; he hadn't had a smoke in almost a week. Yeah, with the way things were going, it was time to have a talk with the Grinder, set things straight. Scather wouldn't admit to himself that he was actually scared of his Second. But he knew if it came to a challenge between them, he would probably end up bleeding out on the ground, and there'd be a new Honcho leading the gang. Well fuck it, he thought, better dead than nutless.

At the sound of the engine Anna Barclay had hurried back to the kitchen, in time to see Art Cavanaugh's jeep pull up by the back door and Art himself burst out of it carrying, of all things, a shotgun. "Art, what's going on?"

"Anna, you alright? Where's Keith?"

"Dad's at the garage, of course. What is it? Were those gunshots?"

Art stepped quickly through the kitchen and into the parlor, looking toward the front window. The front door burst open, a wild figure framed in the doorway. Anna could barely make out any details, silhouetted as it was by the morning sun, but she knew this was no local. He stepped into the room, and she could see him more clearly: greasy jeans stuffed into high-topped boots, muscular arms covered with inexpert tattoos, a leather vest. Designs crawled across his bearded face, as well. He carried a short sword or a very big knife in one hand, a pistol in the other. The man noticed Art and raised the pistol, but Art was quicker. The boom of the shotgun inside the house was nearly deafening.

"Oh my gods..." Anna stammered.

Art Cavanaugh stood staring at the red ruin the shotgun blast had made of the man's head. Art had slaughtered javelina and goats many times, but he'd never killed a human being before. During the last raid, back when he'd been a kid, Art had never actually seen the town's attackers, although they had been described to him. Ravagers had occupied a fearful place in his mind since then, like near-supernatural bogeymen, and now he had killed one. He would have expected to feel elated, having struck a blow in return for the carnage these men, or others like them, had brought to his town so many years ago. Instead he just felt sick and empty. And scared. He shook himself, wrenched his gaze away from the dead man, and looked out Anna's front window. The man had died so quickly and easily; for a moment he considered going out to face the rest of the Ravagers, or maybe trying to gather some of the other men, get weapons, and fight back. Then common sense prevailed. It would be suicide. He didn't know how many there were, how well armed they were. Even a group of townsmen with rifles and shotguns would stand little chance against a troop of outlaws who killed for fun and profit. Anna's safety had to be his first concern. "Come on," he said, taking her arm. "We gotta get you away."

As they headed back through the kitchen they heard Keith Barclay's voice. "Anna! Anna!" The voice suddenly became a high-pitched scream, which was quickly cut off.

"Daddy!" Anna screamed, and headed for the front door; but Art caught her up.

"No, Anna, there's nothing you can do. We have to..."

Art stopped when he saw the look in her eyes, realizing she was not looking at him but over his shoulder, and he suddenly remembered the open front door. He released her, pumping another round into the shotgun even as he turned and aimed at where he expected to find another Ravager coming through the door.

Art was no soldier. He'd only been in two fistfights in his entire life, and he didn't have the instincts of a killer. When the figure in the doorway made no threatening move, he hesitated.

The man was tall and powerful, though not huge. Also dressed in jeans and boots, his head was shaved, his torso covered by a serape draped over his shoulders. The only tattoo visible was on his forehead, three vertical slashes above a squat oval, like the paw-print of some clawed animal. His hands were hidden by the serape, but blood dripped from under the left side of the cloth. The other Ravager's eyes had been crazy; when Art met this one's gaze, he felt like he was looking into Hell.

"Mornin', folks." The man's voice sounded like he regularly gargled with ground glass. He took a step into the room and Art, realizing he'd unconsciously let the shotgun drift downward, brought it back up to point at the man's head.

"Anna," Art said, keeping the man covered, "get to the jeep."

"Stay right where you are, Anna," the Ravager said. She had begun to move, but when he looked at her Anna froze in place. "Anna, Anna... What a lovely name. It's from the Hebrew 'Hannah.' It means 'grace.' Did you know that? Are you graceful, Anna?" He took another step.

"Stop right there," Art said. "I mean it."

"Or you'll shoot?" The man smiled. "Go ahead, hero. Take your best shot."

Art debated only a second. Killing the first Ravager had been easy. Killing in cold blood was a whole different matter, but he knew in his bones that if he didn't take this opportunity, if he gave this man the chance to attack him, he'd never get off another shot. He pulled the trigger. The shotgun boomed again.

Art stared, momentarily stupefied. He knew, he absolutely knew, that it was impossible for a human being to duck a gunshot, especially a shotgun blast at such close range. Yet this man had done it. He not only ducked it, but ducked and came back to the very same position so fast Art had barely seen a blur of movement. Quickly, Art jacked another round. Pulled again. This time, nothing happened. Through the ringing in his ears he barely heard the man say, "Sorry, hero. One shot is all you get."

The Ravager raised his left hand and the serape fell back to reveal something more like an eagle's talon than a hand, its claws dripping blood. With the same unnatural speed the man flew across the room at Art. There was a searing, tearing pain, a flash of black, and a loud rumbling noise, as if someone had dropped a big bag of rocks on a wooden platform. Then Art Cavanaugh was looking sideways across the floor of the Barclays' living room, slowly realizing that the sideways view was because he was lying on the floor. That the noise he had heard was his own limp body hitting the floorboards. He had just time to feel despair at the thought that he had failed to protect Anna, and then everything went cold and black.

The shotgun had clattered across the floor as the farmer fell, throat slashed almost through. The man the Ravagers knew as the Bone Grinder watched him die, knowing that behind him the woman was quietly reaching for the shotgun. He'd seen the intelligence in her eyes; he knew she was a feisty one. She'd know better than to try to shoot him; she'd try to use the gun as a club to batter him from behind. He waited until he could feel the movement of the shotgun through the air behind him, then his clawed hand shot out and caught it mid-strike, stopping it as though it had hit a rock. He turned, twisted the shotgun out of her hands, and tossed it across the room. She shrank back. He smiled again.

"Yes, Anna," he said, "I am one nasty motherfucker. But you don't need to be afraid of me. I like you. You've got spirit." He walked leisurely to the front door. "I noticed your fella's jeep is out back. Motor's running. You want to try to escape? Go ahead. I won't stop you." He looked at her and smiled again. "I won't even tell. Promise."

After a moment's hesitation Anna made her break for the back door. The Bone Grinder watched her go. As she put the jeep in gear, he added, in a whisper, "But I know you'll never make it."

Twilight in the desert, the shadows deep purple shading to indigo, the sun painting the peaks with reddish gold. Scather made his way to the top of a rise just outside the town, where the Bone Grinder sat staring westward over the desert scrub. Behind them plumes of smoke billowed toward the sky, carrying the pungent odors of burning wood, plastic, and flesh. There were occasional shrieks still from the few townspeople left alive. The fighting and rapine had ended by mid-afternoon, the initial wave of looting had died down, and the more organized search for useful parts and equipment would be under way.

"Grinder," the Honcho grunted, and offered a bottle of hooch. "Store bought, not home brew," he added. "Good stuff." The bald man shook his head, as Scather had known he would. No one had ever seen the Bone Grinder take a drink, but it was customary and respectful to offer it anyway. "Long pork, then?" he asked, offering one of the two pieces of roasted meat he'd carried up along with the bottle. "Big gal, mighty tasty." Scather and his boys had come to eat people out of necessity once, when they were starving in the desert, and had decided they liked it. Fat people made the best eating, Scather thought, but you didn't find them in the zones very often. It was a hard life, and zoners tended to be skinny and tough. To their delight, the Ravagers had found one woman in town who was a bit overweight, and wasted no time in butchering her.

Grinder accepted the meat with a nod of thanks and chewed meditatively, staring off at the sunset.

"Good haul, this one." Scather nodded and sat down beside his Second. "Hooch, smoke, plenty of corn, beans, bacon. Even found a water pump Gaffer thinks will fit the Hammer, which is a damn good thing; the beast's fuckin' pump is nearly dead."

Grinder made no reply, merely nodded and continued staring at the sunset. Scather stared at the sunset too, half hoping he'd be hit with some inspirational idea on how best to approach his uncomfortable subject, half hoping Grinder would volunteer himself what his Honcho wanted to hear. After a long quiet interval, Scather decided neither of these miracles was going to occur, so he opened his mouth again.

"Look, Grinder.... We keep going south and west. I think it's startin' to make the boys a little ansty."

The bald man looked at him, then looked back to the sunset. They both knew perfectly well that the Ravagers weren't getting uncomfortable at all. Their raids had been increasingly successful and profitable, and that was clearly all most of them cared about. They were drunk on their own success. Aside from the Bone Grinder, Scather was the only one who really gave any thought to the future, or the implications of the path they were following.

"I mean..." Scather havered. "Well, y'know... We keep on this trail, sooner or later we're gonna be gettin' awful damn close to the coast cities."

"Better pickings," was all the Grinder said.

Scather tossed away the last of his meat, his appetite suddenly gone. He wiped his greasy fingers on his jeans. His stomach felt sour. Fortunately they'd found some tobacco in town, and after noting that he was indeed downwind of his Second, he took out a stogie and lit up.

"Yeah, but..." he started. Sighed. "Look, we get to raiding too close to the cities, eventually they're gonna get wind of us. Next thing you know they'll be sending out a troop of guardsmen with heavy artillery to take us down."

There was another long pause, and Scather had almost decided Grinder wasn't going to reply at all, when the man spoke again, quietly.

"Exactly."

"Exactly?" Scather demanded. "Exactly? What the fuck? You *want* to bring that kind of heat down on us?"

"S'matter, Scather?" Grinder asked mildly. "Don't you want to test yourself against the strongest challenges you can find?"

"Fuck, no!" Scather jumped to his feet. "That's insane, Grinder! Man, you run into guard unexpected like, that's one thing. I'll fuckin' murderize 'em. But go askin' for that kinda fight when it ain't necessary? That's just fuckin' stupid!"

The Bone Grinder showed no particular reaction to Scather's outburst, but sat calmly contemplating the sunset. When he spoke his words were slow and emphatic, as though he was explaining something to a child. "Then 'fucking stupid' is what we're going to be," he said, "because that's exactly what we're going to do. We're raiding south and west until the townies send guardsmen out to get us." He looked up at the Ravager leader now, raised his eyebrows in question. "You got a problem with that?" The Bone Grinder held Scather's eye for a moment, then looked back to the sunset.

Scather hesitated. He'd had a sense it might come to this, but it was happening sooner than he had expected. The leader of the Ravagers was no coward, but he was also no fool. He knew he stood little chance in a fair fight against his Secondman, so he'd prepared himself. If the challenge had come formally, in the company of the group, he was prepared to use his fighting knives—a fair balance, in Scather's mind, against the power of Grinder's hands, which could become deadly claws. But here, by themselves, alone on this hill above the town they'd just raided, the good of the gang superseded Scather's sense of personal honor. He couldn't risk Grinder winning a fight between them, if the formalities of the Ravager gang didn't demand it. It was more important that the gang survive intact than that Scather prove himself the better man. His hand slipped to the small of his back, where the compact machine pistol lay waiting for just such an eventuality. He whipped it out with the speed of a striking snake and aimed it at the Bone Grinder's head. Just before he pulled the trigger, he muttered, "Sorry, man." Then suddenly, he was looking at the stump of his right wrist fountaining blood as his hand, still clutching the machine pistol, tumbled down the hill.

Grinder now stood before him. Scather's left hand groped for his knife, but the Grinder's claw slashed out in a blur of motion. Scather felt pain in his throat, and then he was tumbling to the ground. Everything was going black, he was as cold as he ever remembered being, and as if from a great distance he heard the Bone Grinder's voice say, "No, you're not sorry. And neither am I."

16. BAY CITY

"Kind of on the upscale side for a mutie," Remming mused as they surveyed the clinic from an expensive coffee shop across the street. Dobbs had given Remming and Turrin the mutie's name and address. They'd checked out his records and discovered he worked at a medical clinic in the Thornhill neighborhood. They were looking at a long, low, adobe-fronted building, very clean, no graffiti, several expensive runabouts parked in front. A small brass plaque beside the main entrance informed visitors who drew close enough to read it that this was the Thornhill Medical Center. The streets were free of trash, and palo verde trees shaded the sidewalks at regular intervals.

"Upscale for a mutie, sure, but so's the place he lives," said Turrin.

"But not so much. I'll bet you his neighbors don't come here when they get the sniffles."

"Probably he's a janitor or something."

Remming looked at his partner in disgust. "A janitor? Coming in at eight in the morning in a suit and tie? Not friggin' likely. More like an administrative assistant, or a male nurse or something."

"Well," said Turrin, finishing his coffee, "let's find out."

At the front desk Remming asked for Aguilar Cordoba. The receptionist escorted them to a conference room, offered them coffee, which they declined, and assured them Dr. Cordoba would be with them in a moment. The door closed silently behind her, and the two guardsmen looked at each other.

"Doctor?" Turin said.

Remming just shrugged.

A few minutes later the door opened to admit a tall, well-built man wearing a white lab coat over a light gray shirt and maroon tie. Remming watched the brown eyes behind the silver-rimmed glasses flick from him to Turrin and back again. The man's expression remained carefully neutral. He wasn't twitching with guilt, but he was clearly wary.

"Dr. Cordoba." Remming stuck out his hand, and the doctor shook it with only the slightest show of reluctance. "I'm Guardsman Remming; this is Guardsman Turrin. Sorry to interrupt your schedule. We'll make this as brief as we can. We're investigating a report of cries and shots fired outside your building last night..."

"This building?" asked the doctor.

"No sir, the City Arms. We're checking with all the residents, see if anyone heard or saw anything."

"And you came to my place of work?"

"Well, you know how it is these days, with the killings and all." The guardsmen weren't allowed to use the popular name "the Beast" when talking to the public. "City Plaza wants incidents like this checked out as quickly as possible. Did you see or hear anything unusual last night?"

"No, Guardsman, I'm sorry. I got in a bit late and went right to bed. I didn't notice anything out of the ordinary."

"Okay, sir, thank you for your time. We'll show ourselves out."

Back on the sidewalk in the bright morning sunlight, the two men turned left and headed downtown.

"A mutie doctor." Remming shook his head. "That's fucked."

"He don't look like his picture in the file, that's for sure," said Turrin.

"He can't be a shapeshifter. They don't exist."

"So what, he's a normal who stole a mutie's ident? That doesn't make any sense."

"No," Remming allowed, "it doesn't. Could be he's just a mutie looks especially normal."

"Maybe it's all bullshit," said Turrin. "Maybe Dobbs is

blowing smoke up our arses. You know, he's got something against this guy, and he's trying to set him up."

"Could be. File says he's a mutie, and Dobbs hates muties."

"Can't be that Dobbs is right, can it? This guy can't be the Beast. He don't look anything like what Auden described."

"I dunno. I doubt it. But sure as hell something stinks here."

Surprising for the neighborhood, the steps up to the front door of the Cat's Meow were clean and in good repair. At Morgan's knock the door was opened by a massive mutant in suit pants that were out at the cuffs and a white shirt with sleeves rolled to the elbow. His skin was a pasty, yellowish color, his eyes set far apart on his wide skull.

"Help you?" he said.

"I'm here to see Sally Marks."

"Santa Monica Sal? And you are?"

"Railwalker Morgan."

The man straightened, peering down at her. "Railwalker?" he said.

She raised a hand, palm out. "I know, you don't see Railwalkers around much any more. I get that a lot."

A smile split his face. "I'll bet you do," he said. "Come in, Railwalker Morgan. It's Sal's turn at laundry today." He led her down a hall and gestured to a door. "Down the stairs is the laundry room."

Like the rooms above, the laundry was ancient, but clean and well maintained. The brushed metal of the washing machines gleamed. The walls were clean and white, the lighting some kind of full-spectrum bulb instead of ugly fluorescents. Morgan had never been in the laundry of a harlot house before. She'd expected mountains of flimsy negligees and frilly lace nothings, and there was a basket full of those, but the only mountains in sight were of sheets and towels. Which, on reflection, made sense.

Folding those sheets and towels at the other end of a long table was a skinny blond in hot pink and a shorter, heavier, dark-haired woman with coffee-colored skin. Sal's tan, Morgan noted as she got closer, had that orange tinge that suggested it came out of a bottle rather than from the sun, and her platinum blond hair showed darker blond roots. From a distance she looked like a surfer girl. Up close neither the artificial tan nor the liberal makeup quite disguised the spidery veins of rosaceae spread across her cheeks and nose. The darker woman's makeup was some-what more subtle.

"Afternoon," the blonde said when she looked over and saw Morgan.

"Hi," Morgan said.

The dark woman peered at Morgan's facial tattoo. "Say," she said, "you're one of them Railwalkers, aintcher?"

"Aye," said Morgan. "Morgan am I, Walker of the Rails Between the Worlds. Twenty-three blessings, sister." She held out her hand. The woman shook it.

"Della Santiago."

"Well, what do you know," said the blonde. "Never thought I'd see a Railwalker in this place. Santa Monica Sal am I." She laughed. "Walker of the streets of this city, when I'm not holed up in the Cat's Meow. Member in good standing of the Harlot's Guild. Come freely and go safely, and all that." They shook.

"We should offer you tobacco and coffee, but I think our machine's coffee is probably about as stale as it comes. So maybe you can make do with a cigarette?" She held out a battered package of cigarettes. "No offense."

"None taken, thankee," Morgan said, accepting the proffered cigarette. Sal held out a lighter, flicked it several times before it finally caught flame. Morgan took a token puff, then set the white stick smoldering in the ashtray.

Sal lit up her own and puffed luxuriantly. Della elbowed her in the ribs, and she said "Oh," and slid the pack toward her friend.

As Della lit up, Sal asked, "So what brings a Railwalker

to our humble cathouse?"

"Came to talk to you folks, actually."

"Really?" Sal laughed. Then she looked darkly at Morgan. "Oh, I see. The guard can't track down this Beast, so Roth asked the Railwalkers in."

"About damn time, is what I say," said Della. "Useless fuckin' shits, them guardos."

"I suppose you want to ask us about Suzi," said Sal.

"Suzi Mascarpone."

"Was that her last name?" asked Della. "Thought she might be an Eye-tie. I only knew her as Suzi, or Zee."

"Sometimes," offered Sal, "she called herself Suzi Creamcheese."

"Ain't that a mindfuck, though?" Della shook her head. "You're friends with somebody for years, you never even know their last name 'til they're dead." She sniffed and blinked away a tear. "Man, if anything we got to say can help you nail the fucker killed her, we're so there." She looked at her friend for confirmation, and the blonde woman nodded vehemently. "Whadda ya wanna know?"

"What can you tell me about her?"

"Suzi, she was good people," said Sal.

"Even if she was a fuckin' Marilyn," added Della.

"You don't generally like the Marilyns?"

"Why should we?" Della snorted. "Don't see themselves like harlots, most of 'em. Want to be thought of as priestesses, y'know? High fuckin' priestesses of sex, too good to associate with the rest of us."

"Zee wasn't like that, and you know it," said Sal.

"She could be. Sometimes."

"Besides, there's those in the guild who act like that, from some of the expensive houses."

"Fuck 'em all, we're as good as them any day."

Morgan looked from one harlot to the other. Della raised an eyebrow at her and said, "What, you don't think so?"

Morgan shook her head. "I didn't say that," she said.

Della stepped across to her, her walk a sinuous slide, and laid a gentle hand on Morgan's arm. Even through the woolen tunic sleeve, it felt like a caress.

"Darling," said Della, her voice low and honeyed, "we all do receive the same training, if we're part of the guild." It was as if she'd become a different person, her accents those of the wealthy and powerful. "I can be as sophistic-ated and entertaining a companion as any man—or woman—could want." She smiled, gave a shudder, and stepped away again. "I just don't feel like goin' there on my fuckin' day off."

"Okay," Morgan said, "fair enough. So the Marilyns…"

"Got themselves a fuckin' temple now," Della told her. "Just a cathouse like any other, you ask me, never mind they call it a 'tithe' and do the whole communist thing, sharing the money out. But they applied for that, what-chacallit, tax exempt status, just like a church or temple."

"That's when the Guild voted to throw them out," said Sal.

"The Harlot's Guild expelled the Marilyns?"

"Voted to toss 'em out on their prissy little asses," said Della. "That was Hannah's doing."

"Hannah Caine, the guildmadam?" said Morgan.

Della said, "Hannah said if they weren't gonna pay taxes and be subject to the same rules and regulations as the rest of us, why should the guild look out for 'em? Suzi stood up to her, but it didn't do no good—the whole guild knew Suzi was one herself."

"What made Suzi think she could sway the vote?"

Sal sighed, stubbed out her cigarette, and lit another. She offered the pack to Morgan, who declined. "Well, you must understand, not every Marilyn moved into that tem-ple of theirs. Some of them, like Suzi, stayed working in the houses they were with. Suzi used to say it wasn't about where the money went, it was about how you approached it.

"So," Morgan asked, "Suzi and some of the others wanted to stay in their regular jobs, and also stay in the Temple?"

"Suzi wanted the other harlots in the guild to join their temple, too. She had that whole 'we women should

look out for each other' thing going on. Thought all harlots were priestesses, whether they knew it or not."

"The other Marilyns—the ones at the temple—they
didn't see it that way?"

"Them?" Della snorted. "Fuck, no. They pee rosewater
and shit spun sugar. Some of 'em are worse toward the rest
of us than some of the Witlesses or the Rollers. To them
we're blasphemers, 'cause we do it for money instead of
for their goddess. You know what I think of that? They can
kiss my sweet ass."

"Yeah." Morgan smiled. "That's what I figured. So
where did the vote leave girls like Suzi?"

"Oh, the Marilyns could stay in the guild," said Sal,
"long as they paid their dues and didn't ever work at the
Temple. Hannah would've had them all barred from the
guild on principle, but Suzi and some of the others working the regular houses had enough friends, they carried
that one. Hannah didn't like it, but what could she do? A
vote's a vote, and anyway, she got the main thing she was
after."

"You think Hannah was still pissed at Suzi?"

"Well," said Della, "Zee used to work up at the Gates
of Hell…"

"The Gates of Hell?" Morgan asked.

Both of the harlots laughed. "Hannah's place is called
'The Gate of Heaven,'" Sal explained. "Some of us call it…"

"Yeah, I get it," said Morgan. "Why? Hannah's a
devil?"

"A bitch, anyway," said Della.

"Hannah's very strict and proper," Sal said.

"Full of herself, almost as bad as the Marilyns."

"Anyway," Sal said emphatically, "Suzi was Hannah's
right-hand gal until she joined the Marilyns. Hannah
found a reason to fire her, but Suzi was already a guild
steward, and she couldn't do anything about that."

"Would Hannah have been angry enough to want her
killed?"

"Don't you go saying things like that." Sal punched
her cigarette at Morgan, trailing smoke. "Hannah's hard,

but she's fair, and she's no murderer."

"Chill the fuck out, Sal," said Della. "She didn't mean it like that."

"Then what did she mean it like?"

"Look," said Morgan, "I don't know this Hannah Caine. We have to look at all the possibilities."

"Suzi was killed by the Beast," Sal said. "Even the guardos admit that. Worthless shits that they are, can't even keep the streets safe these days."

"So how did Suzi come to be out on the street that night?"

Della and Sal looked at each other. Della shrugged and looked away. Sal turned back to Morgan.

"She was going to the temple to report on how the vote went. It was a Monday night. Some of the houses are dark on Mondays, so that's when these meetings usually happen. This one ran later than usual, what with all the arguing. I tried to talk her out of it, told her she could go in the morning or just call them, but she'd promised her Marilyn sisters she'd report in person on the way the vote went, and Suzi was a girl of her word. Tried to get her to call a cab, but she said it was only a few blocks. I don't think she ever really thought it could happen to her."

"Yeah," said Morgan. "A lot of people think that way."

"Anyway, she said she had to return Greta's pin."

"Pin?" Morgan asked.

"Her Marilyn pin. They all wear them. Suzi had lost hers a couple of days before, and she'd borrowed one from Greta. She felt she ought to be wearing one at the meeting."

"So the Marilyn pin she was wearing when she died wasn't actually hers?"

"I don't think so," said Sal. "Pretty sure it was Greta's."

Della laughed. "Surprised that bitch hasn't been beating down the doors of the guards, trying to get it back," she said.

"Why?" Sal asked Morgan. "Is that important for some reason?"

"I don't know for sure," said Morgan, "but I've got a

feeling it could be."

Don Whitehouse silently cursed Willa Devlin roundly once more and contemplated ordering another shot. Probably he shouldn't. He sipped at his beer instead. It was one thing to seek a little relief in getting plowed yesterday... and the day before, come to think of it, and if he wasn't careful, again today. It was another thing to develop a regular habit. Without his job to go to, he could far too easily end up spending all his days pickling himself in the Bar of Gold. In fact, wasn't he doing just that even now? He realized abruptly he was already more than half in the bag. It was this damned waiting; it got to a man. And there was no telling when this limbo would end. Of course, he could say fuck the waiting and go look for another position. But not yet.

Don looked up as the front door opened, and was surprised to see the long coat, the eye tattoo, the headscarf that was now draped around the big man's neck like a bandanna. He realized with a start that he was looking at a Railwalker.

The Railwalker's eyes scanned the room and settled on Don. Well, Don thought, I guess I do stand out. The afternoon crowd was scant, mostly old retired guys and rummies, sodden-looking with their worn-out clothes and worn-out lives. Don was the only one there who looked hale and hearty and, if not prosperous, at least currently employed, for all his clothes showed the wear of regular work. Of course he wasn't currently employed, but he'd only been out of work a couple of weeks and didn't yet wear the hopeless look of the terminally unemployed.

The Railwalker nodded to the bartender, ordered a beer, and sat one space down from Don. They nodded to each other.

"Twenty-three blessings," said the Railwalker.

Don struggled to remember what the proper response was. He hadn't seen an actual Railwalker since his teens. He settled for, "G'day, and same to ya, Railwalker."

"Rok," the man said, holding out his hand.

It took Don a moment to realize he was introducing himself. "Oh." Don hastily extended his own hand. "Don. Don Whitehouse." They shook.

"First mate of the *Bay Queen*?" Railwalker Rok asked as the bartender returned with his beer.

"Formerly." Don looked morosely into his nearly empty glass. He didn't wonder how the fellow knew him. The murder of his captain, Arnie Hawthorne, had been all over the newsfeeds when it happened. It had been the first of the Beast's killings, and was revisited every time the bastard offed another victim. Don himself had been interviewed a couple of times, though he took no pleasure from this brief celebrity. He hoped the Railwalker wasn't going to ask him about the Cap's death. The bartender hovered.

"Buy you a round?" asked the Railwalker.

"Be rude to say no."

Rok nodded to the bartender, who refilled Don's glass from the tap. "I noticed the *Queen* was tied up at the guard's impound dock," Rok said, as the fresh glass was placed before Don.

"Yeah. Ought to be out running her nets. It's a damned shame."

"Why isn't she?"

"Ah, don't get me started. You don't want to hear about my troubles."

"I was just wondering why she's in impound. Guards must be through with her by now. They find evidence of smuggling or something?"

"Hell, no. Cap was a straight arrow. Well, mostly. No, you want to know the truth, it's the damned sister."

"What sister is that?"

"Willa Devlin, sister to the Cap'n. She's challenging the will."

"He willed the vessel to you?"

"To his wife. She was to own and manage, and I'd captain for her. I'd have seen her well taken care of, and taken a share for my trouble. Then comes this fuckin' bitch from Santa Brita, the Cap's sister, contesting the will and suing for possession of the boat. As if she'd have any more idea what to do with her than a cabbage with a computer. Tied up in court it is, and the boat stuck in dock, impounded for the duration." He raised his beer. "Willa Devlin, may she rot in Hell."

"Sorry to hear about your troubles," Rok said. "And your captain's death. I take it you liked him?"

Here it comes, Don thought. The Railwalker hadn't acted like a guardsman, though. When the guard started investigating the Cap's killing, Don had been a suspect at first, and he'd had more than enough experience of the guard investigators' approaches to questioning. This Railwalker Rok seemed like a regular guy.

"He was a good man. A little queer in the head sometimes, but harmless for a' that. He was Core Charger for the local Huey Brasse."

"You're not a Huey man yourself? Being a seaman, I mean?"

"No, I don't believe in that stuff. O' course, I'd join in when the Cap raised a toast and gave an offering to the Huey whenever we'd set out. Don't hurt nothin', and you never know. Just 'cause I don't believe it, don't make it not true."

Rok smiled. "I like a man with an open mind. How long were you with him?"

"Oh, we went way back, the Cap and I. Good fifteen year or so. Easy-goin' guy. Everybody liked him. You shoulda seen the funeral. There were more folks turned out... An' not just 'cause of the way he died. No, it was the man himself brought them there. Y'know, even Micah Roth showed up."

"Did he? The city boss? He knew your Cap?"

"Oh, not really, not that well, I guess. The Cap was with him in the Takeover, you see. Not that he was any big shot or nothin', just another soldier fightin' for freedom."

"Sounds like a splendid fella."

"Tell you somethin' about the Cap," Don said, drawing his stool closer to the newcomer and lowering his voice. "He told it me in confidence, one night when we got a bit drunk together, but it don't reflect badly on him, by my lights, and he's gone now anyway. It can't hurt. I mean seein' as how you're a Railwalker and all, it's practically like talkin' to a priest, i'n't it?" He swigged again at his beer, as Rok turned on his stool to face him. "I mean, I can trust you with a secret?"

Rok just looked at him steadily, saying nothing.

Don took Rok's look as a rebuke, that he should ask such a question of a Railwalker. "My Cap," he said, "was the man what killed Wendell Crichton. What do you think of that?"

"Was he?"

"Aye. And anybody else woulda been boastin' and puffing themselves up about such a thing. Me, why I'd have been drinkin' for free on a story like that the rest of my life. But not the Cap. No, he was actually ashamed of himself, that he shot first and didn't try to capture the guy. Can you imagine? Kept it a secret all his life, until he told me. Just a few days before he died. Until then, nobody knew 'cept Cap himself. And then me. And now you, Railwalker. What d'ye think o' that?"

"That's quite a story," said Rok.

Auden looked up from his desk screen when the woman Railwalker sat on the edge of his desk. Her pose, he thought, wasn't provocative in a sexual sense, but it was arrogant.

"Help you?" he said.

"Hope so," said Morgan. "Arnold Hawthorne, the Beast's first victim. You were buds with him, right? You were at his fortieth birthday party at Bar of Gold. There's a DV on his memorial page."

"What of it?" Auden said.

"There's nothing in any of the case files to show that. Isn't that kind of unprofessional, working a case where you've got a personal interest without acknowledging that?"

"I wasn't assigned to the Hawthorne case. I came in on the Fitch case. Gage only made me OIC after Adams died, and Gage got promoted. What's your point?"

"We'd like to borrow the Ortiz pendant. The one from the *Bay Queen*." Auden stared at her blankly. She scowled. "Look, even though you act like a dick, I figure you for one of the straight cops, more or less. So I'm guessing you figured there was no harm when after the forensics guys were done, you took the pendant from the boat as a memorial token of your pal. I mean, you couldn't very well take Hawthorne's own personal pendant. It was entered and logged in evidence. But who'd miss the one from the boat?"

Auden sat back and regarded her, his eyes narrowing. He said nothing.

She continued, "Now, as it happens, the Railwalkers come in and, surprise, things forensics found nothing on, we might be able to get something from."

"Things like the pendant," he said.

"Yeah," she said. "Exactly. Look, I don't need the extra hassle of going through official channels, which would probably mean charges against you. And I totally get wanting a token of a dead friend. So, here's the deal. You loan us the pendant for a couple of days, we bring it back unharmed. Or," she opened her portable comp and turned it toward him, "I can hit *Enter* on one of these two screens."

Auden looked from the screen to Morgan and back again. "Which will do what?"

"One on the left will file an official inquiry into why you removed evidence from the scene without logging it. One on the right will make the record show that you brought the pendant in as additional evidence two weeks ago, and the Railwalkers checked it out last night."

He peered at the screen. "You hacked our system."

"I dunno as it's hacking when you've officially been given access."

"I've officially got access, but I couldn't do…" He looked back at the screen. "That."

"I'm good with computer systems. So, what's it gonna be? You wanna go the hard way, the easy way, or the slightly deceptive easy way?"

"Why would you fake back-dated records on my behalf?"

"Duh. It took me all of thirty seconds to do. Flies, sugar, right? And you are kind of an insect. So what's your choice?"

He sat back again, lost in thought for a moment. "You say having this thing will lead you to the Beast?"

"No guarantees. But it might help."

Auden opened one of his desk drawers and took out a brown paper envelope. "Let's keep it all unofficial," he said. He extended the envelope to Morgan. "Just get it back to me in one piece, okay?"

Morgan shut the comp unit and took the envelope. "Deal."

***

Aguilar Cordoba sensed something was wrong as he fitted his key into the lock and opened the door to his apartment. It was a vague, non-specific feeling, which could have meant his toilet was backed up, or the rent check had bounced. Or it could have meant anti-mutant racists had set a bomb for him. He stepped in and was hit from the side. A heavy body bore him to the floor, one arm twisted up behind him in an iron grip. Aguilar was shocked, but not surprised. He had always known this day would come.

"Gotcha!" shouted a voice in his ear. "Don't move, asshole!"

Aguilar twisted his head to look up and saw a big, bearlike man sitting at his dining room table. "What is this?" he rasped.

"This is an investigation, Doctor," said the seated man. "Or should I say 'mutie'?"

"Fuck."

"Yeah, fuck. See, we came across a strange thing today." The man leaned forward in his seat and, despite his street clothes, Aguilar recognized him as one of the guardsmen who had visited him that morning. "You know every registered mutant has a file at City Plaza, right? Well, we looked at Aguilar Cordoba's file, and guess what? You don't look anything like your picture, Aguilar. You wanna explain that to me?"

The mutant glared at the guardsman. "Not really."

"I don't think you appreciate the grave nature of your predicament, Doc." The big guardsman's voice was companionable, almost chummy. "There are people out there who think the Beast is a shapeshifting mutie. Now, me, I don't believe in shapeshifters, werewolves, zombies, any of that kind of shit. But I do believe in lynch mobs, and lynch mobs often do believe in that kind of thing. And a mob like that might think, a mutie like Aguilar Cordoba, how could he look like a guy like you, unless he was a shapeshifter? You see what I'm getting at?"

The mutant sighed. "Pull my hair," he said to the man holding him down.

"Huh?" said Turrin.

"Pull my hair," the mutie demanded again.

Turrin smiled, shook his head, and grabbed a handful of the curly brown locks. When he heaved back on them they came loose in his hand, revealing close-cropped hair as white as paper.

"Wig," Cordoba said. "Skin coloring. Contacts. It was my boss's idea. He thought the patients at the clinic would feel more secure if they thought I was a normal."

Remming laughed. Cordoba shifted in Turrin's grip. "There's no law against it. I looked it up. We didn't actually tell anyone I was a normal. We just let them come to their own conclusions. There are plenty of mutants who naturally look as normal as I do in this getup."

Remming stood. He nodded to Turrin, who let the doctor go. Cordoba remained lying on the floor as the two guardsmen walked to his front door.

"It ain't a crime," Remming said from the doorway, "but it ain't what I'd call exactly ethical, either. We'll be watching, Cordoba." He closed the door.

On the street outside the apartment Dobbs watched as Remming and Turrin left the City Arms. They didn't take him down, he thought. They made a deal, or he convinced them somehow that he was innocent. He put the runabout in gear and headed for the Bar of Gold.

Walking to their own runabout, Remming and Turrin had already dismissed the subject of the mutie.

"We gotta move," said Remming. "The others should be at the Riverwalk by now. We don't wanna miss the fun." He had determined that the leader of the Railwalkers went for a run most evenings along the palisades of Riverwalk Park.

"Karstairs, what the hell are you doing here?" asked Auden.

Tom Karstairs glanced up from the dispatch desk, a quick, startled, nervous look.

Auden's personal radar went off. He knew that look. He'd seen it too many times on a suspect who'd been caught out at something.

"Uh... Mattingly had something to do, so I switched with him." The guardsman sipped from his coffee cup, then placed it on the desk between them.

"What was it, some kind of last minute emergency?" Auden asked. He knew Karstairs hated working the desk; Mattingly must have come up with something good.

"Uh, I dunno, exactly. He said it was something important, though." Karstairs's eyes shot to the left, and Auden's suspicions increased. Karstairs was lying. He knew Karstairs didn't actually like Mattingly much; the guy hung with Remming, Turrin, and Whaling. Auden didn't care for them much himself. He couldn't prove anything, but he had the feeling they were a little bent. Nothing big, probably. If he had to guess, he'd say they just took a few bucks now and then to look the other way on small-time shit, but the thought still rankled. If Mattingly had managed to pressure Karstairs into covering for him, something big had to be up. If it was something like a family emergency, why was Karstairs being all shifty about it?

Auden leaned over the desk and got in Karstairs's face. "If he's up to something dirty, and you're covering for him, I will personally nail your balls to the wall along with Mattingly and Turrin and anybody else involved," he growled. "Now where the fuck is he?"

Karstairs's eyes went left, then right, then unfocused, obviously struggling with this. Finally he glanced up at Auden. "Okay, but you didn't hear this from me, right?" Auden said nothing. Karstairs continued anyway, "You know they're not happy about the Railwalkers being here..." He trailed off.

"And those guys are out tonight for a game of badger in the bag, right? Think they're gonna teach those Railwalkers a lesson?"

Karstairs nodded. "Something like that, I think, yeah."

Stupid fucks, Auden thought. They'll be lucky if they don't get themselves killed. He'd have been happy enough seeing the Railwalkers taken down a peg, sure, but an assault on Boss Roth's invited guests, on his watch, that wasn't going to look good on his record. And if it came out that the perps were city guardsmen?

"And where," he said aloud, "is this lesson supposed to take place?" Even as he asked the question, the answer came to him: Riverwalk Park. Wolf, the Brick of the team, went for a solitary run there in the evenings when he could.

"I... I dunno," said Karstairs. Could have been another lie, but it didn't matter. Auden moved past the desk and leaned in the door of the bullpen. Looked around to see who was there. "Robles! Holden! Evans!" he shouted. "With me. Right now. Full kit." Without waiting for replies, he turned and stalked back past the desk. "I'll want to talk to you later," he said to Karstairs as he headed out the door.

18. WOLF

Guardsman Fitch had been a confirmed bachelor, with few friends outside of some of the guards and a couple of members of the local Soul-Areist Temple. It was easy to find the two guards who, according to Auden's notes, were Fitch's closest friends in the force, but like Auden they seemed resentful of my inquiries, and had little of value to add to what we already knew. Fitch had been a capable patrol guard, and not much more. He had no enemies anyone knew of, no particular ambitions other than to retire comfortably in a couple more years. During the Takeover he'd served as one of Roth's bodyguard, but had had little contact with Roth since.

The two Soul-Areists it took me a while to track down. One was a manager at a Thornhill department store, the other a laborer at a construction firm. While they weren't resentful as the guards had been, they had little to offer that seemed useful. As I arrived later than I'd have liked at Riverwalk Park, I was feeling like my afternoon had been largely wasted, hoping Rok and Morgan had been more fortunate in their enquiries.

From the top of Riverwalk Park you can see the bay. On clear nights, just before twilight, the setting sun lights up the bay with a blaze that goes gradually from white to golden to bronze. I could smell the river as I watched glimmerings of bronze recede toward the horizon, and I performed the Salute to the Setting Sun. Then I began stretching out.

The Book of Arteology says: "A Railwalker does what is necessary to get the job done. A Railwalker is a good old boy, a righteous brother, a mensch. A Railwalker takes care of business. Every day."

It's not the most popular passage with the women in the order, but they all have the attitude; they're all whatever the female equivalents of those things are. What the hell, the Red Crow was a guy talking to other guys. Of course, there's a common belief that there were female Railwalkers before the time of Brick. Some of the Apocrypha include stories of them. The Canon, as they call it, the basic texts of the order, were written by the First Five, the Ravens who gathered around Brick at the time of the Great Crash. Except for Skywriter, they were all men. Wasn't like they'd planned it that way; it's just how it happened. But they did initiate other women into the order, and most Railwalkers take most of the Apocrypha as seriously as they do the Canon.

Anyway, that passage always seemed important to me. Most of the time I can take care of business just fine. But every now and then, I get to thinking.

You read the tales, the stories of ancient Railwalkers, it's like watching viddiscs or reading paps. High adventure, vanquishing monsters, rescuing innocents, all that kind of thing. But the truth is, those things are only exciting and fun when you're reading about 'em or watching 'em and they're happening on a screen. I can tell you from experience, having a bunch of people out to kill you, or confronting a monster in its lair, is not fun. Exciting, yeah, sure; you're on the edge, dancing with the whirlwind, splashing through Chaos. You live more intensely at those moments than at any other, and some people get addicted to that. But it's not fun, not really. In fact, in some respects, it really sucks.

As the sky turned to purple, I finished my stretching and set out on my run. I wasn't looking forward to the unfolding of this next piece of badness. Wanting to get it over with, yeah, but not looking forward to what that would entail. I knew I was probably going to have to face a monster. What I didn't expect was a bunch of people out to kill me.

The first fucker came out of the bushes to my right and very nearly clotheslined me. He was almost fast enough.

There was no stopping, so I basically clotheslined on my own a nanosecond before impact and spun at the same time, turning it into a flying kick. He went down. I alit on toes and fingers, scanned... Three more coming at me. I moved to meet them.

They had some kind of training, I'll give them that. Rok's better than I am at hand-to-hand. He probably would have taken them down faster and more efficiently, but I did alright. The wide guy in front of me on the path was the more serious threat. Weasel and Schlub coming up behind me were followers; Wide Guy was a leader, dark-haired, bullet-headed, with a look of determination about him. I ducked under his left and jabbed to his ribs as I stepped forward to pivot, putting him between me and the others. The Clothesliner was starting to stir now. Wide Guy came at me again, fast, and I dodged and got in a kick to his midsection that doubled him over, followed by one to the head that put him down. Weasel almost tripped over him, to recover himself and receive a kick that sent him sprawling. Schlub moved in, not fast, but big and beefy, hulking, strong, though not skilled. I broke his nose and one leg. The Clothesliner was now headed toward me, and Wide Guy was stirring. I kicked WG again and turned to meet the Clothesliner, when my head exploded. Either that, or some giant with one of those huge clubs with the big spike on the end had buried it in my temple.

I'd never been shot before. I've been in plenty of fights over my years as a Railwalker, and I'm sorry to say I'd shot a couple of men in my time. I'd been shot *at* before; I've had bullets whizzing by my head in a firefight; but I'd never actually been hit. It was, as they say, a unique experience.

There was an explosion of white light and pain, then everything went black for a moment and I went down. Training must have kicked in despite unconsciousness, and my body must have gotten up again on its own, since the next thing I knew I was upright again as the path swam back into view, my vision blurry.

I took a deep breath, and there was a flash like lightning, or a photo flash. I staggered, but somehow managed to stay upright. Was someone taking pictures? Where the hell was I? I couldn't remember anything. This, I thought, was bad. Several bodies sprawled on the dark path around me. Instinct alone told me they were not my friends, and probably I had put them there. I looked at the big guy getting slowly to his feet. Another one was starting to stir, too. Yeah, this could be very bad. I took another deep breath and saw another flash of lightning. There was incredible pain in my head, but I knew I could turn it off, because I had no other choice. It was seriously time for taking care of business. I could still come out of this alive. I could beat these guys, but it was gonna cost me. Bad.

I realized I was swaying; my body wanted to fall down. My head pounded. I pushed the pain away and focused on staying upright. Go on autopilot, I told myself. Don't think about it, just finish these guys off like you would in the dojo. As I started to move toward the big one, who was actually standing now, a voice shouted, "City guard! Freeze!"

I froze, with one wary eye on the big guy and the other on the one stirring on the ground. It had sounded, I thought, like a familiar voice. City guard... I was in a city. Right, Bay City. Investigator Auden's voice. Several more bodies now appeared out of the darkness; then, everything went black again.

I opened my eyes to see the stars above me. They looked somehow wrong. None of the constellations I knew were there. Then I heard someone crouch down on the gravel beside my head. I knew it was the Wolf.

When the Wolf Spirit first came to me and we joined as allies, he came in the form of a real wolf—a timber wolf, to be precise. Since that time, he's shown up in human form as well; an old black man in a rumpled black suit, a young white guy who looks and dresses like a Ravager from the zones, all beat up leathers and dirty jeans. Then sometimes he's something in between—a man with the head of a wolf. Once, he showed up as a wolf with the

head of a man. I have to admit, that one was a little dis-
turbing.

Mostly I don't let this shapeshifting throw me off. The
Old Ones don't have a real form; they can appear as
whatever they like. Somehow I always know it's him,
regardless of what form he takes. Of course, Wolf's got
nothing on Coyote, where that sort of thing is concerned.
I've met Coyote, too, a few times, and while I sometimes
enjoy his company, I'm glad my ally is Wolf. Wolf's
enough of a pain in the arse as it is.

"You're on a hunt here," he said, "and you didn't
bother to ask my advice?" He was in his wolfman form, a
man's body with a wolf's head, cowboy boots, jeans, and
one of those flat-brimmed hats the Angelos wear. His ears
stuck up through the brim, and I found myself briefly pic-
turing him cutting holes for them, before I realized he
wouldn't have to do that; the hat's no more real than the
rest of his appearance. He was rolling a cigarette.

"Yeah, sorry," I told him. "I hadn't really thought of it
that way."

"What other way is there to think of it?"

"Yeah, well, just color me stupid and make with the
sage advice, okay?" I said. "I'm probably bleeding out on
the Riverwalk back in the world right now, so maybe you
could skip the esoteric lecture and just cut to where you
tell me how to track this Beast down?"

He chuckled, lit his cigarette with an antique Zippo.
"What, you're anxious to get back to bleeding to death?"

"What do you want me to do, prostrate myself before
you in apology?"

"No," he said, suddenly deadly serious. "I just want
you to think like the animal you're named for, you stupid
bastard. You know there's no such thing as a lone wolf. We
hunt as a pack." He didn't say that not consulting him,
leaving the most experienced hunter of my pack out of the
hunt, was a stupid move. He didn't have to.

He smoked in silence for a moment, looking off at the
horizon. Finally he looked at me again. "We hunt in the
territories we know. We hunt the prey we know. If we're

smart, we leave the strongest to breed. That keeps the pool of possible prey growing. Look at the prey. A beast's prey, and how the beast takes it, tells you everything you need to know in order to stalk it."

"Dammit," I said, "I've been looking at the prey, and hardly anything else. I'm not seeing the pattern."

"You're seeing the pattern fine. What you're not seeing is the chaos."

We looked at each other in silence for a moment. There was obviously some profound and important meaning in this that he expected me to pick up on, but it seemed pretty opaque to me. There was a lot of chaos going on in this case. I didn't think I was missing any of that. But it wasn't telling me anything. He meant something else, something that just wasn't clicking. He stood up, pinching out the butt and storing it in a pocket.

"Go deal with your bleeding problem," he said. "Just don't forget to check in later."

Everything went black again.

There were crows on the buildings outside my infirmary room window. I couldn't see them, but I could hear them. As far back as I can remember I've noticed crows around me. I didn't connect them with my dreams and visions at first, just took them as part of the moving landscape, like people and cars, pigeons and ornithopters. It wasn't until my mother appeared to me in a vision that I began to think of them as something else.

The standard dogma is that souls don't revisit the earth. There's no way to come back, no way for the living to make contact with the actual souls of the dead. There are ghosts—snatches of memory caught in the landscape, impressed on the walls and floors, scored into the dirt, memories that replay over and over. There's no real consciousness in them; it's almost like a short DV loop. Then there are shades, which have a certain amount of consciousness—leftover residue from the conscious mind and personality, no longer really informed by the soul. They tend to degrade and dissipate over a fairly short period of time.

The living can only contact the souls of the dead when the soul is between leaving the body moving on into the light. Once they've gone over, they're gone for good. At least, that's the theory.

I never argued with the profs at the Academy about that. Never told them the spirit of my mother had visited me several times over the course of my life. Maybe they were right. Maybe it wasn't my mother, but a piece of my own mind that spoke to me with an imagined voice. Maybe I was just hallucinating. Or maybe it was some other, non-human spirit, appearing in her form; that's been known to happen now and then.

Whatever it was, her advice always seemed to be good. And truth to tell, I wasn't sure I wanted to know the reality of it.

I think I was seven or eight the first time she appeared. About the same time I got her picture from my Pa. Maybe it was some connection through the picture, or maybe the picture just gave me an image to fit where a void had been before. I dunno, really. But I'm pretty sure it saved my life.

It was at a card game in Monteague. One of the players didn't like having a kid around, so I was waiting in the hall that night. I remember sitting on the floor, playing tic-tack on the cheap little handheld my father had given me a week or so before. The wall at my back was old sheetrock covered with about a million coats of paint that sealed in a similar number of coats of dirt. The wall across was cinderblock, slathered with the same puke-colored paint, the mortar lines still visible, but the pores of the blocks so often painted over they were no more than a slightly uneven texture. I looked up from the handheld, and there was my mother coming down the hall. She spoke my name, held out her hand, and said, "Come with me."

I didn't even think about it, just got up and put my hand in hers; we walked out into the parking lot, and across to my Pop's runabout. Just as we reached the vehicle I heard gunshots. I turned around and looked back, drop-

ping her hand for a moment, and saw my father come flying out the window. There were more shots. Pa hit the
ground rolling, jumped up and started toward the door. I
realized he was going back for me.

"Pa!" I shouted.

He saw me, pivoted, and came running toward me. I
turned and my mother was gone. I was glancing around
wildly, trying to find her, when my Pop swept me up and
into the runabout. He tossed me inside, and I crashed
against the passenger door as I heard the engine roar to
life. I was stunned, the breath knocked out of me, and
couldn't protest at leaving my mother behind, but could
only whine weakly as we spun out of the parking lot.

By the time I had my breath back I realized that my
mother was probably dead, and it had been her spirit, not
her physical self, that had saved me. The other thing I realized was that the roof of the building had been swarming
with crows, and for some reason I found myself wondering if they had come there with my mother. I never said
any of this to my father, of course.

I'd learned a lot about the crows since then. All Railwalkers do. We each have our personal connection to some
animal ally, but all of us also have a relationship with
Crow, the totem of our order. As I lay in my bed in the
City Center infirmary, the sound of the crows outside was
a comfort. If I'd been about to die, they'd have appeared
inside the room with me.

Turns out I was lucky. My attackers were disgruntled
guardsmen, out to teach the interloper a lesson, not to kill
anybody, so they hadn't come loaded for bear. Service
weapons had been left behind. The one who shot me had
panicked and drawn his ankle weapon. It was only a .22,
but any gun is deadly if you use it right. He hadn't used it
right. He had clipped the side of my head, resulting in a
wound that bled a hell of a lot and knocked me unconscious, but wasn't horribly dangerous. The doctors were
relieved to find no sign of something they called a counter
coup injury to the brain. I had one hell of a headache and
got occasional lightning flashes in my right eye, which was

so bloodshot it looked like a three ball from a pool table. I remembered stretching out for my run, watching the sun set over the bay, but nothing else until my conversation with the Wolf spirit. They told me the missing memories might or might not return in a few days. Later turned out they were right.

They let me out of the infirmary the following day, though not without some protest from the doctors. Rok and Morgan helped me back to our rooms.

"By the way," Morgan said. "I found the Huey pendant."

"No shit? The one from the *Bay Queen*?"

She held up a bulky manila envelope. "The very one," she said.

"Where'd you find it?"

"Auden had it. He was a friend of Hawthorne's. I promised to bring it back in one piece. Do the docs say it's safe for you to use your Brickish superpowers?"

"Between the injury and the drugs they gave me, last day or so I've spent more than half my time with one foot in another reality. I'm not going to bust a gasket in my head trying to read something. In fact, it would probably be easier than usual."

She handed over the envelope. I tipped it out into my hand. The braided leather thong was stiff with salt. It had a flat pendant of bone carved into the curling "C" shape of Otiz's wave. I closed my hand around the pendant, shut my eyes. A little sense of the sway of a deck at sea, and that was it. No strong impressions. I opened my eyes and said so.

"Should we break out the tools?" Morgan asked. "Go formal?"

"Probably not worth it, unless we take it back to the boat."

"That can wait," said Rok. "You, my friend, are going nowhere, at least physically, for the next twenty-four hours."

***

Since I couldn't get around very well, and any movement aggravated the head pain, I installed myself on the couch in the common room and immersed myself in the materials assembled there.

There were patterns there, dammit. Every victim fit the pattern somehow.

There were the religious affiliations: the Church of the King, the Marilynists, the Campus Crusade for Cthulu, all over the map. Somehow I didn't think we were dealing with a mad atheist serial killer.

All the other patterns were broken somewhere. All but the harlot and the teacher were middle-aged. All but the harlot and the boat captain were connected to Roth. All but the harlot and Czernoff had been killed indoors. All but the harlot had been killed under a waning moon.

All but the harlot...

I saw the chaos. The harlot was the one who cut across all the patterns, threw all the careful correlations into disarray. When does the predator take unusual prey? When it falls in his lap, or he has no choice. It was all so controlled. Yes, the Beast got bolder, took larger chances, came into the Tower, but he did it carefully, precisely. The killing of Suzi Mascarpone had not been careful or precise. It was wild and crazy; it broke the rules.

Did she fall into his lap? Or did he have no choice?

Whichever it was, the harlot broke not just the pattern we were trying to piece together, but the pattern the Beast was working to. If the harlot was a major exception, that left one connecting factor: Roth and the People's Takeover.

Why the harlot? Maybe I could ask her. Morgan had reported that the harlot's friend said the Marilyn pin Suzi Mascarpone had been wearing the night she was killed had been borrowed from a friend. Maybe that's why we'd had no hint of her presence the afternoon we'd visited the tram overpass. The evidence locker would hold other belongings, some of which might allow me to contact her shade.

***

City Administration Tower—Guest Suite

At eight o'clock at night, Bay City was a Yule tree of lights. By halfway through the night, lights had begun to go off again. The office spaces occupied by late workers turned dark one by one. The neon and LED signs gradually flickered off, except for those on a few bars and gaming hells. Residential lights flicked off as the residents turned to bed or headed out for a night of frolic.

In the CA Tower the residential floors retained a few lights. The lights in the suite occupied by the Railwalkers were subdued. Barefoot, in pants and tank top, Rok sprawled on the couch, flipping through files. With the lights turned down, an old pre-Crash western flickered silently on the big screen. Rok found he always did his best thinking while some old movie played silently in the background, hovering in the corners of his vision. He wasn't sure why this should be. Perhaps peripheral awareness of the creativity of those old-time moviemakers who did so much with such primitive equipment somehow sparked the creativity latent in his own mind. Or perhaps it was just the evocation of familiar patterns as background. Many of these films Rok knew by heart, and could recite the lines along with the centuries-dead actors.

He glanced up. Jason Robards looked out at him from the screen. Robards silently mouthed dialogue, and Rok provided the words. "I got a feelin' that when he stops whittlin', something's gonna happen."

Morgan appeared from the hallway, wrapped in a silk robe. "The Brick asleep?" Rok asked.

"Far as I know," she said. "The door's closed, and the light's out."

"Good. Best thing for him."

Morgan walked to the couch and Rok raised his feet. She sank down on the cushions, and he lowered his feet into her lap.

"That was bad," he said. "He should have seen them."

"In the dark, in the bushes of the park?"

"There are always signs."

"Of course. You would have seen them."

"I would. Are you saying I wouldn't?"

"Is that what I said? No, you'd have seen them, alright. And taken them out before they could blink."

"Yeah, well..." Rok said. "Normally he would have, too. This Beast thing has him by the balls."

"It's a bitch, alright," Morgan agreed. She'd taken his right foot in her hands, and now began to massage it.

"Uuuuhhnnnnhhh." His head drooped back as his eyes rolled up.

"You making any progress there?" She nodded at the files in his hands.

He brought his head back up, opened his eyes. "Not really."

"Good."

"Why 'good'?"

"Well," she said, "I'd hate to think I was distracting you just as you were about to put all the pieces together."

A slow smile crept over Rok's face. "Hey, I was just trying to help out. Tracking and detecting, that's not my job. That's for the Brick and the Prof. I'm just a Bear, body and muscle. Feel free to distract away."

Morgan shifted her position on the couch until she was on all fours above him, her face just inches from his. "I was hoping you'd say that."

And she proceeded to distract him quite thoroughly.

19. SANTA BRITA — *Five Years Ago*

He had taken some time getting his Rusk persona right. The shape needed to be big and bluff, but not so powerful-looking as to intimidate too much. Ivan Mikhailovich Raskalov, as he called himself, didn't look at all like Guardsman Caine. He was not so tall, older, had a bit of a paunch. Ivan spent his Thursday nights at the Pivnaya Romanov, drinking and playing *durak.*

"Ivan, come, drink with us," Sascha called. Ivan crossed to where Sacha, Boris, and Pyotr sat at a table in the far corner of the dim bar. It amazed him how these Russians—or Rusk-Mericans—preserved their language and accents even though they had been born into a society that had no contact at all with the Old Country.

"Shouldn't one of you stay sober?" he asked, smiling, as he took the one empty chair.

"When Dima is in this kind of mood, he'll be up there all night," said Sascha.

"Don't call him Dima," Pyotr said.

"You see? Nothing to worry about. Pyotr is sober enough for all of us."

"Sascha is right, though," said Boris. "*Gospodin* Dimitri," he said, using the Russian equivalent of *Mister,* "will probably be upstairs all night tonight." The Pivnaya Romanov was one of several establishments owned by Dimitri Igorevich Prokanazov, the crime czar of West Santa Brita. When the czar came to visit on Thursdays, he would retire upstairs with the Romanov's manager, Sylvia. He frequently did not come down until morning.

"Who's minding the store?" asked Ivan. "Yuri and Georgi?" Prokanazov's bodyguards had come to like Ivan over the last several weeks, and he had become familiar with their routines.

"Georgi had a family problem to attend to," Boris said. "Feodor is covering for him."

"Georgi is always having family problems," said Pyotr. "He needs to get his head straight. He could be out on the street."

"Pah," said Sascha. "He's Dimitri Igorevich's cousin. No way the czar is going to fire him, no matter how much family trouble he has. Don't get Ivan's hopes up."

"Ivan has no hopes. He's too old and fat. He knows that. Don't you, Ivan?"

"Hey," Ivan said. "An old, fat bodyguard is still better than one who's not there."

"You see? He still thinks Dimitri will hire him."

"I'm good. Kabanov used to say I was the best."

"Used to, that's the important point." Pyotr was waving his hands in the air again. "Let the young bulls do that sort of work, *tovarisch* Ivan. You want to work for Prokanazov, maybe we could find you some errands to run."

"I have my pride," said Ivan. "I'm not a messenger boy. I'm a killer."

"Yeah, well, help us kill this bottle, will you?" said Pyotr. "Sascha, deal the cards."

By midnight Ivan had excused himself and left the Romanov. An hour later he was across town, approaching Prokanov's mansion. His runabout was parked on the street some yards from the mansion's gate. But the man who got out did not look like Ivan Raskalov. He looked exactly like Sascha Bylinkin.

"Sascha, what are you doing here?" Feodor asked.

"Open up. There was an accident. The fucking guardos impounded the runabout."

When the door opened, Sascha drove his knife up under Feodor's chin and into his brain. He walked the body backwards into the hallway, and then into a closet.

He withdrew the knife and closed the closet door. Then he hurried up the wide central stairway.

He had studied the floor plan of the house, knew where his objective was, and that Yuri would be in the kitchen grabbing a sandwich and a beer. But Yuri would soon be wondering where Feodor was, and why he hadn't checked in.

The second floor study was a museum. Display cases held every manner of odd memorabilia. There were many weapons, but also documents, an old-fashioned microphone, a skull, several dirty, worn-looking sports balls of various types, a couple of them signed. There appeared to be no rhyme or reason to the collection, but it was all beautifully displayed, and the cases were alarmed.

He suspected Yuri would be looking for Feodor about now. He could hear footsteps in the house. He smiled, kicked in the glass of the case before him. He snatched up an elaborate gold ring from its stand, shoved it into his pocket. Listened. He heard nothing, but was sure a silent alarm had been triggered, and now there was a timetable. He stepped to the door, put his back to the wall beside it. Footsteps were hurrying up the stairs. He grinned.

Pyotr stood by, struggling not to fidget. Dimitri Igorevich Prokanazov was tall and thin, with the mournful countenance of a funeral director and large, bony hands. He stood staring at the broken display case, expressionless. Pyotr could not tell if his stony stare indicated pure disbelief, utter rage, grief, or deep, contemplative thought. Prokanazov finally looked up, scanned the rest of the room.

"You have got to be shitting at me," he said. "He breaks into my house, kills Feodor and Yuri, and with all my belongings at his fingertips, my entire collection at his mercy, he takes only this one little piece? Elvis wept, I have the fucking skull of Arcidemus sitting here. Do you know what that would sell for to the right people?"

Pyotr shook his head. "Maybe he was interrupted—"

"Nonsense. This is a very strange thief. A fan of

Wendell Crichton."

"Who?" Pyotr scratched at his ear.

"A great man from Bay City. Do you know nothing of history?"

"Not much, I confess."

"The ring once belonged to Crichton. Call Murchison. I want a full guard forensics team to scour this place. Everyone is to stay outside until this is done."

"I don't think Murchison..."

"So squeeze his balls with one hand and offer money with the other. Get it done. And have Katarina call the insurance company."

"Oh," said Pyotr. "Katarina said she saw something."

"And you waited until now to tell me this? Send her to me immediately."

Varger Caine sat on his bed, staring at the ring in his hand. It dated to before the Takeover, certainly. It was heavy, but made of some base metal and plated to look like gold. It was set with a piece of black resin intended to look like onyx, into which had been embedded rhinestones, or pieces of glass, in the shape of the Crichton Industries logo. Dozens of these cheap things had been given out to Crichton employees and associates. The Father had never touched this ring. The Rusk had been scammed. He thought briefly about returning the ring to the gangster. Then he tossed it into a corner.

Sascha Bylinkin fought not to whimper or weep. He leaned sideways against the bonds holding him to the chair, but could find no comfortable position. His balls ached, the fingers on his left hand throbbed, the two last fingers pointing at the ceiling like arthritic tree branches. One eye was swollen shut, and his lips felt the size of basketballs.

"He's tougher than I would have expected," said Pyotr.

"Or telling the damned truth," said Boris. "Come on. You were there. He was with us the whole time."

"You were too drunk to notice if he slipped out. You

are calling Katarina a liar?"

"I know what I saw."

"So does she."

Dimitri Prokanazov raised a hand. "Both stories cannot be true," he said.

"Unless," said a raspy voice, "you have to deal with the oboroten." Igor Prokanazov, Dimitri's father, was still big of frame, though stooped by age. He leaned heavily on a stout cane. He shuffled further into the room, gestured at Sascha. "Let this poor bastard go. It's not his fault."

"You can't be certain," said his son.

"You think it's all stupid legends and superstition? I've seen this before. A shapeshifter can look like anyone. Throw suspicion on whoever he wishes."

"If that's true, we're facing a dead end," said Prokanazov.

"Not at all," said his father. "The oboroten can only copy the shape he knows. He must have gotten close to Sascha. Also, he knew your habits, knew which night you'd be away. Look for someone new, who has become close to you or your men in recent days. He will have been studying you."

"Ivan," said Boris.

He had originally thought that Ivan Raskalov might become a regular identity, that he might eventually get papers for him and bank accounts. But he was tired of the Russian character. If he dropped it, if the fellow vanished after the theft of the ring, the Rusks might suspect Ivan, but so what? They'd never find him again, and there was nothing to connect him to Guardsman Caine. Still, his curiosity was great. He burned to know what had happened in the wake of the robbery. Prokanazov had to be aware the ring was a cheap piece of junk. Surely he couldn't believe that City Boss Crichton had ever worn the thing. But he would still be outraged at the violation of his sanctum, the killing of his cousin Feodor, the bodyguard Yuri.

Smiling, he walked to the corner of his room and picked up the ring from where he'd tossed it several nights ago. Yes, he thought, he should return the ring.

The Ivan Raskalov who entered the Romanov Thursday night was somewhat leaner and harder than he had appeared before. Shifting on the fly could be difficult, and he wanted a head start.

They were waiting for him, he could tell. The air in the bar prickled at his skin. Prokanazov's boys were not subtle or deceptive. All the eyes that looked at him as he crossed to the bar were grim.

Sascha joined him as he ordered his usual. The bodyguard's face was battered and swollen, his hand wrapped in bandage. "Ivan," he said, with a patently false smile. "Nice to see you."

"What the hell happened to you?"

"Little family disagreement," said Sascha. "Sorted now." He laid his good hand on Ivan's shoulder, and Boris appeared on his other side.

"Come along, Vanya," Boris said. "Gospodin Prokanazov would like to meet you."

"Good," he said.

At his side, claws were growing from his fingertips as they escorted him through the kitchen and into a back room.

The room was a storeroom, boxes and crates piled to each side. In the center stood a wooden chair, a small table next to it. On the table was a collection of instruments. He put a look of concern on his face, though he was smiling inwardly. It was obvious what they intended. There were several knives, some razor blades, a pair of pliers, a soldering iron, and a thing he recognized as a medical bone saw. On a crate nearby were a pair of manacles, several lengths of rope, and a small rubber ball with a cord threaded through a hole in the middle of it. It took him a moment to realize this last item was a gag. Of course they wouldn't want the Romanov's customers disturbed by his screams. He stopped, staring at the table of torture implements, and Sascha gave him a shove from behind. At that moment, he heard footsteps.

"Ivan Mikhailovich," said a deep voice.

He turned. Dimitri Prokanazov stood there, staring at him with a cold glare. Behind him, Pyotr bolted the door that led to the kitchen. "I cannot tell you how much I have been looking forward to this meeting," Prokanazov said. He did not step forward to offer a handshake. "Please, have a seat."

"I think I would rather stand, thank you, Gospodin Prokanazov."

"But I insist." At a gesture, Boris and Sascha flanked him, grasping him by the elbows and shoulders. They would have forced him into the chair, but he braced himself, and their efforts produced no more result than if they had tried to move a stone statue. The two Rusks looked at each other in puzzlement. As Pyotr walked forward to join them, Ivan formed his right hand into the spearpoint position and drove it into Boris' midsection, just below the sternum. His claw penetrated muscle and organs. Boris gasped, unable even to scream. Ivan pivoted, flinging the dying Russian into the approaching Pyotr, blood spraying them both.

Sascha stared in disbelief, then shook himself and went for his gun. The creature—no longer Ivan; he was morphing and changing into something else—slashed his throat with its bloody claws. Sascha collapsed, gurgling.

Prokanazov drew out a pistol, but the creature was on him before he could use it. His claws ripped through woolen suit and silk shirt, shredding Prokanazov's bicep. Prokanazov screamed as the monster bore him to the floor, clapping a hand over his mouth, smothering the scream. His other hand ripped down the gangster's left arm, leaving both arms now useless.

The monster that had been Ivan sat astride the crime czar's chest, one hand covering the man's mouth, though his scream had now become a whimper. The Russian's feet beat a weak tattoo on the cement floor.

"You thought I had something of yours, no?" the creature said in a raspy voice. "You are correct. And I have come to return it to you." From his pocket he brought out the stolen ring, held it up before the mobster's frightened eyes. "After all, it is worthless to me. How much did you pay for this trinket, comrade? Whatever you paid, you were scammed. This thing never belonged to Wendell Crichton. It's nothing but a cheap souvenir." He shifted his grip, forced the Russian's mouth open, and jammed the ring down his throat. As the man began to gag and choke, the creature leaned close to him. "Perhaps you can get a refund in hell."

Of course, I had to sneak past Rok and Morgan. Normally I'd want them with me on this sort of thing, but they'd have tried to prevent me going out, arguing doctor's orders. I slipped out and rode the elevator down to the first basement level, where the evidence lockup was located. The guard on duty there recognized me, apologized for his colleagues' assault, and told me how nice the Harvest Blessing had been. I mentally gritted my teeth, smiled, and thanked him as politely as I could, impatient to get something of Mascarpone's and go looking for some sign of her.

Rooting through the bin with her possessions, I selected a wristwatch that looked well worn and well loved, and signed it out. Took the stairs back up to street level rather than wait for the elevator. My head was still sore as hell, so I walked slowly and carefully. It took me a while to reach the tram overpass.

When I reached the overpass at Eighth and Alvarado it was after dark, but still much earlier than the time Suzi Mascarpone had been killed. The neighborhood was mixed residential and business, a bit heavier on the business side, most of the buildings adobe brick or limestone, none over six, maybe seven stories. The elevated tram line ran down a long stretch of Alvarado here, eastbound and westbound tracks spanning the wide street, before curving off to the east, to touch down again on the other side of Seventh Avenue, where the ground began to rise toward the city center. In the opposite direction, past Tenth, the numbers on the avenues would give way to names for a few blocks as they approached the waterfront. There were a few pedestrians, but the place looked pretty much as it would have then: The elevated tram line cast huge, black shadows over the roadways and alleys and empty lots it passed over. I hadn't been walking particularly fast, but still I slowed as I came close to the site of the murder, the watch I had taken from evidence gripped in my left hand. I walked toward one of those shadows, then stopped, sniffing. Above the dank of the river and the stench of the nearby dumpster, there was a scent of... ginger. Mascarpone used a ginger-scented perfume. The watch seemed to vibrate in my hand.

I heard a burble of voices, like a group of talking people approaching. Women's voices. I could smell oranges and burnt hair, felt a buzz like a static charge run through me, and suddenly someone gripped my right arm and pressed something into my hand.

"Take this," the woman's voice said in my ear. "There's a killer out there on the streets, you know." I turned, but there was no woman there, only the empty, darkening street. When I looked down, although I could still feel the polished wood and steel, my open palm was empty. I knew exactly what it was, that phantom object. I had held that folding knife with its rosewood grips, which now sat in the same evidence bin where I'd found the watch. I looked up as a tram clattered by overhead. I was staring, seeing my surroundings without registering them. I knew I was looking down the street, at the plascrete columns that supported the tram lines, and several blocks down, there were tiny figures crossing an intersection, but somehow it seemed less real than the high-pitched sound I was hearing like a ringing in my ears, the color of footsteps echoing in the empty street, the sound of the glowing, gray-orange sky above, the feel of the smooth-hard texture of the city night.

Then I was moving, a disorienting sensation, walking along a different dark street while also standing perfectly still, and I knew I'd contacted some piece of Suzi Mascarpone.

"Well, well, what have we here?" a voice called out. I looked to my right, but could see nothing, though I could smell sweat and booze, and a hint of weed, mixed with a cloying, sweet aftershave.

I felt a hand grip my arm again, and a familiar voice said, "You'd best be getting home with no stops along the way."

That one was Rainer Auden's voice. Knowing what sort of thing must be coming, I focused briefly on my own body, my own world, hoping this wouldn't break the connection, while I groped behind me for one of the plascrete columns of the tram line. As my hand found the cold, rough surface, I was grabbed from behind, a powerful arm coming around from the left. Every instinct screamed that my left hand should be shooting up to block, I should be spinning right, my elbow smashing the assailant's face, but instead the arm encircled my throat with no trouble. Small hands with lacquered nails shot up to claw ineffectively at the arm for a moment, before one vanished briefly, to reappear with the folding knife. I felt a tearing pain in my abdomen, and a growl said in my ear, "Be pleased, oh, Lady, be pleased."

The next few moments were a blur, a cacophony of screams and pain and blood, like being caught in a sensory storm, too many images and feelings rushing through me at once to pick out and focus on any one. It seemed to go on for years... Then...

Sitting. I was sitting on pavement. My back was against plascrete, I was staring at a dumpster fifty feet away in the open lot next to a decrepit building whose sign offered "Tech Repair." There was a watch clutched in my sweaty left hand. I was breathing hard, as though I'd just finished a run or been sparring for a long bout. I sat there, getting my breath back, staring at the dumpster. Remembered belatedly to reach for my hara, that point of balance at the center of the physical body, just behind and below the navel. Focused my breathing there until I felt more balanced.

Gradually it came back. Suzi Mascarpone, member of the Harlot's Guild, Marilynist, activist. That's why I was here. She'd been killed on this spot, and I'd just felt that death. That's what all the blood and pain and screaming had been. I wondered if I'd actually screamed aloud. Looked around to find the streets around me still empty. Well, mostly empty. At one end of the block a Latino guy was walking a dog. He didn't even glance in my direction. I watched him disappear around the corner onto Ninth. If I had made any sound, it apparently hadn't attracted any attention.

My head was pounding again. Strange: while I'd been in that fugue state, my head was about the only part of me not experiencing pain. I leaned against the column, closed my eyes, not wanting to do this, but it was necessary. I reached my senses out to the surroundings, searching for some sense of Suzi Mascarpone. There was nothing. The woman's spirit had moved on, and it was likely her shade was gone as well. It happens that way sometimes: A shade will download its traumatic experience into a living human, and then it will dissipate.

Opening my eyes, I reached into my pocket and brought out a packet of tobacco. With shaking hands I dumped some out into a small square of paper, twisted it closed, and set it down on the pavement. Then I produced my lighter and set fire to it. As the tobacco burned, I chanted the Farewell to the Dead.

The tobacco burnt down, the chant done, I got slowly to my feet and began the walk back to the CA Tower, turning the whole experience over in my mind. The killer had said something. Something like "Be pleased..." I thought at first he was talking to me—to her, that is—but it was soft, breathy... like he was praying or something. Unless Suzi's shade had been caught in a loop, he was saying it over and over. "Lady," that's what it was. "Oh, Lady, be pleased. Oh, be pleased..." And then something else I couldn't make out.

"Be pleased, oh be pleased." It sounded like a prayer, yeah, an entreaty. Did this invocation happen at every killing, or just at this one? Just this one, I thought. It's a freak, a fluke, a variation on the pattern, and he's pleading with his Lady, be she goddess, human, or whatever, to continue to favor him, overlook this self-indulgence. "Be pleased." No, not just overlook it, allow it, but take it as an offering, a sacrifice. It's not part of the pattern, but it's still something he's doing for her.

It is the moon, I thought. He broke the lunar pattern. He's getting worked up inside. He's getting close to the end of the pattern, and he's doing it for her, his Lady, his Goddess, and there's something else... What compels the abject worshiper? The worshiped, or its opposite. God—in this case Goddess—or something foul and degraded, a sacrilege. Mascarpone was a Marilynist. Was Marilyn the Beast's "Lady"? Or did he find the Marilynists offensive? There are several goddesses associated with the dark moon. None of them, at least in their more popular forms, would have found the Marilynists offensive. The lunar goddesses tended to be harlots as well as virgins, particularly in the dark phases. Tiamat, Ummu-Hubur, Hebat, Hecate... The killings could be offerings to any of them.

But all that, I realized, was speculation, balanced precariously on one point: my intuition that this killing was a fluke, that the Beast's prayer wasn't the rite that accompanied every killing, but something special. It was a good theory, but still only a theory. Best not to get too attached to it.

I thought back over the earlier parts of the vision, before she was caught by the Beast. The knife pressed into her hand, the hand on the elbow. I had forgotten, the harlot had seen Auden earlier in the evening. And we had only Auden's report of what had happened; there were no other witnesses. Auden was a friend of the fishing captain. Could it be Auden? Could he have had some falling out with Hawthorne? When he met Mascarpone earlier, was he scouting his next victim?

But, no... Auden was with us when Czernoff had been killed. I doubted there were two shapeshifting killers in the city. Was Auden dirty? A human ally to the killer? It didn't seem likely. And if the investigator had been the Beast's inside man, why the charade with the janitor? Auden could have simply let him in. If I couldn't entirely rule out

him as a possible Beast ally, I wasn't about to put that at
the top of my list of likelihoods.

Back at our rooms in the CA Tower, I found Rok still
up, sitting on the couch with a file folder open on his lap.
Something in black and white was showing on the big-
screen DV, but the sound was off.

"Nice sneak-out," he said over his shoulder.

"Thanks." Water was sounding good. As I filled a glass
at the sink, it occurred to me that a couple of aspirin
couldn't hurt, either. I grabbed the bottle from the
counter, shook out a couple and swallowed them, washed
them down with the water, then refilled the glass and took
it back to the main room. I looked at the guy on the DV. It
was Jimmy Stewart. He was ranting silently about something.

"You go to the tram overpass?" Rok asked.

"Yeah."

"She there?"

"Yeah, sort of."

"Any help?"

I thought about what I had experienced under the
tramway. "Maybe," I said. "Hard to tell yet." Eventually I'd
need to fill Rok and Morgan in on what I'd gathered from
the harlot's shade, but I didn't have the energy just then.

"You knew that the fisherman, Hawthorne, fought in
the Takeover?" Rok asked. I nodded. "First mate claims the
Cap'n once admitted to him—deep, dark secret shared late
one drunken night—that he was actually the guy who shot
Wendell Crichton."

"You believe him?"

"I think he believed it. I believe his captain probably
told him that story. Whether it was true or not, who
knows? Anybody can make a claim like that."

I sat down beside him on the couch. "Man," I said,
"you got all the finest, most expensive for-pay DV avail-
able to you on this nice big screen, all at the expense of
Micah Roth and Bay City. Why you watchin' this low-rent,
free channel shit?" The free channels ran a lot of pre-Crash

stuff—no copyrights or royalties involved.

Rok raised one finger, but kept his eyes on the file. "You'd better be fucking joking."

I laughed. It made my head hurt. I'd have to try and remember not to laugh often. That probably wouldn't be too difficult. "Course I'm joking," I said. "Jimmy Stewart's The Man. What's this, *Wonderful Life?*"

"*Mr. Smith.* Get a clue, will ya?"

I took a slug from the water. Rok looked up at the screen. "You ever wonder what it was like, to live back then?" he asked.

"Wasn't like that," I said, nodding toward the screen. "These things are the fantasy those people had of themselves. Hey, how close is the average DV show today to the reality we experience?"

"Yeah," he said. "But it's true, they did have one central government controlled practically the whole continent. That must have been really strange."

"Not if you grew up with it."

"I suppose not."

On screen Stewart was now dumping bags of mail out onto his little desk. For a while there was only the faint hum from the muted speakers. Then Rok said, "You think it's all about Roth, don't you?"

I looked at the thought again carefully. It felt right. "Yeah."

"You think Roth lied about Crichton's pregnant wife?"

"Nah, I don't think he lied. But I don't assume he's right."

Morgan appeared from the other room, her portable balanced open on her forearm. "They're ritualistic revenge killings, that's gotta be obvious," she said.

"Sorry," I said. "Didn't mean to wake you."

"You didn't." She sat down at the table. "Check this out." She gestured at the screen. "Do you mind?"

Rok shook his head. "Go ahead," he said.

Morgan punched some keys on her portable and Jimmy Stewart vanished from the screen, replaced by the image of Morgan's desktop, several old articles open in different windows.

"After the Takeover, the trials focused on Crichton and his top guys," she said. "But you look at the media reports from before the Takeover, they make it sound like Helena Crichton was the real brains of the outfit, the power behind the throne. Kinda like Crichton was the gun, his wife was the hand that pointed it."

I didn't bother trying to read the articles, but took Morgan's word for it. The photos accompanying the write-ups showed Crichton with his wife, a handsome woman with hard eyes.

"They found a body though, didn't they?" asked Rok.

"If anybody could come through a civil war in one piece, I'd be betting on someone like Helena Crichton. Bitch on wheels, totally as ruthless and power-hungry as her husband. More so, probably. It was a war zone. There easily could have been more than one pregnant woman killed in the fighting. I can't find anything on how they identified that body."

"If she did escape," I said, "and gave birth to Crichton's kid, that kid would be..."

"Hitting his Saturn return about now," Morgan finished. It wasn't exactly what I was going to say; I hadn't thought of the astrological implications, but it was close enough. He—or she, I reminded myself—would be almost thirty.

Rok snorted. "Guess that means the New Republic of Bay City is hitting its Saturn return, too," he said. "Makes a certain amount of sense, doesn't it?"

Saturn takes just under thirty years to complete one circuit of the zodiac. Astrologers see the Saturn return as the beginning of true adulthood, the ending of the age of innocence, loss of illusions, the time when the Universe forces you to face a bunch of very hard realities.

"Yeah," I said, "I guess it does at that. How old was Helena Crichton then? During the Takeover?"

"About forty or so, I think," Morgan said.

"Isn't that a little old for a pregnancy?"

"It's pushing it, yeah. Didn't Roth say they'd had trouble getting pregnant?"

"Yeah, he did." I nodded, looking at the screen, where Morgan's cursor was skipping around, flipping through the windows that showed different articles and photos.

"Wait a minute," I said. "What was that? Go back..."

She did. There was a photo of Crichton and another man standing in front of a building that looked like a resort hotel.

"What's that?" I asked. "That symbol?"

There was a sigil on the doors of the building. It looked like two stylized commas bracketing a lower case "i," the shaft of the "i" pointed instead of squared off at the bottom.

"Crichton's corporate logo. I think it's supposed to be C-I-D, for 'Crichton Industrial Development.'"

"Imagine that logo upside-down," I said. "Doesn't it look a little like the mark the Beast has been leaving?"

Rok was starting to twist his head sideways when Morgan clicked on something and inverted the picture. We all looked at it in silence for a moment. "I dunno," Rok said finally. "It's a stretch."

"Yeah," said Morgan. "I guess I can see it, but it is a stretch."

"Maybe I'm just too desperate to make a connection," I admitted. They were right. The logo would not only have to be inverted, but distorted as well, to match the Beast's mark. I stared at the screen some more.

"Okay," said Rok. "Let's say, for the moment, Helena Crichton did escape, and gave birth. Would a woman like that stay here and plot revenge? I'd think she'd be more likely to go somewhere else, start over again. No power to be had for someone like her in the New Republic. Maybe she went to Santa Brita or Bendmond. They were more like the old Bay City in those days. Hell, San Angelus was still practically feudal."

"Maybe she did," said Morgan. "I'm assuming someone like that doesn't lose their taste for power, and that if Helena Crichton survived, she'd be rebuilding her own

little empire somewhere. I've got at least three good possibilities, women who fit her profile, who appeared in
other cities around the right time period. And she doesn't
need to be here, in Bay City, right now. Maybe it's just her
son who came back."

"Could be," I said.

The entire roof of the featherweight dune crawler was
one huge solar collector. The batteries were fully charged
when I signed for it. I turned out of the guard garage and
headed down Fourth Street, south toward the river. Once I
was over the Fourth Street Bridge, moving southwest out
of the city, the buildings got shorter and smaller, going
from plascrete and granite to brick and adobe and even
some old wood frame buildings. After a while they petered
out altogether, and I was speeding through the peninsula
south of the Bay. Now I could see glimpses of ocean
between the oncoming hills.

I could probably have consulted Wolf again in the CA
Tower, but this seemed more respectful. There was an old
sacred circle overlooking the sea at the top of the hill they
called "Chaco Head." The circle of stones wasn't that
ancient—it had been raised sometime just before the
Great Crash—but legend said it had been a sacred site for
centuries before that.

The sun was setting as I parked the jeep a few yards
from the circle. The stones were larger than I'd expected.
Most stone circles you see these days, the uprights come to
your waist or chest at most, but these stones were a good
seven or eight feet tall. Away to the southeast I could see
the cracked remains of one of the great domes that once
made survival possible. Back then bees could only survive
in that artificial environment, which meant only plants
growing under the domes would get pollinated. Almost
any new growth plant in the world today was a descendent
of something that was grown in one of those domes. Their
adoption had saved the human race from extinction
through starvation.

I took off my boots. Bringing my knapsack, I walked

to the center of the circle. Took out a little brazier and some sage, and set the sage to burning. I raised the brazier to each of the four directions. Performed the Evening Salute.

Then I lay down and closed my eyes. Slowed and deepened my breathing. In my mind's ear I heard the beat of a drum, the shaman's drum. It might have been helpful to have an actual drum there, but I'd done this so many times I didn't really need it. In only moments I saw the door, and stepped through it.

Instead of a desert, where I usually encountered the Wolf, I found myself in a walled oriental garden, surrounded by bonsai trees. In size they varied from eight or ten inches tall to some relative giants nearly a full three feet in height. It was like walking through a miniature forest. Some of the trees stood in individual pots on pedestals; others were planted in numbers in large trays that were sculpted and landscaped like tiny parks. The Wolf appeared through a gate at the other end of the garden, this time in the guise of my old sensei, short, bald, and muscular, though he wore a formal kimono rather than the gee I was used to seeing him in.

"Bonsai trees?" I asked.

"Almost every possible style and variation," he said. "Koten and Bujin; Shakan, Kengai, even Netsunari." He gestured at one in one of the larger trays, where several trees appeared to be growing out of a fallen log.

It was weird, hearing Wolf's voice come out of my old sensei's body, seeing the formal movements of the dojo I was used to, but also the looser, more casual body language Wolf used in his human guises.

"Sorry, that's all Greek to me." He raised an eyebrow. "Well," I amended, "Japanese, anyway. I mean, I can count to ten, but..."

"Do you know how bonsai are created?"

"Genetic manipulation?" I ventured.

"No. It is all simple horticulture—pruning, trimming, guiding the branches' growth, taken to the level of an art. Some of these trees are hundreds of years old."

"So they're fragile and delicate Elders."

"Hardly. A well tended bonsai is hardier than a full-sized tree, and will outlive normal trees by many decades. But it still remains an artificial product. Just like you."

"Me?"

"What would you be, if you had not found the Railwalker Order?"

"I dunno. Not an itinerant gambler. Probably I would have continued in construction. Maybe if I was lucky enough or smart enough I'd have saved enough to go to school, become an architect."

"In some ways," he said, "you are like these trees. You have been shaped and pruned by your teachers, your natural tendencies enhanced, energies taught to flow in certain directions they might not have found on their own."

"Okay," I said slowly, wondering where this was leading. "I can see that."

"Now," he said, "in what way are you unlike these trees?"

I pondered that one. I was sure he didn't mean that I could move around from place to place, or that my height was normal for someone with my genetics. Whatever he meant, it wouldn't be something that obvious. I shook my head, shrugged.

"You give up too easily." He smiled. "Sit. Meditate. Talk to the trees. We'll talk again later." He turned and left the garden.

I gazed around the garden, feeling for the right spot, the right tree. There was a warm, comfortable feeling about one particularly gnarled and ancient-looking tree that sat at the end of one of the larger landscaped trays. I walked to it and sat down with my back to the tray, leaning my head back against it carefully, as I would have if I was going to commune with a full-sized tree. I couldn't quite touch the tree, and I wondered if that was important; in all my previous communications with trees I had been in physical contact with the trunk. I closed my eyes and slowed my breathing.

Trees are living beings that house a form of consciousness just as humans or animals do, but they're not at all like us. Communication with individual animals isn't quite like talking, the way the Wolf Spirit and I talk, it's more like a series of feelings and pictures. With trees and plants, communication is even less like talking, and I barely know how to explain it in words. It's more like direct knowing is transferred, and even the content of that knowledge is often strange and unexplainable. This time, however, the tiny and ancient tree infused me with memories. Hundreds of years of memories. For trees time is different than for humans. Days pass for them like seconds for us. Yet in this tree, something was different. It seemed to understand time, if not like humans do, at least in a way that was closer to human or animal perception. That was strange, I thought.

Until the tree's history began to unfold within me, I didn't realize I had already formed expectations. I had imagined the tree as a prisoner, subjected to tortures, distorting its shape and natural intentions into an arbitrary pattern imposed by its gardener. Instead, I discovered a mutual shaping between the gardener and the tree, the human's faster, smaller consciousness adapting to the slower, wider scope of the tree's, even as the tree cooperated with the gardener's intentions. Trees don't have emotions quite like humans or animals, but as close as I could approximate it, this tree seemed almost fond of its original gardener. The gardener had been like a teacher, coaching the tree in understanding something of the humans' faster consciousness. I felt the human consciousness touch that of the tree, exploring, investigating, seeing into the future patterns the tree contained, considering how to reproduce those patterns in miniature in both time and size.

To a tree, the shapes of its branches and the patterns of its leaves are something like the patterns of neurons and synapses in the human brain. The pattern of the tree's growth is the pattern and template of its consciousness. The effect of the bonsai process on the tree was to age and mature it at an accelerated rate. Accelerated aging in humans, as in progeria or Werner's syndrome, doesn't usually affect mental processes; the patient exhibits an aged appearance, but mentally remains their chronological age. While the bonsai might be a fraction of the size of its brothers in the wild, the maturity of its appearance coincides with the maturity of its consciousness. By the time this tree was thirty or forty years old, it held the consciousness and wisdom of a tree hundreds of years older.

I opened my eyes to find myself sitting in the stone circle overlooking the bay. It took me a minute to come completely back to myself and overcome the feeling of being rooted in the earth at that spot. I thought about what I'd learned. On the level of analogy, I had found more parallels than differences between my own training in the order and the bonsai tree's cultivation. Perhaps I had not matured at as accelerated a rate as the tree had, but my training had certainly brought me to a deeper self-understanding more quickly than I would have gotten to on my own, which seemed to fit. Neither the training nor the wired shaping of the tree's limbs had always been comfortable, but there was an equivalency to the knowledge that the discomfort was a necessary part of the process, and a minor inconvenience in the larger perspective.

Then it struck me: The gardener had found the tree and appealed to it to join him in this bonsai process. The Railwalkers did not proselytize; in fact, they would never even extend an invitation. I had sought out my teachers, applied to the order for entrance to the Academy.

Not that I understood what this might mean to my current problem.

Investigator Auden was collecting some printouts from the data center when the tech, Shamir, gave a hoot.

"Son of a bitch! Someone's actually trying to hack Roth's private files," he said to no one in particular.

"You have access to Roth's private files?" Auden said.

Shamir glanced up briefly from the screen as his fingers flew over the keyboard. "Duh, no, idiot. But they send me a signal if someone's cracking them."

Auden stepped into the hall, pulled out his communicator, and called the Railwalkers' suite. Rok answered.

"Give me your prof," Auden said. "Emergency."

A moment later Morgan was on the line. "This isn't really a good—"

"Are you hacking Roth's files?"

"How did you—"

"Get out now. You've been nailed."

"Shit," she said.

He heard the clacking of keys. From the data center, he could hear Shamir's voice. "Shit! I lost him."

"I'm out," said Morgan. "Talk to me."

"I was in the data center when the tech caught wind. Now you talk to me. Why were you hacking Roth?"

"You never know where information is going to lead."

"Your boss Wolf thinks this all has to do with Roth's history, doesn't he?"

"If you knew that, why did you ask? And how did you know that?"

"Guards talk. Look, you believe that?"

"Enough to try to hack Roth, see what I can find. He's not telling the whole truth about something."

"You don't think he's involved?"

"No. We think he's the ultimate target. Whatever he's concealing may have nothing to do with the Beast. But then it may."

There was a long silence. Finally, Auden said, "Okay. As long as you share anything pertinent you come across. Try again around ten. The night guy is a lot less conscientious. He likes to toke up and play games."

"Thanks," said Morgan, and disconnected.

22. THE ZONES — *Ten Years Ago*

He traveled in his human shape, which made things a little more difficult, but he was used to hardships. There had been training excursions with Evreyt into Bay City, and sometimes into the nearby desert, but he had never traveled this far alone before, nor had he ever ventured so far from the Cave, or the Baja Bay area. He was now many days' walk into the zones, carefully following the directions he had been given. For long stretches he was able to follow the ancient roads, in one place walking for nearly two days along a parallel pair of roads, wide expanses with four lanes each, though the pavement was broken in many places, scrubby plants and grass poking up. Now and then he had to make his way around the rusting hulk of an ancient vehicle, sometimes a group of vehicles. Once, when a scaledust storm blew up, he took shelter inside one of them, covering up with his tarp.

As the wide, flat spaces with Joshua trees and creosote bushes had gradually given way to higher desert, rolling hills dotted with sagebrush, scrub oak, and juniper, he had sighted the range of mountains he was looking for, the profile of which had been drawn for him, and which he had memorized.

In the foothills of those mountains lay the House of Katana.

Its back to the slope of a foothill, the house looked out over the desert, and the distant mountains on the opposite horizon. It was a moderately sized adobe house, with a small barn and a large garden. Beside the front door was a plaque with the kanji for "Katana." No one answered his knock at the front door, so he walked around the side of the house to the garden.

There was a figure bent over in the garden, an old woman wearing a wide-brimmed straw hat. Tiny and birdlike she crouched, pulling weeds.

"Excuse me," he said, "I'm looking for the Master Katana."

"See that well over there?" She pointed without turning, her other hand continuing to pull weeds. "There's a bucket behind you. Go fill it and bring it here."

"I was supposed to meet the Master Katana and become his apprentice."

Now she stopped and looked up at him. "No shit?" she said. "Well, I don't see no Master Katana here. Just me. I'm the mistress of this house, and until the Master Katana sees fit to put in an appearance and invite you into his dojo, you belong to me. Understood? Good. Now go get that water."

The woman put him to work, helping her weed and tend the garden. She would answer no questions about the Master. When it became too dark to work, she gave him bread and water and pointed him to a sleeping palette on the ramada of the house.

Days passed, and the Master did not appear. He soon fell into the routine of chores around the small farm. There were chickens and goats to be tended to, the garden to be weeded and watered, food to be prepared. He found time to work out as well, doing his exercises and kata daily, as well as his rituals for the Four Quarters of the Day. As the days went by, he began to wonder if the Master would ever appear.

Then one day, when he had been there several weeks, he was taken by the idea that there was no Master Katana. Either that, or the old woman herself was the Master. Perhaps she was testing him. He decided he would test her in return. He would strike at her with something—a broomstick, perhaps. If she was indeed the Master, she would block it easily. If not... Well, if it turned out she really was just an old housekeeper, he could pull his strike and avoid hurting her. But he didn't expect he would need to.

To his astonishment, he did have to pull the strike,

but he hit her anyway, and she went down on the brick paving of the ramada. She was up again pretty quickly for an old woman.

"What the hell is wrong with you, you stupid bastard?" she howled. He apologized profusely, but she told him to get out of her sight for the rest of the day.

The following day, the old woman acted as if nothing had happened, and would not let him mention it, either.

Two days later, she broke his fingers.

He was carrying wood for the fireplace and she appeared from nowhere. She laid a broom handle across his right fingers, so fast he hardly saw it, only heard the resounding crack and felt the pain. The wood nearly fell, but he got his left arm around it, holding his right hand out to one side. He didn't cry out or grimace with pain; he was already too disciplined for that. But he looked a question at her.

"You're right-handed," she said. "Get over it. Make your left as strong and smart as your right."

He stared at her. "But...." he said, "you did not block my strike."

"Expectations are weapons, like surprise," was all she said.

There was no further pretense. The next stage of his training had begun.

23. WOLF

My Pa didn't like the Railwalkers, or the supernatural stuff they often dealt with. "I don't mess with that sort of thing," he'd say, holding his palm out like a guardsman's "stop" signal. But kids notice everything, particularly the things you don't want them to notice, so naturally I realized early on that he never actually said he didn't believe, even though he sometimes seemed to imply that. To my child's mind, it seemed my father chose to avoid this aspect of life as a matter of practical good sense, the way you'd avoid taunting a dangerous animal, or drawing to an inside straight.

He had his own superstitions, his lucky cigarette lighter (he'd never gamble without it), and his lifetime membership in the Order of St. Bernardine (the patron saint of gamblers, naturally), but he avoided the Railwalkers, never went to the High Holiday celebrations. He would acknowledge some of the holidays, giving presents at Winterpeak or taking me to see the fireworks on Forge Lie Day. Generally, though, Pa kept himself, and me, out of the way of any sort of religious or spiritual activities. Which is why I managed to live twenty years before having more than a brief glimpse of a Railwalker, or even an All-world priest, come to that.

First time I saw an actual Railwalker, I was working a construction site outside the city of Two Suns. The building was to be both warehouse and offices for a transit company. We'd had lots of problems putting the thing up. So much so that the bossman on the job was starting to look worn and harried. Slim Harnett wasn't really all that slim, but he was one of the tallest men I'd ever seen, and his extreme height made him seem thinner than he actually was. A saturnine fellow with short salt-and-pepper hair and a goatee, Slim wasn't one for talking much. He usually spoke just enough to convey whatever instructions he needed to give the hands. Unless you caught him off-hours and got him started on hunting. Slim was an avid hunter, and this was the one subject he would sometimes open up about. During work hours, however, he was silent and taciturn. Not rude or curt; he was always polite. In fact, the second time the northeast end of the framing fell down on this job was also the first time I'd ever heard Slim swear.

"Fucking butthole-sucking architects."

I stared at him. I was just some guy pouring plascrete for Slim's outfit, who happened to be standing there. It was none of my business what Slim muttered to himself, but I stared anyway, as this was such an uncharacteristic outburst, even uttered quietly the way it was. He noticed me staring. Then he spoke to the air again. "They didn't have a Railwalker check the site first."

It was hard to tell whether this was for my benefit, or he was still talking to himself. Slim had this odd quirk of never looking at you when he talked. He'd be talking to the air over your shoulder. I wasn't sure I should venture a question, but it popped out anyway.

"Are they required by law to do that?" I asked. I was still learning the business. Construction laws varied greatly from city to city, zone to zone. In some places the laws were convoluted and labyrinthine. Having a Railwalker or a Feng Shui practitioner check over a potential construction site was not uncommon; it was possible some city ordinances required it.

"Nah," said Slim. "It ain't required, but it's customary. And smart."

Slim set a crew to cleaning out the mess. Turned out the plascrete of the foundation in that section was bad; it had crumbled like there had been too much water in the mix, though I had been there when Red Avery was making up the mix, and it looked to me like it was fine; if anything, a little dry. Once it was cleaned out, Slim set us to working on the other end of the building for the rest of the day, ignoring the northeast corner.

We were shutting down for the night when Red Avery noticed an animal lurking around the edges of the desert chaparral.

"Shit!" he cried. "That's the biggest goddamn coyote I ever seen."

"That's no coyote," said Armando. Unlike Red, he pronounced the word "Coy-oh-tay." He shook his head. "Es un lobo—a wolf."

I looked over Red's shoulder. I had never seen a wolf, though I had seen plenty of coyotes over the years. This animal was certainly bigger than any coyote I'd ever seen, heavier for his size, with a fuller ruff around his shoulders. He seemed to be looking directly at me.

"Bullshit," said Red. "Ain't been no wolves in this area since before the Crash."

"Armando's right," said Slim, who had come up as we stood gawping at our watcher. "That's a wolf. I seen 'em plenty of times when I was hunting up north." He grunted. "Strange alright, seein' one of 'em around here. Especially by himself."

"What," said Red, "you never heard of a lone wolf?" He laughed.

Slim's glare silenced him. "Lone wolves are a myth," he said. "Wolf is a social animal. They travel in packs. Wolf by himself, without a pack, usually don't live long."

I could see Red was skeptical about this, but no one was going to challenge the bossman on his wildlife knowledge. Red kept his mouth shut. The wolf, or big coyote, or whatever it was, vanished into the chaparral.

The following morning the wolf was back, watching us from the undergrowth. By noon it was gone again. Then, just after lunch break, the Railwalker came walking out of the desert.

When I first noticed him, I looked up from the plasteel framing I was bolting together and saw a pale, dust-colored figure off in the distance. I continued to bolt plasteel, glancing up at the approaching figure now and then. As it got closer I could make out the long duster, the headscarf, with the long tail pulled over his lower face like a bandanna. All one color, the shade of the reddish brown desert dust. A pair of crows soared in the air above, circling.

By the time the figure had reached the construction site we were all watching him. He stopped a few feet from us. "Who's the bossman here?" he asked.

Slim stepped up. "That would be me," he said.

The stranger unwrapped the scarf from around his face, and you could make out part of the eye tattoo under the dust.

"Hear tell you could use a Railwalker."

"I 'spect we could," said Slim.

"Slate am I, Walker of the Rails between Worlds, charged by Corvinus, fifth of his line from Brick, the Red Crow. Twenty-three Blessings of Soul-Are on you and yours, brother. Say your need."

We were all sent back to work as Slim brought out coffee and tobacco, and the two of them sat down to talk.

While I worked I watched them covertly. The stranger was almost as tall as Slim, and much leaner, practically skeletal, but tough and wiry looking, skin browned by the sun 'til it looked like leather. His lined and hollow cheeks were covered by stubble, though it wasn't clear whether this was a short beard or a long five o'clock shadow, but from the rest of his appearance, I was guessing the latter. He shared coffee and tobacco with Slim, and then they walked over to the northeast corner where the framing had collapsed and the 'crete gone bad. They looked it over together, then the man from the desert nodded. He walked a few yards out from the site, then began a slow circuit of the place, pacing a large circle around the whole site. When he reached his starting point again he spoke a few words to Slim, then walked off to sit in the shade of a nearby palo verde tree. Slim returned to work.

Come quitting time I hung back as the others left. I walked over to where the stranger was still sitting under the palo verde. "'Scuse me," I said. "Can I ask you something?"

"Sure, you can ask." He looked up at me. His eyes
were so pale blue they were almost colorless. "Don't guarantee a good answer."

"Fair enough." I hunkered down next to him. "So," I
asked, "you know why that foundation gave way?"

"Pretty sure." He wasn't giving anything away for free,
this guy.

"So... Why did it?"

He looked at me, then looked around at the landscape
as if checking to see who was listening, though there was
no one around, and nowhere for anyone to hide nearby.
He looked back at me again, a long, considering look.
Made me feel like my Pa's look did sometimes when I'd
done something wrong.

"See that depression with the brush growing around
it?" He pointed to a spot a stone's throw from the northeast corner. "There was a waterhole there once. Still water
there, deep down below. They're planning to sink a well.
Part of the reason they chose this spot, I reckon."

He stopped speaking as if that had explained
everything. I waited a bit. When it became clear he wasn't
going to say any more without urging, I asked, "So, what
does that mean? You saying the ground's not stable?"

"Stability got nothing to do with it. Waterholes got
spirits. This one may be dried up, but the water's still there
deep underneath, and the spirit's still there with it. This is
her land, that water spirit. Not respectful to go building on
it without her permission."

I thought that over. "The plascrete acted like it had
too much water in it," I said. "That was her doing?"

"Reckon so."

"And you're going to.... What, talk her into letting us
build here?"

"If I can," he said.

"And that'll solve the problem, just like that?"

"Mebbe. If she agrees. 'Course, likely she's more than
a little pissed off right now, so your Boss Slim will have to
make some offerings. Probably good to make 'em pretty

regular until the work is done. Even better the owners come down and do that."

"Somehow," I said, "I don't think that's like to happen." I'd seen the owners once when they toured the site. Suits from downtown Two Suns. They didn't look like the type to come out here and burn tobacco, or whatever it was the spirit needed, on any kind of regular basis.

"Well," he said, "what happens once the building's done is their problem, then, isn't it?"

I laughed. "I reckon so," I said, unconsciously imitating him.

He peered at me again, those pale eyes boring right into me. "You don't really care, do you? That's not what you really wanted to ask me about."

My stomach turned over. He was right. I'd been silent about my strange experiences for so long, it was like I didn't have the first idea how to open up on that subject. He took out a small, ropy cigar, lit it with a tarnished silver lighter. Watched me struggle, not helping, just sitting there, waiting, puffing his cigar.

"I..." I started, and faltered. Gathered my courage and plunged ahead. "Sometimes... I see things."

"Uh-huh."

"Things that ain't there. Or at least, nobody else sees 'em. Things that haven't happened yet, sometimes."

He nodded. Then it all spilled out. I found myself telling him about the visions, the dreams, the visits from the spirit of my mother. All the weird stuff I'd been silent about for so many years. Once I'd got started, it wasn't hard at all; it just all kind of burst out of me. When I'd finished, he said nothing for a while, staring off into the distance.

"You got someplace to be tonight?" he asked finally.

"No place particular."

"Better if you fast, but if you gotta eat, eat light. Then come back here after sunset."

I arrived back at the site exactly at sunset. The Railwalker was standing to the west of the site, his arms up, saying something. I didn't know the Salutation in those days, but I knew instinctively this wasn't something I should interrupt. I stood back in silence until he finished. Then he turned to walk to the northeast corner. I could see he'd prepared a small fire about halfway between the site and the depression in the ground he claimed was once a waterhole. He crouched down to apply a light to the piled branches and twigs. I thought he hadn't seen me, but once the fire had caught, he stood, and without turning called out, "You gonna stand there all night?"

I hurried over to the Railwalker and his fire. As I got closer, I could see other things on the ground nearby. A couple of blankets, the Railwalker's backpack, a bowl of water, a smaller, shallower bowl that held loose tobacco, and a tin cup with some rock salt in it.

"Sit down," he ordered, pointing to one of the blankets. I sat. He picked up the bowl of water, walked a few steps away, and held it up as though offering it to the sky. He muttered something I couldn't catch, then walked around behind me and repeated the gesture. Two more times brought him back to his starting place. He then plucked a flaming stick from the fire and repeated the same process with the stick. By the time he set fire to the tobacco and took that bowl around, I'd figured out he was stopping at the four compass points. A pass with the cup of rock salt apparently completed the procedure. He returned to the fire, spread his arms, and declared, "Soul-Are be with us." Then he looked at me and raised his eyebrows.

"Oh..." I said "Uh..." I stumbled to my feet, imitating his pose as best I could, and repeated, "Soul-Are be with us." He nodded and smiled briefly. Indicated I should sit again.

Opening his pack, he produced a small, leather-wrapped package. Unrolled, the leather revealed a carved stone pipe and two cloth pouches. He filled the pipe with some sort of herb from one of the pouches. He lit the pipe, took a lungful of smoke, and held the pipe out to me. I looked at it dubiously.

"You want to learn about these experiences?" he asked. "This is the door to your first schoolroom. Take it or leave it. It's all the same to me."

I managed to keep my hand from shaking as I took the pipe from him. I sucked in the smoke, expecting it to choke me. I wasn't a smoker, and my previous experiments with smoking had not been pleasant. I didn't know what this herb was, but in my travels with my Pa I'd seen people smoke a great many different things. This wasn't tobacco, and it wasn't pot, hash, corn silk, or any other substance I was familiar with. It tasted a little fruity, with a sort of sour undertone, but it went down easy, and to my amazement it didn't make me cough. It wasn't that hard to hold the smoke in my lungs, either.

The Railwalker chuckled. "It ain't mary-gee-juaner. You don't have to hold it in."

I let the smoke out with a gasp. That made me cough. The Railwalker laughed out loud. "Careful, kid. You'll blow the damn fire out."

He took another draw from the pipe, and handed it back to me. When we'd each smoked from the pipe three times, he emptied the rest of the herb into the fire, held the pipe up to the sky for a moment, then cleaned it and wrapped it up again. By that time I was starting to feel pretty strange. If it wasn't pot in that pipe, it was something that would alter your consciousness, of that I had been pretty sure. Now I was absolutely certain. Sitting across the fire from me, the Railwalker began a low chant, rocking his body in time to it. The words were so long and drawn out I couldn't tell what they were, or even if they were Merican, Mayacan, or some other language.

Things were starting to take on a funny glow. The creosote bushes seemed to crackle with something like electricity. The palo verde had a soft, pulsing light to it. The Railwalker's pale eyes, staring into the fire, seemed to give off sparks. In my peripheral vision I saw lines of light. They vanished when I looked directly at them. As I watched the Railwalker, I became convinced that he saw them, too. His eyes seemed unfocused, though he appeared to be gazing into the fire. I took a cue from that. I didn't want to look at the fire, and have my night-sight destroyed, so I looked out over the darkened desert instead. I fixed my eyes on the middle distance, trying not to focus on anything in particular. Keeping my eyes still, I shifted my attention to my peripheral vision.

Immediately, I saw it: a web of energy, pulsing lines of light running everywhere, from everything to everything else.

Movement at the edge of the chaparral attracted my attention, and I lost sight of the web of light. The wolf we had seen in the morning—I was certain it was the same one—was standing there watching us, the firelight making his eyes glow red, which reminded me so much of an effect from a bad DV movie that I laughed out loud. My laughter quit abruptly, though, as I realized that whatever the smoke was doing to me, this wolf had been seen by others and could possibly be real and capable of killing me; it would be easy in my drugged state. My whole body went cold; I was rooted to the spot.

Then the Wolf spoke. "Is this a private party, or can anybody sit in?"

A talking wolf, or a spirit wolf, or whatever. I would have expected him to sound like an Indio or a Mayacan. This thing sounded like a guy from the eastern cities, or from one of those old pre-Crash gangster series. I would have laughed again, had I not been too appalled. Besides, I was a stone. A statue next to the Railwalker's campfire. The Railwalker glanced over at the animal.

"Always a place at my fire for Brother Wolf," he said. "Got no meat, but there's water and tobacco to share."

"Thanks, I'm good," the Wolf said, as it padded to a spot next to the fire and settled down. It looked at me. "You're a hard soul to connect with, little crow." My name wasn't Wolf yet, but it wasn't "Little Crow," either.

A huge, gray-blue moth fluttered past my face, its wings flashing blue and gold as they beat in the firelight. It fluttered away again, and the Railwalker stirred himself.

"If you gentlemen will excuse me, I have an appointment." He stood up. My pulse began to race. The Rail-walker hadn't actually told me much, but he was my guide to this strange world, and he was about to abandon me, leave me alone with the wolf. Panic must have shown in my face.

"Don't worry," he said. "I'll be back."

I watched him walk off to disappear into the brush around the dry waterhole, trailed by the fluttering light smudge of the moth. The Wolf's eyes followed mine. "That's his appointment," he said. "This is yours." Firelight sparkled around the edges of his fur, giving him a golden nimbus.

"Listen, kid. You got the Sight, okay? You figured that part out. Now you get two choices. You can walk away from it, pretend it doesn't exist, and keep yourself out of the deep end. You'll probably get regular weird coincidences, the occasional prophetic dream, maybe a vision or two. But if you ignore it hard enough, it won't be so bad.

"On the other hand, you could embrace it, learn to deal with it, just like you learned to deal with card games or pouring plascrete. You'll eventually end up in the deep end, but by then you'll know how to swim. You might even be good at it."

I found my mouth was no longer made of stone. "Huw..uh.... How cnn..." Okay, I wasn't ready to audition for newsfeed anchor, but it got the point across.

"Well, I can teach you some stuff. But, diggit, kid. This is the deal. I come to you this time. Next time, you have to come find me. And I ain't talking about bumming loco weed off Railwalker Slate, either. Got it?"

And just like that, he was gone. I was looking down a vast wall that seemed to extend as far as I could see in all directions. It was studded with rocks and odd frothy growths, and an eerie orange light came from somewhere far below. I heard footsteps, and then saw the Railwalker, striding across the wall, walking on it at a right angle as though it was a floor, his boots miraculously adhering to the vertical surface. I wanted to ask him how he was doing that, but couldn't get the words out. He drew near me and leaned over, and the entire world shifted.

I was sitting at the fire, the Wolf gone, the Railwalker crouched beside me. He shifted himself over to sit on the other blanket, reached into his pack and withdrew a bottle. When he uncorked it, I could smell it was water. I'd never noticed clean water had a smell before, but it was clear and distinctive, no doubt in my mind what it was. The Railwalker offered the bottle, and I took it greedily.

"Three small sips," he said. "There'll be more later."

I was glad I had followed his instructions when my stomach informed me that it wasn't altogether certain it shouldn't have been only two small sips.

"It'll pass," the Railwalker said, taking back the bottle. He took three sips himself and set it down. Drew out his cigar and lit it. I expected it to smell nasty, but it was actually a quite pleasant aroma. There were still flashes of the web in my peripheral vision. "Good talk with Brother Wolf?"

"I guess," I managed. "Did you...?" I gestured toward the waterhole.

"Yeah, you can pour your new plascrete tomorrow. In the morning, I'll give Slim instructions on the offerings."

"Give me the instructions. I'll do it. Hey, I'm gonna have to deal with this stuff. I may as well get started."

He shook his head and smiled. "Good you're willing, but no. If it's not gonna be the owners, it's gotta be Slim. He's their surrogate here, not you." He held out the bottle. "Three more sips. Then sleep."

It was something of a start to wake lying on a blanket outside the construction site. The Railwalker had boiled water, and was making zoner coffee in the tin cup and the water bowl. I took the extended cup, for once not minding at all that it was probably pure chicory.

"Where did you learn about this stuff?" I asked.

"An old hoodoo man lived near us when I was a kid. Spent some time with an old Indian guy, too. But most of my training came from the Railwalker Academy."

"There's a whole school?"

"Where did you think Railwalkers come from? The sky?"

I'd never thought about it before, but it made sense. Just like lawyers and doctors and engineers, Railwalkers had to learn their trade somewhere. Why not a school?

"How do I get in? What does it cost?"

"Don't cost anything, except a lifetime commitment if you want to graduate. Apply to join, and if the crows vouch for you, you're in."

"The crows?"

"They're the gatekeepers. And some of the best teachers."

I thought about my previous strange encounters with crows. They had always seemed to be on my side. "Approved by the crow," I mused. "Might not be a big problem."

Later in the morning, once the guys started rolling in, Slim arrived with a motorcycle strapped into the back of his transport vehicle. The bike was a frankensteinien creation, HF cell-powered, cobbled together from a variety of makes and models of various ages. Much of it was rusty and dented.

"Project of my kid's," Slim explained, as he set about removing the straps. "From way back when he lived at home. He don't want it anymore. Told me to sell it or trash it." He turned to Slate. "It still runs, figured maybe you could use it, give your dogs a break."

"Thank you," said Slate. "Thank you kindly." Together we wrestled the bike down from the vehicle bed. The Railwalker strapped his pack to the back of the bike, mounted, and fired it up.

"Come freely and go safely, Railwalker," said Slim.

"Twenty-three Blessings on you and yours, Slim Harnett."

Railwalker Slate gunned the bike and rode out of Dodge. Er, Two Suns, that is.

INTERLUDE: SOUL FRAGMENTS

During the first century, a Railwalker named Cristoff Rydel proposed what would become known as the "Projected Fragment Theory," or sometimes simply "Rydel Fragmentation." Rydel suggested that under a number of specific conditions, particularly those of extreme trauma, either physical or emotional, pieces of the soul could actually split off to form an independent entity. Generally, Rydel fragmentations were supposed to consist of the shadow selves, rejected and dissociated aspects of the soul. Fragmentation Theory was generally regarded as a crackpot fringe, except during the second century post Crash, when it enjoyed some brief popularity.

Yet, in fairness, it cannot be said that Fragmentation Theory has ever been disproved, or even entirely rejected by orthodox Railwalker theorists, and it is worth noting that Rydel's own conclusions were relatively conservative, with the wildest speculations attributable to later theorists following Rydel's lead. In his famous work *Fundamentals of the Rails*, Prof. Porte allows for the possibility of such fragmentation, under the conditions Rydel describes, but adds, "As such a combination of conditions is likely to be extremely rare, so is the occurrence of fragmentation likely to be rare, and such fragmentations would undoubtedly tend to have less cohesion and coherence even than the typical shade; though, admittedly, they might have more longevity."

During the third century there arose a religion based on Rydel fragmentation, the Church of Ecstatic Union. The Ecstatic Unionists believed that true integration of the soul required fragmentation into separate entities, followed by reuniting of the fragmented parts. They developed rites intended to facilitate both fragmentation and reunification. Critics suggest that the rituals of the Ecstatic Unionists are no more than elaborate psycho-drama, but adherents insist on their legitimacy. The CEU had its heyday in the latter half of the third century. It began to collapse in 279 PC, when Frederick Tahns, the reigning Prime One, absconded with the CEU's not inconsiderable treasury. From that time on CEU member-ship began to dwindle, and as of 387 there were barely a handful of CEU Unification Centers left, most of them concentrated in the city-states of the northeast.

Netpedia entry,
"Rydel Fragmentation"

24. WOLF

When we arrived at the conference room, Auden was waiting for us outside.

"Come up with anything on your little fishing expedition?" he asked Morgan.

"Not much," she said, "Plenty of blackmail material, if anyone cared about his love life. But nothing that seemed relevant to the Beast. He had very few records went back as far as the Takeover. But thanks for the help."

Auden just nodded, turned, and led us into the conference room.

Keeping the Wolf Spirit's earlier advice in mind, I was trying to think of this as a hunting party, or a pack, but it seemed more like a council of war. Maybe, I thought, that wasn't so wrong either. For the Beast this was a war, a personal war against Roth.

The man himself sat at the head of the conference table, where he'd sat each time we met in this room, the large gold circle with its wave looking down at us from the wall. Sarah Weldt sat to his left, Gage to his right. Auden, Morgan, and Rok were ranged around the table. I paced. The opposite end of the conference table was too far away, but I had to keep a dominant position for this to go the right way. I didn't feel right sitting on the edge of Roth's conference table, so I compromised and stayed on my feet.

"We think the Beast is targeting Mr. Roth," I said. "The victims have all been people associated with him during the time of the People's Takeover."

"Wait a minute," said Roth. "I didn't know the fisherman. Or the harlot."

Rok answered him. "The fishing boat captain, Hawthorne, was the first kill we know of. He fought for you in the Takeover, and at least once he claimed to have been the man who killed Wendell Crichton. If we're correct, that might not need to be true to make him a target."

"Hawthorne to Castro to Finch to Adams to Czernoff," I said. "Each killing getting closer to you. One of your soldiers in the Takeover, then an officer, then a current-day guardsman, your Chief, and finally the Treasurer."

"And each on a waning moon." Rok added.

Roth turned toward me. "And the harlot?"

"She's the one anomaly," I told him. "She breaks every part of the pattern. I think she wasn't really part of his campaign against you. She ran afoul of him somehow, presented some threat to his plan, and that's why he eliminated her. She's the only one without an association with you, the only woman, and it's the only time he's killed under a waxing moon."

"Yeah? Or maybe he killed her as a favor to a friend. I'm sorry, Railwalker, this theory of yours doesn't hold up very well."

"But it does," said Weldt. "Except for Suzi Mascarpone, it does. Five out of six is close enough for our purposes. We have to assume they're right; you are the ultimate target. Chief Gage..."

"I'll assign bodyguards."

"Hell," said Roth. "If this is true, then we have to contact anyone who might become a target, protect them."

"But discreetly," I said. "I'd prefer the Beast didn't know that we've sussed out his pattern."

"What," said Roth, "you think this animal watches the newsfeeds?"

"Yes, he watches the newsfeeds. And scans the net, too. He does his research, plans carefully. He probably knows the floor plan of this building better than you do. Don't let his appearance and his savage mode of killing deceive you. He may be a beast, but his body houses a calculating, human mind. He's patient, careful, and thorough, as well as being ruthless. He's a soldier, a warrior for a cause."

"And that cause is revenge? For the Takeover?"

"For Crichton's defeat and death, yes, I think so." I let them digest that for a moment. Then I said, "We're going to set a trap for this beast. You're going to announce a post-Summersend dinner at Hartshall for yourself and a few select friends."

Rok produced a sheet of paper. "Here's the guest list," he said. There were only five names on the list, all that were left of Roth's inner circle from the Takeover days.

"None of these people will actually be present two nights from now at Hartshall," I assured Roth. "They'll be replaced before they leave home by guardsmen dressed in their clothing."

Roth didn't look happy. "And the guardsmen will be the bait in this trap?"

"Armed and dangerous bait," I agreed. "But yes, bait nevertheless."

"I have to be there," he said. "No body double for me. I can't ask my guards to do something I'm not willing to do myself."

Gage shifted in his seat. "Not possible, sir. Too much risk."

"You could too easily be killed or taken hostage," I said.

Roth glared at me. "Railwalker," he said, "I am still the boss of this city, and I still go where I choose."

Gage gave orders for guards to be assigned to protect the five people on our list, and we sat down to plan out the particulars of the trap.

"You want to keep the whole plan under wraps," said Morgan, "but the people we're sending guards to protect, we'll have to tell them something."

"We have reason to believe they may be targets," I said. "That's all they need to know."

Several hours later I arrived at Riverwalk Park for my evening run and found Robles there, warming up. "What," I said, "does Gage think I need a bodyguard now?"

"Nah, I'm here on my own lookout."

"You think I need protection?"

"Karstairs says you do Parker running."

"Yeah."

"Not many Parkerers around Bay City. You mind some company?"

Even though the sweats weren't as tight as her guard uniform, somehow they did more to set off her figure. Or it seemed that way to me. Maybe it was the softness of the fabric and the loose cut; it came across less like armor, had me seeing her as a woman instead of just a guard. I smiled. "Think you can keep up?"

She grinned back. "Look out for your own self, Railwalker." She dashed off across the park.

"Hey!" I shouted as I started after her. "You didn't give me time to warm up!"

She turned, running backward for a couple of steps. "I thought Railwalkers weren't supposed to lie. You're warmed up already!" She turned again and continued her sprint.

"I didn't say I wasn't," I muttered, grinning, and put on a burst of speed.

We ran the length of the upper park. Sometimes Robles was in the lead, sometimes I pulled out ahead of her. As we started down the hill that led to the waterfront, Robles, ahead of me, veered to one side and vaulted the park fence to the sidewalk beyond. I followed as she dashed across the street and ducked between two buildings. For the next few minutes she put my Parkering abilities to a more serious test, going over fences and through passageways, across empty lots and down alleys. I let her keep the lead, since she clearly knew where she was going.

We reached a street that had been converted to a pedestrian mall, all brick cobblestones and decorative streetlights that looked like old gas fixtures. She slowed to a panting stop.

I jogged up beside her. "Nice route," I said, catching my breath.

"Only one knows these streets better than me is Gage." She grinned, nodded toward an expensive-looking coffee shop. A sign in the window read "100%." "You like real coffee? My treat."

The coffee at the CA Tower had been good, but the last time I'd had actual one hundred percent real coffee was almost four months back at Almagordo. I followed her.

"You're pretty enthusiastic about your job," I said when we were settled at a small, round table, steaming cups of rich black brew before us. "You from a guard family?"

"Sort of. My Dad was a guard, back before the Takeover."

"Did he fight for Crichton?"

"No, he'd mustered out by then. Went into law school. Ended up as a Councilman. He died a couple of years back, heart attack."

"I'm sorry."

"Yeah, thanks."

"You planning on something similar?"

She snorted. "Dying of a heart attack? Well, I hope not."

"No, I meant law school, politics."

"Me? Nah." She laughed. "Career guard, that's my path." She looked at me like she was expecting disapproval or challenge. "I know," she added, "kind of a cop-out."

"Why?" I was honestly mystified. "Guard's a respectable career."

"Yeah, it is," she allowed. "You know, there are pieces of paper, they got the right writing on them, can kill you sure as a bullet. I'm not talking about juju. I mean legal documents. Fighting the bad guys on the street is easy. They bang, you bang back. It's cleaner and clearer than politics. Fighting the bad guys in City Hall, that's harder, messier. It's like fighting knee-deep in mud, with cheap weapons that can explode on you."

"You really believe that?" I asked. She raised her eyebrows and shrugged, as if to say "doesn't everybody?" I shook my head. "Like nobody on the street ever lies or backstabs or cheats? You can handle yourself on the street because you know the street. You know the physics of violence, how it works. That's why you're good at it. Your Pop knew the rules of politics. At least I presume he did. Was he good at it?"

"Not good enough."

"Good enough for what?"

"To accomplish everything he wanted to."

"Few men ever are. Doesn't mean they're not still good at what they do."

"Yeah." She looked down at her coffee, nodded. "Yeah, he was good at it, actually. He believed in the law. He was an amateur historian, you know? Had all these books on the history of the guard, the ancient police and military. Had a whole collection of antique weapons and badges and stuff like that." She paused and sat back in her chair. "Do you believe in the law, Railwalker? Consider yourself a lawman?"

I shook my head. "Two different questions," I said. "I believe laws can help people live together amicably. I've also seen them used to oppress. So no, I don't consider myself law enforcement. As a Railwalker, I'm in service to the community. Sometimes that means doing rites for the dead, sometimes mediating conflicts, sometimes it's helping to build a barn or dig a well."

"And sometimes tracking down a serial-killing monster?"

"Yeah," I allowed, "sometimes."

She leaned forward, her crossed arms on the table. It did nice things for her breasts under the sweatshirt. I made myself look at her face.

"Scuttlebutt in the guard says you talked to the Old Man's ghost. Is it true?"

"Not exactly. We recorded some electromagnetic residue of the chief's passing. What we call a shade—a little like bloodstains, only instead of a piece of his body it's a piece of his mind, his personality that's left behind."

"But it talked to you."

"Yeah, after a fashion. Told us some things that may help."

"I guess, in a sick sort of way, that's kinda cool. The Old Man getting to help you find his killer, I mean, even though he's dead and gone. Way to go, Chief Adams." She glanced at her watch and stood. "Gotta run. Don't want to be late for lit class."

"Lit class?"

"Adult ed over at Bryers'. Can't spend all my time beating up on people. Gotta acquire a little culture now and then, keep the brain limber, too. Same time tomorrow?"

"Barring unforeseen circumstances."

She nodded, grimacing. "Yeah, roger that." She picked up her coffee and left, giving me a little wave over her shoulder as she hit the street. I enjoyed watching her walk away. The back view was every bit as nice as the front.

Was she interested in me? I wasn't sure. Didn't really matter. Either way, she'd be an interesting woman to get to know better. And right now, the sheer relief of indulging in basic human contact, chatting over coffee with minimal reference to a series of brutal murders, was really nice. I sighed. Okay, I thought, recess is over. Time to perform the evening Salute, and then back to obsessing about a series of brutal murders.

Some days I really love walking the rails. Other days, not so much.

"Suspended!" The Tankard was filling up with the early evening crowd, and Nickas Turrin was on a verbal roll. "Fuckin' suspended without pay! If that ain't a big old shit sandwich..."

"Stop whining," the burly man growled.

"What, you sayin' it's right?"

"No, I'm sayin' stop fuckin' whining!" Remming put his beer down hard, the sound like a gavel falling. Several other patrons glanced in their direction, then quickly looked away. They were mostly guards; they knew what had happened in Riverwalk Park, and about its aftermath. Remming lowered his voice. "We both knew what could happen if things went wrong. Well, things went wrong. Deal with it. Just be glad that with the Beast running around, they couldn't afford to suspend us for more than a few days. And be glad you're not Mattingly, sitting in a cell without bail."

"What'd he do that for, anyway?" Turin asked, returning to the subject of their disastrous attack. "We agreed no guns."

"What do you want me to say? He panicked."

"Yeah. Well, I gotta admit, the Railwalker surprised me. Never seen anybody move that fast. Fair broke my wrist."

"That was one fucked-up night."

"Yeah." Turrin looked at the dregs in the bottom of his beer glass, signaled the bartender for another. "Hey," he said to Remming, "you tell Dobbs he was wrong about that mutie he thought was the Beast?"

"Like I needed to."

"What do you mean?"

Remming took a deep breath and mustered his patience. He basically liked Turrin, but the guy could be dense at times. "You didn't see Dobbs sitting outside the City Arms in his runabout, the night we braced the mutie? He knows we're not moving on the guy."

"Huh." Turrin digested that. "No, I didn't see him. Dobbs seemed pretty certain about the whole thing. We don't move on the mutie, you think he'd actually go to Kabanov with it?"

"Nah." Remming snorted. "Dobbs wouldn't go to Kabanov if the ruskie had the only hooch on the west coast." He sat thinking for a moment, then added, "But he might take his fuckin' amateur guards out to do something about it."

"The Citizen's Safety Committee?" Turrin laughed. "Bunch of lame-arse wankers. What are they gonna do?"

"Individually, not much. But he gets a whole gang of 'em together, there could be real trouble." Remming finished his beer, fished out his wallet, and dropped some bills on the bar. "Maybe we better pay Dobbs a visit after all."

Turrin looked up from the beer he'd only sipped at as Remming stood up from the stool and started to move toward the door. "Hey," he said to Remming's back, "we're suspended without pay. Not our problem."

Remming stopped and turned, stared at his companion for a moment. Then he slapped Turrin on the shoulder, and Turrin yelped. "Fuck's a matter with you?"

"Me? 'Smatter with you, dickhead? We're city guard, suspended or not. A lynching in Bay City isn't our problem? Fuck that. I'm going to see Dobbs. You can come or not as you please."

Turrin quickly chugged about half the remaining beer and followed in Remming's wake.

"Jezus, Elvis, and JFK, am I glad to see you guys!" Betty hauled her girth out from behind the bar and waddled toward Remming and Turin. A solitary old man stared into his drink at the back of the bar; otherwise, the place was deserted. That had to be a first even for a Tuesday night in the Bar of Gold.

"Oh, fuck," Remming muttered.

The fat woman clasped her shaking hands in front of her as if trying to still them. "Dobbsey made me promise not to call you, but you're here now, and I'm so worried they're gonna hurt that guy..."

"The mutie?" Remming asked.

She nodded. "Dobbs was shooting his mouth, you know, the way he does, and—"

"How many people?'

"I dunno, thirty-five, maybe forty."

"How long ago did they leave?"

"Five, maybe ten minutes."

"Turrin, call it in."

"What?" Turrin snorted. "We're suspended. Besides, I don't got a radio."

Remming backhanded his friend's shoulder. "Then use a phone! It's a fucking lynch mob, Turrin! Call it the fuck in!"

Turrin did as he was told.

Auden had just taken a mouthful of gyro when his radio went off. One-handed, he fumbled the radio out and grunted at it. Listened, swallowing hard. Took a sip of coffee, and said, "Patch me through to the Railwalkers." He looked up at the counterman. "Can you wrap this for me, please?" He tossed a few quid onto the counter. "Yeah, Railwalker Wolf? Auden. Seems some dickhead down Water Street thinks he's found the Beast, a mutie who lives on Hallard. He's leading a lynch mob to get the guy now. On the outside chance the dickhead is right, I figured you might want to know." He listened for a second as he accepted the wrapped gyro, and then headed for the door.

Minutes later, Rainer Auden pulled his runabout into Hallard Street to find it full of people. The dispatcher had told him the caller reported forty or fifty people in the mob, but their numbers had swelled along the way, and now nearly a hundred people crowded the street before the City Arms apartments. Auden blared his siren and bulled the runabout through the crowd to the building.

Someone had been on the ball, he thought, seeing several uniforms had arrived before him. One runabout and one of the few full-sized guard autos were pulled up on the sidewalk, forming an impromptu barricade. Half a dozen uniformed guards held the crowd back, and farther down the sidewalk two more uniforms were holding back a couple of newsfeed anchors. Sergeant Roberts, who would have been the ranking officer until Auden's arrival, stood at the front, arguing with Hanover Dobbs. Roberts was clearly doing his best to keep hold of his temper as Dobbs worked himself up to an apoplectic rage, ranting and shouting at him. Auden stepped up behind Roberts and put a hand on his shoulder. Dobbs stopped yelling and looked at Auden.

Rok and Morgan were out to dinner together when Auden's call came in to our suite. I agreed with Auden that it didn't seem very likely some average citizen had discovered the lair of the Beast in an upscale apartment in the North End. And I seriously doubted the Beast was a mutie. Still, we couldn't afford not to check it out. I decided not to interrupt my partners' dinner, but to leave a message for them and go myself.

Rush hour might be over, but the streets around the City Plaza looked heavy with traffic. The address Auden had given me on Hallard Street was only a few blocks away, in the North End. I decided I'd make better time on foot.

I left the tower heading north on State. Within a block or two I was certain I was being followed. I reached the next intersection and dashed across against the light, one or two horns blaring at me. I kept my eyes on the store window opposite, watching to see if anyone tried to mimic my move, but no one did. I took a corkscrew path through the city streets, mindful that I was costing myself time, but determined to flush out my follower. Nothing.

Traffic was thinning out now. I stopped on the corner of Hale and First. Dammit, I knew there were eyes on me; I could feel them. I looked down Hale and saw a woman standing at the mouth of an alley, staring directly at me. She was small, slight, with wavy, blond hair. She wore huge, baggy jeans and a sweatshirt much too large for her. Her face was in shadow, but she seemed familiar. I took a step toward her, and as she turned to retreat into the alley, I saw her face clearly for an instant. It was Suzi Mascarpone. I dashed down Hale and crossed to the alley.

The alley was empty. I ran to the other end. Another alley led crosswise there, the length of the block. There was no one in sight. No wait, there to my left... a movement vanishing between two buildings. I raced to follow. Another empty alley. This one took me to Kurzweil Boulevard, a wider street, more trafficked than Hale. There were a number of pedestrians, but there was no sign of the harlot. I heard soft laughter behind me. It wasn't a girl's, but a man's. I turned and looked. The man watching me from the other end of the alley was Arnold Hawthorne. He wore the same jeans and sweatshirt Suzi had, though they fitted him much better. Not a spirit, then. A shapeshifter. A crow cawed above me, and the man glanced up. I charged down the alley, and he fled.

By the time I turned the corner he was gone again. I ran until I hit the next cross alley, and glanced down it. No figure, but I heard the laugh again. I stopped, looked around.

"Give it up, brother Railwalker," a gravelly voice called. It echoed through the alleyways, impossible to trace the source. "You cannot win. And I'd rather not kill you."

"Why not?" I called back. "What makes me different? I'm working for Roth, too."

Laughter. He was above me somewhere. I scanned the building tops, saw nothing. As the laughter faded, it seemed to be coming from the roof to my left. I leapt up, caught the edge of the lowest fire escape, and scrambled up. It was impossible to climb the fire escape quietly and quickly both, so I settled for doing it fast as I could.

"I will kill you if I have to," called the Beast as I climbed. "And I will eat your brains."

I reached the roof, a flat expanse broken up by Tesla receivers and air vents, which otherwise appeared empty. I made a circuit of it anyway. No one was hiding behind the receivers or the vents. There was a flash of black in the air and something thumped down by my feet.

"Take heed," the voice called, this time seeming to come from a greater distance. The broken clump of black feathers at my feet had once been a crow. Its neck was broken.

I walked to the edge of the roof where a thigh-high wall bordered it. I looked down, searching the alleys, and up, scanning the roofs. No sign of the Beast.

I heard cawing. A crow alit on the wall beside me. Then another. I turned back to the roof, and the air was filled with black feathers and raucous calls. A moment later they had all settled, maybe forty of them, black shapes in the twilight with gleaming black eyes, eerily silent now except for the occasional rustle of feathers. All of them facing me, and the motionless black body before me. I knelt down, gently straightened the broken wings and neck. Then I began the Chant for the Dead.

It might never be entered in the files of the Bay City Guard, but I considered the Beast had just committed another murder. He had issued a challenge, killed one of my crow brothers. He knew what he was doing, I thought. I was always going to hunt him down, take care of business, do what a Railwalker does. But now the Beast had made it personal.

I finished the chant, bowed to my crow brothers, and climbed down the fire escape again, leaving them to take care of their fallen comrade.

Elvis wept, thought Remming, what a fucking mess. The mutie's street was filled, one end of the block to the other, with angry bodies. He had no idea where Turrin had got to, but if not Turrin, someone had called it in. He could see the colored lights of the guard runabouts flashing off the buildings, and at the opposite end of the block the big dish antennas of two newsfeed vans.

He was able to walk barely twenty feet down the street before the press of bodies slowed his progress. This was as bad as City Plaza on New Year's Eve, he thought as he began forcing his way to the front of the crowd. Worse, actually. New Year's Eve revelers didn't carry baseball bats, broken bottles, and the occasional firearm. It was like swimming through mud. He applied his elbows and fists, throwing his weight into the task of shoving bodies aside and moving forward between them. He was cursed and yelled at, but fortunately no one actually attacked him. He reflected he was lucky to be out of uniform. For all these idiots knew he was one of them, or it might have gone differently. The bullhorn blared again, a familiar voice— Roberts maybe, or Washington; the bullhorn distorted the voice too much to be certain—telling the crowd to disperse and go home.

After what seemed like hours he saw the front lines, the guard runabouts, and, jeez, they'd brought out one of the full-size cars—parked on the sidewalk, the guards ranged along them between the crowd and the building. He hoped they'd thought to put someone on the back entrance. He shouldered past Carter Evans and John Macchio. Macchio gave him a look, but he glared back, and the man backed down. Remming stopped directly behind

Dobbs, as Dobbs shouted at Roberts, carrying on about bringing justice to our streets, and the monster the guard were protecting, yadda, yadda... Beyond Dobbs and Roberts, he saw Auden approaching from behind the vehicles.

Dobbs stopped shouting when he saw Auden step up behind Roberts. This was not good, he thought. Just when he'd been thinking they might bully their way past the guards to get to the mutie, here comes Investigator Trouble Auden. Well, the guards were still outnumbered, if it came to that. Maybe it was time to cry havoc and let loose the dogs of lynching. He was taking a breath to shout for the mob to charge when he felt the barrel of a gun pressed against his spine.

"Back down," Remming's voice said in his ear. He turned his head slightly, caught Remming's eye out of the corner of his own. "Back down right now," Remming repeated, "or I swear I'll blow your guts all over this street and take my chances with your mob."

Dobbs knew Remming well enough to know the guard was not bluffing. The burly bastard was just crazy enough to kill him there in the street, and then take as many of the mob with him as he could before they brought him down.

Dobbs didn't hesitate. "We know that mutie in there is the Beast!" he shouted at Auden. "Why aren't you arresting him? Why isn't he in custody?"

Auden looked at Dobbs with a deadpan expression. "He is in custody," he said. He didn't add that it was protective custody. The guard would look into the possibility that the mutant Cordoba could be the Beast, but they weren't expecting to find much evidence to support Dobbs's contention.

Dobbs nodded slowly, a big pantomime gesture, as if he was thinking about Auden's answer. Then he stepped closer to the guards, Remming moving with him. He turned toward the crowd and threw his arms wide. "Friends!" he shouted. "Fellow citizens!" Only the few

people in his immediate area appeared to be listening. He
stretched out a hand to Auden. "Bullhorn," he demanded.

"No fucking way."

"You want them dispersed or not?"

Auden looked at Dobbs, and then at Remming, who
was pressed up closely against the barkeep. Remming nodded. Auden took the bullhorn from Washington and held
it up before Dobbs. He placed his hand over the mic end,
and said, "Send 'em home. Fuck with me on this, you will
regret it."

Dobbs leaned toward the bullhorn and tried again.
His amplified voice rang out over the street. "Friends! Fellow Citizens! This is Hanover Dobbs, chairman of the
Safety Committee." The crowd quieted somewhat. "You
have succeeded. We have forced the guards to do their
duty and arrest the Beast. Investigator Auden assures me
that the Beast is in custody even as we speak. He will now
be brought to trial for his heinous crimes." There were a
couple of ragged cheers, and a lot of grumbling murmurs.
"Thank you all for your help. Thanks to you, the city is
now free of this criminal's reign of terror. This calls for a
celebration. Everyone back to the Bar of Gold. First round
is on the house!"

The cheering this time was a little more widespread
and heartfelt. Dobbs backed off from the bullhorn, glared
at Remming. "I won't forget this," he said quietly.

Remming's grin was nasty. "Make sure you don't."

Dobbs moved off, slapping backs and pressing flesh,
hurrying people along toward his bar.

Auden had seen Remming step up behind Dobbs; he
knew Remming had to be responsible for the troublemak-
ing barkeep's abrupt change of heart, and had a good idea
how the suspended guard had probably accomplished it. A
bulge in Remming's jacket told Auden the man was armed.
Technically guards weren't supposed to carry firearms
when they were suspended, but Auden couldn't blame the
guy. Not the way things were just now in the city.

The two men eyed each other as the mob slowly dispersed; the guards remaining started to relax. Auden stepped closer to Remming. "You want to earn back the respect of the guard?" he asked quietly. "Got an assignment for you. Could easily get you killed, but it's yours if you want it."

"Doing what?"

"Playing bait for the Beast."

Remming thought for a moment, then shrugged. "Fine," he said. "Let's do it."

Auden was heading back to his own runabout and his now cold gyro when the Railwalker arrived.

John Hamblin stowed the flask away in his pocket, confident that the waitress had not seen him tip a measure of hooch into his coffee. In this Hamblin was mistaken. Hamblin's habit of drinking while on duty was an open secret amongst the employees of the various diners and restaurants he frequented on his rounds.

Hamblin was glad to have dodged the bullet. He'd been on an accident when the general call to all units came for a possible riot. By the time the ambulances had left, and he'd finished his report notes and pointed his runabout toward Hallard Street, the all-clear had been called. Now it was almost nine, Hamblin reflected as he took a sip of the fortified coffee, so he'd be off duty soon and could get down to some serious drinking. Technically he was on call tonight, so he should probably stick to vodka, just in case he got called in. There'd be hell to pay if Robles, or gods forbid Gage, smelled liquor on his breath. He scowled down at the brew in his cup, wishing the Ten O'Clock Diner would get themselves some decent Java. This crap couldn't be more than ten percent; it was mostly chicory. The hooch helped a little, though. Eileen placed his fried chicken before him as his radio squawked.

"Two-five-niner, this is Central, over." Guard Central Dispatch, calling his badge number. He frowned. Five minutes before quitting time. This could not be good.

"Hamblin here. Go, Central."

"Your on-call has been called on, Two-five-nine." It

was Miriam on dispatch tonight. "Ten-nineteen for an eleven-eighty-six."

Ten nineteen meant return to headquarters, but Hamblin always had trouble remembering the eleven codes. "Ah, hell Miriam," he said, "speak English. What's up?"

"Special detail, that's all I know. Robles wants you back here ASAP."

"Dammit," he grumbled. "I ain't had a night off in a month." Which wasn't strictly true, but they'd all been pulling extra duty since the Beast started his killings. "Ain't Richardson on call tonight? Get him."

"Already got him, Hamblin. All the on-calls are being pulled in. Just get your lazy butt down here."

He acknowledged and signed off. He knew better than to pump Miriam for more information when something big was going down. The night dispatcher was generally friendly and agreeable, especially since Hamblin often plied her with her favorite chocolate rolls, but when things started hopping she got all rigid and by-the-book. He sighed and signaled for the waitress. "Can you wrap this for me, honey? I gotta run. Duty calls."

Hamblin took a shot of breath spray, just in case the smell of the hooch might be detectable over the chicory coffee. Moments later, the grease of his extra-crispy chicken and fries already beginning to stain the bottom of the bag, he marched out the door of the Ten O'Clock Diner to find his runabout missing.

"What the blazin' hells?" He looked up and down the street and noticed the tail of the runabout just visible in the mouth of the alley a few yards to his right. He wondered who would have the balls to mess with a guard runabout. He scanned the street again, but there were no obvious suspects. "Fuck," he muttered to himself as he clumped down the sidewalk toward the alley.

INTERLUDE: W.S. JACKSON

The Railwalkers were not, of course, the only heroes who answered the call to battle the strange creatures and bizarre phenomena that appeared in the wake of the Crash. Other warrior-shamans arose from the ranks of the Namericans, the Neopagans, Santerians and Mayacans, heroes who are often referred to as Railwalkers, despite their having no connection to the formal Order of the Railwalkers founded by Brick. The most famous among these, however, is from a somewhat later period.

In the twenty-seventh year after the Crash, a woman in the village of Corteone, on the outskirts of Bay City, saw a five-year-old child walking out of the desert zones. The child could not speak, and there was no evidence to give indication of where he had come from.

The woman, one Agnes Jackson, adopted the child as her own and named him William Stuart Jackson. The boy had an unpromising early life. He seemed a slow learner, last in his classes at school, but he grew large and strong, and Agnes Jackson had hopes for a future for her son as a guard, and when he turned eighteen she took him to Bay City.

Young Will was enrolled in the City Guard Academy, barely passing his entrance exam. Then the revenants struck Bay City. Arcidemus, popularly known as the Revenant King, was a sorcerer who began his career as a Ravager in the zones. He gathered to himself an army of the living dead, and in 145 A.C. he moved on Bay City. The city guard was totally unprepared, and the city very nearly fell in the first day. Many guard officers, as well as the city boss, were killed.

It was William Stuart Jackson who rallied the remaining guards and, along with students from the academy and a ragtag assembly of citizens, staged a counterat-tack. Rising literally overnight from obscure lower-than-average cadet to city hero, Jackson led his impromptu army to victory over the revenants, killing the sorcerer Arcidemus himself. In the wake of the victory he became City Boss.

By all accounts, Bay City flourished under Jackson's administration. Some years later, Jackson traveled to the City of Two Suns to do battle with a Glaeken, which had arisen from the Chiricahua Mountains to plague the desert city. The tale of Jackson's struggle with the Glaeken would later become a staple of DVs and comanga.

Jackson's war with the Mayacans, however, was an ill-considered step. The Mayacan leader, Juan Zorr, was crafty as well as powerful. Just before the decisive battle of Nogales Jackson was betrayed, ambushed and killed. His quixotic quest and ignoble death left Bay City leader-less, and the city-state fell into chaos and disorder until the rise of the House of Crichton some years later.

Randall Cottone
Creatures of Chaos:
Heroes and Monsters of the Post-Crash Years
Historica Books, Gatesville, 0326

I arrived late to the party. When I reached Hallard Street, there was little sign of any impending lynching. There were still a couple of guard vehicles pulled up on the sidewalk blocking access to the City Arms apartments, and uniformed guards stood behind them. In the street, however, only a handful of people milled about, reluctantly deserting the scene. In front of the guard vehicles I saw Auden, bullhorn at his side, talking quietly to another guy in plain clothes. As I approached them I recognized Cort Remming, the purported ringleader of the guards who'd jumped me the other night. We eyed each other for a moment, then he turned and walked away.

"You missed all the fun," said Auden.

"Was Remming involved in this?" I asked him.

"No," he said. "In fact, he may have saved our bacon. I'm pretty sure he had a gun on Dobbs, forced him to back down."

"Really?"

"No shit. You should probably know, I offered him a piece of the action at tomorrow night's shindig. He's a dead ringer for Jim Shaw." We'd be substituting guards for Roth's friends Shaw, Carter, Weldt, Armstrong, and Tyburn. I'd seen a photo of Shaw in his file. Auden was right. Remming had the same bullet head and wide, sloping shoulders. We still needed to find an appropriate ringer for Weldt. There weren't many female guards anywhere near the policy advisor's size, and we were contemplating putting a male guardsman in drag.

"Well," I said, "that would be Gage's call. As long as Remming can contain his dislike of us and not let it interfere with the job, I won't object if Gage doesn't."

"Appreciate that," Auden said, his face expressionless. I wondered if not for his severe sense of duty, would he have been tempted to join Remming and his cronies in trying to teach the outsider a lesson. If so, I'd have to get past that resentment somehow. As the Wolf Spirit had reminded me, this was a hunt, and on a hunt you have to utilize the skills of the whole pack. "The strength of the pack is the wolf, and the strength of the wolf is the pack," as the old saying tells. Whether I liked it or not, Auden was part of our pack for this particular hunt.

Two guardsmen came down the front steps with a tall man between them. He had dark, curly hair and glasses, and didn't look much like a mutant of any sort. The heavyset guardsman said to Auden, "It's his daytime disguise. We thought he'd be safer if he wore it." I looked a question at Auden.

He almost smiled. "Dobbs thought Dr. Cordoba here was the Beast because he goes around disguised as a normal."

"I'm no murderer," the doctor said sullenly. "And dressing as a normal isn't illegal."

"You're not under arrest, Doc," said Auden. "Not yet, anyway. At the moment you're in protective custody. Consider yourself lucky. You could be strung up by the neck about now." He nodded to the guards, who escorted Cordoba to the car. "We'll check out his alibis," Auden said to me, "but I don't expect he's gonna look very good for it."

I had to agree. Nothing about Dr. Cordoba suggested he was our Beast, whatever Hanover Dobbs might think. Auden's communicator buzzed. He pulled it out, listened for a minute. "Who's on call?" he asked. Listened again. "Okay, send 'em to the Allworld Temple. I'll swing by Tyburn's place and then meet them there." He signed off and stowed the radio.

"They haven't been able to locate Tyburn," he said. "He's not at his office, not answering his page. He's supposed to be conducting services at his temple about now, but they haven't heard from him either." Guards had been assigned to all five of the people we considered the Beast's next most likely targets, but Tyburn's guards hadn't found him yet.

"Byer leave, I'll come along," I said. "The Beast is about. I think I saw him briefly a few blocks from here."

"And you didn't nab him?"

"Like you did?" Auden nodded, a wry look on his face. I gestured to his runabout. "I'll fill you in on the way."

He signaled two of the uniforms to join us, and I followed him to his transport.

Tyburn's home was a large townhouse in Thornhill, which he shared with four other Allworlders. One of his roommates had arrived home moments before we got there, so we didn't have to break in. The roommate, a sharp-faced, petite woman in jeans and a synthleather jacket, opened the door for us and stood back. The house was impressive, lots of synthwood paneling and antique carpets, fancy home theater and an office full of computer equipment. No signs of violence, but no sign of Tyburn, either.

The roommate didn't seem too concerned. "He's been having runabout trouble," she said. "He's probably broke down somewhere." When Auden raised a skeptical eyebrow, she added, "His runabout's a piece of crap. He doesn't maintain it. He could afford to fix it, or get a newer one, but he never gets around to doing anything about it. Procrastination's his middle name."

We left one of the patrol guards on watch there and headed for the Allworld Temple, keeping an eye out for a broken down runabout on the way.

About halfway between Thornhill and City Center, the Allworld Temple wasn't as big as some of the old Christer cathedrals, but it was bigger than most churches and temples. The outside was all granite and marble pillars, wide stone steps leading up to the massive brass-bound doors.

The service had apparently just ended. Allworlders of every race and station were filing out and down the steps. We made our way up the steps against the current. For all their apparent weight and size, the doors swung open easily.

Inside, the granite and marble gave way to synthwood paneling and wall-to-wall carpet. The vestibule looked more like an expensive club than a temple. We stepped into the Circle Chamber. It was a large, circular room, several levels leading down to a central platform upon which stood a round, silk-draped altar. On the altar were a large crystal bowl of water and several silver goblets for the Watersharing. The carpeted levels leading down to the altar featured scattered cushions and pillows. Here and there Allworlders were still sharing water, some in quiet conversation, a few in even more intimate activities. The Allworlders are a cuddly, touchy-feely bunch.

Tyburn stood at the altar, wiping down the goblets and putting them into one of several velvet-lined wooden cases. Another Allworld priest gathered up goblets from around the room. Just inside the entrance to the Circle Chamber stood two more guards, the on-calls Auden had sent here earlier: a black fellow whose name tag read Calder and a plump white guy I'd earlier been introduced to as Hamblin.

"They said he wasn't here?" Auden said.

Calder shrugged. "He was here when we got here."

"You talk with him yet?"

"The service just ended," said Calder. "We figured better not to interrupt."

The four of us approached the altar. Auden and I stepped up onto the dais; Hamblin and Calder stopped at the edge of it. Calder just stood there, thumbs in his belt, but Hamblin struck a parade rest pose, hands behind his back. It was more formal than necessary, but maybe he wanted to earn back some credit, seeing how Czernoff had been killed practically under his nose.

"Brother Tyburn," I said. "We need to talk."

"Certainly." The Allworlder smiled. "I just have to finish up here."

"We have reason to believe," said Auden, "that you're the killer's next target."

"Me?" Tyburn paused in his wiping and packing. "I

don't understand. Is it because I found Phillip's body?"

"We're not at liberty to explain why," I told him. "But please trust us. We have our reasons."

Auden nodded over his shoulder. "These are Guardsman Calder and Guardsman Hamblin. They, or others who'll relieve them later, will be with you at all times over the next few days, until we determine that you're out of danger."

"Excuse me," Tyburn said. "I just have to put these away, and I'll be right with you." He picked up several of the wooden cases.

"I'll help you with that," said Hamblin. He grabbed up the remaining two cases, then followed Tyburn to a door at the back of the chamber.

"You going to try to get him into the security suite at the Tower?" I asked Auden. Gage had spoken of moving all the potential victims into the VIP guest suites in the CA Tower for the next two days.

"I'll offer him the option," Auden said. "Shaw's there, but Carter refused." Weldt already lived in a suite in the City Administration Tower.

Tyburn's scream sent all three of us tearing across the room. Auden was first, I was close behind him, with Calder taking up the rear. Just outside the door Tyburn and Hamblin had stepped through was a short hall. A cupboard stood open at the near end, the wooden boxes of goblets piled in it, one smashed open on the floor. At the far end of the hall lay Tyburn. The wall above him was splashed with his blood. Hamblin was nowhere to be seen. We raced to Tyburn's side. Auden slid to his knees as he reached him, groping for a pulse. At that end the hall turned right and led to an exit door. There was a smear of blood on the crash bar. I headed for it.

"Tyburn's dead," Auden said to Calder. "Hamblin is MIA. We're in pursuit. Call it in!"

I was already out the door. In the alley I caught a flash of movement as Hamblin went over the fence at the far end. Hamblin was not MIA, I thought as I raced down the alley. He's probably dead, and we're in pursuit of a shapeshifter who's assumed his appearance. I sprang up, catching the top of the fence and hauling myself over it. I found myself in a sort of courtyard with multiple alleys running off it. Hamblin—or the Beast—was already at the other end, vanishing into an alley. I followed. Out of the alley, across the street, runabout horns blaring. The Beast actually cat-vaulted over one runabout and slipped into another alleyway. He was shifting as he ran. He'd shifted his hands to claws earlier; that was why he'd kept his hands behind him in the parade rest position. Even now he was already larger in the torso and shoulders than Hamblin, his tunic unbuttoned or torn loose and flapping behind him.

It would still be a while before he could shift completely to the form Auden had seen. Shifting while you're running, that would take a lot of concentration, I thought, as I pounded down the alley to find an even taller board fence. I made it three steps up the fence with a dash jump, caught the top with my hands, and reverse-vaulted over. I came off sideways to rebound off a mound of dirt, roll, and come up running. I was in a construction site, and the Beast had already reached the other side. Some of the framework of the building had started to go up, but there was no floor as yet, just the gaping pit of the basement, divided by retaining walls like a rat maze seen from above. I ran out on the top of one of the basement walls.

The trick of running on top of a wall is you don't slow down, and you don't look down. Keep your eye on the way ahead, trust your peripheral vision to place your feet. I had to change direction twice, but still made it across in half the time I would have by going around.

The Beast had already climbed the fence on the other side, jumped from the top of it to a fire escape on the next building, and was climbing upwards. There was a crane parked on that side of the lot. Its top end looked to be only five feet or so from the roof of the building the Beast was climbing. I didn't stop to think. I didn't dare, or I'd never do it; I just clambered up the crane's arm as quickly as I could, eyes forward. At the top I checked my footing, then spotted for the jump. From there it looked closer to ten feet to the top fire escape. The Beast was already there, scrambling from the fire escape onto the roof. I gathered my will as well as my strength with a deep breath and put everything I could into the leap.

I was airborne and weightless for long moments before I realized I wasn't going to make it across. My hands didn't even brush the edge of the railing. From below, the next level of the fire escape leaped up to meet me, catching me in the midsection. The wind knocked out of me, I grabbed desperately, upper arms over the rail, body hanging down, swinging, feet scrambling for purchase. I hauled myself over the rail, let myself exult for just a split second as my diaphragm opened up so I could breathe again. I was on the next to last level of the fire escape. I headed up the last flight of metal stairs to the roof.

Damn! All that, and I'd hardly gained on him at all. He was already going off the other side of the roof. I ran after. At the other side there was a gap of only six feet or so, and a drop of closer to eight to the next roof. Below and beyond, the Beast was weaving his way through the maze of air vents, Tesla receivers, and solar collectors. I leaped, hit the roof and rolled, came up running.

The next building, slightly higher, was further away. The alley was eight or ten feet across, and I wasn't sure if I could make the jump even with a running start. The Beast made it fairly easily, catching on with his hands and monkey-vaulting up and onto the higher roof. I veered, jumping onto a solar collector near the edge to gain a little more height, sped up as I approached, leaped again, managed to catch the cornice of the next roof.

I didn't quite translate my forward momentum the way the Beast had. I had to muscle myself up, but I was gaining now. This was a flat roof, covered by gardens.

I couldn't see the next building until I reached the next ledge. It was much lower, and closer. I saw him hit and roll. I did a reverse vault, hanging from the cornice again to minimize the height before I dropped. The move might cost me what little ground I'd gained, but I couldn't stay in the chase if I broke an ankle landing.

This would be the last building on the block. There was nowhere to go now but down into the street. He went over at the corner. I raced after him, and looked down. We were now three stories up. He was clambering down a vertical sign mounted on the corner of the building. A perfect target, and for a second I considered using my gun. But Auden's shots had barely phased him, and if mine had no more effect, he'd lengthen his lead. Over I went.

As I shifted from building to sign and began scrambling down, I could hear guard sirens approaching. How they knew where we were was beyond me, but I couldn't worry about that now. The sign, not made for climbing on, was vibrating, and the metal supports cut at my hands. I kept glancing down to keep track of him. He reached the street and tore off westward.

A runabout braked to avoid hitting him, and the truck behind it couldn't brake fast enough. It swerved over the curb and I chose my moment, jump-falling the last ten or twelve feet to the truck's roof. The force of the impact drove me to hands and knees, and the truck's brakes chose that moment to bring the thing to a shuddering halt. With no traction or purchase, I went tumbling over the truck's cab, bounced off the hood. Pavement rushing up, a flash of lightning as I tucked and rolled. I barely managed to come up running. It had been too many sharp impacts now; my head was throbbing. This wasn't good. When your one rule is keep moving, you can ignore a whole lot until later. Keep moving, Railwalker. Take care o' business. The truck driver was shouting behind me. I probably left a serious dent in the hood, but the city could afford it. I wasn't about to stop and give him a number to call to lodge his claim.

I dodged more runabouts, made the other sidewalk of the cross street. We were on Alameda. The Beast was halfway down the next block, vanishing into another alley. I was on him, I was right there... But the dead end alley was empty except for a bulkhead with the city crest on the door. Yeah, unless the sucker could fly, he was in there.

I jerked the door open to find a flight of steps leading down. I plunged down the steps. At the bottom, straight ahead, a blank plascrete wall. Tunnels led away left and right. I chose right. That was west, toward the water, the direction he'd been heading all along. Ten steps along I hit a cross tunnel. I stood in the tunnel, my eyes closed. Faint sounds, yes, receding footsteps, to my left. Within just a few paces, I had to slow. The faint glow from the bulkhead door I'd left open didn't travel far once the corner was turned, and this new tunnel quickly became pitch black. I could hear only the faintest scuffling further down the tunnel as I edged forward. Ahead, a slightly rectangular gray blur against the black. A shadow moved across it. It could have been something else interrupting the light source. The Beast could be lying in wait for me in the darkness somewhere between here and there, but my gut told me not. That was him, the shadow I'd seen. I hurried my pace.

The gray blur resolved into a much bigger cross tunnel as I reached it. It was a tramway line, two sets of tracks, a faint green dot to my right. That would be back uphill, toward City Center. To my left there was a definite glow. I went left, toward the water again. The green light behind me told me no trams would come from that direction. Anything rolling on this track I'd see coming.

I could see well enough to run again, and set off down the plascrete walkway beside the gravel track bed. The air was damp and smelled of the ocean. This tunnel had to date way back; the big I-beams between the tracks and along the walls were not plasteel or graphcomp, but actual steel, studded with large rivets, multiple layers of paint peeling to reveal blackened metal and rust. The rails were gleaming silver lines running between them.

As I got closer to the bright glow ahead it resolved into the tunnel's mouth, an arched opening showing a view of the docks and the bay beyond. In the center of the picture was the silhouette of a running figure, veering left. I leaped from the walkway, crossing the tracks, following his lead.

Outside, the tracks curved sharply to parallel Water Street, one going left, one right. He broke into sunlight, crossing the left-hand track. I put on a burst of speed and hit sunlight, heard the train. I wasn't even close to making it across as the tram cut off my sight of him. I slowed my run, counting cars, seven of 'em, and then I was across the tracks. He was still in sight, pelting across Water Street and down the quay between a docked cargo vessel to one side and the open water on the other. Crossing Water Street, dodging another runabout, with the tram and its noise vanishing into the tunnel, I could hear the sirens again. Yep, he did just what I was afraid he'd do, dammit. When I reached the end of the dock, I dove in right after him.

The water wasn't as cold as I'd expected, but it was still a shock. Under the surface, treading water, I looked desperately around. The water was pretty clear. No sign of him.

When I came up for air I realized I was done here. I had blown it. In the time it would take to get an organized search of the area going, he'd be long gone. For all I knew he was growing gills and swimming away underwater at that very moment.

There was no convenient ladder at this end of the dock, so I had to swim the length of the ship back toward land to find one. When I reached it the thing was slick and hard to get a purchase. I reached the street level to find several guard runabouts parked at the entrance to the dock, and Auden approaching across the tarmac. I sat down on the asphalt, catching my breath, still seeing an occasional white flash. Seawater running from my clothes formed a puddle around me.

Auden stopped a couple of feet away. "Lost him?" he asked.

"Looks like."

"Probably no point in searching, but I'll put a few men on it anyway." He barked orders at the uniforms coming up behind him. They hurried away.

I looked at Auden. "How'd you get here?" I asked.

"I kept you in sight from the street until you went into the tunnels. That bulkhead accesses a maintenance tunnel for the Water Street line. Unless he doubled back on himself, he was going to end up here." He took a case from his pocket, took out a cigar.

"And if he did double back?" I asked.

"I sent men to Point Street Station, just in case. But my bet was here."

"Your bet paid off. For whatever that's worth."

"Yeah," he said, lighting the cigar. "I'll be sure to put my winnings in my retirement fund." He fished in his overcoat pocket, pulled out a small package. Looked like a paper-wrapped sandwich. "They found John Hamblin, you know. His dead body was stuffed in a dumpster over on fifth." He looked down again at the package in his hand. "Fuck," he muttered, and threw the package hard at a nearby trash can. It hit the side, and the contents splattered over the pavement. I was right, it had been a gyro. He sighed, walked over and picked up the paper, dropped it in the can. The gulls would take care of the rest. I could see one eyeing the remains of the sandwich already.

"Lost my appetite anyway," Auden growled. "What I really want is a drink. Four years without a drop, and the goddamn Beast drives me back to it. You want a drink, Railwalker?"

"Yeah. But it doesn't sound like a healthy choice for you," I said.

"Fuck that," he grunted. "I'll worry about healthy when the Beast is in the ground."

I couldn't tell the guy how to live his life. But an alcoholic is not the man you want at your back. Not when he's drinking, anyway. I stood. The lightning flashes had backed off, and my head was pounding a little more softly. I really did want a drink, but it probably wouldn't help the headache. The hell with it, I thought. The Beast has killed Tyburn and gotten away; there's little enough more we can do tonight.

"I haven't eaten yet," I said. "I'll join you for that

drink, if you'll join me in a meal." He nodded. I added, "But so help me, the day you fail to back one of us up because you're drunk, it will become my mission to make your life a living hell. Assuming I'm alive to do that."

"Fair enough."

Auden's runabout held a spare set of clothes, jeans and a sweatshirt. The jeans were a little long for me, and the sweatshirt a little tight across the shoulders, but they'd do well enough for grabbing a bite to eat. My boots still squelched a bit, leaving damp footprints behind, but I could live with that for an hour or two. Auden knew of a place not far away, said it looked like a dive but served excellent burgers and moderately good whiskey. He was right on both counts. We demolished the burgers quickly, Auden's appetite apparently having returned. When we sat back with our coffee and drinks Auden's look was evaluating.

"Tell me something," he said. "Byer leave, I get the impression you've dealt with Boss Roth before. But I haven't seen a Railwalker in Bay City for many years, and then it wasn't you. How and when did you meet Roth?"

I told him.

I was about twelve when my Pa nearly lost me to Wendell Crichton in a card game.

Until that happened, I never quite knew what I really meant to my Pa. Sometimes he'd call me his "lucky charm" and swear the only times he won were when I was with him. Other times he went the other way, claiming I jinxed his luck, made him lose. I never knew if he was going to insist I sit by him through a whole night of gaming, and I'd be nodding off to the low murmur of men's voices growling out bets and the smell of hooch and tobacco, or whether I'd be sent out to sit alone in a parking lot behind some anonymous bar or casino, waiting for him to come collect me when the games finally ran down. It was pretty confusing for a kid. It seemed like I was somehow responsible for whatever the Fates threw at my father, good or bad. That's a heavy load for a kid to carry, especially when your Pa loses more often than he wins.

Pa had been on a bad losing streak that spring when we rolled into Bay City. Did I say "rolled"? I misspoke. We walked. Pop had lost the jeep back in some berg or other; I don't remember the name. I do remember the place had only one small bar where the games went on, where Pa had been playing with hard men who smelled of animals and grain. We left there riding on a donkey who could barely carry the two of us. Pa lost that animal in the next town over, which I remember was called Sitio Ancho because it sure didn't look much like a city to me. From there we ended up walking into Bay City, which did look like a city, in spades. I don't know who Pa got to stake him to the first couple of games he played in Bay City, but he must have found someone, since his losing streak, if it didn't turn to winning, at least eased up some. We had a room where the roaches would actually run and hide if you turned on the light, instead of hissing at you to back off and get out of their face.

I guess I've been presenting a kind of one-sided picture of my father here. I've been citing all the bad stuff, and none of the good. It wasn't like he was an evil man. He never mistreated me, not really. Oh, he walloped me a few times. Sometimes I probably even deserved it. Now and then, when he was losing regular, and drunk, he might light into me for no other reason than that I was a convenient target. But if he was stupid and unconscious sometimes, and a slave to his addiction, he could also be wonderfully charming and loving and generous, too. He had what my profs at the Railwalker Academy called "the glamour." I've seen him lose money he never had to men who would have killed you for looking at them wrong, and not only escape with his life, but charm them into lending him tram fare to get home. That's how we ended up with that donkey.

Still, life with my Pa wasn't all roaches and sticky carpets and dingy sheets. I've been talking mainly about his losses, but he sometimes won big, too. There were times we spent weeks in the most expensive hotels in the western cities, catered to by uniformed servants, and indulged in whatever fancies crossed our minds. When Pa was on a winning streak, nothing was too good for his kid. And because he did have his winning streaks, and he knew how to work them, my Pa had a reputation in the gambling community. Which meant that when the chips were down, he could sometimes get into high-stakes games on nothing more than his name, and his winning smile.

I can't say I know it for a fact, but I can guess that that's probably how he got into that game in Bay City that time. If you'd made a list of the players sitting at the table that night, except for my father, your average Bay City resident would have assumed it was some sort of high-level city conference. And for all I know, it may have been; there were many games my father attended where much more than just gambling went on. You've heard the cliché about how deals are made in smoke-filled rooms... Well, my father and I were there for many of those deals. We weren't parties to the negotiations, just to the card games, games which served as the excuse for certain persons of power to gather together in an informal setting.

This particular night there were many powerful men present, and a couple of women, but I would remember only two of them. One was Wendell Crichton. The other was Micah Roth.

Pa was losing badly that night. I could tell by the way his leg was twitching. Not that I couldn't have followed the play—by the age of nine, I knew the games and the odds almost as well as my Pa did. Poker, jackflash, crops, round-about, you name it, I knew it. But I wasn't really following the play, not in any conscious, intentional way. Tired and sleepy, sitting on the floor by my father's chair where he could touch my head for luck now and then, the leg told me all I needed to know. Pa was not doing well.

I came alert again when I heard my father say my name. He wasn't addressing me, he was talking to one of the other players. "He's a good boy," I heard him say. "Smart, industrious, worth a fuck of a lot more than twelve K."

Alarm bells went off in my head as I realized suddenly what was happening. I now knew exactly what my father thought I was worth: twelve thousand bucks.

"No," said another voice. "I'll cover."

"I didn't hear the man ask for anyone to cover for him," said another.

I dragged myself to my feet, looked around the table. It was clear immediately what was happening. The others had all dropped out. It was down to my father and the two men who had spoken. One was big, blond, and balding, with the face of a man used to getting what he wants; the other was smaller, but denser, with the build of a boxer, lank black hair, piercing eyes, and thick, stubby fingers, a man who looked used to physical labor. I would later learn that the blond man was Wendell Crichton, the boss of Bay City, and the darker man was Micah Roth, head of the Federation of Labor Unions. At that time, however, to me, they were simply the Dark Man and the Light Man. And intuitively, I knew that the Dark Man was on my side, while the Light Man was an enemy.

The atmosphere around the table crackled like static on a frigid day in February. Everyone was staring at my Pa. I looked at him too. He glanced at me, then back at the other players. At last he said, "Sure. Thanks, Micah. I appreciate it. I'll accept your cover."

The blond man looked disappointed, and the dark man didn't exactly look pleased, either.

Later, as we were leaving the place, the dark man approached us. My Pop started to voice his thanks again, but the dark man, Micah Roth, put him up against the wall of the building, his forearm across my Pa's throat.

"Spare me your thanks, arsehole," he said. "And know this. I may not be able to track all your movements, all your games and all your bets, but I will have the word out to watch you. And if you ever wager away this child's life again, and I hear of it, I will find you, and I will make you regret it. Do you understand me?"

Pa nodded, so far as he was able with Roth's forearm pinning his neck to the wall. Roth released my father, glanced briefly at me, then walked away.

Seven years later, at the age of sixteen, I left my Pa and went to work with a construction company in Santa Brita. It took me another three years to save up that twelve thousand, but I finally did it. When I had the total amount I traveled down to Bay City and looked up Micah Roth. By that time the People's Takeover had happened, and Roth was now the City Boss in place of Wendell Crichton.

As it turned out, it took some doing to reach Roth, even with the money I had to offer. When I finally made it past the secretaries and official filters and dropped the cash on Roth's desk, it was clear that he remembered me and my Pa, and what this was all about.

"You didn't have to do this," he said.

"Yes," I said, "I did."

He examined me with that laser gaze for long moment, and then said, "Yeah. I understand why you did. Thank you."

"We square?" I asked.

"Yeah, we're definitely square."

"Good." I walked out of his office.

Auden had listened quietly to my story. When I'd finished, he nodded. "Yeah," he said, "that sounds like Micah Roth."

"Funny," I said. "I paid off my old man's debt, but I still feel like I owe Roth something."

"Yeah," he said. Took a sip of his drink. "That kind of thing, it's about more than money. Roth and Adams both stood behind me when I needed it. You can't ask more than that from a boss." I looked my question at him. He made a sound somewhere between a chuckle and a snort. "What," he said, "you don't know? Well, it's not like it's some kind of secret. It was all over the newsfeeds at the time."

30. AUDEN

My Da was a guardsman, back in the day. You probably know the guard were divided over the Takeover. Lots of 'em had had their fill of Wendell Crichton. Anton Robles, George Adams, and my Da among 'em. This bunch of buds fought alongside Roth and his people. When the fighting was over they formed the core of the new city guard. Da retired from the guard not long after that. Wasn't a long retirement. His heart got him within a couple of years.

My younger brother, Clay, he was always a heartache to Da. All kids go through that rebellious shit, but Clay never grew out of it. Ran with a rough crowd—Bar of Gold, Danny's Place, that sort of thing. In the days after the Takeover, the loyalists who stayed in the city gravitated to the rougher streets, so Clay ended up hanging with that sort, too. Said some harsh things about our Da, and the guards, and Roth now and then. 'Course, that was other people talking through him, I knew that. Clay wasn't ever a thinker, a reader, the type to make speeches. He just memorized bits and pieces of his favorite loudmouth's screed. He was like one of them guys chop up bits of other people's music and make a song out of it. But then, some of them guys actually come out with some cool stuff. They apply some creativity, where with Clay, it was just regurgitated pap, y'know?

Anyway, that's neither here nor there. Kid had a good heart. But he lost it somewhere along the way. There was this loyalist cell, called themselves the Bay City Traditionalist Wing—most called 'em the City Trads—that Clay got involved with. Jeff Coltrin, they called him Fariff, the leader of the City Trads, he'd turned them from being a fringe political party into practically a religious cult. He used hypnotic indoctrination, drugs, sex, whatever worked best for the mark he was brainwashing. He got Clay hooked on crackers. I knew the kid was doing them; you can't miss the shakes crackers give you. But what could I do? Give him a talking-to as his older brother? Like he was gonna listen to that, right? Don't think I didn't try.

Long story short, one afternoon, we got a tip-off. The Trads were planning to assassinate Mears. He was a famous Labor leader who was about to set off on a five city-state tour. I got the call; I went out with a squad, met with Mears's people as they were about to set out. It was our responsibility to escort him to the intercity train station. After that he was somebody else's problem, right?

The City Trads, they decided to take him at the station.

There was a Railwalker in town about that time... I think he did the Mayday Ceremony. Big strapping blond guy named Baze. Kinda full of himself. Either he had Chief Adams convinced he was hot shit, or Adams let him think he had. Either way, he was with us when our people arrived at the station.

When the hit came down, the City Trads had maybe a half dozen in the field. Real amateurs. They tried to look like regular travelers, but they were sending off signals like they might as well have carried neon signs. My guys took 'em down, no problem. Except one of 'em, he grabbed a hostage, this six-year-old girl. He was holding a gun to her head. And as I got a little closer, I could see it was Clay.

Now, I was thinking like Clay was still in there somewhere. If I could talk to him, I could get him to see how he shouldn't be doing this, how this little girl is innocent. She has nothing to do with his fight; he's gonna be betraying his own cause if he hurts her, right? I mean, can the cause really call itself righteous if they murder innocent kids? I still think I might have stood a chance to talk him down.

But before I could even move, Railwalker Baze stepped up, and he walked toward Clay and the kid, talking to him the whole time, putting a Force in his voice, working on Clay, trying to get him to stand down. What he didn't realize is, that kind of voice trick, it wasn't gonna work on this kid, 'cause he'd already been brainwashed. Fariff had got his mind in a steel trap, and nobody else was getting a finger between those jaws. Not with fancy esoteric mind tricks, anyway. All Baze did was piss him off.

I looked at my brother's face, holding his gun on this girl, and our eyes met. And I saw my brother wasn't there any more. I wasn't looking into Clay's eyes, I was looking into the eyes of a disease, an addiction, a sickness. And I knew that that sickness meant he was not getting out of there alive. And I knew, I absolutely knew, that he was going to take that little girl with him when he went.

He raised the gun and capped off a shot at the Railwalker, which knocked him down.

Before he could bring the weapon to bear on the kid again, I shot him through the forehead.

Clay wasn't really a good shot, so he had only winged the Railwalker. The kid was fine. Mears came out of it with his hair barely ruffled. Newsfeeds had a field day with it, of course. Most called me a hero, and some—the more loyalist-oriented—made a lot out of the fact he was my brother.

Auden was silent for a while.

Finally, I said, "I'm sorry about your brother. And I'm sorry one of our order interfered."

"Baze was a dickhead," said Auden.

"Yeah, probably," I said. "The order isn't perfect. We can't avoid that entirely."

"Avoid what?"

"A few dickheads taking the tats now and then."

Auden snorted. "I guess you can't. The guard has our share of dickheads, too. As you discovered."

"I won't hold that against you, if you won't hold it against me."

"Fair enough."

We were both silent for a while, wrapped in our own thoughts.

"Y'know," said Auden finally, "I tell myself that my brother died long before that day. That what I killed was a disease, a monster. But even if he was really my brother at his core, the monster was gonna make him kill that kid. I couldn't let him do that, could I?

"No, you couldn't."

"Don't change the fact that I killed my own kin."

There wasn't anything I could say to that.

31. BAY CITY

Nita Robles stood in the door of the locker room, looking into the gym, watching the female Railwalker, Morgan, work out. She had been doing sword work. She didn't work with the wooden bokkan or shinai that were racked on the wall, but Iado-style, with her own steel sword. Robles admired her moves. She was fast and slick, faster than most swordsmen or women Robles had seen. The city guard were drilled in sword work, and wore swords with their dress uniforms. It was one of the weapons they had to qualify with, but it wasn't a preferred weapon. Most guards carried batons and guns, and trained most heavily at baton and hand-to-hand. Robles was the odds-on favorite in the inter-city competitions coming up this fall.

After a while Morgan set her sword aside and began her empty-hand kata. Robles watched with interest. The woman had power, no doubt about that, a lithe strength. Her moves showed some influence of Baritsu, but were mostly derived from a hard style: Shotokan, Nita thought, or perhaps Kyoku. After watching for a while, as the Railwalker finished one set of kata, Robles walked into the gym and to the edge of the mat. The Railwalker nodded with an inviting gesture. The guardswoman stepped onto the mat and the two bowed again and squared off.

Robles let the woman come to her. Since the Railwalker's kata had been hard style, Robles stayed soft, avoiding, circling, redirecting attacks. 'Kido and wado moves mostly, the adjustment of vectors, use of the opponent's strength and energy against them. When she thought she'd taken the Railwalker's measure, gotten a sense of her personal style, Nita shifted to offense and moved in on her. Kicking, punching, blocking, the two women pursued each other across the mat. Nita moved in for a one-two combination and Morgan stepped inside it. There was a flurry of knees and elbows, stunning blows, and Robles was slammed to the mat. Morgan knelt above her, poised for a killing stroke, as the guardswoman slapped out.

They stayed frozen for a moment, Nita Robles glaring up at Railwalker Morgan. Since she'd won her first black belt at eighteen, no one had ever taken Robles down that easily. The Railwalker's eyes were steady and level, revealing no emotion.

Nita Robles began to laugh. "That," she said, "was cool. Show me."

Morgan smiled, stood, and handed the guardswoman up. "The close-in stuff comes mostly from the later pre-Crash street systems like Keysi and Bakbakan," she said. "You want to really learn that style, you should talk to Rok. He's amazing with it. But yeah, I can show you a few things."

They spent the next half hour with Morgan coaching Robles through some of the moves she'd used, and some other techniques. Robles was a fast learner, and despite the fact that much of what Morgan showed her was very different from the fighting styles she was used to, she took to it instinctively.

Later, their hair damp from the showers, Robles and Morgan stood in the locker room dressing, the Railwalker in her tunic with the crow patch on the shoulder, Robles into civvies for her lit class.

"So," Robles asked, "you're married to Railwalker Rok?"

"Uh-huh," Morgan confirmed.

"How long?"

"Twelve years."

"You must have still been at the Academy when you married."

Morgan nodded. "Yep."

Nita sighed inwardly. After the workout session, she'd

thought she might be able to establish a connection, get some friendly camaraderie going with Morgan. That might still be possible, but she could see the Railwalker was going to make her work for it. "Are there many married Railwalker couples?"

"A few." Morgan looked at the guardswoman, then sat on the bench stuffing her workout clothes into a small duffle. "Not many of them are out on the routes, though."

"So how's it happen you guys get lucky?"

The look the Railwalker shot her suggested Nita was on the verge of prying, but after a moment she answered. "I was a couple of years behind Rok and Wolf at the Academy. We got married just before the two of them took over the north shore route, with another Prof, a guy named Sparks. A year or so later they lost Sparks in a firefight outside Redmond. You probably know, numbers are down in the order these days..."

"Yeah," said Robles, "you don't see Railwalkers around that much. Not like in my Dad's day."

"Right. There's not many full teams left, and the order doesn't pressure a team to replace a lost member."

"They don't get assigned by the order?"

"The order makes recommendations, but it's up to the team to make a final decision. Wolf and Rok waited until they could request me."

"So, the other guy, Wolf, what's his story?"

Morgan chuckled and raised an eyebrow. "Depends on what you're looking for."

Robles looked away, embarrassed in spite of herself. She hadn't thought she was being that transparent, but she should have known better.

"You're not exactly his usual type, but I'm sure you could catch his eye if you put your mind to it. Question is, do you really want that?"

"Why? What's his usual type?"

"Blond, busty, and brainless. Disposable. He likes to fuck 'em and forget 'em."

Robles' chin went up. "Yeah? Well, that gives us something in common, I guess."

"Really?" Morgan looked at the other woman with a question in her eyes.

"Well, you must know how it is," Robles said. "Career guards don't usually do too well with marriage. I forget the exact numbers, but something like eighty, ninety percent end up in divorce. No surprise, really. It's gotta suck, being married to a guard. Civilians never understand us, no matter how hard they try. They don't know what it's like, being in this life. And it's the same thing with us as with you. It could all end in a second. With you, married to your partner, at least the chances are you'll be with him when it happens. Could you stand it if you were sitting at home, never knowing when you're gonna get that call, knowing you could be going to a funeral tomorrow?

"Anyway, I figure the odds are against me. No percentage in looking for Mr. Right. If I did find him, it would probably end up a disaster. So I became the queen of one night stands."

"Yeah," Morgan said. "I guess that's one way to deal with it."

"Ooh," said Robles. "Do I detect a tone of bitterness there?"

Morgan's eyes snapped at the other woman, but her voice was calm. "Probably." Her tone said, you got a problem with that?

Nita Robles raised her hands, palm out. "Hey," she said, "none of my business."

Morgan's look softened and she chuckled. "'S'alright. 'S just I still feel bad, y'know? I used to needle Wolf about his shallow relationships. Maybe it had nothing to do with me and what I said, but a few of times he's taken it into his head to get serious about relationships, and every time it turns out to be some psycho bitch who ends up cutting his heart out with a rusty spoon and serving it to him on toast."

Robles thought about that for a minute. "Hey, we all make our own choices."

"I know," said the Railwalker. "The Book of Brick even says something like that. Doesn't stop me feeling bad about the whole thing. I know he'd love to have something like what Rok and I have. But he hasn't got a clue about how to go about getting it, and, frankly, neither do I. Far as I can tell, Rok and I just got totally fuckin' lucky."

"Yeah, maybe," said Robles. "But luck could only put the two of you together. It's the two of you have to keep making it work day by day."

Morgan laughed. "Yeah," she said. "Ain't that the truth?"

His very first memories, of course, were of his Goddess. But very early came Evreyt. Trainer, teacher, window on the world beyond the Cave and the Island, Evreyt bounded his day with rituals and exercises, taught him how to read and how to kill, how to swim and to fish, how to sew clothes and wounds, to cook and to cauterize. At Evreyt's command he would run across the sea rocks at night, never sure when his teacher might appear from the darkness to attack him. He stood for hours holding heavy stones at arm's length while doing his sums, hung from the bar while reciting his histories. He performed pushups, Evreyt kneeling on his back, while he conjugated verbs in Spanglish or Japanese. At times, as he grew older, Evreyt would take him on expeditions to the outer world. Sometimes these trips were exercises in stealth and camouflage, where he would have to move unseen through the darkness, a shadow among shadows, slinking through the desert to slip undetected into barns or even houses, or lurking through Bay City's alleys and tunnels. On other forays they would travel in disguise to the city, at first dressed as father and son, and later as separate characters, Evreyt tracking his progress from a distance. Even when they walked in full view, the object remained the same: to pass unnoticed, to become a part of the background, to hide in plain sight. And always there was the Cave, and the formal training: kata, kumite, jiyu kumite, the forms and the sparring.

If Evreyt was his sun, his surrogate father and mentor, the Goddess was his mother the moon. She appeared almost always late at night, when Evreyt had retired, to share with him the intimate secrets of her magicks: the shifting of form, the re-shaping of bone and muscle. Where Evreyt's histories were dry recitations of facts and dates, his Goddess shared with him magical tales of his own life; tales of her wanderings in human form; stories of his father, a great hero and acolyte of the Goddess, who brought peace and prosperity to the world until he was betrayed and brought low by the Evil One. It was his Goddess who taught him of his true destiny, his lifelong mission to avenge his father's betrayal and restore the Goddess's perfect world.

He was perhaps fourteen when he experienced his first Ritual of Teocatl. Together, he and Evreyt constructed the circle, performed the ablutions and the chants, and Evreyt prepared the sacramental potion. When he had drunk the sacrament, Evreyt retired. The world shifted. The cave, formerly dark, lit by flickering candles, became filled with light. And She came to him, his Goddess, his Moon, his Mother, his Hnahna. He chanted her secret name, and she unfurled the Multiverse for him, immersing him in excruciating joy and pleasure such as he had never imagined possible. When he awoke in the morning he returned to his training with renewed passion. He was a man now, a priest of the Sacred Goddess, an anointed hero.

He trained with Evreyt for another three years. In that time their relationship grew gradually to be strained. He had no idea where Evreyt went when away from the Cave and the island, had no notion of what Evreyt's relationship with the Goddess might be. The man was an acolyte, certainly, but how far was he initiated to the Goddess's service? Surely not far, he thought, for Evreyt was a teacher, not a hero, not a demigod. The thought plagued him.

He was eighteen when he surpassed his master and killed Evreyt in a sparring match. Once the man was dead he was filled with dread, and felt something like guilt for the first time in his life. But soon the Goddess came and blessed him for his courage and wisdom, and told him that this was the sign. It was time for him to travel far from his cave, out into the wide world, to find the House of Katana, where he would complete his training and take his first steps on the road to manifesting his unique destiny.

33. WOLF

So I was going to face a monster tonight.

I was concerned, but not afraid. I've never been afraid of monsters, ghosts, mutants, any of that sort of thing, not even when I was a little kid. Maybe that's because as a kid I felt like a monster myself. Eternal gypsies, an itinerant gambler and his son, we were outsiders everywhere we went, and to be an outsider is already halfway to being a monster. Then I started having those weird experiences: visited by my mother's spirit; followed around by the crows; animals talking to me; visions of the future—or possible futures, like the guy with the suicide jack. Like I say, I never talked to my Pa about any of this. Early on I knew he wouldn't approve. Later on, as I got older and understood more, I was even more certain of that. He had no use for "visions and curses and ever-filled purses, prophecies, potions, and knells," as he quoted once from some old song (damned if I understood what knells might be, but I knew about the rest of those things). Such opinions were adamantine, glistening, sharp edges to his personality. None of that stuff was welcome in his life, thank you very much.

To my child mind this could only mean one thing: if he ever found out about my strange experiences he'd give me away, or leave me somewhere. He wouldn't want me around him if he knew. He'd already nearly gambled me away once. How much could I mean to him?

Chances are good I was wrong. As an adult I realize that blood ties, particularly parent-child ties, can motivate people to transcend their prejudices and fears. And sometimes they don't. The homophobe may put aside his disgust when his own child comes out; but then sometimes he may dispossess and deny his child. So I can't be sure, not a hundred percent. I hadn't spoken with my father since just after I joined the Order, so maybe my childhood fears had been realized after all.

Point is, those fears, that adamant position my Pa took, made me feel the Compleat Monster. Rejected by society as a gypsy kid, rejected by my father (although he didn't realize it) as a weirdo, I was truly damned.

So I never feared the monsters and the spooks. That's not to say I was without any fear. I had plenty of fears in my anxiety closet. Fears of abandonment and isolation (for all I embraced isolation often enough). Fear of water (I died by drowning once as a child and was brought back), fear of dogs. I was petrified of heights at one time. I got over many of those fears just by facing them down. But monsters? Not a problem.

Roth's presence, though, had me fearing for his safety.

It would be a night for monsters, I thought, as I watched the fog begin to rise. The restaurant had been closed since Chief Adams's death, but now floodlights illuminated the long sea grass, the parking lot, the carved wooden Hartshall sign. Below the sign hung a "closed for private party" notice. The building looked like it had been converted from a big old summer house. A wide porch, which could be set with tables in season, ran completely around the place. The first floor held the main dining room, with the smaller dining room running off it to create a fat "L" shape. Inside the angle of the L was the kitchen, which communicated with both dining rooms. Between the kitchen and the main room was the bar. Above, a second floor office and another private dining room opened to a mezzanine overlooking the main room.

Trying to make the whole affair look as natural as possible, Roth and the three ringers had met in the kitchen, where they'd talked and drunk while Roth cooked. The guards who had escorted the "guests" took up positions. One was in the main dining room, one in the kitchen, and one on the front porch. Rok kept watch from the mezzanine. In the office, Morgan watched the infrared perimeter and coordinated our communications.

I had four guards hidden with me in the bushes outside the building, watching from the perimeter. We were an open hand, and when the Beast stepped in we were going to grab him. I was the opposable thumb that was going to make sure he didn't twist out of our grip.

An hour had passed, and the fog was really rolling in now. I hadn't experienced fog in some time, and the dampness that soon coated me was an unpleasant surprise. Hartshall wasn't quite a blur in the grayness, but its details were becoming vague. As fog lowers the visibility, it conducts sound better. Listen, Railwalker.

34. THE BAY

Through the fog, he comes.

The oarlocks of his boat are muffled. The boat slows, gliding through the mist to beach itself with the softest of grinding noises.

Across the sand, up over the rocks, he comes. The fog seems to rise with him as he climbs, spilling over the edge, lapping through bushes and across long sea grass. Where the sea grass ends the mown lawn begins to fill like a bowl, the mist blurring the shapes of the glowing, lighted windows.

He can smell them. There, in the bushes. There, in the tall grass. And then over there—he sees the one in the clump of trees move slightly. They smell of gun oil, tobacco, aftershave, sweat and grease. They are not important, but he is careful. He takes the two closest quickly—first the one in the grass, then the bush-lurker. Then he waits for the fog to thicken, as he knows it will, before taking the hider-in-trees.

And now he comes to the building, the home of light and laughter, and the Enemy. He had hoped to come against the Enemy in his Tower, but this was better. The Tower might be the outer stronghold, but this place was the Enemy's Heart Home. Yes, this was much better.

A guard was coming around the corner of the house, and inside, he sensed, bodies were moving...

35. HARTSHALL

Cort Remming had not been this close to City Boss Roth since the man had pinned his badge on him ten years ago at his induction ceremony. Back then, that occasion had been nothing like this. Back then, Remming was just one among a dozen guard academy graduates being inducted that year.

He leaned against a counter in the Hartshall kitchen, savoring the aromas of grilling meat and spices. The city boss moved about the kitchen, keeping up a steady stream of stories, comments, and anecdotes as he prepared the meal.

The Railwalkers' plan had called for the illusion of an intimate dinner for Roth and his three remaining cronies from the old days: Jim Shaw, Harold Carter, and Sarah Weldt. Remming had to shave his mustache to impersonate Shaw, but he figured he had the easier end of the deal when he considered Brewster's plight. They hadn't been able to find a female guard as large as Sarah Weldt, so Rob Brewster had to dress up in drag, in a silver dress with a long black wig. Jaffa Armstrong, who needed only the application of a little gray to his kinky hair for him to sub in for Carter, had kidded Brewster that he ought to consider moonlighting as a Weldt impersonator at the Drag Strip, a transvestite club in the south end. Brewster had not been amused.

Remming was surprised that this scenario should mean Roth himself was doing the cooking, but he shrugged and took it in stride. To each his own. If Roth liked to cook, Remming just hoped the man was good at it. He wasn't particularly anxious about the whole night. Auden had implied that this assignment was a dangerous one, that he could easily end up dead, but Remming wasn't buying that. Assuming the Railwalkers were right about the Beast's objectives, and assuming that the Beast was stupid enough to fall for this trick, Remming had no doubt the guy would be taken down before he got anywhere near Roth and the guards pretending to be his cronies. And the fact that Micah Roth was playing himself in this little charade convinced him that this was so. Remming was sure Gage would never have let Roth participate in this farce if there was the slightest chance of the city boss being in danger. Still, danger or not, Remming was just as happy to feel the weight of his pistol under his armpit. They were all armed, the guards with the standard .9 mms, Roth with an ancient .357 magnum, a real museum piece.

The old man continued to talk nonstop, taking the responsibility off the guards for doing any acting or impersonation. He kept up a running commentary on the state of the city and the progress of the dishes he was preparing, all interspersed with stories and recollections. Remming had to give the man that: He knew how to tell a story and make it entertaining. And his liquor was good. If the food was as good as the talk and the liquor, with the other guys outside poised to take the Beast down, Remming figured he and the others were in for an enjoyable night, though it would probably end abruptly once the Beast was caught. He promised himself he'd get as much out of this assignment as he could before the shoe dropped.

Between stories Roth had explained the various steps to what he was doing with the food, though they hadn't really registered with Remming. Remming didn't cook, beyond tossing a frozen dinner in his micro or boiling coffee. Roth was preparing some sort of venison steak inside a pastry shell, with asparagus and roasted potatoes to go with it.

"So the landlord points to a sign on the wall, 'cash today, credit tomorrow,'" said Roth, spinning out another story. "And Cochrane, he's got no money, but he knows if he doesn't buy drinks for this crowd, he's not getting their vote. So he tells the landlord to hang on a minute, and steps out into the desert. He looks around and sees a raccoon climbing into the tavern's garbage. He's in the zones, so naturally he's got his gun on him. So he pulls it out, pots that old 'coon right off the garbage pail. Pulls out his buck knife, strips the hide, and takes it back into the tavern.

"Now you have to understand, in those days a recoon skin was as good as a couple of gold pieces…"

Remming raised his glass, then stopped. Armstrong was looking half drunk already. It was part of the role they were playing to drink Roth's booze, but it wouldn't do to get potted while you were supposed to be guarding the city boss, even if it worked out you weren't called on to pull your piece. He put the glass down, vowing to watch his own drinking. Damn, but it was hard not to get carried away when the city boss had such good stuff. He'd have to look into whether there was anything like this hooch that was affordable on a guardsman's salary.

"So about the fifth round," Roth was saying, "Cochrane's traded the landlord that same coonskin five times now. So he figures he better call it quits before the fellow catches on. He gladhands all around, pulls up stakes, and moves on, leaving a party in his wake. Naturally he won the election, and a few months later he gets to thinking that landlord is now one of his constituents, too. And he's probably figured out Cochrane's scam by now.

"So what does Cochrane do? He sends that landlord the full price of the drinks he bought on that coonskin that night. But the landlord, he sends it right back, with a note that says, 'That coonskin is mounted on the wall in my bar, and the story I get to tell out of this is worth more than the price of the drinks. You got my vote any time you run for office.'"

They all laughed—some legitimate laughter, in appreciation of the joke, some dutiful, because it was the city boss who told it, and Remming was amused to note which guard laughed which way.

Roth transferred the baked pastry containing the steaks onto plates, which he handed around. "Gentlemen," he announced, "and lady, our steaks are done. Let's repair to the dining room. Jim, if you'll get the asparagus," he said to Remming. "Harry, the potatoes there? And Sarah, maybe you could grab that sauce? There's a ladle for it in that second drawer."

The guardsmen, dressed as Jim, Harry, and Sarah, complied and made their way in procession into the dining room. They ranged themselves around the table, placing their respective dishes in the center and their personal plates at their own places, and Roth took his place at the head of the table.

"Lady and gentlemen," said Roth, still standing. Remming wondered if the rest of them should stand up again, but no one else seemed about to, so he kept his seat. "Though we gather as private individuals, the truth is, we are here to continue the work we do for the benefit of Bay City."

This is it, thought Remming. If it's going to happen, it happens now, or very soon.

Then the lights went out.

36. WOLF

"They're moving," Morgan's voice said in my earpiece. Roth and the ringers were going from the kitchen to the private dining room. More time passed.

I kept thinking I saw something move, but when I focused on it, it was only the wind rippling the grass. Then I thought, wait a minute, there isn't any wind, as the voice of the Wolf Spirit said in my ear, "Believe your eyes, not your mind." I looked up and saw Hancherow come around the corner of the building. It seemed as if the grass suddenly surged up toward him and he went down. A ripple moved away from him across the grass.

"Bogie, northeast corner," said Morgan. The ripple of grass had shown on infrared.

"Move in!" I said quietly into the headset.

Only two of the five responded. I had to assume the others were dead, or at least out of the action. As I began to move, the lights in the building went off. I broke into a run. Robles appeared from my left, and a strangled cry came from my right. Anders was down, his leg caught in what looked like a bear trap. I didn't stop to wonder how the Beast had managed to rig that.

"Robles," I said, "get him loose." I headed for the building. I could see the stark white glare of the emergency lights inside. As I reached the door I heard breaking glass and shots being fired.

"Breach, room zero," said Morgan. The small dining room. Bursts from an automatic, and twice the blast of Roth's hand cannon of a revolver. I flung open the front door and stepped in as Rok vaulted the mezzanine railing and dropped to the main floor. We converged on the door to the private room and I threw it open. Only two figures still moved inside.

One emergency light was out. The other was skewed at the opposite wall, limning the wall beside it in sidelight. The room had been redecorated with what I thought was a rather tasteless splatter effect. At the center of the room stood the silhouette of the Beast—tall, rangy, naked, moving like a panther. Long, light-colored fur stood up on his back, which I realized with a start had been his camouflage; this had to be the moving grass I'd seen earlier. Armstrong, Remming, and Whaling lay bleeding out on the floor. Beyond the Beast Roth was stirring, struggling up from the floor, the big, old-fashioned revolver in his hand. The rime of the emergency light outlined his figure. The Beast carried two swords in his clawed hands. I wondered why he bothered, having seen what his claws could do. Then I saw it. They were Railwalker blades.

"Roth," he growled, stone grating over stone, the abrasion of mountains. "Micah Roth."

Roth came to his feet and raised the revolver. His voice was hoarse and harsh when he spoke. "I know you. I know where you come from. I freed this city from Crichton and ran it for twenty-seven years. Did you think I wouldn't defend it with my life?"

The hand cannon roared twice in the confined space of the room. The Beast spun backward, staggered. He straightened, and Roth fired again, twice more, solid body shots, as the old man found his eye for shooting. But this time, though the bullet struck his chest, the creature only shuddered back a step.

"Roth!" I shouted. "Head shot!" But Roth's next pull clicked on an empty chamber.

The Beast turned and saw me where I stood in the doorway, one hand still on the opened door. I saw his teeth in the dark as he smiled and growled, "The Railwalker!"

Two Railwalker blades in the Beast's hands. Then I knew: the Hicks Junction massacre. The guards from Monteague and Santa Brita, Wiley and the Boar. The swords were Death Singer and Whisperer, and there was no doubt about how the Beast had acquired them. Call me a fool, but I holstered my gun and drew Windsteel. The sword whickered as the blade came free. Bullets seemed to have little effect on this creature anyway. If this Beast thought he could kill me with my fallen brothers' stolen blades, let him try.

He launched himself at me. I stepped back, and as he reached it I slammed the door, throwing all my weight against it. He struck it with an enormous crash and a crack, and the wood of the door gave. I jerked it open again and aimed a sword stroke at where I thought he'd be, but with an amazing recovery he dove under it, tumbling to his feet in the main dining room.

Even as he came to his feet Rok was on him, his blade singing. The Beast backpedaled, parrying, then halted his retreat, standing his ground as he and Rok exchanged a flurry of cuts and parries, weaving a web of bright steel in the glare of the emergency lights. I couldn't help feeling a certain anxiety. With firearms or hand to hand I'd never seen Rok lose a fight. But the sword was not his best weapon.

Rok ducked under the Beast's stroke, came up inside, and struck with the pommel of his blade, snapping the monster's head back. The Beast staggered, and Rok followed, staying close in, striking hard with elbows, fists, and hilt. The Beast got in one shot to Rok's face with his left sword hilt. Rok's own speed of reaction spared him having his skull split open, but he couldn't dodge the blow entirely. The force of the blow threw him across a table. Blood sprayed in his wake.

The Beast sprang after him, and Rok came up to meet his cuts, blood flying from his wound. A shot rang out, and the Beast staggered back. A large groove had been chewed out of the horny plating that covered his chest. He screamed a song of rage and pain in a language I'd never heard.

Morgan stood by the base of the stairs. Her Gunspire magnum smoked in her hands. She calmly took aim again, but the Beast turned, hurling one of his stolen blades as the gun went off.

A sword can't be thrown with any accuracy, so throwing it is just a distraction, an inconvenience. Rok knows this as well as I do, so he should have ignored it and attacked again immediately, instead of glancing at Morgan. Maybe the Beast's apparently supernatural prowess had him thinking he could do something impossible. I don't know.

And maybe he was right. Morgan parried the thrown sword with her gun, and in passing the blade sliced her arm. Those blades are so sharp, it doesn't take a lot of power to cut with them, and the Beast had put a lot of power into that throw. She dropped the gun and clutched her arm. And then she screamed, but not with pain.

In the split second Rok's attention was diverted the Beast had lunged, driving his blade into Rok's chest. Rok's parry was late, and my Bear went down. There was another shot, from the other side this time. The Beast staggered, and Auden advanced through the front door, firing his service piece repeatedly at the Beast. The rounds were like thunder inside the restaurant, and my ears rang. The shots jolted the creature, staggered him back away from Rok, but did not seem to penetrate. The slide on Auden's pistol locked back—he was empty.

I moved in, cutting at the back of the Beast's neck. He either heard or sensed me. He turned as I came in, slapping my sword aside with Death Singer, which he still held.

Auden leaped to Rok.

The Beast and I faced each other en garde. He shifted the sword from his left hand to his right. So he wasn't perfectly ambidextrous. That was good to know. Beyond the Beast I saw Morgan rush to join Auden at Rok's side.

I dismissed my wounded brother from my thoughts. Morgan and Auden would do everything they could for him, and I couldn't afford to become distracted as he had. The Beast and I circled each other, swords poised.

The Beast lunged. I backed away, batting his cuts aside, watching how he delivered them. Once I thought I had a feel for his style I moved in hard. I feinted, got past his guard with a cut that should have handed him his head. He twisted his shoulder into it. The blade glanced off, though it shook him. Horny growths like organic armor covered much of his body. Like the bullets, my sword only bit chunks out of this stuff and did not penetrate. His quick return tried to serve me a steel dinner, but I wasn't biting, and danced away.

The stolen sword he carried, Death Singer, keened as it slashed through the air. Its tone sounded sour to my ear, and I remembered that the Beast was not bonded to this blade as Wiley would have been, or as I was to Windsteel. The blade might not actually work against him, but it wouldn't play to his strengths as Windsteel would to mine.

We fought back and forth across the restaurant floor. He got through my guard, barely—a glancing cut to the arm—and again; now my cheek stung, my vision swam. We stared at each other. I was bleeding now from the cut on my face, and where he'd caught my left arm with a shallow cut. Head pounding, panting, flashes of lightning in my eyes. He was grinning, breathing easily, looking like he'd just rolled out of bed.

The Beast charged me again, lunging. I parried, sidestepping, and took a big chance on a disarm move. It worked. Death Singer went sailing. His left claw flashed out at me, and I leaned back. The claw missed my face by a whisker.

You'd think that the man with the sword had the advantage in this situation, but I didn't. The Beast had two hands he could use independently as weapons, five razor-sharp knives on each, and he could parry my strokes with his armored limbs. I had one weapon for both offense and defense. I concentrated on avoiding those claws and finding vulnerable points to slash or stab at. I slashed at his throat. He ducked and delivered a kick to my midsection that dashed me over a table and into the wall. The impact brought another of those flashes of lightning. I came up again, rebounding off the wall. My head was pounding, and I could hardly breathe. I cut at his head and he slipped sideways, spinning. His elbow caught me behind the head, and lights exploded before my eyes as I went down. For a moment the pain lancing out from my head obscured everything else. I didn't feel my body hit the floor.

There was a snap, and Windsteel shivered in my hand. I rolled away, nothing but the instinct for survival driving me now, my vision swimming. I forced myself to my feet and brought up the sword, to find it was half a sword.

The Beast stalked me slowly, smiling, sure of his kill. I was stunned. Windsteel was a Sierra Mutant blade, forged by a sixth-generation Osoto. Sierra blades, and Osoto blades especially, did not break. It must have been against the floor, and the Beast had stamped on it, using the lever-age provided by the tsuba, the hand guard, against the floor. I shook sweat and blood out of my eyes and dismissed the thought.

The Beast lunged at me. This time I moved under him, gripping the broken remains of my sword, edge turned up. I buried it in his armpit, then worked it like a lever, slicing muscle and tendon. Blood sheeted from his armpit. He twisted away and kicked. I followed him as he moved, but his kick connected. My legs went out from under me as if I'd been hit by a tram. We both went down. I landed on top of his arm, the remains of my sword skittering away.

The Beast roared and surged upward, gushing arterial blood. I grabbed onto that arm and was dragged up as he staggered to his feet. For a moment I thought he was going wherever he wanted, taking me along; but then that horny armor that was all that still connected the arm to his shoulder gave way. I fell to the floor again, clutching the arm. Through another flash of white light I saw him fall to his knees. He pitched forward onto his face and lay motionless as the blood pumped sluggishly from his shoulder. It slowed to a drip.

37. HARTSHALL

Darkness.

Hnahna.

She was Creator and Destroyer, the great snake that encircled the world, the vast ocean that could engulf, the cosmic cunt that gave birth and sucked all things into death at her pitiless bottom. She was Mother Goddess, but never Mother or Mama. From the very dawn of his awareness, she had been Hnahna. Arbiter of his pleasure and his pain. Center of his heart and of his universe. Giver of milk, and drawer forth of milk. Hnahna.

He had failed her.

He had always feared this very thing the most. He had failed her, and she had turned her face from him. The world grew dark and cold, the many realities he had inhabited in his life narrowing down to this single pinpoint of light, vanishing into darkness. No ecstasy, no Hnahna to embrace him, just the cold and the dark. The no-thing.

Nothing.

I lay panting, covered in the monster's blood, embracing his severed arm. Then Morgan was at my side, asking, "Are you okay?" I nodded and she vanished again, presumably returning to tend to Rok.

Gage appeared, crouching. His hand snaked warily to the Beast's throat. He looked up, saying, "He's done."

Roth appeared too, at the edge on my vision, the big revolver still clasped in one hand, a towel in the other. He looked from the body of the Beast to me. I dragged myself into a sitting position. Roth offered the towel. I took it and wiped at my face.

Light flashed again. I thought I was seeing more lightning, then realized it was the spotlight from an ornithopter shining through the windows. Morgan had already signaled someone to come for Rok. The doors burst open and EMTs rushed in. They loaded Rok's inert body onto a stretcher and hustled him out to the 'thopter. I nodded at Morgan, indicating she should go with them, and she hurried out in their wake. Auden stood looking after them, his hands red to the wrists from his attempts to slow Rok's bleeding.

I listened to the ornithopter take off with my two partners, then levered myself to my feet, looking dazedly at my broken blade.

"So," said Roth, looking at the body of the Beast. "He was a mutant after all."

I looked over at the body. "No," I said. "He was a shapeshifter. Look at his shoulder. He was trying to close the wound over before he bled to death." It was obvious when you looked at it. Smooth, pink skin had formed all around the edges of the wound. But it hadn't worked.

"You take any serious damage?" asked Roth.

"I don't think so."

"Look like you could use a drink, though."

"I'll see about the power," said Gage, and he headed out the back.

"I need a wash," said Auden, and he turned toward the men's room.

Without speaking Roth and I shuffled wearily toward the other room. Neither of us really wanted to have our drink over the Beast's body. Roth opened the door to the private dining room, glanced at the carnage inside, and shook his head.

"Kitchen," he said, letting the broken door swing shut. I followed him into the kitchen. He was handing me a glass when the regular lights came back on. We both blinked in the new light, and the emergency lights went off. Roth was pouring the third glass as Gage returned from the kitchen door. A moment later Auden joined us, and Roth poured another.

We all drank in silence. Then Roth sighed, and said, "So you were right on both counts. He was after me."

"No, I was wrong," I said. "You may have been his mission, City Boss, but in his heart, he was after us all."

I needed a shower and about twenty-four hours of uninterrupted sleep. But first, the hospital.

Rok looked shrunken amongst all those tubes and wires, half his face covered by bandages. I'd have expected him to look like Frankenstein, a warrior of his size lying there in the hospital bed. Instead he looked like a shriveled old man, an ancient fairy caught in a web of technology. Morgan sat beside the bed, clutching his hand.

I looked down at the man who, for the past decade or so, I'd never seen seriously injured or wounded. Sure, we got in scrapes; he took his share of bruises, cuts, and an occasional bullet wound. Nothing like this, though. Nothing life threatening. I admit it was a little frightening. It comes to us all, of course. And it's not just intellectual knowledge when you've seen humans shot, stabbed, beaten and crushed to death, torn apart by animals, and otherwise savaged by life and their fellow life forms.

I knew this. I even knew the odds were always in favor of Rok's dying before I did. In a Railwalker team, though we're all martially trained, the Brick's primary job is to deal with the magickal, the visionary, the numinous. And that often means an altered state of consciousness. At those times, you can lose sight of what's going on in this world, so your Bear is there to watch your back while you're altered, and to take point on martial encounters. A Bear is twice as likely as a Brick or a Prof to get killed in the line of duty. I always knew, somewhere in me, that this moment was coming. But somehow, some part of my mind had conspired to ignore that fact.

When he spoke his voice was weak, reminding me of the shade's voice on the telephone.

"My Brick..."

"My Bear."

"Morgan says the Beast is dead?"

"His body's in the morgue, several floors below."

"Good deal. No regrets, Wolf. We took care of business."

"We did that." I nodded.

"Twenty-three blessings, brother. I'd like a moment with Morgan."

"Sure thing." I left the two of them alone, stepped out into the corridor.

The walls of the hospital corridor were painted the same puke color as the hall where once, waiting for my Pa, I first saw my mother's spirit. Or at least it seemed that way to me.

After a moment, I heard Morgan sob, and then her shaky voice began the Chant for the Dead. I raised my voice to join hers, walked back into the room. As we sang, the crows gathered at the window.

39. WOLF

I was too restless to sleep. Morgan's door was closed, the light out. I left the suite, went down to the street, and started walking. Aimlessly, wandering the streets, paying no particular attention to where I was going. I was somewhere in the area where City Center becomes the North End when I started thinking this was stupid and pointless. There was a bar and casino open on the corner ahead. I should have a couple of drinks, then go back and sack out. I stepped inside.

The place was divided into two fairly large rooms. The front room was the bar, in the back was the gaming room. I ordered a shot and took it with me to stand at the entrance to the game room. It had been a long time. I'd seen plenty of cards and other games of chance go on in bars out in the zones, but it had been years since I had been in an actual game room of this type. There were tables for jackflash, crops, and poker, a wheel of fortune table, and even a couple of slot machines pinging away in the back.

It was a shock when I looked at the men sitting around the poker table and saw my Pa. He'd aged badly. He was gaunt as a corpse, with great caverns carved out under his cheekbones. When I'd last seen him his hair was starting to recede and turn gray at the temples. Though he hadn't lost any more hair, it had turned snow white. His eyes were still bright, though, peering out at me from beneath shaggy white brows.

He put down his cards.

"Gentlemen, I'm out," he said. "If you'll excuse me for a bit."

I stared in stunned silence as he got up from the table

and walked over to where I stood. "Long time no see," he said. He looked me up and down and added, "Railwalker."

"Yeah," I managed.

"Buy you a drink?" he asked, then he gestured and led the way to the bar.

We found stools and sat in silence until the drinks were delivered. He raised his glass to me and nodded, and I did the same, and we both drank. Then we looked at each other for a long time.

"So," he said at last, "Howyadoin'?"

That phrase, run together as one word, at once was foreign and familiar. He still hadn't lost the accent of the northeastern cities he grew up in, so reminiscent of the dialogue from DVs of pre-Crash gangster movies. I'd heard him utter that phrase—or that word—"How-yadoin?" a million times when I was young. In exactly that tone. And this was part of my father's magic. Each time he uttered it, the person he was asking knew deep down in their gut that he really did want to know, that there was nothing more important to him in that moment than how you were doing. Being his son, knowing what I knew about him, I also knew perfectly well that an hour from now, when he was looking across a card table at an opponent he thought was bluffing, the information he was now requesting would be irrelevant and forgotten. But right at this moment, it truly was as important to him as it seemed.

"I'm okay," I said.

"Bullshit," he grunted. "But you always were a good liar. You're a Railwalker now. Roth called the Railwalkers in to hunt down the Beast. You gotta know the whole city's talking about that. You found this Beast yet? Got him under lock and key?"

"No," I allowed. "But the job is done. He's dead."

"So?" He sat back. "That's good. Why do you look like you just lost your best friend?"

"Because I did," I said. "He was killed by the Beast."

"Oh," he said. "Sorry to hear that. Then I was right. You're not okay. In fact, you're very fuckin' far from okay."

"Alright," I said. "In that respect, no, things aren't okay. I thought you were asking about the bigger picture, y'know, how my life has been, how it is being a Railwalker, that sort of thing."

He laughed. "I know how the fuck that is. It's good, or you wouldn't still be doing it. You're like me in that respect, anyway. You're not going to stick with something doesn't suit you. Oh, I know, you'll fulfill any obligations you made, but once the debts are paid, you're done. Am I right?"

"Yeah," I said. "You're right. But I'm not a liar."

"Not constitutionally, maybe," he said. "But you're good at it when you need to be, just the same. Remember how you used to become different characters from the DVs you saw?"

I only vaguely remembered having played at being some of my heroes as a kid.

"You were totally convincing, completely in character. You'd be Batman or Captain Arclight, or Brick, for days on end sometimes. Quite the little method actor, ya were."

I remembered using towels as capes, and recalled a particular hotel we'd stayed at in Fresh Springs that had dark-colored towels that worked better than the white or cream-colored towels we found in most places.

"Thought sure you'd become an actor. That worried me some. That's not a real secure job. Hard to make a living."

"Oh, yeah, and gambling is real secure. You got yourself a pension fund squirreled away somewhere, Pa?"

He snorted. "That's just the point. Never wanted you to grow up to be a bum like me. I was real happy when you went into construction. Solid future in that business."

"It wasn't for me."

"Yeah. I shoulda figured that. I saw Bobby a year or so after you left. He told me you'd joined the order."

"Railwalker Academy isn't exactly hard to find, Pa. In the five years I was there, you never had a game near New Frisco?"

"You know I don't do good with that ooky-spooky shit."

"Not even to visit your own son?"

"Bad enough you're all into that shit now. Sitting down with you today ain't the easiest thing for me, just on that basis, never mind our history. I wasn't going to walk into a whole campus full of that."

I heard the anger in his voice and realized it was as much anger at himself, at his fears and frailties, as it was at me for having embraced the "ooky-spooky shit." Suddenly I was looking at the man before me not as my Pa, but just as a man—an old, burnt-out gambler, probably an alcoholic, who lived with a lot of regret and struggled with his own fears and anxieties. A man who felt himself a failure.

I thought back to my youth and remembered how he'd always avoided Railwalkers, witches, and psychics, except for Patty Morris. And even his friendship with her had been an uneasy one; he'd been much closer to Bill than to Patty. It was a common enough thing amongst gamblers, as I ought to know. Most of them were intensely superstitious. They'd carry their rabbit's foot or St. Bernardine medal, maybe mount a plastic Elvis on their dashboard. The bravest among them might visit a desert witch to get a custom luck charm. But they all avoided any active involvement with anything that smacked of the occult or the spiritual. I pulled my attention back to Pa, who was speaking again.

"Blood will tell, they say. Guess you'd pretty much have to turn out to be either a gambler or a Railwalker. Probably Patty was right, I shoulda left you with her and Bill. You'd have had something like a normal life in Alturo. 'Cept Patty woulda probably started you down that road all the sooner." He shook his head. "I dunno. Hell, I guess it's better this way. At least you're doing something helps people, contributing something to the world. Better that than turning into a drunken old gambler."

I could see he was perched on the precipice of self-pity, and I wasn't going to go there with him. Besides, something he'd said had stuck in my head like a burr on a coattail.

"What did you mean, 'blood will tell'?"

He looked at me for a long minute before replying. "Patty used to say you had the Sight. Guess she was right. You got that from your mother. She trained to be a Rail-walker, you know."

I hadn't known. He chuckled at my expression.

"Close your mouth, kid. You'll be catching flies. Yeah, Irena trained at the Academy for a couple of years, but she never took the Oath or got the tattoo. She dropped out, or whatever you call it."

I was baffled. I couldn't imagine my father in a romance with a Railwalker trainee. Talk about "ooky-spooky shit."

"How did you...?"

"Get together?" he supplied. "I started dating your Ma before she went in. Her visions and dreams and stuff were like her dirty little secret in those days. She didn't talk about them. I didn't know anything about it until it was too late. She already had me, hook, line, and sinker.

"I think she wanted to forget it, leave that shit behind, but it wouldn't let her go. Went from dreams and occasional flashes of vision to full-blown fits that would have her out of it, lost in some other world, right out in broad daylight. Things eventually got so bad she couldn't hide it, had to talk to me about it. 'Course, I was spooked. It scared the shit out of me. But I wasn't gonna walk on her at that point, leave her to deal with it by herself. Eventually we agreed she had to get help, had to get some kind of training to deal with it, and that's when she decided to go to the Academy. We both thought that meant we were all done, our life together was over. I drove her to the Academy, dropped her off. Thought that was the last I'd ever see of her."

"And where was I during all this?"

"You? You weren't even a gleam in either of our eyes at that point. You were an egg that hadn't dropped, a sperm that hadn't swum upstream. Couple of years later, I was playing in a casino in Freno, and she comes walking up to the table. 'Hi, Doc,' she says. 'You up for a different kind of game?'"

"She'd left the Academy?"

"Yeah, she'd left. Learned enough to get control of the shit, or so she thought. Wanted to have a life, raise a family. We were both still young enough in those days. We thought we could pull that off. I even tried getting a regular job for a while. Not that that worked out any good."

"So what happened?"

"Whatdye think? Ooky-spooky shit happened. A couple of years after you were born, the visions got out of control again. She never did explain it all to me, but something she'd seen convinced her that if she stayed around, you were going to be drawn into that world, and it was gonna be bad for you. Said you'd be swallowed by the dragon, or some shit like that. She thought if she left, and I did my best to keep you away from that kind of stuff, you could have a normal life." He shook his head. "Guess we both should have known better.

"I never talked about this because, you know, trouble between men and women is always that he-said, she-said shit. I have my feelings and opinions, and I coulda told you what they were, but I wasn't the person to present her point of view, and I didn't want to poison your mind against her. She was your ma, after all."

"Poison my mind?"

"I wouldn't have done it intentionally, but when you're a kid, you listen to what your parents say. It weighs more with you than it ought to. If I'd have told you the whole story, even if I'd tried to be fair, you'd have heard my side, but not hers."

I was stunned. He'd never told me anything about my mother because he was afraid he'd unfairly prejudice me against her? "Look, Pop," I said, "I've learned a bit about how reality looks different to different people. I think I'm a bit old to take my father's word as absolute canon verity."

"Fair enough," he said, and he sighed. Looked at the bottles behind the bar, at the door to the games room, the front door of the place, everywhere else he could before finally looking at me. "Your mother," he said at last, "was a hard woman to love.

"Not hard to fall in love with, y'know. That's different. Gorgeous she was, with that soft smile and those big, luminous eyes. You've seen her picture. She was like some elegant DV star. You know, some women that beautiful, they develop this attitude, like they're somehow privileged and better than everybody, because all their life people have given them everything they wanted, just because they were beautiful."

I nodded. I'd known a few women like that.

"Your mother was never like that. Modest, self-effacing, when I met her. Easy to fall for. But falling in love, that's nothing. Loving, once you're in a day-to-day relationship, that's another thing entirely. When you're playing partners, and things get rough, the world don't exactly deal you all the best cards. Tension builds up. You get anxious and edgy, and you start blaming each other.

"I knew how that went, of course, but when Irena and I started at each other, well, she could say things. Things that weren't true, that she didn't even believe were true. Just to hurt you, to score a point. Especially when she was drinking."

My mother had a drinking problem? This was new to me. I mentally laughed at myself. Everything and anything about my mother was going to be new to me, since all I actually knew already was her image from that one photograph.

"I'd been around the block a time or two even then. You'd think an old dog like me would have run into that before. But dumb as it seems, the truth was, I hadn't. I'd known guys would lie to get the upper hand in an argument, say shit that was total lies, but never a woman who'd do that to hurt her man. I think it was that more than anything had me ready to agree, and to let go, when she decided to hit the road."

I wondered again about the spirit I'd seen that I'd always accepted as the spirit of my mother. This didn't sound at all like her. But what did I know? That spirit appeared now and then to pull my irons out of the fire, and then vanished again. I didn't deal with her on a day-to-day basis, like I did with the Wolf Spirit or the Crows.

"So why did she leave?"

He sipped from his drink and looked me up and down. "You want to know my honest opinion, she left to chase her own ambition. Washing out at the Railwalker Academy did something to her. She'd seen something there that she wanted: power, influence, authority. Oh, she gave other reasons for leaving at the time. All that stuff about a vision, a prophecy about you. Supposedly she was worried about that, trying to avoid it. You were better off without her. But you ask me, the reality was, she thought it was her was better off without you and me.

"When the weird stuff started up again, after you were born, I could see that instead of resisting it, this time she was accepting it. She was determined to turn it to her advantage, gain herself some power. On a path like that, a gambler husband and a baby were just encumbrances. Toward the end, you could see her getting harder, nastier. Like she was trying to rid herself of compassion, empathy, softer feelings like that. Back then I thought it was the booze, but now I think the drinking was a symptom, and a tool. I think she'd come to see those kinder feelings as weakness. Drinking gave her some distance, some insulation."

I thought about that. I'd known more than a few people like that in my time.

"So the whole prophecy about me was a made-up excuse?"

"Hell, no. That was a legitimate vision. I was with her when it happened. Unless she was a much better actress than I thought..." He paused. "Which I guess is a possibility." He shook his head, denying it to himself. "No, I think that vision was real. I just don't think it was the reason she left."

"So what exactly was this vision? I'd be swallowed by a dragon?"

"Something like that. Couldn't tell you the details." His eyes widened at my expression, and then narrowed again as he leaned toward me. "Look, okay, I know, you and your cohorts, you pay attention to visions and prophecy and all that shit. You can't imagine how somebody could actually forget something like that. But you gotta remember, at the time I was scared shitless of that crap, and I did my best to avoid and forget anything associated with it."

I noticed he'd used the past tense. "So you're easier in your mind with 'that crap' today?" I asked.

"Yeah," he said, "I am, actually. The older you get, the more you realize Old Man Death is sitting in on every hand. You tip to the fact he can collect up the pot any time he feels like it, the other weird stuff don't seem all that scary anymore.

"I'm sorry I forgot that prophecy. If it was today, I'd mark it down and remember it. But back then, last thing I wanted was to remember. And I'm sorry I never told you anything about Irena. That wasn't fair. Though, truth to tell, you never actually asked."

Once you made it clear such questions wouldn't be answered, I thought, but I bit my tongue. What's done is done. Instead, I said, "You know she's dead now."

"You got inside information on that, or you just guessing?"

I thought about that. My heart was sure that, yes, she was dead, and I had been visited by her spirit. My head wasn't so sure. I knew that both heart and head can be deceived, especially when you're feeling desperate; and what could be more desperate than a young child who wants his mama? Even when—maybe especially when—he's never known her.

"No," I said finally, "I don't know for sure. I'm just guessing. Call it a feeling."

He stood, emptied his glass. "Sorry, but I am working," he said, nodding toward the game room. "And the cards call. Nice to see you again. Sorry to hear about your friend."

I watched his narrow figure walk back into the game room, thinking, that's so typical. A big revelation, a heart-felt apology, and like a switch was thrown, that's done, good, back to business as usual, bye, seeya.

I walked back slowly toward the Tower. Meeting my Pa had been weirder than any trip I'd taken to meet with the Wolf Spirit. I would have thought I'd be angry and bitter toward him. I was, but not as much as I'd have expected. Seeing him from an adult perspective changed that. I understood a lot more about people and life than when I'd last seen him over twenty years ago. When you're a child your parents are like gods. And even though as you get older you realize they're not, you still carry some of that with you. On some unconscious level you still expect your Pa or your Ma to be superhuman, heroic. When they prove to be merely flawed human beings, it's like they betrayed you personally. Tonight I had looked at my father the way I'd look at any man I'd met in my travels. And while he wasn't any paragon, he also wasn't a monster. Just a tired old gambler, doing the best he could. It took some of the fire out of my anger.

I'd also realized that in my younger mind, Pa had suffered severely by comparison to my mother. Oh, there was anger and disappointment about her leaving us, sure. But without regular day-to-day exposure, I was able to keep my happy fantasies of what she might have been like, to build a mental image of a perfect goddess. Her occasional appearance as a spirit, ghost, vision, or whatever the hell she was, did nothing to tarnish that image. You might think my Pa's account of her having attended the Academy might have polished that image even further, but the truth was, it brought her down to earth for me. She hadn't finished her course at the Academy, had never taken the tats or been granted the coat and the sword. She'd dropped out —to have a family, sure, but apparently when she aban-

doned us, she didn't go back to it. And if Pa was to be
believed, she was a drinker, and could be cruel sometimes.

Reaching City Plaza, digesting all this new information, these new feelings, I wasn't ready to go indoors yet.
Now that Summersend was over the Guy had been disassembled and the fountain had become a fountain again. I
sat on the rim of the circular pool, listening to the sound
of the falling water behind me, and the faint music and
voices that trickled up State Street from the Tankard a
block away. The sound suddenly got louder for a moment,
as several figures came out of the basement entrance,
seeming to grow up out of the sidewalk. They milled
around in the street for a moment, saying their good-
nights, I imagined, and then drifted apart like slow pool
balls dispersing from a cue.

As my anger at my Pa had deflated some, my compassion toward him had grown. Like I say, he had this ability
to be totally concerned, totally focused on the person he
was with—caring and concern that seemed to vanish the
moment you were out of his presence. I'd always seen this
as a failing, thought it was false or insincere. Now I realized it was quite sincere; I could remember times when
he'd seriously put himself out for someone, despite the
fact he might still forget them afterward. It was, I realized,
like having a peculiar existential blind spot. Or perhaps
lack of peripheral vision would be a better description. If
it wasn't immediately in front of him, it really didn't exist.
I'd learned long ago that I had to take my Pa for what he
was, appreciate the attention and caring when I was with
him, and not expect more than he could give. But I now
realized my frustration with the support he couldn't provide had interfered with my appreciating what he could.

"Hey," said a voice. I'd been peripherally aware that
one of the figures that had come out of the Tankard was
drifting up State in my direction, but I hadn't been focused on it. Now I looked up to see Robles standing beside
me. She was in civvies, or what passed for them with her:
cargo pants and a leather jacket. Her usually skullcap-tight
hair was unbound, floating about her face like black foam,

and I was surprised at how long it was.

"Evening," I said. "Been out celebrating the Beast's demise?"

"That, and raising a glass or two to the dead," she said. In my grief over Rok, I'd forgotten the guards had lost people tonight as well. Seven, all told. She sighed. "Had a couple of drinks, whipped some arse at pool. You play pool?"

"Yeah," I said. "I like pool better than cards. It doesn't depend on luck or percentages. It's all about your skill and accuracy."

She raised an eyebrow at my tone. "Guess you don't feel much like celebrating. I'm really sorry about Rok. He seemed like a standup guy."

"Yeah. He was..." I groped for words, or even a word, that would come close, but found none. "My friend," I finished lamely. She sat down beside me on the fountain's rim. "I'm sorry for your loss, too."

"Yeah, thanks," she said. "You'd think it would get easier." She shook her head. "It was their choice. You always know it could happen to any of you, at any time. You try to be okay with that, but it's hard, especially when the good ones get taken. Armstrong, he was a good guy. Not a great guard, but a decent human being. Hell, even guys like Remming... He was a dick, but he didn't deserve to go like that."

"Nobody does."

"Yeah, guess you got that right." She peered at me in the lamplight of the plaza. "How long you know him? Rok, I mean?"

"We were partners along the rails for ten years. Known him closer to fifteen."

"That's a long time. No wonder you're sitting out here grieving alone."

"I'm not, really," I said. "Oh, yeah, it started out that way. But just now I was thinking about my father." She didn't say anything, but her look was questioning. "Ran into him down at the..." I realized I hadn't noticed the name of the place. "Well, some bar and gaming house down that way." I gestured.

"I didn't know you were from Bay City."

"I'm not," I said. "Just coincidence we were both here." I explained a little about my Pa, and my upbringing on the road, Pa's aversion to the Railwalkers, and all that 'ooky-spooky' stuff.

"Y'know," she said, "I could never do what you do. Dealing with spirits, and the dead and stuff. Not that ghosts scare me. I'm not like your dad, wanting to avoid any contact with it. But I don't want to know about death. Death, and what comes after, if there is anything. If I don't just turn off like a light, I want the next thing to be a sur-prise. It's like, you walk down a strange street in a strange city, you don't know what you're going to meet there. Could be you get shot dead, could be you meet somebody who will be your best friend forever. There's just no telling. Until you actually walk down that street, you don't know. The possibilities are infinite. That's how I want to go, when the time comes. It should be like walking down that strange street. Infinite possibility, and you just roll with whatever comes along."

Her hands were on her thighs. I reached over and covered her left with my right. "Let's hope," I said, "that you don't find out too soon." Sounded to my own ears like a tacky line, but it was what I was thinking.

She leaned toward me, smiling. "I intend to be around a while," she said. "But y'know, if it happened tomorrow, I could be okay with that. I got no regrets."

Ooo-kay. She not only didn't pull her hand away, she leaned into me. I realized my heart was speeding up a little. How long had it been since I'd been with a woman? And was I doing the right thing, moving in that direction? It's a classic, of course; when confronted with death, we want to affirm life. And what better way to do that than with sex? Was it really Robles turning me on, or was I just jerking my knee in reaction to all the death around me? Or was I just plain horny? Did it really matter? I looked into her eyes and thought I saw similar thoughts racing behind them. Yeah, I thought, given a little time, we'd have ended up here eventually anyway. All the emotions stirred up by the death surrounding us just stepped up the schedule a little.

"Let's go to my place," she said.

We did.

41. AUDEN

Rainer Auden stepped out of the front door of the CA Tower and looked around. Down State Street he could see the spill of light and hear the music and raucous voices coming from the Tankard, where guards often gathered. He didn't want to go home, but he wasn't in the mood for the company of other guards. He took a deep breath of the night air, walked down the steps, and started down First. What he really wanted, he thought, was some down time in a neighborhood bar. He didn't want to talk to the bartender, shoot the shit with the regulars about the latest news or yesterday's victory for the Crushers. And he sure as shit didn't want to field questions about the Beast. He didn't want to participate in camaraderie and community. He just wanted to sit somewhere and bathe in that atmosphere, undisturbed by the patrons who created it.

It was a strange mood, Auden reflected. He didn't really want a drink any more than he wanted actual company, which surprised him. A couple of blocks along, he heard the music coming from Taffy's. Auden remembered that the old Armenian who ran the place, for all he served up all sorts of drinks to his clientele, was famous as a teetotaler himself. He stopped, hesitated for a moment, and then stepped into Taffy's.

Taffy's was an Irish bar. The proprietor, Tavtag Nahigian, though of Armenian descent, loved Celtic music, and had opened an Irish bar hoping to attract Celtic musicians to play there. In this he was fairly successful. It was only after Taffy's had been established for some time that Tavtag, whom everyone had by that time come to call "Taffy," discovered that "Taffy" was not actually an Irish name but a derogatory term for a Welshman. By that time,

Taffy's was well established, and Tavtag declined to change the name.

The place was fairly crowded, and the band was in full swing, playing a jig now, or a reel—something fast and danceable. Auden hardly knew one type of Celtic tune from another, though he enjoyed listening to them. A number of people were dancing in what little space there was between the low stage and the ring of tables. He made his way to the bar, saw Taffy was working, and got the man's attention. The little round Armenian pointed his prominent nose in Auden's direction and approached with a wry smile.

"What can I get for you, Investigator Auden?" he asked.

Auden leaned close and spoke quietly. "You got one of them fake beers, the non-alcoholic kind?

"Oh-dat!" said Taffy. "We got dat, yes! Can do!" He turned away to fill a mug for the Investigator.

Auden snorted and forced a smile onto his face. Truth was, he resented the barkeep's smug condescension. "Oh-dat" meant "ODAT," the Anti-Alcohol Association's slogan, an acronym for "One Day At a Time." Auden didn't consider he was getting with the program, back on the wagon, he just didn't feel like drinking tonight. Maybe, he thought, if he was lucky, he wouldn't feel like drinking tomorrow night, either. The barkeep was right, he realized in spite of himself: Deal with what's here and now, and worry about tomorrow when it gets here. One day at a time. His resentment dissipated, and his smile, when Tavtag returned with the near-beer, was more genuine.

Auden leaned against the bar and surveyed the room. The band took a short break, and when they reassembled Auden noticed the personnel had changed. The slightly heavyset fellow with thinning hair and scruffy beard who had been playing the drum had been replaced by Rail-walker Morgan. The drum she played was wide and flat— Taffy, in one of his instructional moods, had once told Auden the name of it, though he couldn't remember it now. Like the other fellow, she played it with a short

drumstick with a head on both ends, which Auden remembered was called a tipper. They launched into something fast and raucous.

Though Auden didn't know much about music, he
did know something about human nature, social groups,
and pecking orders. Listening and watching, he could tell
the rest of the band was a tight-knit group of friends who
were used to jamming together, and Morgan was the newcomer. The regulars, he thought, were testing her and
challenging her with the way they played, introducing
weird sudden changes of tempo and rhythm, segueing into
unusual local versions of commonly known tunes. The
Railwalker, however, was up to the task, and stayed right
with them, never missing a beat.

After a little while the dynamic changed. Morgan had
apparently passed the test. She and the other musicians
seemed to quit playing "can you top this" and settled down
to enjoying making music together. More people were
crowding the dance floor, and Auden found himself smiling, his toe tapping. He also found his glass was empty. He
turned back to the bar, avoided the eye of the younger bartender, and caught Taffy's. The old Armenian refilled his
glass of fake beer and moved off again.

Eventually the music stopped, there was a round of
applause, and then a shuffling. As the sound of conversation began to grow, there was suddenly a startlingly loud,
high, bell-like tone. Auden whipped his head around to
find the source of the sound.

It was Morgan's drum. She sat alone on the stage now,
the drumstick discarded, and she began to play the drum
by hand, with finger rolls and snaps high and clear near
the rim, and deep bass tones resounding from the center.
In her hands the frame drum became an almost melodic
instrument, and though the deep beats and high tones
came fast and numerous, the overall pattern they created
was of a slow, somber song. Morgan began to hum, and
then to sing wordlessly, a slow, sad melody.

The bar fell quiet as Morgan played and sang, even
the rattle and clink of glasses and bottles fading to silence.

Her tuneful murmurs became discernable words, and as she sang, Auden realized he'd heard the song a time or two before. It was an old traditional lament called "Lowlands," the story of a woman who dreams of her man's death at sea to awaken and find her dream has been prophetic.

> He made no sign,
> no word he said,
> Lowlands...
> Lowlands awa' my John,
> and then I knew,
> my love was dead,
> lowlands awa'...

But of course, Auden thought, the name in her head was not John.

She finished the song. The silence that followed was a palpable object in the air. A single tear escaped Morgan's eye. She turned upstage, away from the crowd, to wipe it away. Someone began to clap, and then another and another, until the applause was thunderous. Morgan stood, nodded to them all with a small, rueful smile, and stepped down from the stage to return the drum to its owner.

"Thanks," she said quietly. Fending off congratulatory remarks, she stepped to the bar and ordered a double scotch. Soon enough the jam band had regathered on the low stage and begun to spin more lively, dancing tunes again.

Auden pushed away from the bar and began making his way slowly toward the back of the room. He smiled and nodded at the few people he knew, but kept moving, not stopping to get engaged in conversation.

Railwalker Morgan sat alone at a small table in a dark corner in the back. She was looking down, and looked like she was writing something on an object in her lap. Her tunic was draped on the back of her chair, her shirt sleeves rolled. On the table before her sat a half-empty glass of liquor and a dark lump that, in another moment, Auden

was able to identify as a loose braid of hair. He realized
with a start that her hair was shorter now. She'd evidently
cut off her braid—and probably just recently, or it
wouldn't be sitting on the table. As he got closer, he realized it wasn't a pen or pencil in her hand, but a knife,
which she held by the blade, using the point to score
something into a surface below the table level.

The woman was kind of a bitch, he thought; but she
had just lost her husband. He ought to at least offer condolences. She was absorbed in her task, and the noise level
was relatively high. Auden didn't want to surprise her, so
he shifted an empty chair noisily as he approached, and
she looked up.

"Railwalker," he said with a nod.

"Investigator Auden."

She'd stopped what she was doing, and placed her left
hand palm down on the edge of the table. Her right still
held the knife by the blade, like a pen. He looked again at
her left hand. Blood was gathering on the table.

If he'd stopped to think about it, he wouldn't have
laid hands on a Railwalker, but Auden's move was instinct-
ive. He leaned over and grabbed her left hand, turning it
over. The bare forearm was scored up and down with cuts,
blood running freely from them. The cuts looked like
some sort of runes or an alphabet Auden wasn't familiar
with.

In an instant she twisted the captured hand around,
and then she was holding him, his wrist gripped in her left
hand, the knife flipped over in her right, held in a fighting
grip, point at his throat. "Don't push your luck, grackle,"
she said.

He stared into her eyes for a long, silent moment.
Finally he said, "Why do you people call me that? I never
understood that."

Morgan released her grip and sat back, chuckling.
"Grackle's a bird the ignorant could take for a crow," she
said. "It's a term for Railwalker wannabes."

Auden laughed. "What made y'all think I was a wannabe?"

"The coat," she said. "And your use of the Voice."

Auden looked down at his overcoat, realizing that it did indeed look something like the Railwalkers' crow coats. He looked at her again. "Never thought of that," he said with a shrug. "Just thought it was a nice coat. As to the Voice, it's just a trick I picked up from an old man I knew once."

"Not really a wannabe?"

"Nope. Never really cared much for the weird stuff, ghosts and omens and such. No offense."

"None taken."

"Never really wanted to be anything but a guard investigator." He looked over the bar, then back at her. "Mind if I sit?"

She nodded toward the empty chair. Auden shifted the chair and sat where he could face Morgan and still keep one eye on the rest of the bar. The Railwalker noted that, and nodded. She reached out and plucked the glass from the table, drained it, and then signaled a passing waitress for a refill. The waitress picked up Morgan's glass and then raised her eyebrows at Auden.

"I'm good, thanks," he said, waving her off.

Morgan looked at her bloody forearm. "Some cultures," she said, "a widow cuts off her hair, tears her clothing. Some even cut themselves."

Auden nodded, his eyes on the braid of hair lying on the table. "Your man Rok seemed like a decent guy."

"Oh, smooth segue, Investigator. Let's draw the widow out. They give you a psych course in the guard for dealing with bereaved family members?"

"I wish." He snorted a laugh. "We're stuck figuring out for ourselves how to deal with that shit."

She sighed. Stuck the knife point-down in the table, where it stood up like a tombstone. The waitress returned with Morgan's drink. She looked dubiously at the knife stuck in the tabletop, glanced at Auden. As Morgan stared at the tabletop, Auden silently mouthed, "I'll cover it." The waitress shrugged and headed off again.

"Yeah," Morgan said finally. "I'll tell you about Rok."

She picked up a napkin to wipe the blood from her fore-arm. "He saved my life. Many times. I would have been killed by a bunch of Ravagers in Carlito Flats if not for him. Pulled me out of the path of a runaway truck once, in Malpaso. Of course, I saved his arse more than a few times, too."

When she reached up to push her now shorter hair back from her face, Auden noticed keloid scars on her right forearm. Cutting herself was obviously not a new activity for the Railwalker woman; the scars were old.

"But that first time, you know why that was the most important? Because all those other times, those were all outside threats. That first time what he saved me from was myself."

She reached around to the pocket of her tunic and brought out a flat, leather-covered case, large for a cigarette case. She opened it. It contained little cigars, the kind they called "Clints." It was what Auden had seen Rok smoking.

Morgan brought the open case to her face and inhaled the scent of the tobacco. She looked at Auden. "You want one?" she said, offering the case. "I don't actually smoke 'em. I'm just carrying them around 'cause they were his." Her voice didn't break on the last word, but it grew thick.

"Thanks." Auden took one and lit it up. As he exhaled smoke, he saw her close her eyes and breathe it in for a moment. Then she looked at him.

"Before Rok, I never met a man I really trusted. I'd had a few lovers, but I never really let myself get attached, never really opened up to them, 'cause I always expected they'd either start abusing me somehow, or they'd up and leave, or both. Most of 'em left, of course. Hard to keep up a relationship where somebody never really lets you in. 'Course, I didn't see it that way at the time. Back then, I just figured they were doing what men do, and leaving. I couldn't see how that was a sort of self-fulfilling prophecy." She made a sound that was almost a laugh. "Don't mean some of them weren't also arseholes. I picked some real winners." She swallowed a large slug of her drink, and when she put the glass down, it made a startlingly loud rap on the tabletop.

"Tried women for a while, too," she went on. "For some reason I thought that would be different. And it was, in some ways. But even with women I couldn't really give my trust. I always kept 'em shut out. And guess what? They'd leave, too.

"Rok, he really was different. He had all the patience in the world, and he just wouldn't leave, wouldn't do the sort of bullshit stuff I always expected men to do. He just stayed there, steady and regular, and totally committed. I gave him every opportunity to cut out. Even tried to drive him to it. But he wouldn't. He said if I wanted to end it, I'd have to leave him.

"When I finally faced the truth, I realized I didn't want to end it. I wanted what he was offering. And I'd put together enough of my own self-worth by that time to think that maybe I even deserved it. Things started to get a little easier from that point on."

Auden watched the Railwalker still turning the cigar case over in her hands, lost in thought or memory. She was very drunk, though she didn't show it much in her demeanor—except that her zoner accent had gotten stronger. Of course, hiding how drunk you were was easier when you were sitting down, as Auden well knew. He had a feeling she'd be staggering if she tried to walk. "How'd you come to be a cutter?" he asked.

"When I was four years old," she said after a long pause, "my parents died. Mother of zone fever. You ever seen zone fever?" Auden shook his head. "Nasty stuff," she said. "Cooks your brain while it eats your body. Makes you crazy, gives you hallucinations, paranoia.

"Anyways, parents dead, they put me in an orphan-age." She stopped suddenly. "Shit, why am I telling you this? You really want to hear this?"

"I asked, didn't I?"

"You did that." She nodded. "A'right. Well, the short version is, I hit a series of foster homes, five different families in the next few years. I was a problem kid. If I didn't run away, they got fed up with my bullshit and shipped me back to the orphanage. Didn't help that a couple of the husbands turned out to like little girls. Fucking diddlers."

Auden nodded. He knew about foster parents who abused their wards.

"But it was after that I got started burning and cutting myself. Guess I was about thirteen, fourteen. Something about it was just so cool. It was, like, so good to be the one in charge of inflicting the pain, y'know? And it was like it released me from feeling the pain on the inside.

"When I was sixteen, legal at the time in Two Suns, I ran away for good. Kicked around a while, lived in a squat... Then the ghosts started to catch up with me, and the crows started talking to me. It was either assume I was crazy and check myself in to another institution, or go to the Railwalkers and ask them how to manage that shit."

"Guess you chose the Railwalkers."

"Yeah." Morgan smiled and looked down at her arm. The cuts still seeped blood, and she patted them with the napkin again. "They broke me of cutting myself, mostly. Eventually they let me participate in some of the body modification rituals: tattooing, piercing, scarification. But only after I'd proved it was a conscious choice, and not a compulsion anymore."

She pulled up her right sleeve and raised her arm. It was covered with complex designs, some tattooed, some keloid scars, the two types of markings braided together and interwoven.

"When Rok and I got married we exchanged rings, but we also got matching tattoos." She indicated a complex design that looked like a bracelet, running entirely around her wrist. Auden noticed that there were burns and scars incorporated into the inked design. "We designed it together, to include some of the cuts and burns I already had. He got cuts and burns to match them." Her eyes filled with tears. She blinked them back, took a deep breath. Reached for her drink, missed it, tried again. This time she managed to pick up the glass, and drained the half inch or so of liquor remaining in the bottom.

"Railwalker Morgan," said Auden, "you are totally shit-faced."

"Yeah."

"You should get some sleep. I'll walk you back to the Tower."

The woman looked at him like she was going to argue, then appeared to think better of it. "Yeah," she said. "Thanks."

They rose. Morgan made her way unsteadily to the ladies' room. Auden paid for their drinks, then waited by the bar, reflecting that it was probably good that Taffy's was only a couple of blocks from the CA Tower. When she rejoined him they wove through the crowd toward the entrance. Once outside, the cool night air seemed to help her a little, and he didn't actually end up carrying her back, though it was a close thing. In the end he wondered if carrying her might not have been easier. It took her three tries to slide the electronic key through the reader. She turned in the doorway.

"Y'know," she said, "for a grackle, you're okay." She aimed a light punch at his shoulder, but it struck only glancingly.

Auden chuckled. "Get some sleep, Railwalker." She nodded and staggered into the suite. Auden wondered if she'd make it to her room, or end up sleeping on the couch, or even passing out on the floor, but figured his responsibility ended here. He pulled the door closed. Let Railwalker Wolf take it from here, if he was in. The investigator turned and walked back to the elevator.

Back out on the street Auden found he was not interested in much of anything but sleep. As he started down First Street again heading for his own apartment, he noticed two figures seated in conversation by the fountain: Railwalker Wolf and Anita Robles. He smiled to himself, thinking Morgan might sleep on the floor tonight after all, since it was a good bet Railwalker Wolf wouldn't be back at their suite any time soon.

42. PARKVIEW APARTMENTS, BAY CITY

It wasn't often that Nita Robles got annoyed at the conditions of her job and life. Being a woman in the guard meant you wore your strength on your sleeve just to survive. But of course that meant that all the men, hardcore gamblers at the poker game of life, had to up the ante, be stronger-than-thou. Even the ones like Gage, or the Old Man, who were a little more subtle about it, danced that dance. Mostly Nita could live with that. You were a survivor, you took life as it came, just did your best to get by and not lose any more self-respect than you had to.

But now and then, it seemed like you ought to get to take a breather. Stop and smell the damn roses, or whatever. These days her bars were the Tankard, where the guard tended to gather, or the Ring, down in half-wharf, where the fighters—boxers, martial artists, guards, bouncers, rent-a-cops, what have you—would congregate. When she came home with a man, it was hot and fast and no-holds-barred. Half the time it started in the stairwell, and by the time the door of the apartment shut they'd be naked, or good as, a two-backed beast staggering to the bedroom. Or not bothering, but collapsing there on the hardwood floor into sweat and hunger and bodily juices.

So why was she hesitant and nervous bringing Railwalker Wolf to her apartment? They'd been talking, and she didn't crawl all over him as they started up the stairs. Nor, once the door closed behind them, had she jumped his bones. Instead, she had offered him a drink. He'd asked for cold water.

What, she wondered, is the matter with me?

She ducked into the kitchen area, ran the water, and went to the fridge for ice. She'd overfilled the ice cube tray again, and they were going to be hard to get out.

It's because he doesn't wear his strength on his sleeve, she thought. He was gentle, polite and friendly, but firm about most things. Like the instructors at the guard academy tried to teach their guards to be. Most of them pretended to be that way, and many fooled the civilians; but this guy was the real thing. His strength was a tool to be used when needed, and left at rest when not, like senseis would teach you your limbs and mind should be. When she twisted the plastic tray, the ice cubes slipped out in one mass, a few separating as they struck the counter. She collected the loose ones, dropped them into two glasses, and filled the glasses with water with only a single glance at the fridge, where the beer was.

Yes, she thought, she'd asked for a breather, and here it was. A man who could not only match her on the mats (probably), but who could talk about things other than methods of hurting people and sports statistics. Railwalkers knew all sorts of ancient lore, and were given the equivalent of a college education.

43. WOLF

When Nita walked back to the living area with the two glasses of water I was still looking over her bookcase.

"You've got a full set of Malvern," I said. "And the Master Sayings. Annotated."

"My Dad thought it belonged in any law enforcement agent's library." She handed me the glass and sat on the couch. "Have you studied his period at all?"

"The 'Master' of the Sayings? A little."

"Victorian was an odd period. Strange that a man of such insight and wisdom came from a society so screwed up. The Victorians were very uptight about sex."

I walked to the couch and crouched beside her. "Are you feeling uptight about sex at the moment?" I asked.

"Strangely, yes." She looked me in the eyes, and I realized her brown eyes had green rings around the pupils. "But that doesn't mean I don't want it."

"Come to Hartshall for an evening before you leave."
Roth's voice faded in and out, static spiking from time to
time. He must be on a portable unit. "The place is cleaned
up. We'll gather upstairs, light a fire in the fireplace, raise a
glass to the dead."

"Gotta admit," I said, "I don't feel much like partying
just now."

"I know your man just died. We all have to honor and
mourn our dead, and that's something it's good to do
together. Besides, it's probably the last chance we'll get to
relax and talk about things other than the Beast. And it's
important we do that before you leave. Besides, we've got a
ceremony to do, don't we? Closure on your gift of aid to
the city?"

"I'm not sure we're ready—"

"I'll see you at seven," he said, and he hung up.

I was a little surprised to find that Morgan had agreed
to go too. "What do you want me to say?" She shrugged
where she lay on the couch in our suite, staring at the ceiling, fiddling with Rok's cigar case. "The Rothster is very
fucking insistent. Plus he asked for Ceremony. We're sort
of obligated, aren't we?"

Yeah, we were. Roth was the one who summoned our
help. It was right we do the closure thing on that. Except I
wasn't sure we were really near anything like closure. I'd
been about to point that out to Roth when he'd cut me off.
I pointed it out to Morgan now.

"Fuck it," she said. "If Roth is satisfied, then fine. Let's
give him his ceremony and get the hell out of this place."

This wasn't like Morgan. Usually once she got her

teeth into a mystery she was tenacious as a zone badger until she had all the answers. I watched the light flash off the silver edges of the cigar case as she turned it in her hands.

"I thought we were agreed there was more to this than one bloodthirsty shapeshifter," I said. "What about where the Beast came from, why he was after Roth? What about Helena Crichton?"

She sighed. "Helena Crichton," she said. She didn't look at me, kept her eyes on the cigar case. "She'd be, what, at least seventy by now? If she was behind all this, without her pet beast, she's nothing but an angry old woman. Sometimes you need to let the past bury the past. We did what we said we'd do. We stopped the Beast. *You* stopped the Beast. We've done enough. We've lost enough." She opened the case, looked at the little cigars inside.

"An angry old woman could have other servants, partners, co-conspirators," I said. "We have an obligation to make sure the city is safe."

Morgan snapped the case shut and stood. "Fine. You're the Brick. It's your call."

I watched her stalk away and vanish into the room she'd shared with Rok. I shook my head. I could understand grief smothering Morgan's intellectual curiosity about the mystery of the Beast's origins, and his master or mistress, if he'd had one. But whatever her mental state, I'd never known Morgan to not take her obligations as a Railwalker seriously. Granted, I'd never seen her grieving for a dead husband, either. The loss of Rok was like a large stone weighing down the center of my being, the loss of Windsteel close beside it. Rok had been my friend, my Bear, and my partner, but not my lover or husband. Maybe I really just didn't understand what she was going through.

I grabbed up my tunic and headed for the door. Whatever was going on with Morgan, eventually either she'd open up and talk to me, or I'd figure it out myself. Or not. In any case, I wanted a look at the Beast's body.

I don't know why I'd expected the guard morgue and

forensic lab to be in the basement. I'd watched too many mystery DVs, maybe. Turned out it was on the ninth floor of the tower. Once you were inside, though, it might as well have been in the basement, since it had no windows.

The man in the white coat was heavyset, with a mop of curly brown hair and bright, intelligent eyes behind square glasses. "Railwalker Wolf," he said. "Doctor Bill Barnet. Call me Bill. Fascinating specimen you sent us. Thank you so much."

"I didn't send you a specimen," I said. "I killed a living being. The guard brought his remains to you."

His face fell. "Of course, of course," he said. "We must respect the dead, even our fallen enemies." He brightened again. "But this particular fallen enemy really is quite amazing." He led me to the table on which the Beast's body was stretched out. "These armor-like growths are keratin based..."

"Can you tell me where he came from, anything about who he was?"

"Oh... well." He blinked. "He was human. At least, he's got human DNA. Of woman born, as the saying goes. Unless, of course, he was 'from his mother's womb untimely ripped...'"

"MacDuff was still a human," I said.

"Right. As is this guy. Apparently. I can tell you a lot about his peculiarities, but unfortunately, I can't tell you much about *why* he's so peculiar."

"He was a shapeshifter," I said.

"We haven't got a lot of data about shapeshifters, and we don't understand them very well. Keene dissected a few back in '03, '05 or so. Didn't find out much. We still can't tell you why they are able to shift their molecular structure."

"It's magick. It won't show up under your microscope."

"No such thing, Railwalker. Oh, I know, the phenomena are real. But it's not magic in the sense you mean it. The 'unnatural' is by definition impossible. It's all natural. We just don't understand it yet."

I was looking at the Beast's body. On his forehead was what the guard had come to call the "beast mark." It was drawn on the skin in some sort of paint or makeup, which had partially rubbed off, and yet...

I looked closer. I reached out and rubbed at it with my thumb. The doctor held out a rubber glove and said, "Umm..." I ignored him.

There was something underneath that painted mark, something hard-edged just under the skin. I rubbed some more.

"Doc, take a look at this," I said. He looked, then took a scalpel and ran it around the edge of the area. It didn't bleed much. He drew something out of the wound with a pair of forceps.

It was a piece of metal, the size of a large coin, but wafer thin. A cutout of the Crichton Industrial Development logo. It was inverted, and so still looked to me like the prototype of the "beast mark."

"Now I suppose we have to wonder if this guy really was born," said Barnet, "or if he was hatched in a lab. I didn't see any tattooed bar code."

"No," I said, "he was born. This was inserted later in life. It was part of an initiation, like a tattoo. The metal was so thin it didn't really show, so he reinforced it with war paint." I wasn't sure how I knew that, but I was certain of it.

Roth was right. Hartshall had been cleaned up thoroughly, and the only obvious suggestions of the violence that had gone on here two nights ago were a window paneled over with plywood and the faint scent of blood beneath the sharp odor of cleaning fluid. I hadn't really appreciated the upstairs private dining room when I'd been here before, and it had been untouched by the fight that went on downstairs. Paneled in light wood, the room had a stone fireplace at one end and a gathering of mission style couch and chairs. The dining table was in the same style, and seated six.

And there were just five of us... Roth, Sarah Weldt,

Morgan, myself, and Weldt's daughter, Rochelle, with one empty place at the table. Roth was also right about the food: The venison chili was amazing.

The meal finished with coffee and tobacco. We performed a brief, heartfelt Ritual of the Given and Received, and then shared a cup and bowl with the dead. Formalities concluded, the atmosphere relaxed and we took our cups and bowls to the fireside.

The girl, Rochelle, had not gotten to act the Javamama, but she did refill my coffee cup for me now with formal ritual intent. It was obvious Roth and Weldt had worked out their differences after their divorce, and it had been the girl's choice to keep the Roth name. She was very serious at twelve, with long, dark hair and large, luminous eyes.

"Rochelle is training with Hannah Caine," Roth said, as his daughter refilled my cup.

"It's not as if I want to be a harlot when I grow up," she said, and I saw Roth and Weldt exchange a glance. "But they do have the best social graces. And I'm sure those will be useful, whatever I become."

Roth laughed and hugged the girl. "Gets that calculating mind from her mother," he said.

"I thought you didn't get along with the Guild-madam," said Morgan. There was something in her voice when she said that. She'd actually varied the flat monotone she'd spoken in since Rok's death. I knew that tone. It said she knew this wasn't good news, but she wasn't willing to say so yet.

"There's lots of things we don't see eye to eye on, politically," said Roth. "But certainly we respect each other. And she is an old mistress of her craft. Who better to teach Rochelle her social skills?"

Roth broke out his expensive scotch. Weldt and Morgan both chose to stick with their wine, and Rochelle had a small glass of lightly spiked punch. When the drinks had been distributed, Roth asked Morgan if she'd tell a tale. Any Railwalker can spin a story, of course, and we all know the traditional Brick tales. But the Profs are usually the ones who have a passion for it, who carry the lore and know all the old and obscure stories, the history tales and such that aren't part of the central canon. Roth would know this, and I wondered if it was a guess or just a good bet on his part Morgan would be one of those with a real passion for it. At Morgan's expression, I thought perhaps Roth had been too clever for his own good; it was early days to be trying to draw a grieving widow back to herself, especially one who was sharp enough to know exactly what the city boss was doing. She started to shake her head, then stopped herself. If Roth made the request formal, she'd be honor obligated to agree to it, and there was no way Morgan was going to allow herself to be forced into something she didn't want to do.

So she hauled out her frame drum, settled herself by the fire, and began to play. She set a rhythm, played with it for a few moments. Then she began to speak, first nearly singing the words, and then settling down into the prose of the tale of Huck and Heather, and the troubles of Farr City:

> Two cities in mountainous countryside,
> They come to a place where they both decide
> They'd be better off if they was allied,
> Sister cities, as you might say, side by side.

Farr City's Blues tells the tale of two rival cities who forge an alliance over a marriage, but like in Romeo and Juliet, along come Tybalt and Mercutio—in this case a young buck named Rant and some unnamed guy from the other city. They start a fight, and next thing you know it's war again, blood running in the streets.

They nearly recover from this, both sides wanting and needing peace. But the heroine, Jess, is put in a position where no matter what she does she betrays someone. Many of the protagonists die, victims of someone's idea of honor. It's a sad tale, traditionally told in alternating sections of prose recitation and almost-song like punctuated rhyme.

They stand that way for a good long time,
While the tension continues to slowly climb.
You could hear the sound of a pin or a dime if you
dropped it.
Jess looks at Rant, and the rest look at Jess,
And Rant got his eyes closed in major distress.
He's lookin' in the eye of death, I guess,
and prayin' to some old god to bless his dyin' soul.

Morgan spoke and sang the tale in the traditional way, accompanying herself on the frame drum. It was amazing, the variety of sound she could get out of that little drum. She'd make you hear whatever was in the story: rain, waves on the beach, gunfire, the cries of birds, a train, an ornithopter, or the grass growing. By the time she reached the passage where Huck gets killed Sarah Weldt was mesmerized, a blank expression on her face. Rochelle had gotten moist eyes back when Jess lost Nate, and was wiping at the tears now. Roth shifted uncomfortably in his chair—Huck and Nate were city bosses, both murdered.

Jess ain't proud of what she's wrought,
And she knows what kind of trouble she's bought,
But the truth is all her choices were fraught
With confusion, betrayal and fear.
So vengeance and blood and pain were sown,
And the cities both figure the gauntlet's thrown,
And it's back to a hatred that cuts to the bone,
Each city now alone, against the other.

And that's the story, or so I've heard,
So you tell me, was Jess true to her word?
She betrayed one man to avenge the other,
Killing Huck for Heather's brother.
Nate, her city boss and lover,
Wanted cities allied one to another.
Hatred and vengeance ended that plan,
And the life of many a woman and many a man.
Two cities in mountainous countryside,

Failed to keep themselves allied,
And many good folks died,
In sister cities, as you might say,
Side by side.

Morgan finished, and the last beats of the drum faded away as those assembled applauded.

"Helluva tale," said Roth.

Weldt nodded. "It is a classic," she said. "And beautifully performed." Morgan nodded her thanks.

"But Jess was stupid," said Rochelle. "Huck didn't kill Nate. And he was mad at the guy who did, and offered to kill him. She shouldn't have killed Huck."

"In the old days," said Roth, "they set a great store by the honor and fealty you owed to your city boss. Not to mention she was married to Nate. Huck may not have wanted Nate killed, but it happened in his city, and ultimately he was responsible. The folks of Danz River would have seen it as a betrayal if Jess hadn't sought vengeance."

"I still think it was stupid."

Roth shrugged, with an expression that said, "Kids! What are you gonna do?"

"You're right," Morgan said to the girl, "it was stupid. I've always thought that tale was a warning about the dangers of being too rigid about obligations and protocol."

"I could use some air," said Roth. He turned to me and added, "Walk with me."

He led me out of the room, down the stairs, and out onto the deck overlooking the bay. I'd been expecting something like this, some kind of private talk Roth wanted to have with me, but I'd halfway thought he'd manage it by wanting to show me some new kitchen tool he'd acquired or something. I should have known he'd make no pretense. He'd been a city boss for over twenty years. He was secure in his power base and getting ready to retire. What did he need with pretense?

Roth looked out over the view of the darkened bay and set his glass on the deck railing. Without preamble he said, "You know that Traveler is going to die soon. Not now, maybe not for a couple of years—but three years at most."

I was surprised, but mainly because the news had come to me from a city boss, and not through the Railwalker network. Traveler was the Elder Raven of the Railwalker Order. He was a hundred years old or so. His health hadn't been great last I heard, but there was no talk of impending death.

"When Traveler goes, there must be a Raven to take his place." Roth stared me in the eye. "A reasonable, balanced Raven."

I could see where he was going with this. If Groute took control, he would withdraw the order from the world, make the Nests into closed monasteries. If Kane became Elder Raven, he'd be politicking and maneuvering to acquire more civil power and authority for the Railwalkers. I could see Roth didn't like either alternative, and frankly, neither did I, though probably for different reasons. Roth was thinking of the stability of the status quo, the usefulness of the Railwalker Order to the city bosses. I was thinking of the order itself, of its integrity—although I admit, I shared Roth's concerns about the bigger picture.

The Cities Alliance was a loose federation, not a central government. It could only advise—and sometimes pressure—local governments, but it couldn't compel. The Railwalkers were independent, and the sort of authority the cities granted them was traditional—as well as limited and voluntary.

Still, there were some laws on most of the cities' books. Railwalkers could be asked to act as mediators and judges, if both parties in a conflict agreed to it. Agreeing to it was voluntary, but once the agreement was made, the Railwalker had final say in the case, in most cities. We could be consulted as healers, but, again, once a physician handed a case over to a Railwalker, according to most areas' laws, the Railwalker was then in total control until he handed the patient back to the physician.

Then there were cases like Roth's: crimes where the

city guard were without any leads. Or crimes where mutant or otherworldly forces were thought to be involved. Here again, we couldn't march in and take over, but once we were asked in we were in until we chose otherwise, in as far as we chose to go.

The whole thing was in precarious balance right now. Looking ahead, I could see serious trouble for all of us—Railwalkers and everyone else—if the authority the cities and regions granted our order was given too easily, in too many civil contexts. If that happened, all it would take was a little luck for one unscrupulous type—or one well intentioned but misguided sort—to rise eventually to Elder Raven, and there'd be hell to pay. Even today, if we'd chosen to, our order could probably "disappear" people we deemed a threat, manipulated and pressured certain governments into certain actions. Not that I thought Groute was capable of such a thing. But I wondered suddenly if that had ever happened. If members of the order had ever actually turned so far from the order's precepts. I didn't know of any, but that didn't mean it hadn't happened. It was a sobering thought.

Roth broke in on my thoughts. "You're one of the few Railwalkers qualified to stand for the job."

I'd known that was coming. I shook my head. "I'm too young to be a Senior Raven, let alone Elder."

"What are you, thirty-six, thirty-seven? Put in a couple of years as a Raven, maybe the Western Warden, you'd be forty by the time you're confirmed," said Roth. "That's all that's actually required by your rules."

He'd obviously been doing his homework, thinking about the situation. I should have known he'd know what the rule said. By custom, Elder Ravens were generally in their fifties or sixties, but there had been a few decades there when life expectancy had been down all over the country, and the rule reflected those times. The unspoken message here was that if I chose to eventually make a bid for the position of Elder Raven, he would support me. City bosses had no official say in the election of the Elder, but it was no secret that the Corvine Council and the

Raven Parliament would take the opinions and preferences of the various city bosses into account when making their decision. Like I say, diplomacy was part of the job for the average Railwalker, and it was even more so for the Elder Raven. It behooved the order to select an Elder with whom the city bosses could get along.

"I walk the rails, Mr. Roth," I said. "I never aspired to a position of authority in the order. I'm not a politician."

"But I think you're also not a man who will walk away from his order, or the peoples of the cities and the zones, when they're in need and you can help them."

I had to admit he had me there. But was he right? Did the order really need me, or was my ego listening to strokes from a retiring politico who wanted an advantageous alliance he could pass on to his successor? It wasn't something I could sort out here and now. And Roth recognized that.

"Think about it," he said.

I nodded. We stood looking out over the sea.

"You haven't mentioned a closing ceremony," he said.

"Not sure we're ready for that," I told him.

"Why not? The Beast's dead, isn't he? Might be interesting to know who he was and where he came from, maybe, but is it really important?"

"I'm surprised you have to ask. He was after you. His forehead had a damn metal Crichton Industrial logo embedded in it. Doc Barnet says he was in his late twenties at the most. His grudge against you can't be from personal experience, and it can't date to the Takeover. He was indoctrinated and trained by someone whose grudge against you does go back that far. The Beast was a puppet. The puppet master is still out there somewhere, and might have other puppets."

Roth looked away, turned toward the sea. He took a drink. He was too intelligent not to see it. "Damnit. Gods damn it, wasn't this enough already? You're right, Railwalker, we do have to find this nemesis of mine. Do what you have to. We'll do closure on it when you're ready."

45. WOLF

On the way back to City Plaza in the back of a chauffeured runabout, I asked Morgan about why she'd sounded odd at the mention of Hannah Caine.

"I'm not a hundred percent certain yet," she said, and sighed. "But I think she's Helena Crichton."

"And therefore, probably the mother of the Beast."

"Yeah," she said, with an odd look I couldn't identify. "I think so."

There was clearly more to it. Something was bothering her. I was about to press her further when her head snapped up and she said, "What happened?" She had caught the energy before I did. She'd had less to drink.

I picked it up a second later, the buzz of energy, as we turned the corner into City Plaza, which was ablaze with lights; guard runabouts, autos, ambulances. I looked at all the flashing lights through a light-haze-of-Scotch distance, took a deep breath, and felt the hooch receding fast. Something serious had gone down here.

A patrol guardsman named Howard came to the side of our runabout.

"The Railwalkers?" he asked. "Got orders from Chief Gage. You're to go right up."

"Up" turned out to be the fourteenth floor, where the V.I.P. suites were.

As the elevator doors opened, my breath caught in my throat at the smell. The place was awash in blood and littered with corpses. Guard techs in white coats and face masks whisked back and forth with brittle efficiency, trying not to think too much about what they were documenting.

Gage stood not far from the elevators, some kind of

white cream on his upper lip. I assumed it was something to kill the smell. He held out a small jar.

"I haven't let them move anything," he said, "until you got here. But the techs are done with the bodies in the hall."

I was right, the jar was some sort of mentholated cream. I passed it back to him unused. The smell was unpleasant, but if I was going to pick up anything from the energy here, I didn't dare confuse my system with Gage's menthol.

Five of the dead were guardsmen. A guardswoman lay half in, half out of one of the doorways along the hall. One smear of blood along the wall, left by a falling guardsman, seemed to point toward the woman.

Every door had been blasted open. Every living being had been killed. Entenman, the rookie guardsman who had drawn a shift on the front desk of the CA Tower, had been shot through the forehead. The four guards in the hallway were cut down by automatic weapons fire. The millionaire importer who was thinking of relocating his warehouses to Bay City was cut almost in half by a spurt of bullets from a full auto pistol. The visiting secretary of commerce for Santa Brita was shot through the forehead, like the rookie in the lobby. The wife of the councilman from Corteone was decapitated.

It was Harold Carter and Jim Shaw who suffered the most. They were the two men on the floor who were supposed to be at Hartshall the night of the Beast's defeat, the two who were the real reason for the extra guards posted on the fourteenth floor. Shaw's legs and arms had been cut off, and he'd been left to bleed to death. Carter was eviscerated, his entrails pulled out and draped over his right shoulder. Forensics would later confirm that this had been done while he was still alive.

Ashes. All I could taste or sense was ashes. At the end of the hall, Nita Robles lay twisted at the juncture of wall and floor, service automatic loose in her hand, the slide locked open, which meant she had emptied the clip. A line of dark stain across the front of her tunic, black holes dotting the line. They hadn't hit her face, though it was splattered with blood.

I knelt beside her, staring, realizing that I was facing the same paradox she'd mentioned to me the night before. How many times had I sat beside dead bodies? Why was it still so hard to accept when it's someone you knew and cared about? Every death should affect me this way. Rok did. Nita Robles did. But many others didn't, except in some abstract way. That seemed wrong somehow. But this, this emptiness at the core of me, that seemed right, the only reaction possible to the absolute absence of Rok, of Nita.

Much as I didn't want to, I sat down at the end of the hall, began to slow my breathing and heighten my senses to the point where a new sense would emerge.

The place tasted of the Beast, but different—something older, something larger. Of course, I thought to myself, it was his mother. The woman. Helena Crichton, or whatever she called herself now. Hannah Caine, if Morgan was right. I opened my eyes.

"Are there security tapes?" I asked Gage.

He nodded. "Of course. Boss Roth is on his way. He'll meet us in the media room."

I didn't like the way his eyes looked. He'd seen the tapes already, and clearly he didn't like what was on them. I didn't ask. I'd know for myself soon enough. We followed him back to the elevators.

The media room Roth joined us in was small, cramped, and jammed with screens and consoles. A technician played back the surveillance videos. From an elevated perspective near the ceiling we watched a woman step from the elevator with an automatic weapon in each hand and begin shooting.

Roth stared at the image on the screen. "Hannah Caine?" he said. "Hannah fucking *Caine*? I can't believe it."

"You might remember her better as Helena Crichton," Morgan said.

Roth turned his gaze from the screen to Morgan, but

it was still the same disbelieving stare. "Helena Crichton died..." he started.

"Not," said Morgan. Her voice was flat and monotone. "One week after the People's Takeover, she surfaced in El Tope, a small town just over the Mayacan border, with her newborn son and a suitcase full of cash. She hired some local thugs, had the local headman assassinated, and took over the town. Two years later, calling herself Hannah Caine, she bought her first brothel in Catalina, bought her way into the Harlot's Guild, and then expanded to a place in Bay City."

"And the rest is fucking history," Roth said. He blew out his breath. Then he focused on Morgan again. "You knew this and didn't tell me? Elvis wept, she's been tutoring my kid!"

"We couldn't be certain," I said. "Think about it. Suppose we'd been wrong. That's a heavy accusation to lay against the Headmadam of the Harlot's Guild."

Roth let it go. He clearly didn't like it, but he was a practical man. He turned back to the screens and blew out his breath again.

"Damn. I had no clue that woman would be capable —mentally, or physically. Unbelievable. And what about the Beast?"

"She took his body from the morgue on her way out," Gage answered.

"Her son," said Morgan. "Varger Caine. He served as a guardsman in Santa Brita during the Union Riots."

I didn't know where Morgan had come up with that, but I didn't doubt she was right. "And," I said, "he ran with a gang of Ravagers in the zones. He was responsible for the Hicks Junction massacre."

Morgan looked at me. She had seen the swords the Beast had carried, so she must have realized this before. Or maybe not. Maybe it never sank in, distracted as she was over Rok.

I stared at the tape again, studying the woman. "She didn't shift. I thought sure she was his teacher."

"She was," said Morgan. "Look closer." She leaned

over, took the controls from the tech, ran the tape back and stopped it. "Look at her wrist when she reaches here. That's not normal human musculature. She's, like, half-shifted."

"She had to know about the security cameras," Roth rumbled. "She wants us to know what and who she is."

"Where will she go now?" I asked.

"Not to the Gates of Hell, I'm sure," said Auden. I hadn't realized he'd joined us.

"Excuse me?"

Morgan said, "Her offices in the city are at her main hostelry, the Gate of Heaven. Some people call it the Gates of Hell."

"No," said Gage, "she won't go there, but we'd best send a team there anyway. Could be evidence there."

"Or resources we should cut off," I added.

"Call Judge DiCerto," said Roth. "Get a warrant." Gage was already on the phone.

Morgan was staring at her comp unit. "She has three brothels in the city," she said. "One with an attached gaming hell, two hotels here, one in Santa Brita, and a house in Anderson."

"We'll cordon off the routes out of the city to the north and east," said Auden.

"This woman won't retreat to Santa Brita," I said. "She's not finished. Roth is still alive, and we've killed her Beast—her son. You throw your cordon up, Investigator, but my bet is she's not going to leave Bay City. Let's check those hotels and brothels."

"She was probably operating out of the house in Anderson," Morgan said. "It's right near Hartshall. She'll have cleared out of there by now, though."

"The place on the south side," said Auden. "Lot of rough trade down there. Less chance of bloodstains and weaponry attracting attention."

Gage shook his head. "But more chance of her expensive car and clothing being noticed," he pointed out.

Something clicked. The Beast was a bonsai. And Hannah Caine—Helena Crichton—was the gardener.

"He thought like she does," I said, "like she taught him. She'll think the same way. She'll have a beat-up looking vehicle with a solid motor and a downscale wardrobe ready. Auden's right. Send teams to the other places, but I'm going to the south side."

"Byer leave," said Auden, "I'll come with."

We all started for the door, except for Morgan. "Wolf, a minute," she said.

I waved the others on and turned back. Her look was grim, and she wouldn't meet my eye.

"You need to see this." She turned her portable so I could see the screen.

"What am I looking at?" I asked. There were two Citizen ID forms on the screen, and they looked very similar, and somehow familiar. I looked closer.

"I ran a pattern recognition match for faces on picture IDs," Morgan explained, "and came up with this match. The one on the right is the earliest record we can find on Helena Crichton, nee Hebat..."

The one on the left was my mother.

The photographs were identical.

"How long have you known about this?" I asked.

Irena looked across the cab at Miguel driving the truck. He was tall but not bulky, his slim figure giving little hint of the strength it held. She'd seen him break a man's spine once. Miguel had been useful this past year, and he seemed genuinely devoted to her. It would be a shame to kill him. She shook off the brief weakness. Reminded herself he was almost too strong, she would have to take him by surprise, kill him quickly.

Compassion, she thought, that was the problem. It weakened you, made you soft, and unable to deal with the harsh realities of life—especially the realities of magic and the supernatural.

The truck's electric engine was beginning to struggle with hauling the old rustbucket up the steep mountain road. Outside Miguel's window the stone of the mountain's side had ceased to flash by, and was moving past sluggishly. Irena glanced out her side, where the edge of the road fell away into a vast canyon. Though she couldn't see it past the mountain, she could tell the sun was beginning to sink in the west, and it would be dark soon. The mountain air was taking on a chill.

The Railwalkers had been full of compassion, and it made them weak. Oh, some were strong of arm, and some full of knowledge; training with them had been useful enough. But in the end they would be brought down by their compassion, always subject to the whims of the public they served, of the crows, of the spirits they dealt with. Spirits, Irena had decided, were to be commanded, not to be commanded by. The crows and the spirits were not the wise councilors they pretended to be; they always had their own agenda. And why not? In this world, she had discovered, you were either predator or prey, user or used, the one with the power or the powerless. And she was sick to death of being powerless. Tonight would fix that forever.

The truck slowed even more, the engine's sound turning to a high whine. Shit, Irena thought, we could walk faster than this. "Stop the truck," she said. "We'll walk from here."

"Lo siento, Señora," said Miguel, pulling over. He hit the button and engine's whine died.

"Nothing to apologize for, it is what it is. The truck won't take it." She shouldered her pack and got out, walked back to the bed of the truck. "Come on, get out," she said.

The two figures in the truck bed stirred. The kid, full of fear, scuttled to the gate of the truck bed and jumped off. The woman followed more slowly, her eyes full of resentment above the gag that bound her mouth. Unlike the boy, she had trouble getting out of the truck with her hands tied, and almost fell. Irena watched, not moving to help. Miguel appeared and took the woman by the arm, leading her past the truck and up the road. Irena nodded at the boy, and they followed.

By the time they reached the wide plateau at the top of the mountain, the woman was breathing hard, and stumbling often, and the boy was flagging. Irena herself was feeling the effects of the thinner air, but she refused to let on, and did not acknowledge the others' discomfort. She could see it in Miguel, too, but he hid it well, and no one who didn't know him as well as she would have recognized it.

When they stopped, the woman fell down, wheezing. The boy sat on his haunches. Irena shed her pack, opened it. She took out the two stakes and a ball of twine. She planted one stake at the center of the plateau and tied the twine to it. She measured out four and a half feet, cut the twine with some to spare, and tied it to the other stake. Digging into the dirt with the second stake, she began to scribe a circle on the ground. She left a two-foot gap at the north.

"Harina?" asked Miguel, holding up a bag of corn-meal.

"Start in the east," she said, nodding to where she had started the circle. She glanced at the boy, and the woman. Neither had moved.

The boy was maybe six. They'd picked him off the street in one of the last zone towns they'd passed through, the woman already hidden under tarps in the back of the truck. Irena's own son would be half that age, she thought, traveling with Doc now, roaming the southwest as the man gambled and drank his life away. For a brief time Doc had convinced her that it was possible to forget the other world, live a life without visions or magic. Live like normals. It was all an illusion, of course. Now, if she had her own kid here, that would be a sacrifice that would cement her power unequivocally. If you could kill your own son, that would be proof positive you had purged yourself of love, compassion, all those softer feelings that made you weak, made you prey to the various blind forces of the world.

She wanted a drink, desperately. Just as well she'd forbidden Miguel to bring anything. Like compassion, her addiction to hooch was a weakness. She'd purge herself of that tonight, too. She watched Miguel fill the line she'd scored with cornmeal. The white meal seemed to glow in the twilight. She took the twine and stakes and began another, smaller circle to the south of the first one, almost touching. Within this circle she scribed a triangle. This time she left no opening or gap.

"Now," she said, when Miguel had outlined both circles and the triangle with cornmeal, "let's get started."

The woman who opened her eyes to the new dawn had once been called Irena, but had no name now. She lay on top of a mountain, at the center of a circle scribed in the earth and filled with cornmeal, much of the area within stained with blood. She sat up, blinking into the rising sun. Around her were the bodies of a man, a woman, and a child. Each had had their throats cut, their bodies sliced open, their entrails dragged out. The living woman looked down at herself. Her arms and hands were dark with caked, dried blood. She looked again at the carnage about her, and felt nothing. Yes, she thought, just as I should.

She glanced at the smaller circle and triangle to the south. There was no sign of the wraith that had appeared there, screaming, the night before. That was good. She had rid herself of her weakness, embodied it in that wraith, and destroyed it for good.

Her path to power was clear of obstruction.

47. WOLF

I was still trying to get my mind in gear and sort out my thoughts and feelings as I stepped out into the corridor, following Gage and Roth. Distantly, I heard Gage clear his throat.

"Um... sir?" he said.

Roth stopped and turned.

"If I might have a moment with you and Railwalker Wolf?"

Roth nodded. Gage turned to look back toward me. He looked concerned.

"Railwalker? Are you okay?"

I took a deep breath, dismissed my confused thoughts. "Yeah," I said, "I'm fine."

Gage didn't look like he believed it, but he gestured at the conference room door. "If you would? For a moment?"

I shook myself, nodded, and the three of us filed into the conference room.

"Mr. Roth," Gage asked, "do you trust me?"

Roth looked at him for a long moment before answering. "The trust I had in Chief Adams was built up over the course of thirty years of working together," he said finally. "I trusted Adams's judgment, and Adams trusted you, so I was ready to give you the benefit of the doubt. So far you've done nothing to make me regret that. That's the best I can tell you right now. Why? What's this about?"

"Sir, I'm going to have to ask you a personal question, and the answer is something I think both the Railwalker and I need to know, if we're going up against this woman. I'd appreciate it if you'd give us a straight answer."

Roth sighed, pulled one of the chairs out from the

conference table, and sat down. He looked tired. I suspected the city boss knew what was coming.

"Why," Gage asked, "is this woman so vindictive? It's become increasingly clear that this whole business is directed at you. The Beast was working his way toward you, killing people who were closer and closer to you each time. Railwalker Morgan says Hannah Caine is really Helena Crichton. That may well be, but this isn't a campaign to reclaim her lost power in Bay City. This is revenge, revenge against you, and I for one don't buy that it's only for the People's Takeover. It's more than that. It's personal. So I'm asking you: Why?"

Roth sat back in the chair and scrubbed a hand across his face. I said nothing, stood by listening, watching. For a moment I thought Roth was going to tell Gage to fuck off. Then he sighed and began to speak. His voice was low, hoarse.

"I had an affair with her," he said. "This was back just before the Takeover. I used her to get information on Crichton, his plans, his security routines."

That hung in the air for a while, all three of us silent.

I could see it in my mind, the ambitious woman preparing to transfer her loyalties from the fading star to the rising one; the future city boss letting a potentially troublesome partner go down with her original ship. Twenty-seven years ago, I was what, nine at the time? Roth would not have warned her ahead of time when the Takeover was about to happen, I realized; and when the fighting started, she'd have been trapped with Crichton's forces. And later reported killed. It was a shitty thing to do, even if the woman was doing something shitty herself.

"That would explain something of her motive," said Gage.

The cold lead weight in my stomach had just gotten heavier and colder.

"You told me," I said, "that the Crichtons hadn't been able to have children, that the child she was carrying when she supposedly died was a sort of miracle child for them." I saw Gage's eyes widen as he realized the implications of my question. Roth's expression didn't change. "Could it have been yours?"

Of course, Roth would have thought of that as soon as he realized Hannah Caine had once been Helena Crichton. "I don't know." He sighed. "I don't think so. But I don't know." He scrubbed his hands over his face again.

Could the Beast have been his own son? I couldn't blame him for not wanting to think that. Hell, I didn't want to think that the madwoman who had raised that monster, had engineered this campaign of killing and revenge, might be my mother. Was the Beast my half-brother? And I had killed him? Gods damn. Maybe I could form a club with Auden.

"Thank you for your candor, Boss Roth," said Gage. He shook himself, and turned to me. "We should get moving."

Auden and I departed the tower with two uniformed guards, in a full-sized auto. On the way, the questions screamed in my mind. What did Morgan's discovery mean? The photos were both clearly my mother, and looked exactly like the picture in my crane bag, like that spirit that had saved my life several times. Yet if my mother had become Helena Hebat, and then married Wendell Crichton, who or what was the spirit I'd seen? Not a sending from a living woman, surely, for a sending appears the real age and appearance of the sender, while my ghostly visitor had never aged. If my mother was dead, and my visitant truly was her spirit, who was this Helena Hebat Crichton, who had become Hannah Caine? Why was my mother's picture on her ID?

Since I couldn't construct any logical answers to these questions, I slowed my breathing and silently repeated a chant for a while, giving the whole question over to my unconscious, hopefully leaving my conscious mind free to focus on the solvable problems of here and now: pursuing and capturing the woman responsible for all this violence. It worked. Mostly.

Across the Fourth Street Bridge, we entered the south

side. Shorter buildings, adobe brick and plasteel, strip malls. It wasn't as grim as Alphabet City, but it had its own gritty, depressing charm. The Accord Hotel was one of the taller buildings, a full six floors, built in the Velasco style, which was popular eighty years ago. The adobe bricks were tinted a rust red, the plascrete ornamentation around doors and windows and the edge of the roof a dull gray. The metal frame on the wire-reinforced plasglass door was probably dark brown originally, though now it was a muddy non-color where it wasn't chipped and rusted. Graffiti edged around the corners from the alleys on either side.

Knowing the skills of the Beast, and what abilities this woman had shown, I had to go first. None of Gage's men would have stood a chance. And my Bear wasn't with me, except perhaps in spirit. I'd have to be my own Bear now, as many other Bricks had done before me. I drew my gun and stepped through the door. Auden followed right behind me.

The carpet in the lobby was sticky. I advanced on the cowering desk clerk, keeping him covered. "Where's Caine?" I demanded.

His eyes got even bigger, if that was possible. He caught my eye for just a moment, then stared down the barrel of the gun.

"P-p-penthouse..." he stammered.

We left Rogers to cover him and rode up to the top floor. We burst through the door, guns at the ready, to find ourselves facing an empty suite. She'd been here. Blood-stained clothes littered the place. Some power bar wrappers and a couple of empty water bottles. And nothing else.

Auden and I looked at each other.

"Where?" I asked.

Auden shook his head, shrugged. "She must have places that aren't on the books, or are in some other name."

Auden's radio buzzed. He answered it, and cursed roundly. Then he said, "We're just clearing up here. No, nothing. Yeah, meet you there." He switched the radio off and turned back to me. "Rochelle Roth is missing."

"Caine's got her."

He nodded grimly. "That's Gage's assumption. Turns out the girl had a lesson this morning and never came back from it."

"If she's not going to kill the girl immediately, she'll have to stash her somewhere."

"Why not kill her now?"

"I'm sure she'd love to kill her, but she's more valuable as bait for Roth than as a body. It's Roth she really wants. She can always kill the daughter later. Or better yet, in front of Roth."

"You really think this bitch is that sick-minded?"

"Auden, the Beast was her idea, her creation. What do you think?"

We stood in silence for a moment, considering.

"What about Crichton's old properties?" I asked. "Maybe a remote estate, a summer house, something like that?"

"No," he said. "Crichton's estate was razed. There's a factory there now." He sighed. "Shit," he said, his head coming up sharply. "Cali Isle. Come on!"

Trusting his instinct for the local scene, I followed him out of the hotel. "Kali Isle?" I asked, once we were under way. "As in the Death Goddess?"

"No, Cali as in 'Hot Cali.'"

I looked at him and waited.

"There's an island a couple of miles or so to the south," he said. "Supposedly haunted. Fishermen avoid it like the plague, but every so often some teenagers row over to it and scare the bejeezus out of themselves. I guess it was part of the mainland at one time. There was a luxury hotel out there, the Hotel California. Supposedly owned by a famous band who were into some demonic cult, back before the Crash. Somehow it survived the quakes of the Crash, but there was a lot of damage, too, and the sign lost some letters. So now it says 'Hot Cali.' Used to be people called it 'Hot Cali Island,' but it's just Cali Isle these days."

He glanced over and trailed off, seeing my angry expression. "What?" he asked.

"Let's go," I said, and we hustled into the auto.

"What?" he repeated as Guardsman Rogers gunned the engine.

"You've got a supernatural killer on your hands, and a reputedly haunted island a stone's throw from the city, and you didn't see fit to mention this?"

"Didn't think of it." He shrugged.

"So what made you think of it now?"

"Crichton owned it. Had part of it cleaned up and refurbished at one time, but somebody died at one of his parties out there or something and he closed it down again. If Caine is really Helena Crichton..."

"She'd know the place," I finished for him. "And it would make a perfect bolt-hole."

48. THE ISLAND

She walks through the corridors of the ruined hotel. The cavernous room she enters holds many ancient treasures, all, she thinks, valuable to others for their monetary worth, but their true value meaningless to any but her. So this, she thinks, is what her life has come to. A final stand, in a rotting building amongst the meaningless trappings of former glory. She could kill the Railwalker, probably, and may yet. But what would that avail? The tyrant Roth is without honor. If the Railwalker dies, he will send another mercenary, and then another. She might kill them all, one by one, but what will that mean? Eventually they will come in force and drag her down by sheer numbers. She is old now, beyond her prime, and there will be no others like Varger, her favored son.

It was the Railwalker, she thought, who had done this. And he her own blood, too. Without him her plan would have succeeded. Roth would be beneath her heel, and she would be the true boss of the city, returning it to its former glory. Now that glory would never happen.

It was infuriating. If she had only broken free when she was younger, rid herself of that small-minded, conventional bitch she had been earlier in life, she might have made the Railwalker hers as surely as Varger had been. Instead he had grown up to become her nemesis. Galling.

Ah, well, she could not have done, in those days. The boy was born several years before she had made her way to the Mayacan mountains of the south, performed the needful rituals. When she had cast off those useless parts of herself, expelled them forever, her conscience, her empathy, her compassion, she had seen them personified briefly, retreating before her new self's fierceness. And the freedom that followed its dispersal...

And it was dispersed, she was sure. The twinges she'd experienced since, the momentary convictions that the little bitch was looking over her shoulder and judging her, or that she was out there, somewhere, doing... something. That had all been nonsense, a natural anxiety provoked by the seriously dangerous nature of the game she was playing.

At the other end of the corridor a form appears. The vision is a woman, young, elegant, in a white blouse with the collar turned up.

Be gone, ghost, she tells this vision. You are long dead, and have no power here.

The figure vanishes, leaving her alone in the dank hallway.

49. WOLF

Cresting the hill on the deserted coast road, Rogers slowed and our auto rolled down the other side of the hill, the electric motor only a quiet purr. Before us stretched the salt marsh, a field of fog with stands of reeds and cordgrass punctuating it. On the horizon, the dark shape of an island, which became less prominent as we descended, finally fading into the fog. Rogers extinguished the headlights and turned on dim yellow fog lights. Auden sat forward in the shotgun seat, peering into the darkness and fog. "Slow," he said, though Rogers was already proceeding slowly. "I see him."

Ahead, a flicker of orange light. The auto pulled over near where a man stood lighting a cigarette. Behind the man a runabout was visible, a trailer linked to its tail with two boats lashed to it. The man nodded as Auden got out of the car, then turned back to the trailer and began unlashing the boats.

We had agreed that a frontal assault, driving to the island in a guard launch, would accomplish little. Hannah Caine would have an escape hatch arranged, and if she knew she was being raided she might kill the girl. Our only alternative was to approach with stealth. Auden had called a man he knew, a fellow who owed him a favor, and arranged to have two flat-bottomed punts brought to the edge of the salt marsh. We'd be approaching the hotel and the island from behind.

The boats were set afloat in the shallows of the salt marsh creek. Auden walked to the trunk of the auto, then returned with a sword, which he held out to me.

"You might be wanting this," he said. "A little better quality than the standard guard issue." He was right. I'd been feeling half naked without Windsteel, and had requisitioned one from the city guard armory, but they were mass-produced blades, nowhere near the quality I was used to.

I took the blade, drew it partway from the sheath. It was a Sierra blade, more than a century old, unless I missed my guess. It might not have been Windsteel, bonded to me in ceremony, but it was a superb blade, beautifully balanced.

"It's called Mist Razor," Auden said. "Been in the family a long time. It'll do more good in your hands than on my mantelpiece. Just take good care of it, will you?"

I groped for words, but there didn't seem to be any appropriate to the moment. I nodded.

He turned toward the boats, and I removed the guard sword. I placed it in the auto and slid the Sierra blade into my back rig. We climbed into the boats. Auden's guy returned to his runabout and settled down with another cigarette, a flashlight, and a magazine.

We slipped into the fog, floating down the channels between ranks of tall cordgrass and reeds, and within seconds we could no longer see the shore or the glow of the man's cigarette.

The channels of the salt marsh were like twisting corridors, walls of tall cordgrass looming up out of the fog on either side. The scent of low tide stung our noses. The water was shallow, and once or twice there was a shudder and a low shushing sound as we glided over a barely submerged sandbar. A couple of times we had to use our oars like barge poles to move forward. Then we were out into the deeper channels, and began to make better speed.

I heard a faint splash and turned, just in time to see a large, dark form explode from the water beside the boat following ours. It sailed over the boat, snatching Rowlands up on the way, and disappeared into the water on the other side with a louder splash.

"Fuck!" Auden gasped. "Bay gator!"

Gator? The thing had jaws like an alligator, but its body had been more dolphin-like.

"Get down!" hissed Rogers from the front of our boat. As I turned back to him, another dark form surged from the water. This one didn't have the force or momentum of the first, but it grabbed Rogers in its maw and fell back, trying to drag him with it into the dark water. Rogers braced himself, and the two of them hung half in, half out of the boat.

I'd never seen or heard of a creature like this. The thing was like a cross between a dolphin and a crocodile, with slick, dark-gray skin, a torpedo-shaped body, and a long snout full of nasty teeth. I couldn't see its back end, which was underwater, but its front had vestigial limbs with sturdy claws, with which it grabbed at Rogers as well. In one movement I drew the blade Auden had loaned me and lurched forward, slashing down at the thing. My cut mostly severed the head from the body, and its jaws opened in a silent scream, letting Rogers fall back into the boat. It hung for a moment, body in the water, head in the boat, a raw strip of flesh and muscle connecting them across the gunwale. Rogers kicked at the head and the whole creature vanished into the black waters.

I turned back to look at Auden as the first creature surged up again. Auden took aim with his oversized gun. I heard a sound like that of an arrow, and the bay gator's head exploded. The remains fell back into the water and silence descended again.

Auden raised the pistol. "Old Silent but Deadly... Air powered, loaded with hollow points." He shrugged. "I thought we wanted to be quiet." He scanned the water as if seeking other targets.

"Pairs," Rogers muttered. "Bay gators hunt in pairs."

His arm was shredded, pumping blood into the bottom of the boat. He had taken his uniform belt off and was fumbling at making a tourniquet of it. I stepped to his side, knelt, and finished the job, using an oarlock to lever-age it tight.

Auden had pulled his boat alongside. "He needs help," he said. He was right. Rogers wouldn't survive without medical attention, and soon. "We'll have to take him back.

Backup will be here in a few minutes."

"You take him back," I said. "I'm going in."

"Alone? All due respect, Railwalker, I've seen what you can do, and it's impressive, but..."

"Rochelle Roth is in there alone," I said. "She's only twelve."

"You said Caine wouldn't kill her yet."

"I was guessing. What if I was wrong? We can't take that chance."

It was true I'd just been guessing about Hannah Caine's motives. For all I knew the girl was already dead. But I was like a man riding a bull; the gate had been opened, the bull released, and there was no letting go at this point. I had to go on. Had to meet whatever was waiting for me on that island.

Finally Auden nodded. We both glanced at Rogers, and then Auden stepped over into my boat, and I took his. It was easier than trying to move Rogers.

"Take this," said Auden, holding out the air gun. I took it, and he held out a hand.

"Good hunting, Railwalker."

We shook.

"Take good care of Rogers," I said. As Auden maneuvered my boat around, I took the oars of his and struck out.

50. WOLF

Soon the air freshened a bit and I realized I was nearing the estuary. I backed the oars and brought the boat to a halt. Before me the reeds fell away. The fog hung above an expanse of open water between me and the island, a dark shape rising out of the fog. Beyond the island I could hear surf.

I would have to be even more careful now. The fog would help, but I would no longer have the cordgrass for cover. I examined the air gun. I hadn't used one like this before. A compressed air canister jutted from the handle like an extended magazine, while the actual magazine was mounted in front of the trigger. Two rounds were already missing from the magazine. I wondered how much air it had. I was guessing one canister powered one magazine's worth, and probably it was full before Auden used it tonight. But that was two guesses, and I wouldn't want to bet my life on them if I had a choice. The thing looked cheaply manufactured. No telling how reliable it was.

The island was an elongated teardrop shape, nearly a peninsula, as the southern point of the teardrop nearly reached the mainland. Crichton had built a causeway off the southern point to connect to the mainland, which still stood, though it was seldom used. The estuary and the marshes spread out to the east, and to the north the estuary deepened, then joined the ocean in the west. On the horizon clouds were gathered, and I didn't like their bruised purple color. There was scaledust incoming, and quickly—even as I watched, the clouds grew larger and closer. I crossed the open water as quickly as I could.

Auden had mentioned two possible landing points on the landward side, but if the investigator knew of them,

Caine would too, and she'd have them watched. The northern extent of the landward side was cliff and rocks. I headed for that. Normally I wouldn't take a boat in among the rocks like that, but the estuary chop was minimal, and I was in no danger of being smashed on them. Coasting through the fogbound rocks was like sailing through one of those Chinese paintings, where the mountains rear up out of fog banks.

I found a spot where there was a foot or so of shingle between the rocks and beached the boat. I was about to tie off to a rock when a scuttling noise made me turn, drawing the blade.

Facing me was one of the strangest mutants I'd ever seen. It had a body like an enormous centipede, fully eight feet long, armored with shell-like segments. Half of its length reared up like a cobra about to strike. At the top, its head looked like a crab, its last pair of legs, closest to the head, like huge crab claws. It hissed at me like a leaky steam fitting and lunged.

I sidestepped and brought the sword down, catching the crab claw leg at the shoulder joint and severing it. The thing whipped around, scary fast, and slashed my leg with the tip of its other claw, though it didn't catch a grip. It hissed again and reared back, and I lunged after. I drove the sword into its throat and levered hard, nearly severing the head. Black blood gushed from the wound, and the thing collapsed. I collapsed as well.

I sat up, examined my wounded right leg. It was a shallow slash across the outside of my right thigh, painful, but not dangerous or debilitating. I tore a strip off my headscarf and bound it up. Then I stood again, favoring my wounded leg, and looked around. I realized I was hearing a slightly hollow sound, almost an echo of the lapping waves. I looked to my right, and there it was. Across the water some yards away, where it would have been concealed from the view from the open water, I saw a cave. I returned to the boat and rowed my way over to it. As I did I could hear the peculiar wheezing sound the wind takes on in a scaledust storm. What light there was was tinted purple now. I could see no dust in the air yet, but I knew it wouldn't be long. I rowed faster.

I risked shining my battery torch into the cave for a moment. It was deep, and at the back I saw a gleam of metal. I guided the boat inside.

Not far into the cave the ceiling dipped, and I could see by the high-water mark that come high tide the boat wouldn't fit. Auden had assured me high tide was a couple of hours off yet.

Beyond that point the cave opened up again. Then it rose and turned. There was a dock, but no boat. Gage's men had found a small boat on the beach below Hartshall, and it looked as if the Beast had arrived in it. I wondered if it was normally kept docked here. I tied up at the dock and got out.

I was in a vast chamber. At the far end a faint light flickered, a small flame. I drew Auden's air gun and stood still for a moment, letting my eyes adjust.

At first I didn't understand what I was looking at. Strange sculptures hung on the rock walls. On a closer look the sculptures resolved into collections of body parts —heads, hands, internal organs. Some were mounted with steel spikes, some bound with ropes, some simply hanging there as if in defiance of gravity, although some sort of adhesive had to have been used. All the parts had been dried and preserved, leaving them with no charnel odor. Further along, where the floor of the cave was flattest, there was a large clear area, around the edges of which were scattered the familiar accouterments of a dojo: waki-mara; heavy bag; barrels of rice and pea gravel; and a rack holding swords, spears, staves, canes, billies, and a variety of knives.

At the back of the cave, to the right, was a large ward-robe, a chest of drawers, and a single bed. To the left, a wide double circle had been inscribed on the floor. Some sort of runes I didn't recognize were written in the space between the inner and outer rings. Beyond that a solidly built wooden staircase rose up to a landing, where a door was set into the wall of the cave.

At the very back was the shrine. An altar with a cauldron on it; above it, suspended by chains, was an oil lamp, the source of the light. This hadn't been left lit by accident. It was an eternal light. It represented the Beast's idea of god or goddess or something, as well as his devotion to it.

To Her, I corrected myself. I was being too careful, thinking like a lawyer or a scientist. I knew perfectly well what the Beast believed in. This was a shrine to his goddess, his mother, a woman who took a child and twisted it into a killer, compelling the kid to worship her, do her bidding. She had denied that kid the basic things the poorest humans take for granted: community, family, human contact. She'd turned the poor kid into the killing machine we called the Beast, and turned him loose on Bay City, just to get back at Roth.

And maybe she was also my mother. Which meant that there, but for the grace of Soul-Are, went I. Instead of a Railwalker facing one of his hardest challenges, I might have been a Beast, dead under a Railwalker's sword. Did I have it in me to become something like that? Yeah, I thought reluctantly, given the same brainwashing and conditioning at an early enough age, I might have. It wasn't a comfortable thought.

And if Helena Crichton was my mother, that meant that the Beast I had killed was my brother, or half-brother at least.

I climbed the stairs, staying close to the edge to avoid creaks. There were none. The place was well maintained.

At the top of the stair I put my back to the door and narrowed my senses, reaching out to feel the energies of the place. Something was alive here, to the southwest of where I now stood. I drew the air gun and eased the door open. Stepped through the door.

It was dark. I could dimly tell I was in a long corridor with doors on either side. Faint light glowed at each end of the corridor. I took out my torch, and before turning it on, dialed it down to its lowest setting.

The corridor I found myself in was not well maintained. From what I could make out in the dim torchlight it was exactly what you'd expect in a hotel left abandoned for twenty or thirty years: filthy, cobweb ridden, the carpets rotting, sconces fallen from the walls. It smelled of rot. I moved through the darkened corridors, keeping to a southwesterly direction. The place had obviously been an expensive hotel when it was new. The halls were wide, the doors hand-carved. Ahead of me light seeped into the corridor, and I could hear the howling of the wind louder now. Mindful that parts of the hotel might be open to the storm, I dug out my breathing filter and put it on.

As I got closer to the glow, I realized that it was coming through a glass wall with French doors. Many panes were broken. The glass that was left was milky, dirty and smudged. The doors led to a wide courtyard, now overgrown, with a large pool in the center. Scaledust swept though the open space like purple snow. At the opposite end of the courtyard steps led up to another set of French doors. Peering across the open space, I could see something of the room beyond, a large function room of some sort. I couldn't make out the source of the glow at the back of that room, but the blue-white color of the glow suggested an artificial light source.

The French doors were unlocked. I eased one open. It creaked slightly. I froze and waited. There was no sound to indicate anyone had heard it above the sound of the wind. I slipped through the door. Scaledust could burn your skin if you were exposed to it too long, but as long as you had a gasmask or breathing filter you wouldn't suffer permanent damage.

I left the door open behind me. There was no telling how many people might be in the building besides Hannah Caine and the kidnapped girl, but I was guessing it was just the three of us. In any case, the risk of Caine or any cronies she might have with her finding the open door was less than the risk of a second creak being heard.

Chances were, Caine was near that light source.

I walked quickly toward the light. My skin was already stinging from the purple dust swirling through the air. As I approached the pool there was a splash. A bay gator hauled itself up out of the dark water, its beady eyes fixed on me. It scrambled toward me much faster than I would have thought the ungainly looking creature could move on land.

A single shot from the borrowed air gun splattered half the gator's head across the flagstones. The body scrambled forward a few steps before collapsing on the flags. I crouched, drawing back into the shelter of a creosote bush. For long moments there was no sound except the wind playing through the leaves. The bay gator hadn't roared or made any vocal sound, but the noise of its progress across the stone floor had been louder than the wind or the creaky French door. I wondered if Caine was not, after all, near the light. Perhaps the room I was approaching was empty. Or perhaps Rochelle was tied up in there, and Caine was elsewhere. No telling.

I stepped past the gory splatter that had once been a nasty amphibious predator and started across the courtyard again. Passing the pool, I could see more of the room ahead. It was large, with a raised platform or stage at the back. The light source was a portable camping lamp, set on the edge of the stage. In the center of the room was some sort of high table, draped with a cloth that hung to the floor. Under the cloth was an irregular shape—a body. Rochelle? No, too large for a twelve year-old girl. The Beast, maybe?

I heard a splash of water again. As I turned, my right leg exploded in pain as it was jerked out from under me. I crashed to the flagstones, the air gun flying from my grip. The bloody cheap thing discharged as it hit the flags. One of the French doors ahead dissolved in a shower of glass. I'd forgotten that Rogers had said bay gators hunt in pairs. The bay gator dragged me backward, toward the pool. Air gun out of reach, I twisted and whipped the sword from its back scabbard. The bay gator lurched backwards, and I was just able to snatch a deep breath as it dragged me over the edge into the pool.

I'd expected I might be submerged, but hadn't expected the pool to be so deep. The gator swum down, dragging me by the leg. Above us the small circle of dim light that was the surface of the pool got smaller, and then I was yanked sideways into darkness. My free foot and my elbows and hands banged off rock as the gator surged forward through the underwater tunnel. I couldn't see, couldn't get an angle to bring my sword to bear. I gritted my teeth on the breathing filter, determined not to lose it, though I wasn't sure how immersion might affect it. My lungs felt about to explode when there was suddenly light again as the tunnel opened into another pool. The monster slowed, and I bent at the waist and slashed at it. My cut took it behind the head, severing the spinal cord. A cloud of blood billowed out. It stopped moving but did not let go. Its small, black eye rolled up to stare at me. The damned thing wasn't dead, just paralyzed from the neck down. I reversed my grip on the sword and plunged the point into the creature's eye, driving steel into its primitive brain. The beast uttered a sound something between a sigh and a squeal, which echoed weirdly in the water. I was pretty sure it was dead. But it still did not release its grip on my leg.

My chest was on fire. I couldn't swim to the surface for the weight of the bay gator's body dragging me down. I struck again, once, twice, and the body fell away, drifting to the bottom. I was drifting up now, despite the weight of the thing's head still attached to my leg. I swam up, broke the surface and blew out through the filter, spraying water, and then heaved in the air. The filter gurgled but allowed me to breathe.

My face began to sting. Once I had my breath back I swam to the edge and pulled myself out, dragging the bay gator's head with me. I lurched out onto flagstones. As the gator's head struck the edge of the pool the pain made me scream, and I lost the breathing filter. I started to inhale involuntarily, stopped myself as my throat began to burn.

Holding what little breath I had left, I grabbed for the breathing filter, but it skittered away and dropped into the pool.

My face and hands had begun to sting, and then burn, and my lungs were aching again. I looked around. I was in a large patio overlooking the sea, more exposed to the storm than the confined courtyard had been. The air around me was thick with the purple dust. The pool I'd come out of was larger than the one I'd gone in through.

Half crawling, half limping, I dragged myself and the head that gripped my leg to one of the six glass doors that gave onto the patio from the hotel. Only two of them were boarded over, the rest missing only a pane or three apiece, and I wondered why more of this glass had survived than in some of the interior doors. It didn't make sense.

My head was spinning, my lungs screaming. The doors were unlocked. It didn't have to make sense, I thought. This was Wonderland, Hell, Chinatown, the Hotel California. I had to treat it like I'd treat the Otherworld if I wanted to survive. Hannah Caine's world would operate by Otherworld logic. I fell inside. With my free foot I shoved the door closed behind me.

I crawled down the rotting carpet of the interior hall until I was away from the purple dust that wafted in through the broken panes. Then I finally took a lungful of air. Heaven. I took off my headscarf and did my best to wipe the dust from my face and hands. The fine, soft cotton felt like sandpaper, and made my skin burn harder for a moment, but after a few moments it subsided a bit. I made careful to let the dust touch only one side of the folded cloth, and shook it out as best I could after. I was going to need it to bind my leg, and didn't want the dust getting in my wounds.

Dissection time, I thought. Glancing around me frequently, wary of any reaction to the noise I'd made, I inserted the end of the sword between my leg and the back of the bay gator's jaws and began sawing away at the jaw muscles.

Minutes later I was cursing my ignorance of amphibian anatomy. Apparently the muscles that held the jaw closed weren't where I'd expected them to be, and cutting from inside the mouth I'd have had to cut through bone to reach them. I stopped for a moment, looking around and listening. Nothing. No sign of Hannah Caine or anyone else. My lungs still felt scorched, and I wondered if I'd inhaled any dust.

I turned back to the bay gator head. I withdrew the blade from between its jaws and began cutting at the thing's cheek. That did it. As the animal's blood seeped from the cuts I'd made, staining the carpet black in the feeble light, I could feel a slight loosening on the side toward me. Now I had only to reach the other muscles, on the side of the thing's face that was toward my foot. That was a lot harder, trying to angle the sword into the muscles of its cheek without slicing my own leg as I worked.

Finally the pressure on my leg released and I was able to move the jaws apart and examine the damage. Fortunately I'd severed the thing's spine before it was able to get to work shaking its head and chewing and worrying at my leg, shredding it the way the other bay gator had shredded Rogers's arm. The wound was a series of ragged holes on either side of the leg. It was bleeding a lot. I bound it up with my head scarf. I hoped no scaledust had gotten into the wounds. They hurt like hell but didn't burn, so I was thinking I'd been lucky. The skin of my face and hands felt scorched, but that would heal. As long as I hadn't inhaled any, or gotten any dust in my bloodstream, I should be good. I wasn't sure about that, though. The fire in my lungs might be just from the punishment they'd taken. All I could do was hope that was true.

Taking stock was not encouraging. I had been wounded twice in the right leg, scale-burned, possibly poisoned, I had lost my breathing filter and both guns— the air gun back in the courtyard, my Gunspire somewhere in the underwater tunnel. All I had for weapons now was the sword Auden had given me. At least my left leg was still functioning, if a bit bruised. I got to my feet.

Took an experimental step or two. Yeah, it wasn't comfortable, but I could walk. I hoped I wouldn't have to do any running.

I had no idea how far the bay gator had dragged me, but my guess was that the courtyard we'd left from was at the center of the building, and now I was in the western end.

I advanced down the wide corridor. I was dripping. This wouldn't do. I stopped to wring the worst of the water out of my tunic. At least Caine wouldn't hear me slosh as I got near her.

The compass in my head told me to go straight ahead —that the tunnel the bay gator had dragged me through led back this way.

Soon I saw a glow ahead. I had been right. I was approaching the same courtyard again, from a different angle. This glass-paneled door did not squeak as the other had. I approached the pool slowly, limping. My wounded leg was getting really unhappy. I told it to shut the hell up.

The storm was letting up. The flagstones of the courtyard were dusted with purple, but the air was no longer colored with the dust. I looked around, trying to locate the air gun. It wasn't where I'd thought it had fallen earlier. When the French door had been shattered most of the glass had fallen inside the room, but a scatter of glass fragments decorated the steps, strewn among the fallen leaves on the cracked stones. But no air gun. I peered into the overgrown foliage to either side of the doors and steps. Still no air gun. I was sure the gun had gone off on impact, that my dropping it as I fell couldn't possibly have sent the gun itself through the glass of the door. The broken door yawned on its hinges. It had been closed before. The shot would not have caused it to open.

This did not bode well. Could someone—Hannah Caine, or one of her people or creatures—have stepped out, grabbed the gun, and retreated back into the room while I was being dragged away by the bay gator?

I stepped through the shattered door and into the room.

Hannah Caine appeared on the low stage at the other end of the chamber. I'd expected her to be dressed down for her escape through the city, but she was in a long, flowing robe, open, over a tunic and loose pants. Somehow, despite the squalor of her surroundings, she managed to look immaculate. I'd expected to see her pointing the air gun at me, but instead she carried a sword. An ancient one, by the look of it. Possibly an original Osoto.

She walked to the body on the table. "Welcome to the Hotel California..." she said. "Son."

What could I say? "Thanks, Mom?" Or, "I'm no son of yours?" Gods, did *that* sound like a tired cliché from an old DV show. So I said nothing.

"You look like shit. Don't you know better than to go running around outside in a scaledust storm? What's the matter, boy? Nothing to say? You had plenty to say at Summersend. Cut quite a rug, you did. Embarrassed at getting a hard-on over an old woman? Worse yet, over your own Mommy, the quim that brought you in?" She chuckled. "Poor little Oedipus, wants to kill his daddy and fuck his mommy. And you did want to kill dear old daddy, didn't you? When you met Doc in that game room? Of course I knew he was here. I felt it when the two of you came together. Bitterness has such a lovely tang when you drink its emanations."

She stepped closer to the table and drew the shroud back from the body. The cloth slithered to the ground. It revealed the body of the Beast, the half-healed shoulder wound still looking like raw meat. "His name was Varger," she said. "A book of names would tell you that it means 'outlaw' or 'outcast,' which is certainly appropriate. Do you know where that name comes from?"

Almost involuntarily, I shook my head.

"It is from the German 'warg,' meaning 'wolf.' You've joined your new friend Auden as a kinslayer. You've killed your brother wolf, Wolf."

"Many times," I said. "Every man is my brother."

"Oh, bullshit. Don't read to me from the Book of Brick. I didn't leave the Railwalker Academy because my scholarship was deficient. You have killed your blood brother, the son of your mother."

"My mother is dead."

"Well," she said, "I suppose in some sense that may be true. Certainly I am not that innocent, confused young girl who gave birth to you. She did truly die, many years ago. And I can't even truthfully say that she ever lived in this body. After all, science tells us that our sense of bodily continuity is mistaken. Every cell in the body dies and is replaced over the course of seven years. So this is, what? The fifth new model we've each occupied since you came into this world as a squalling babe?

"Even so, your very newest cells contain my DNA. There is some continuity after all, isn't there?" She held a hand up before her. "These seven-years-new hands bear the same fingerprints the old ones did, unless I make a point of changing them. I'll bet that just like that baby, you have the same little mole under your left arm, and the same crook in the ridge of flesh that runs from your arse-hole to your balls."

I was trying to keep my expression neutral, but I must have shown some reaction to this. Or she wanted me to think I had; I truly wasn't sure which.

She smiled. "What, you didn't think I'd washed your arse, rubbed the sleep gum from your eyes, wiped your spittle and snot and puke? You were too young to remember, of course. But you're a Railwalker now, and a Brick at that. You could reclaim those memories, if you chose to."

It was true. We were taught a technique for recovering lost memories—any memory, no matter how deep or clouded over. We can even work this technique on others.

Not that it was something I felt inclined to use here and now, about this subject.

She looked down again at the body. "Tell me, Railwalker, are shapeshifters born, or are they made? I suppose that nature versus nurture debate is old hat to a sophisticated Railwalker like you. But then, you aren't really a shapeshifter yourself, are you? Oh, I'm sure you've become a wolf on occasion, maybe even done crow a time or two. They all do. It's probably a requirement these days. But that's just borrowing another creature's shape. True shapeshifting, creating your own new and original shape, crafted to meet your needs, that's an art even the Railwalkers haven't mastered."

"I am what I am," I said. "It suits me."

"And that's all what you am? '*What* I am'? Not '*that* I am'? You are too modest, crow son. Besides, Popeye, are you not also the manifestation of Soul-Are?"

"For that matter, so are you," I said. "So was your son the Beast. Didn't stop me from killing him. Won't stop me from killing you, if you force me to it."

She smiled. "I suppose you could try," she said, and stepped away from the body, her sword raised.

I raised my borrowed sword, and a youthful voice cried, "Stop!"

To my left stood Rochelle Roth, pointing the air-powered gun at me. "You're not going to hurt my teacher," she said.

I stared at her. We'd thought her kidnapped, but it now seemed she had gone willingly. She couldn't think this was a field trip. Had her teacher brainwashed her? Turned her against her own father?

"You don't understand—" I started.

"Put down your sword," she demanded.

Hannah Caine glided to her side. "Best do as she says, son," she said. She turned to Rochelle, taking the weapon from her hand. "That's all right, Rochelle, you did well. I'll take that." She pointed the weapon at me. "Put it down."

I slowly placed Auden's family sword on the floor.

"Kick it away." I did. "Good. Now, the guard must

have given you cuffs of some sort. Put them on."

They had. The guard used plastic handcuffs that were similar to cable ties, and Auden had given me several of them. I wasn't going admit this to Caine, so shook my head. To my surprise, this caused her to lower the gun. Then I realized that she was casually pointing it at Rochelle Roth's leg. Rochelle didn't seem to notice.

"Come, Railwalker," Hannah Caine said with a smile. "We wouldn't want anyone to get hurt."

With a sinking feeling in my gut, I slowly reached into my tunic pocket. The fabric was like sandpaper on the raw skin of my hand, but I refused to let that show on my face. I brought out a pair of cuffs and placed them around my wrists. I left them loose enough that I could still slip out of them, though I didn't expect that would fool Hannah Caine for long.

"Good," she said. "Now lie on the floor, hands out in front of you." As I complied, she turned to Rochelle. "Go wait in the parlor, there's a good girl. I'll be along shortly."

With a last glance at me, Rochelle left the room. Hannah Caine walked to where I lay on the floor. With the gun to the back of my head, she put one knee on my back, and then leaned forward and jerked the cuffs tight. The tightening of the plastic against my scaledust-burned flesh was agony, and I nearly screamed. She stepped away from me. I tried to get up, and she stepped forward and delivered a kick to my midsection. I fell, tumbling into the shards of glass from the shattered door.

"You should have been my Varger," she snarled, "should have been the instrument of my vengeance. Instead you killed him, destroyed my work, and would destroy me if you could. You, my own blood, a whimpering hireling for Micah fucking Roth." She delivered another kick. "You are beneath contempt."

Groaning in pain, I rolled over, holding my burned hands away from her. I grabbed one of the glass shards, hiding it with my body as I applied it to the cuff. The glass cut my fingers but I didn't care; it was less than the pain of the plastic on my burned wrists.

"They're coming, aren't they?" she asked. "Gage, Auden, your partner, and a whole phalanx of city guard with prodigious firepower."

"Yeah, they're right behind me."

"Nonsense. My creatures would have warned me."

Her creatures? Did she mean the bay gators? Or the centipede crab thing? Was she somehow in control of them? Or at least in communication with them? Or were there other creatures as well?

"We have half an hour at least before they arrive," she went on. "What should I do with you in the meantime, my prodigal? Perhaps I should take your arm, as you took my Varger's arm. Let you bleed to death, as he did."

I was through the cuffs; my hands were free. I kept them together, showing no sign, keeping the plastic cuffs draped across my wrists. She stepped toward me again and raised the air gun. I tensed, then rolled to my feet. Pain shot through my wounded leg. I refused to believe it wouldn't hold. I kicked out at her just as she pulled the trigger.

I wasn't fast enough. She would have killed me, except that instead of firing, the gun made a popping noise and exploded. A spring and the upper casing flew up and the air canister shot down out of the grip and ricocheted off the floor as my kick connected with her arm and sent the rest of Auden's broken gun flying.

Hannah Caine barely flinched. Before the remains of the gun had even left one hand, the other was bringing her sword around at me. I dove under the strike, fetching up against the table, where the drapery lay. I grabbed the cloth and spun it toward her like a matador's cape, then let go as I stumbled and fell within arm's reach of the sword I had earlier kicked away. She batted the drapery aside, but I'd gained my feet, sword in hand, and we both froze, eyes locked. I could feel the blood running down my leg and soaking my boot. That wasn't good. Blood loss would weaken me quickly. My face and hands burned from the scaledust. My breathing was painful, and purple spots roamed through my blurry vision. Dammit, I had inhaled some of the scaledust. How much, I wasn't sure. Probably it didn't matter; I'd never heard of anyone surviving inhaling even a little. In any case, I wasn't going to be much good for very long. Get this over as fast as possible, I thought.

She leaped across the intervening space between us, her sword flashing out in a flurry of cuts that drove me back against the wall. Sloppy of me letting her surprise me like that. For a moment I'd gotten arrogant, thought of myself as the warrior, and her as an old woman, a pencil pusher and a bureaucrat. She must be what, seventy? But I should have known better. Now, as before, I was entirely on the defensive, without a split second to riposte. The Beast had amazed me with his speed, but his mother was even faster. One moment she was bearing down on me with cut after vicious cut, and the next she was standing across the room again, with barely a flutter of her robes to suggest she'd ever moved at all.

She nodded slowly. "You're almost as good as my poor Varger. Better by definition, I suppose, since you killed him. It's a shame I didn't take you away from Doc when you were still young, suggestible, malleable. I could have molded you into such a weapon."

I thought again about what she'd done to the child who became Varger Caine, the Beast. "What are you?" I asked.

"I am that I am." She laughed. "Poor little Wolf, you want to codify and define. You want to put me in a little box, a pigeonhole with a neat little label."

But her eyes answered my question. They looked like the eyes of the Old Ones I've met, like Wolf, or Crow or Coyote. She was no longer human, but something primal. A spirit, even a goddess, perhaps: Kali, Baba Yaga, Roggenmutter, the devouring mother, vicious and angry and mad as only the gods can be mad. And I had killed her son and avatar. Oh, boy. Lucky me.

"Oh, fuck this," she said. And she began to change.

I'd never seen a shapeshifter change so quickly. It wasn't instantaneous, but it was quick, like watching time-lapse photography on fast forward. Her form was similar to the Beast's: large, muscular, with horny plates standing in for armor. Where he had been bald, however, she had a mane of white fur.

She charged, drove me back, her cuts coming so fast and fluid it was like a dozen swords coming at me at once. I parried like a madman, retreating, but one got through, then another, stinging pain and blood springing from my forearm, now my thigh. Then I could feel the wall was behind me. I dove under her next cut to roll to my feet behind her, but she had already spun about. I backpedalled, bleeding from both of her cuts and the gator bite. My head was throbbing again. I was getting intermittent flashes of light. I felt cold and tired, probably from the blood loss. My face and hands burned, and her shape was becoming blurrier. This was no good. I couldn't afford to lose this one.

She charged again with an overhead cut. In parrying, the force of it drove me to the floor. When she reversed her blade to come down with a thrust, I risked everything on a dicey move sensei had shown me once. As her blade came down I rolled into her, against her feet. She stumbled over me and her blade point hit the floor. I rolled forward again, snapping the blade out of her hand and bringing my own blade up. Her momentum carried her forward, impaling her on it. She screamed and straightened, taking the blade with her, out of my hands. I rolled away, grabbing up the sword she'd dropped. It quivered with battle fire energy.

I rolled to my feet to see the creature that had been Helena Caine kneeling, impaled by Auden's blade. She reached up and grasped the blade, and began slowly to pull. I gaped. Her breath was an extended growl, her face a rictus of pain, as inch by inch, like a man pushing an auto up a hill, she drew the blade out of her body.

Then I realized what she was doing. The dying Beast had tried to heal his severed arm, and his mother was now healing her wound around the blade as she withdrew it. If she had pulled it out quickly she would have died of blood loss like her son, unable to heal the wound fast enough. Withdrawing it slowly, the blade itself prevented the torrent of blood, and she could seal and heal the wound behind it. For a moment I could do nothing but stare, amazed by the audacity, the determination, and the force of will involved in such an effort. Her face was a mask of pain and concentration, her knuckles white, blood running freely from her fingers where she grasped the razor-sharp blade.

My trance broke when I noticed the smoke rising from the metal. Her blood on the steel was hissing and bubbling like acid, and where the blade had been inside her body, the razor edge was now corroded, uneven. Her own words had warned me. She was no longer human. There was no word for what she was now.

Before she could get Auden's blade free, I shook myself, stepped forward, and slashed with the Osoto. The ancient sword sliced through the muscle and tissue of the creature's throat, stopping with a chunk as it bit into the spine. Her growl became a hiss. Bubbles appeared in the blood that gouted from the wound. I drew the blade back and slashed from the other side, cutting upward now. This time it passed through all the way. Her head toppled and fell to the floor with a thump. Blood sprayed into the air as the body slowly collapsed.

It seemed like an eternity that I stood frozen in place, sword still extended in the follow-through from the cut. I had killed Hannah Caine, I had killed a monster. Two monsters, my mother and my half-brother. Blood will tell, my Pa had said. What kind of son kills his own mother? My childhood fears were confirmed. I was a monster, just like them.

I lowered the sword. Some part of my mind half expected to see her hands begin groping toward the head. Some atavistic fear whispered that I could cut the body into small pieces and each piece would still live, still creep after me, reaching out to claim revenge. But it did not happen. The body lay still, spilling a torrent of blood out onto the wooden floor. Slowly the torrent became a pulse, and then a trickle. The dark red pool spread across the dusty floorboards. Oddly, it didn't seem to eat the wood as it had the steel.

When I looked up I saw for a moment the image of the spirit I had always thought of as my mother. "Who or what the hell are you?" I cried. "Are you my mother? Or was she?" The figure simply spread her hands, shook her head, and vanished. I was left staring at a paneled wall. What the hell did that mean?

My legs were shaking. I fell to my knees. My head pounded, and the lightning flashes were back. My back ached. My arm and thigh throbbed from Caine's cuts, as did the bay gator bite on my lower leg. My skin burned from the scaledust, and every breath was a labored bellows feeding a hot furnace. I looked down to see one arm and one leg soaked in blood. The leg was near useless. I tried to focus through the haze. I should bind up the cuts Caine gave me. How much blood had I lost? Was I going into shock? I wasn't shivering yet. I couldn't let that happen. Couldn't relax into a nice, oblivious shock state. Not yet. There was more to be done still. For a moment I couldn't remember what.

I knew I had promises to keep. What had I promised? I had promised I would look after Auden's family sword, right. I already blew that one. That sword lay now with only its tip inside the creature's chest. Most of the blade was now corroded through. I looked at the Osoto in my hand. It, too, had begun to sizzle from the blood. Small pieces dropped from its edge as it corroded. I wiped it on Caine's robe, careful not to get her blood on myself; if it dissolved metal, what would it do to flesh? Even the pressure of wiping it proved too much for the blade. Its temper and integrity had been undermined by the creature's caustic blood. It snapped off halfway down. I wiped the broken end again and held it up. The blood seemed to have stopped eating the metal.

Promises to keep, right. And miles to go before I sleep, or something like that. What promises? Roth's daughter. Of course. I was here to get Rochelle Roth. Using the broken sword like a cane, I struggled to my feet. Fortunately, the blade held my weight. I turned, swaying, to see Rochelle Roth standing in the doorway, staring at me. I wondered that she didn't run screaming away. My face and hands must have looked like raw hamburger; I was dirty, disheveled, and bleeding. Surely I looked more like a monster to her than her Hannah Caine had.

"You killed my teacher," she said. "Will you now kill me, too?"

"No," I said, "of course not. I'm here to take you home."

"Ah, yes," she said. "The hero come to rescue the princess. Just like in the fairy tales. I suppose you expect to marry me, and rule my father's kingdom."

"What?" I said, none too brightly. "No. But I think your father will be here with the city guard soon."

Hannah Caine had been right. It was about a half an hour.

We went to all the funerals, of course. Gage wouldn't hear of a mass funeral, and Roth didn't fight him on that, so it took days. We performed the Chant for the Dead, and the Passage to the Crows, where the soul of the dead is offered into the keeping of the Crows for transport to the Land of the Dead. Morgan said she'd be okay doing the Passage for Robles, but I did it myself. I felt like I owed her that, at least. We'd already done the ceremony for Rok, although there would be another one when his ashes arrived in New Frisco.

A lot of this I passed through in a sort of a daze. And I was avoiding anything stronger than aspirin, since my natural state of shock was altering enough. One of the things you learn as a Railwalker, and as a Brick especially, is to manage to seem normal and attentive when you're actually in an altered state. Falling down with your eyes rolling up may be impressive in a shamanic healing, but it doesn't encourage confidence in your order if it happens in a public ceremony like a wedding or funeral, or a Blessing of the Crops. So you drill, and you learn to present as normal when you're far from it. I was like a zombie, going through the motions, but only the closest ones—Morgan, Roth, maybe Weldt—realized this. Morgan knew what was up with me, of course, but I had not told the city boss or his advisor what killing Hannah Caine had really meant to me. Hell, I wasn't sure myself.

And of course, that face kept appearing in shadows and reflected in windows, and overlaid on the faces of people who looked nothing like the spirit I had believed was my mother's.

I'm not given to a lot of wallowing in guilty feelings.

I've done things I wasn't proud of. The earliest ones were done out of youthful stupidity, the later ones out of the belief that it was somehow for the greater good. In my career as a Railwalker I'd killed a number of men, a couple of women, some animals, and several creatures not entirely of this world, some of which weren't even in the *Concordance Monstrum*. I remember all of their faces, even those of the animals and the unknown creatures. I remember all their names, at least all the ones that had names that I heard. Their souls are passed on and any shades have been dispersed, so when they do haunt me now I know it's not coming from them, but from inside my own mind.

I don't allow them to haunt me much. I can't afford to. You let yourself dwell on that sort of thing too much, you'll drive yourself mad. Now and then, though, you have to let those faces come out of the shadows. You have to think about them and remember. It's what keeps you from allowing yourself to take life lightly, to kill because it's expedient rather than truly necessary. To remember that it's always a choice, and you take responsibility for it, accept the consequences.

I knew I'd be seeing that face loom out of the shadows more frequently than the others. Hannah Caine, Helena Crichton, Goodnight Irene, the Amazing Vanishing Mother, Demon Goddess, Vengeful Wife and Spurned Woman. I wondered how often, if ever, it would be overlaid by the face of the Fairy Godmother, or whatever she was, who appeared to me over the years.

And what about her, anyway? Was she a figment of my imagination? A spirit of some sort, masquerading as my mother? A Rydell fragment of herself my mother had thrown off? If she ever showed up again, I supposed, I could try to ask her. Not that she had ever given me time or opportunity for questions.

I watched Morgan tapping away at the keyboard of her portable unit. She was sitting cross-legged on the couch, the unit on her lap, our satchels packed at her feet. Now I thought I understood why she'd tried to persuade me to leave once the Beast was dead. She had already known—or had a strong suspicion—that Helena Crichton was also my mother. She'd been trying to avoid having to tell me, hoping to protect me from the knowledge. She'd thought that if we called the case closed, left the city, went on with our lives, I might never have to know what kind of monster dear old Mom had become. That's what she'd meant when she'd said, "We've lost enough." With Rok gone, even in the midst of her own grief, she'd tried to save me from this further loss.

But you can't protect people by denying them knowledge, or denying them an informed choice. Morgan had realized that. That's why she'd told me at the last.

I'd said we'd talk about this later, but I realized now there wasn't any need. Ultimately she'd done the right thing, and that was what counted.

"We're to return to New Frisco ASAP," Morgan announced, looking up from the screen. "They've convened a Raven Parliament. You are requested to attend."

"They want me to give evidence?" I asked.

Morgan frowned. "There's only twenty-two other names on the list."

The Raven Parliament consists of twenty-three members: a Murder of seventeen Ravens a Pentangle of five Senior Ravens, and the Elder Raven. If someone had appointed me a Raven, no one had told me about it yet. I thought of my late-night conversation with Roth. And I wondered... Did he know something I didn't? Did he have a contact inside the order?

"By the way, Roth wants to see you before we go."

I found Roth sitting alone in the conference room where we'd first met. The westering sun cast gold highlights on the edges of things in the room. The large circle on the opposite wall positively glowed. Before Roth, on the conference table, lay the hilt of the ancient sword I'd used to kill Hannah Caine.

"You know what this sword is?" asked Roth. The hilt and what remained of the blade threw off sparks of fire from the evening sun.

"I'm an expert at using them, not at appraising them. I can tell it's the oldest piece I've ever seen, probably an Osoto."

"It's older than that," said Roth. "It's an original Isao Suddeth. Look at the menuki here." He pointed to the side of the handle. "Suddeth used very simple, stylized shapes, we think in reaction to having used the traditional, intricate carvings for so many years. They went out of use in the second century, and sword makers went back to the older style. And the tsuba," he indicated the round hand guard, which was decorated with a bas relief of crows and leaves. "Those leaves are sugar maple, which only grows in the northeast. Take this hilt apart, and I'd be willing to bet you'll find the tang of the blade stamped with Suddeth's mark. It's not Ravenwing, but it's of that period. Possibly belonged to one of the First Five."

"I didn't know you were such an expert on antique swords."

"Everybody needs a hobby." Roth laughed. "Look at this. There's a story in these engravings. You see this face here? With the runes under it?"

I'd seen it. I could read the runes. "It says 'memory,'" I said.

"It means 'remember.' And the face is a mask. Just before the Crash there was a class war developing. It was the corrupt government officials, the puppets of the petrobarons and wallbankers who created the economic disasters of the period. This mask was a symbol of the folks who rose up against them.

"It's important for a city boss, or a leader of any kind, to have a clear sense of history," he said. "Look at the great disasters of the past and eight out of ten times you'll see that a crucial component in making the disaster is a leader who's not thinking straight, one who makes decisions on the basis of what benefits themselves and their cronies, rather than what's best for their community. Consider in our own era the fall of Redmond, the collapse of Charlotte, even what happened here with the Takeover. If

Crichton's priority had been what was good for Bay City, the People's Movement would never have been necessary."

"But don't you think," I asked, "that it's possible for a leader to have his constituents' best interests at heart, and still make the wrong decisions?"

"Of course. Anyone can make a mistake. Hell, I've made some major mistakes myself. And they do come back to bite me in the arse." He lifted the hilt of the sword. "Case in point. My actions with Hannah Caine, Helena Crichton that was, were driven by tunnel vision, concern for my immediate objectives, without considering the price of those objectives. If I had counted the human cost of those actions, even just the cost to Helena Crichton herself, it might have prevented much of what has happened here.

"It's all about your people, Railwalker, about your relationships, your community. When I began the People's Movement, I sought out associates who weren't afraid to argue with my decisions. That's what keeps a leader honest, keeps the power from going to your head. But your associates can only help you with that if you clue them in. I said nothing to anyone about my affair with Helena Crichton. It was a secret from even my closest friends. No one ever had the chance to tell me I was being an arsehole."

"Sometimes you have to figure that out for yourself," I said.

He nodded. "Your partner has told you you've been called to New Frisco?"

"Yeah. There's a Parliament."

"You know they'll ask you to fill a post. Probably Warden of the West."

He paused to let that sink in. It did. He was right. Morgan had called it. Dahlia was even older than Traveler, and she wanted to retire, and she was looking at me to replace her. I'd never wanted any sort of office. But Morgan was right, I had to admit. The alternatives were not pretty. If Kane or Groute became Warden, they'd be one step away from Elder Raven.

"Your Prof, Morgan," said Roth. "Does she say you

frankly?"

"Yeah." I laughed. "She lets me know when I'm being an arsehole, that's for sure."

"Good," said Roth. "Good enough. Keep her with you if you can, and seek out others like her for your staff as Warden. You need the ones who'll call you on your shit.

"Once you're Warden, you'll be dealing with me, and people like me, a lot. But when you're making your decisions, make them for Suzi Mascarpone, and Arnie Hawthorne, for the people of Maricopa, and the other places you've visited in the zones. Make your decisions with all of them in mind."

He slapped his open palm on the table. "Enough lecture!" he said, and stood. "You've done a man's job, sir." He produced a small valise, slid it across the desk toward me. It was heavy. I looked inside. Gold pieces gave it the weight, and there were bundles of intercity scrip.

"That's an awful lot of money," I said.

"You saved my skinny old arse, and saved my city and my people from a pair of monsters," he said. "Take it. If you won't take it personally, deliver it as my contribution to your order."

"Thank you," I said.

He extended his hand, and I took it. Roth knew nothing of the fact that I'd killed my own mother. His thanks were unmitigated by any doubt or second thoughts. He would not be haunted by what had happened. Or would he? Maybe, I thought. He may not have killed his own mother, but the woman I killed had once been his lover, and had become his most fervent nemesis, and Roth was a man who clearly saw how his own actions had sown the seeds of his near-destruction. Yeah, I thought, he'd have his own ghosts to deal with.

"Many thanks, Railwalker Wolf," he said.

"Just doing my job," I said in the ritual response.

"Go safely, and return as the crow flies."

"I will as I may. Twenty-three Blessings of Soul-Are on you and yours, City Boss Micah Roth."

***

We stepped out onto the roof in the half-light of early evening. The sun was a narrow crescent of orange on the edge of the bay to the west. Morgan and I turned toward it and performed the Salutation to the Setting Sun. When that was finished we stood still, watching the final slice of the red orb sink into the bay. Then we turned toward the ornithopter.

That was when I noticed the figure in the wheelchair. She saw me notice her, started her chair, and rolled over to me.

"Oculus," I said. "What are you doing here?"

"You don't know me, Railwalker," she said. "You don't know nothing 'bout me, or my homies and contacts. How's this crippled old mutie come to be on the roof of the City Admin Tower, chair and all? Like to remain one of them mysteries. But I tell you true, Railwalker, word and pledge on it, I had a vision 'bout you. Your Momma, she dead these many years, no?"

"Not so sure about many years," I said. "But she's dead, that's for sure."

"You're a fool, then. You Momma, her spirit come to me, coupla days ago. She showed me a vision. She feared for you, Railwalker. You face many trials ahead. Then one of these days, you'll meet that old Glaeken. And your Momma feared for your fate at its hand."

A Glaeken was something like a dragon. There were tales of them in the Railwalker Canon, but no one had seen one in living memory. The Glaeken was also often used as a metaphor for other forces: the unconscious, the darkness, the things that dwell in shadow. It wasn't clear how Oculus, or my mother's spirit, meant this to be taken. I sighed. Again with the obscure mystification.

"But here's the important thing," Oculus continued. "What she wanted me to tell you. Don't try to stand against the Glaeken alone. You can't defeat it by yourself, so don't even try. When the day comes, reach out to your people, Railwalker. That's the only way you will conquer."

She peered at me, apparently gauging how well I was listening. I nodded slowly.

"Go safely, Railwalker," she said.
"Twenty-three Blessings, Grandmother."
I turned and followed Morgan to the ornithopter.

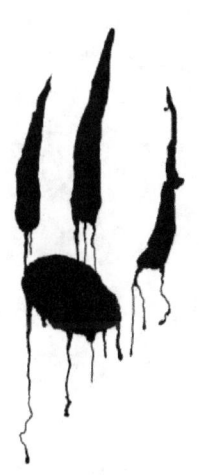

ACKNOWLEDGMENTS

Nearly every acknowledgments page I've ever read (and, yes, I always read them) trots out the old saw about how novels are not created in a vacuum, and it takes lots of help and support to make them happen. It's not as if I ever scoffed at this idea, but writing *Darkwalker* and seeing it through to publication certainly underscored the validity of that oft-repeated claim. I'm deeply grateful for the help and support of a number of folks who contributed in one way or another to the making of this novel.

First and foremost, my profound thanks to my best friend and sometime collaborator, Rev DiCerto. He was there at the start of *Darkwalker*, and gave invaluable feedback and input during the writing of the initial drafts. I think it came as a bit of a surprise to both of us when he ended up becoming my editor on the final drafts, but I couldn't have asked for a better editor.

A major shout-out is due to my crow-bro Gregory A. Gallo, one of the finest artists and the finest men I've ever known, without whom the Railwalkers would never have existed.

Thanks also to Rose Mambert, for believing in *Darkwalker*, and offering it a home at Pink Narcissus. Profound appreciation to my early readers and critics: Kelley Braheny, Jane LeCompte, Juniper Talbot, and Sarah Eaton. Also to James D. Macdonald, for some of the most practical, pragmatic and down-to-earth writing advice I've ever been gifted with.

Though I don't know Howell Chickering personally, I nevertheless owe him a debt of gratitude, as it was his essays and annotations to *Beowulf* that first opened up that famous epic poem for me, and got me delving further into the critical literature about it.

And deep gratitude to my life partner, Moira, and my daughter Kelley, for their unflagging belief, love, and support.

ABOUT THE AUTHOR

Author and artist Duncan Eagleson has had a checkered career which has included working as an advertising copywriter, private detective, astrologer and cartomancer, actor, stage combat choreographer, painter, sculptor, screen printer, book and comics illustrator, and mask maker. He is best known for his artistic contribution to Neil Gaiman's *Sandman* series, his graphic novel version of Anne Rice's *The Witching Hour*, and the masks he created for Wes Craven's *Cursed*, the Big Apple Circus, magician Jeff McBride, and the WWE wrestler Kane. He lives just outside Providence, Rhode Island (former home to Poe and Lovecraft) and spends most of his time in his basement studio, surrounded by far too many drums, swords, books, and DVDs. He no longer owns any pets, and refuses to explain why, but has been seen talking to crows on numerous occasions.

He can be found online at duncaneagleson.com, eaglesondesign.com, and maskmaker.com.

Other Pink Narcissus Press titles featuring Duncan Eagleson

ELF LOVE: An Anthology
The best of the lot was "Goodnight, My Lady", penned by Duncan Eagleson and inspired by Raymond Chandler's "Farewell, My Lovely" wherein hardboiled detective Philip Marlowe is hot on the trail of the vanished lover of a dangerous ex-con. Although it is a 35-page short story, the pages fly by fast and the story goes down like a shot of Hennessy Cognac.
-Bob Heske, *IndieCreator*
ISBN: 978-0-9829913-0-5

IMPOSSIBLE FUTURES
The subtitle emblazoned across Duncan Eagleson's pitch-perfect, retro-kitsch cover of Impossible Futures *promises its readers a "Return to the Future that Never Was!" It's a promise that this new anthology fulfills several times over...This wholly satisfying collection delivers an entertaining, engrossing, even exhilarating reading experience.*

-*ForeWord Reviews*
ISBN: 978-1-939056-02-3

RAPUNZEL'S DAUGHTERS
and Other Tales
Duncan Eagleson's Viking Snow White retelling, "Snovhit" [has] an authentically ancient feel. [... A]ny fairy tale fan will find something to enjoy in this collection.
-*Publishers Weekly*
ISBN: 978-0-9829913-1-2